Praise for *Forget You Know Me*

"Gorgeously written, suspenseful, and full of characters who feel like old friends. I loved this book and didn't want it to end." —Michele Campbell, author of *It's Always the Husband* and *She Was the Quiet One*

"It's been a long time since I've been so lost in a book that when I looked up I had to remind myself what day it was. I'm delighted to say that this happened several times as I read this book. From the very first page of *Forget You Know Me* I was putty in Strawser's hands. From her portrayal of the changing nature of adult friendship to the seemingly harmless secrets we keep in marriage, *Forget You Know Me* is that book you can't put down, and can't stop thinking about when you are finished." —Sally Hepworth, *USA Today* bestselling author of *The Family Next Door*

"A fantastic, tautly paced novel that will have you racing to unravel its many questions and half-truths."
—Liz Fenton and Lisa Steinke, bestselling authors of *Girls' Night Out*

"Friendships crack, marriages erode, and dangerous deceits rise to the surface in this twisty, emotionally complex, powder keg of a tale."
—Emily Carpenter, bestselling author of *Burying the Honeysuckle Girls* and *Every Single Secret*

"Sinister, sophisticated, and teeming with secrets . . . completely irresistible."
—Hank Phillippi Ryan, bestselling author of *Trust Me*

"A taut and immensely satisfying novel of domestic suspense. Come for the sinister premise, stay for the insightful portrayals of a friendship crumbling apart, a marriage strained to its breaking point, and at least one character who finds themself suddenly—and dangerously—in over their head."
—Kathleen Barber, bestselling author of *Are You Sleeping*

"Masterful." —*Publishers Weekly* (starred review)

"Strawser is a clear master of the craft." —*Booklist*

"A great hybrid of women's fiction and suspense . . . strong character development and unpredictable plot." —*Library Journal*

ALSO BY JESSICA STRAWSER

Not That I Could Tell

Almost Missed You

FORGET YOU KNOW ME

JESSICA STRAWSER

ST. MARTIN'S GRIFFIN
NEW YORK

This is a work of fiction. All of the characters, organizations, and events portrayed in this novel are either products of the author's imagination or are used fictitiously.

Published in the United States by St. Martin's Griffin, an imprint of St. Martin's Publishing Group

 Printed in the United States of America. For information, address St. Martin's Publishing Group, 120 Broadway, New York, NY 10271.

www.stmartins.com

Designed by Devan Norman

The Library of Congress has cataloged the print edition as follows:

Names: Strawser, Jessica, author.
Title: Forget you know me / Jessica Strawser.
Description: First edition. | New York : St. Martin's Press, 2019.
Identifiers: LCCN 2018036268| ISBN 9781250184467 (hardcover) | ISBN 9781250184474 (ebook)
Subjects: LCSH: Domestic fiction. | GSAFD: Suspense fiction.
Classification: LCC PS3619.T7437 F67 2019 | DDC 813/.6—dc23
LC record available at https://lccn.loc.gov/2018036268

ISBN 978-1-250-25297-5 (trade paperback)

Our books may be purchased in bulk for promotional, educational, or business use. Please contact your local bookseller or the Macmillan Corporate and Premium Sales Department at 1-800-221-7945, extension 5442, or by email at MacmillanSpecialMarkets@macmillan.com.

First St. Martin's Griffin Edition: March 2020

10 9 8 7 6 5 4 3 2

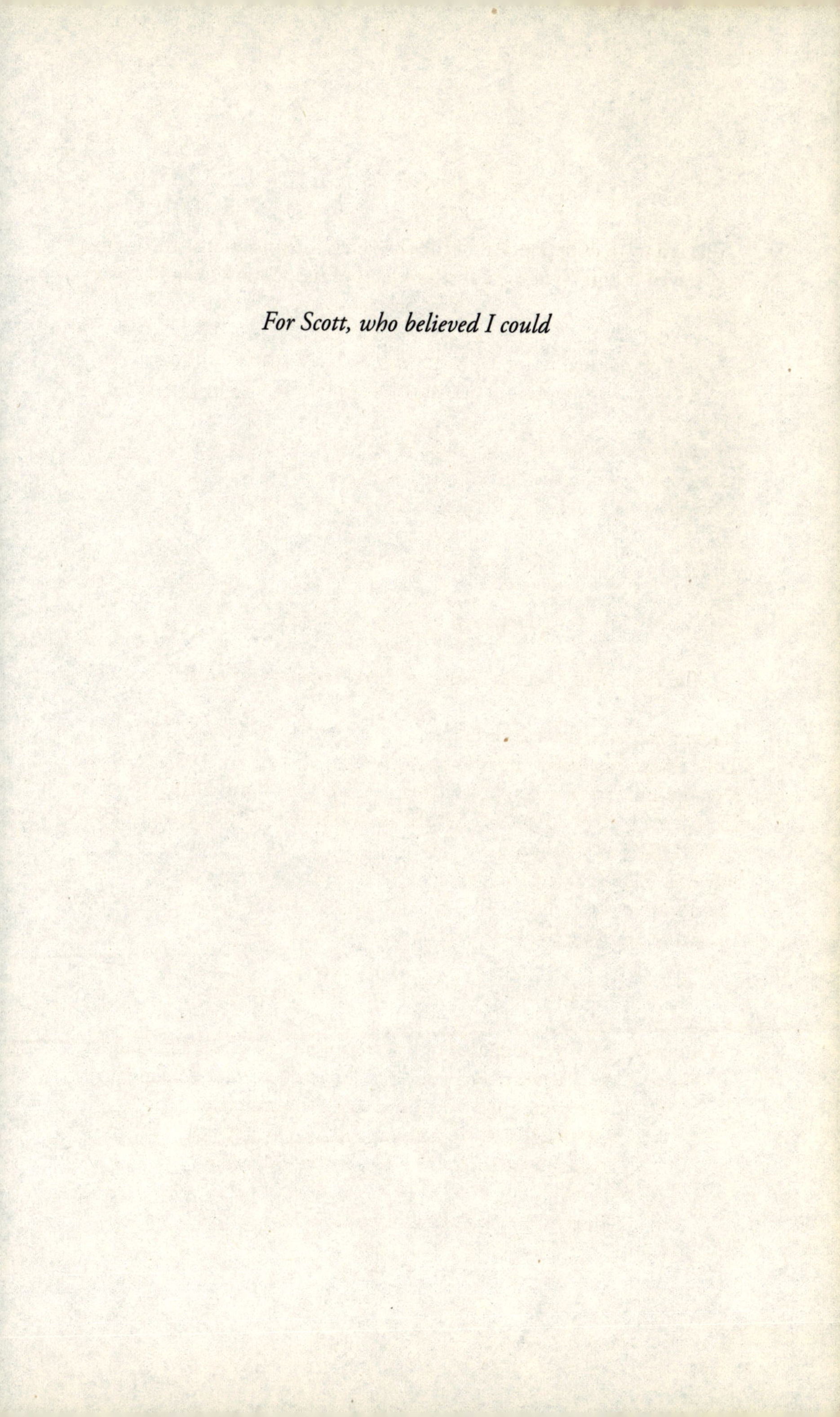

For Scott, who believed I could

1

LIZA COULD TELL RIGHT AWAY THAT MOLLY'S SMILE WAS FAKE—AND NOT fake in that courageous way that tired moms of young children sometimes muster a grin, either. That, Liza would have understood, even empathized with. *This* was that ultra-polite, too-bright sort of smile-on-cue reserved for less than welcome social situations—the corners of her mouth pulled up too stiffly and the rest of her face forgot to match the purported emotion behind it. Liza squinted into the flat-screen of her laptop, hoping maybe it was just the awkward angle of the webcam or the dim light in Molly's living room, where her friend sat in a halo of yellow lamplight on a ridiculously suburban-looking plaid sectional a few hundred miles away. But no. Liza could read Molly's face with the indisputable clarity that came with years—most of a lifetime, really—of familiarity, even as she numbly lifted her own hand in a halfhearted wave.

"We finally did it!" Molly said in a tone that matched her cringeworthy smile. "Girls' night."

After a long stretch of "We should really . . ." and "Maybe after the kids are in bed?" and other overtures they both tried to pretend were not empty, one of them had at last called the other's bluff, and here they were: set to catch up with more than an offhand text—their first real chat in who knows how long.

Well, Liza knew how long. But she wouldn't admit to keeping score.

"Girls' night," Liza agreed. She was already wondering, and simultaneously *chastising* herself for wondering, why they'd bothered—and not just because girls' night was no rarity for her, though she was usually the only one taking part. She missed Molly. Really. She did.

It was just that the woman currently lifting her glass of red wine in a virtual "cheers" was not the Molly she missed. The image on Liza's monitor was Molly 2.0—the version you eventually have no choice but to upgrade to but then can't figure out how to navigate.

"Tell me everything," Molly said with a mischievous shimmy of her shoulders. There. There she was. The old version, just for an instant. "Start with the Canadian."

Liza took a long sip of her own wine, then tipped her glass toward her friend's in the air. "No can do on the Canadian. He was deported."

"What? *Why?*"

"Long story. But," she said gently, "not one worth telling. That was like three guys ago."

"Girl, you work fast!" Molly's eyes lit up. Liza knew the drill—that her married friends liked to live vicariously through her dating escapades. It wasn't their fault; she'd painted them into the role by having so many story-worthy nights in the first place, and by embellishing her retellings with such gusto. Being the lone scout out on the hunt, sending missives to her fellow soldiers at the base camp, had been fun for a while—a long while. But she'd grown tired of giving the play by play.

Which was when she'd realized she was tired of *living* the play by play.

"Not that fast. It's been months." Molly's face fell. Liza had broken the unspoken rule of not acknowledging how disconnected they'd become, how little they'd come to know about each other's daily lives. In junior high, they'd collaborated on a whole playlist's worth of alternate lyrics to their favorite pop songs, serenading their lunch table with

"Give Me Just One Bite (Uno Nacho)" and their still-loved stuffed animals with "GUND Must Have Spent a Little More Time on You." In college, they'd held back hair over porcelain basins, mopped up tears with cheap liquor and late-night pizza, giggled their way through *General Hospital* sprawled on the shabby carpet of their living room. They'd gone on to help each other learn to, well, *adult,* even sharing a family data plan to make their cell phone bills manageable. That they would ever have to fill each other in on months of life at once, let alone reach for something to talk about, was unthinkable then. Laughable.

Liza never should have moved to take the job here. Chicago still seemed out of reach, even though she was right in the middle of it.

"Oh, God," Molly moaned. "It's really been that long. I'm officially the worst friend ever. Too busy competing for my Mother of the Year award in the Frozen Waffles for Dinner category."

"That's the best category. Kids love that category."

"Being Mother of the Year isn't about doing things kids *like.* It's more of a competition in legal forms of torture, like those vegetable medleys that are all broccoli stalks and no florets." They both laughed, but Molly's didn't last long. She pulled a face. "Liza, I really am sorry."

"Don't be. It's better to stick with the highlight reel anyway. Of which—brace yourself—there is currently none. I'm taking a break."

"A *break*?" She looked so confused, Liza's fears were confirmed: This hiatus, by its very nature of being unthinkable, was long overdue. "From sex, you mean? Not from *dating.*"

"From everything." She held up her empty hands as if to display proof. *I've got nothing. And by choice!*

Well. It was by choice if you didn't count the years of failed efforts preceding this period.

"Don't you know my husband is away on business? This call is meant to take the place of the rom-coms I binge when he's gone. What now?"

"Tough one." Liza leaned forward on the futon and drummed her fingers dramatically on the coffee table where her laptop sat in front of her. Thanks to her mother's overzealous gift of a whole box of flameless candles—with a note gushing about how magical they were, and how *safe,* and "what will they think of next?"—the open space of her loft glowed all around her. She loved how the simulated candlelight gave the exposed brick of the converted warehouse a nostalgic café type of feel, in place of the dingy disrepair that the renovation had never quite hidden from the daylight.

She was about to suggest that the husband himself might be a suitable topic when Molly perked up. "I know. How's Max?"

Liza couldn't help but smile. "Maximizing his Maxiness, as usual."

How telling, in retrospect, that she'd met her closest friend here through indiscriminate dating—the very thing she'd pledged to do less of in order to seek more friends. If Liza were to leave Chicago, Max would be the only person to truly miss her. She supposed that this, too, was why she clung to what was left of her friendship with Molly. Because she might barely have it anymore, but she didn't have anything else close. At this rate, she might never again.

"I still think he'd be a perfect match for you, if only . . ." Molly sighed.

"Kind of a big *if only.*" Liza wasn't about to beguile Molly with colorful new Max tales, though she had a whole rainbow of them. She liked to keep him to herself—in part because she knew how well Molly remembered both the promise and disappointment of their sole date.

They'd met over a slow, talkative dinner at the kind of middle-of-the-road restaurant that could be surprisingly satisfying under the right circumstances and Liza had already been thinking ahead to what might come next when she excused herself to freshen up while waiting for the check. If the ladies' room line hadn't been so long she decided to skip it, she might not have returned to find Max in intimate conversation with their waiter. Their red-faced, furious, *male* waiter, who was demanding to know why *her* date had not returned *his* calls.

Knowing any second Max would turn and see her, Liza had stood, stricken, as the server stormed off. Part of her wanted to slink away, but she couldn't summon the politeness *not* to confront what she'd witnessed. All she could think was, *Damn. I liked you.* The date wasn't just going well; she hadn't had this much fun talking to anyone since she moved here.

Max did turn then, and he looked just as caught as she'd feared he would. For a glimmer of a second she'd almost dared hope that it wasn't what it looked like.

"So you date guys, too?" she'd asked quietly.

"No!" His expression turned funereal. "I mean, not anymore."

"I've seen my share of scorned exes"—it was true, though they didn't usually belong to her but to the otherwise affable men she was attempting to date—"and that one seemed fresh. Recent, I mean."

Max averted his eyes. It had been just a phase, he said. He was straight—definitely straight, he said. But he looked cornered, trapped. And her instinct, her own feelings aside, was to reach in and free him.

"Look," she'd said, thinking fast. She was usually honest to a fault, but she really did want to see him again. "I was working out how to tell you. I've had a lot of fun tonight, but I'm not feeling the chemistry beyond a friendship level." Did it show that minutes ago she'd been angling for a look in the bathroom mirror, wondering if he might invite her to his place? Being openly bisexual would have been one thing. But she wouldn't risk *this:* dating someone who was either confused or in denial, marrying him, having three kids, and *then* finding out that she was a beard and he had some *waiter* on the side.

No thanks.

"Friends then," he said.

And just like that, they were. A couple years in, she still couldn't say whether he was gay, straight, or something in between. But they'd never had trouble keeping things platonic, and she figured that alone said something.

Something Liza didn't want to spell out for Molly all over again.

"Speaking of perfect matches," she said instead. "How's Daniel?"

"Oh, you know." Molly sipped her wine, then squinted and

massaged her temple with her free hand. "Actually, it was kind of awful when he left this morning."

"What happened?"

"Grant." Liza smiled at the mention of Molly's five-year-old. When he was born on her own birthday, Liza had proclaimed him a kindred spirit—and so far, he didn't disappoint: surprisingly kind for his age, in spite of having zero inhibitions and a wicked sense of humor. "Daniel woke him up to say good-bye—it was almost time for him to get up for school anyway—and he flipped. I mean, really flipped. 'I'll be back soon,' Daniel said, and Grant sobbed, 'No you won't!' He was hysterical. He kept yelling, 'You're never coming back, never!' Over and over." She shivered at the memory.

"Yikes. Those exact words?"

"Those exact words."

"What did you do?"

She rolled her eyes. "Daniel was staring me down, I mean *boring* into my eyes with this look that said, *Whatever you do, don't acknowledge this: Just pretend it isn't happening.* Like I don't know better." Molly *did* have a way of freaking the kids out with her own reactions—Liza had seen it—but now didn't seem the time to side with Daniel, which had gotten her into trouble before. Excuse her for liking the guy her friend had married. She was guiltier, she supposed, of knowing full well that Molly could be . . . well, Molly.

"I keep hearing Grant's tiny voice in my head, though," Molly continued. "He sounded so sure."

"Do you usually worry about Daniel when he travels?" Liza tucked her legs under her, glad of her stretchy yoga pants, the evening uniform she almost hadn't donned tonight. Feeling self-conscious in Molly's presence was still new to her, but she'd had oddly embarrassing visions of her pajama-clad self dialing in to find her friend in business casual. She needn't have worried—Molly was in lounge clothes, too, though cute ones, a heather gray jersey wrap over a lace-trimmed cami.

"A little. Not Liza-style worrying, though," Molly teased. Liza didn't worry about everything all day long, but when something did take hold of the worst of her imagination it would cling for dear life, keeping her up all night. Few people knew the extent of her *almost* anxiety, as she called it. And fortunately, it usually seemed silly even to her in the morning.

Except for when it didn't. That's when she knew she was in trouble. She was no longer worrying; she was intuiting. And her intuition was kind of a show-off sometimes.

Molly turned serious. "Bad as it sounds, I've actually come to look forward to him being gone. I am *never* alone."

"Do we count as alone right now?" Liza refilled her wineglass. "I mean, are we drinking alone?"

"Oh no. Friends don't let friends drink alone. And you're stuck with me. Because I plan to drink the ever-loving living bejesus out of this wine."

"The ever-loving *living* bejesus. Wow."

"Sometimes the regular bejesus isn't going to make a sufficient point."

"The regular bejesus doesn't even *know*."

Molly shook her head sadly, and Liza hid a smile, wondering if she'd gotten a head start on the bottle before the call. She didn't know how responsible it'd be for Tipsy Molly to be on her own with the kids, but Tipsy Molly was kind of a riot. A quaint midwestern drunk, prone to launching into expressions Liza never heard anyone under the age of sixty use in normal conversation. *I'll be a monkey's uncle. Whoopsie daisies!* They'd once had an earnest 2:00 a.m. conversation about what the phrase *dollars to donuts* means.

"Well, count me in. What's the occasion?"

Molly gestured dramatically around the room, her wine sloshing dangerously close to the edge of the glass. "You better be in! This. This is the occasion. Girls' night." There was a challenge in her eyes, one Liza suddenly had no interest in backing down from. "The thing about Daniel is—" She stopped short and squeezed her eyes shut tight.

"What?"

Molly put her finger to her lips.

"Mommy!" The child's voice calling from upstairs was faint, but still Liza jolted at the sound of it. The call came as a demand, not an unkind one, but not a question, either.

Did Liza imagine a flash of relief passing across Molly's face before an eye roll fixed it in a look of annoyance?

"Never fails," Molly sighed, not moving, as if the child might give up and go to sleep, an occurrence even Liza knew had happened roughly zero times in the history of cared-for children calling out for reasonable things.

"Mom. Me!" Each syllable got its own sentence this time, and Liza strained to discern which child was calling. Grant would probably just pad on down, which made his little sister the likely culprit. *Is it too much to ask,* Molly's expression seemed to be saying, *to get through one lousy call while I'm here with you kids on my own?*

Liza might have argued *Is it too much to ask?* on her own behalf, too, but she was afraid of the answer. It *was* too much these days, it seemed, for Molly to be present—really there, and glad to be—for more than an occasional glimpse of their friendship. And it wasn't even *entirely* Molly's fault. So instead, she said, "Go ahead, go to her. I'll wait."

"I'm going to give her a minute and see if she gives up."

Almost as if on cue, it came again: "*Mommy?*"

Liza raised an eyebrow.

"I just wanted one night of peace." Molly looked directly at her then, and to Liza's surprise, there were tears in her eyes. "She's relentless. It's like she knows when I'm weak—not feeling well, or Daniel isn't home—and *that's* when she strikes."

"Maybe she's just thirsty?"

"Mom! Me!"

Molly shot her a look that conveyed in no uncertain terms what an amateur Liza was.

"I really don't mind," Liza said. "It's not like I'm going anywhere. I can even watch TV until you get back if I want."

"God help me if it takes that long," Molly said, getting to her feet and bending down to give her a sad smile. "Sorry. Back in a jiff."

Liza looked around at her own quiet living room, debating whether to break the silence after all. She liked it this way, candlelit and serene. It was Molly who'd never liked being alone, who'd been the sort to turn on every light in their old shared apartment when Liza had a date or a late class. She'd play a radio in one room and a TV in the other and pay no mind to the clashing of sounds, which drove Liza mad. For the new Molly to relish solitude was telling, and Liza found herself mustering unexpected sympathy for her friend, who she more often wondered if she should envy. Molly's life seemed so crowded that Liza never wanted to intrude from afar, but now she wondered if she'd taken the wrong tact, as these years away had flown past them both.

She should invite her up for a weekend; that's what she should do. Was it fair, anyway, to resent Molly for not visiting when she didn't go out of her way to encourage her to? Maybe she could work it out with Daniel for them to surprise Molly together—he could pack her up and put her on the Megabus one day, promise to handle the kids, and she would arrive unburdened to do all the things Liza had once anticipated she herself would do on the regular here but rarely did. They'd walk Navy Pier. Window-shop the Magnificent Mile. Hit the Art Institute, score Second City tickets. Take selfies at The Bean.

If she *had* turned on the TV, or stood to get a glass of water, or even flipped through the notifications on her phone, she might have missed it. It was dumb luck that she was staring blankly into the portal of Molly's waiting living room, feeling something akin to relief to discover she was warming after all toward her friend—long distanced but not long *lost,* after all—when the back door swung soundlessly open into Molly's kitchen.

Liza jumped, so sudden and startling was the motion. There in the background, across the stretch of white ceramic tile sprawling behind the couch, gaped an ominous rectangle of darkness. Had a gust of wind blown open the unlatched door? Perhaps one of those feral cats Molly was prone to feeding had come begging and jarred it open? Her mind was busying itself to put the pieces of the picture back into place when a tall, broad-shouldered figure stepped through.

He was dressed head to toe in black, a ski mask tight over his face.

Liza's tongue recoiled into her throat with a gasp. Her lungs shuddered mid-breath, terror shooting lightning-quick warning signals from one muscle to the next until she was under its siege, unable to move.

He shut the door behind him.

Without a glance in her direction, he began to make his way slowly around the kitchenette, his eyes on the hallway through which her friend had just disappeared to go check on the kids.

Oh, God. The kids.

She understood all at once what people meant when they said they were too scared to scream, as everything within her constricted—her veins, her windpipe, her courage. The black-clad figure did not hesitate, did not take stock of his surroundings or stop to get his bearings. He merely headed for that hallway, and Liza realized then that she could not afford to stay frozen. She had to act now. She had to act as if she were there, in the room.

Because in a way, she was.

"Hey!" she yelled.

His head whipped around as he halted, mid-step. The just-visible circles of his eyes fixed themselves on the computer.

"Leave," she commanded, her voice cracking, shaking, forsaking her. He moved brusquely toward the screen, and Liza's eyes flicked down to her lap, where she'd rested her phone. She clutched the smooth rectangle in her fist and thrust it toward the webcam.

"I'm calling the police!" She was already crying, willing him to change course, to back out, to slink away. As he stepped closer to the camera, his head disappeared from the frame, then his torso, and in an instant she was staring at a black pant leg that came to a stop right before her. She dove forward and seized her laptop in both of her trembling hands, lifting it to her face, skimming the hardware for the dots marking the location of the microphone.

"Molly!" she screamed into the machine. "Molly! There's a man! He's—"

A swift diagonal of darkness sliced down the screen as an unseen hand slapped Molly's laptop closed.

The connection went dead.

2

"MOM! MOM! MOM!"

Molly put her hand on her hip to steady her back as she conquered the last of the stairs. The pain was relatively mild compared to some days, but still enough of a nuisance to slow her methodical, carefully aligned climb and to remind her she was overdue at the chiropractor—a visit she'd been putting off intentionally, in hopes of convincing herself she could do without.

"Coming!" she called back, echoing Nori's cadence. "Come! Ing!"

Even when its touch was lightest, Molly hated the pain. Hated how it made her feel decades older than the other moms running after three- and five-year-olds. Hated the exhaustion from not sleeping undisturbed in—well, it must be years. Hated the way Daniel looked at her when she capitulated, bowing out or asking him to take over, as if she were being difficult on purpose, as if she didn't hate it even more than he did.

Rotten luck, her doctors claimed. The stubborn slipped disk was the frothy crest in a wave of things that threatened to give out on her, one after the other, so many that she could hardly blame people when they seemed to suspect she was pretending, or exaggerating, or a head case: Debilitating migraines that began during her first pregnancy.

Gestational carpal tunnel that accompanied her second, so bad she could scarcely hold Nori in those first months without the support of a pillow or armchair. Months-long bouts of jaw-popping TMJ syndrome, carrying with its facial pain waves of tinnitus—incessant ear ringing, unpredictable dizziness. Early arthritis in her knees, which seemed to belong to a much older woman and had developed the ability to predict rain. And still this disk in her evidently flimsy spine, which never found its way back into place for long.

It was all real, of course: all diagnosed, confirmed via various scans. Though she'd never admit aloud there *did* seem to be a correlation between the severity of her discomfort and her mood some days.

Like today. As she beelined down the hall toward Nori's dark doorway, she was already regretting the phone call. Every awkward pause was a reminder of what she'd lost, what she didn't know how to get back.

And not just in her friendship with Liza.

"Here I am!" She stepped over the baby gate into Nori's room as her young daughter let out a squeamish sort of squeal loud enough, Molly feared, to wake Grant. A halfhearted pat back to bed never sufficed. Molly would have to appease her completely if she didn't want this return trip to be the first of many.

How long would Liza wait? Molly had grown impatient with other people's impatience, but hadn't yet quite figured out how to let go of the guilt it so readily inspired.

"Mom! It's an alligator!"

"It's not a—" Molly stopped short as her eyes reached the ceiling. The shadow encroaching from the corner did in fact look *exactly* like an alligator.

"I can fix that," she assured her daughter, and made a show of gathering the curtains and tucking them into the blinds. Above her, the alligator was now a narrow triangle. The best she could do, with the night-light at this angle. "See?" she said hopefully. "Better."

Nori looked at her with evident skepticism. "I want to sleep on the floor," she said, and without awaiting a response hopped out of her toddler bed, trailing her pillow. "Help me with these animals, Mom," she ordered.

Molly didn't know what unsettled her more: her daughter's recent dropping in casual conversation of the *-my* from her name, which sounded so *teenage* in combination with Nori's bossy toddler tone, or the image of her sleeping like a puppy, curled at the foot of the gate in her doorway, as she inexplicably had every night this week.

"But the floor is so much less comfortable than your bed."

"No it *isn't.*" Nori pointed impatiently at the mound of stuffed animals on her mattress, and Molly heaved a sigh of defeat and started volleying them onto the carpet where Nori was arranging her pillow with a satisfied smile.

"What are you doing downstairs?" Nori asked, sounding almost suspicious. Molly had always been rattled by Nori's uncanny ability to tap her emotional state, even when she'd felt sure she hadn't offered a clue.

"Talking to your aunt Liza."

"Who's Aunt Liza?"

Molly cringed. She could hardly believe it had come to this point, where the kids scarcely remembered Liza's last visit. She'd assumed they'd always be a regular part of each other's lives, raiding each other's refrigerators without asking, meeting for head-clearing walks after work, bringing each other lattes just because. Now they were—what? How long could you hinge a relationship on a history of what had been?

And whatever the expiration date was for a neglected friendship, could sheer will extend the "best if used by" stamp on a marriage?

She sank to her knees next to her daughter and started arranging the plush toys around her, tucking a blanket over the whole soft mound. "Liza has been my best friend since I was a kid."

"I had best friends when I was a kid, too," Nori said, nodding.

Molly smiled. "You're still a kid, pumpkin."

"I'm three now," she said defiantly.

"Exactly."

"Is Grant a kid?"

"One of the best. Like you."

"Is Aunt Liza a kid?"

"No, but I knew her when she was one."

Nori cocked her head, considering this. "Is she *here*?"

"Nope, I'm talking to her on the computer. Like we do with Granny and Gramps."

"Is she at Granny and Gramps' house?"

"No. She's even further away."

"Do you miss her?"

Something tugged at Molly's heart. Even when she was *talking* to Liza, she missed her.

"Time for bed, little alligator wrestler. Dream of something sweet."

"Like Daddy coming home?"

"Exactly like that."

She pulled her daughter into her arms and was glad of the darkness as a swell of emotion overcame her. It wasn't so long ago that her own sweetest dreams had revolved around Daniel. The introduction into their marriage of two children in close succession and years of chronic pain had taken a toll, not bit by bit, the way she might have recognized and stopped, but in a sneak attack, when one day she'd awoken to find a wall of resentment constructed between them. The mortar seemed to have set overnight, and she hadn't the first clue as to how to go about breaking it down.

"Will you sing me a song?"

"Aunt Liza is waiting, baby." She shouldn't have left her on hold. One of the most striking changes that had accompanied motherhood was the degree to which she was constantly underestimating things—how long they would take, how simple they would be.

What effect they would have.

Nori ignored her and launched into "Twinkle, Twinkle, Little Star," keeping the meter slow and deliberate to give her mother a chance to catch up. After the first verse, Molly joined in—at least it was a short one. She'd learned the hard way that arguing with Nori would end up taking longer than just singing the damn song.

She couldn't fault her daughter for her strong will because Molly had asked for it, literally. In high school, Liza had gifted her a book of Eleanor Roosevelt quotes when they were both on a feminist kick that, looking back, should have been not some foray into progressive thinking but their regular state of mind. (How many times had they reinvented themselves to suit whatever silly teenage boy had caught their eye?) Its pages were worn now from aimless turning in search of inspiration, sticky notes flagging gems such as *No one can make you feel inferior without your consent,* and Molly had named her daughter for that gumption, choosing a less common nickname for Eleanor to set her apart from all the Ellies and Ellas on the daycare roster.

I have spent years of my life in opposition and I rather like the role, Ms. Roosevelt had famously said. Nori seemed to have gotten the message along with the name, and three years in, Molly was torn between admiring her daughter's conviction and feeling utterly defeated by it.

"Bedtime," she said firmly when the last notes of the song had been sung for the third time. "You need rest so you can grow."

That, Nori rarely argued with. Stubborn though she might be, at heart she was a classic little sister: forever trying to catch up with Grant.

As Molly made her way down the stairs, the sheer-curtained windows at the bottom began to flash: a blur of blue light, a flicker of white, a glow of red. She was squinting at the pattern, taking it in, when the pounding came, so hard the door shook in the frame. "Mrs. Perkins?" came the muffled bark of a masculine voice, and she hurried to pull the curtain aside. Two uniformed officers peered back at her, their cruisers alert at the curb.

She pulled back and closed her eyes, a parched, sandy lump catching in her throat. When she opened them, the room around her swirled. Her shaking hand reached for the knob, hot tears already falling down her cheeks, as if they'd known all along.

Never coming back, Grant's voice echoed in her ears, hysterical and sobbing as he'd been that morning, as she suddenly was now.

"Is it Daniel?" she choked out before they could speak, and they looked past her, into the house, hands on their holsters.

Never coming back, never.

"We got a call," one officer said, looking at her expectantly. "A report of an intruder."

The wave of relief that came with the words was already breaking with dread.

3

LIZA WAS OUT OF HER MIND.

Over and over, she rang Molly's phone.

Over and over, it went to voicemail.

Acquiescing to her tearful begging, the gruff woman on the other end of the Cincinnati police line had promised Liza a call back from *someone,* preferably Molly but if necessary the dispatcher herself, after they'd checked things out, and yet Liza had scarcely brought herself to put her phone down since—thus dooming her hyped brain to another level of second-guessing. What if they'd tried to ring her back and her incessant dialing stuck them with the busy signal?

Still, nearly an hour in, she couldn't stop herself from placing the call again and again. It was the only thing within her power to do. Her bumbling alert to the confused dispatcher might have saved her friend from—what? Or it might have been futile. Hearing Molly's voice would be the only thing that could reassure her that everything was okay. That every*one* was okay.

She set the phone next to her on the futon, where she'd returned from pacing the room, and dropped her head into her shaking hands, beginning again to cry. In her panic, she'd downed the rest of her wine too fast, and her misguided effort to squelch her nerves was now churning in her stomach, much the way an ill-considered choice nagged at a guilty conscience—as if she were inevitably going to pay for this later.

What a luxury it had been to be merely *annoyed* with Molly going into tonight's call. And what shortsighted annoyance, at that. All friendships went through out-of-sync patches. What if they never had a chance at another girls' night—long distance or otherwise—and Liza had squandered half of this one swallowing bitterness about . . . what? That her friend, bogged down by the responsibilities of wifehood and parenthood, was more of an adult than she was?

Her phone chimed loudly with a text—she'd cranked the volume as high as it would go, as if there were any danger of missing a call while staring rabidly at the thing—and she fumbled with the log-in screen. Relief flooded her at the sight of Molly's name even as the anxious air thickening the room tightened its grasp around her. She tapped the icon.

Police just left. House was clear. Not sure what you saw . . . maybe camera/tech glitch? Scared that living bejesus back out of me tho.

A technical glitch? She must be joking. Liza called Molly again, but again it went to voicemail. No sooner had she hung up than another text pinged.

Sorry our girls' night didn't pan out. Really beat. Rain check soon, K?

Didn't pan out? Understatement much? She typed back furiously.

Need to talk—can't wait. Call me.

The response was immediate.

Sorry, kids upset from all the excitement. Maybe tomorrow.

Maybe? Maybe? Then, on the heels of that one, another, just as she was typing: *They're not the only ones. . . .*

Off to bed. Night.

A deeply troubled feeling took up where the panic had been. Of course the kids would be upset—officers in the house, their father away—but how could Molly *not* want to talk to her, even for a minute, about what she'd seen? To ask for details, to share a *what the actual fuck* moment, to acknowledge that Liza had been frantic for over an hour? A text message was hardly a substitute. There had to be something going on here. Something not good.

How could Molly bear to even stay in the house, much less *go to bed*?

The phone rang, and Liza's heart lifted for the split second it took to register the unfamiliar number, then hung in a perilous balance.

"Hello?"

"Cincinnati Police, returning a call about a disturbance?"

It was the dispatcher from earlier. "*Yes.* What in the *world*?"

"No signs of forced entry, or of an intruder. The homeowner seemed baffled."

Liza's mind raced. "But the laptop—it was shut on the coffee table, as I described it, right?"

"Homeowner said she was unsure whether she'd shut it herself before heading upstairs."

Why would Molly say that? She knew damn well she'd left Liza on hold.

"She did not shut it. A man in a mask did." Liza was incredulous. "Please. Are you sure she's okay? Something isn't right." Did they not believe her? It seemed ludicrous that she'd need proof to back up her story. "Maybe the video chat host keeps a record of calls?"

"Even if they did, we don't have real grounds to request it. Aside from your account, there's no evidence of a crime. But we're keeping a cruiser outside through the night as a precaution. If there's no doubt about what you saw, chances are he got spooked by being caught on camera and ran. We weren't secretive about pulling up, so I'm sure he won't be back."

"But—"

"That's all I can tell you. You'll need to talk to your friend."

The call disconnected, and Liza stared at the silent phone, weighing her options. If she were in Cincinnati, she'd go straight over—she'd already be there—but what more could she do from Chicago? What if Molly was in some hidden danger, right now? What if the intruder had threatened her to find a way to get rid of the authorities and Molly had succeeded? What if he was still there, inside the house, having escaped detection? What good would a cruiser *outside* be then?

She should call Daniel, maybe. But surely Molly would have already done that. Liza scrolled through her phone contacts to the Ds and found that his number wasn't there. When she'd upgraded her phone last year, only some of her address book transferred, and she'd only made a point of re-adding the numbers she actually called. She tried to remember if Molly had said where he'd gone—the name of a city, a hotel—but was pretty sure she hadn't. What good would it do to track him down, anyway? What she needed was someone in town.

Ignoring the low-battery warning—her phone was evidently as ill equipped as she was for marathon panic sessions—she scrolled to a different name.

"Liza?"

"Luke. I know it's late, I'm sorry to bother you. . . ."

"This isn't the greatest time." She'd never understood why people answered their phones if they couldn't talk. If you can't talk, don't answer. As if reading her thoughts, her brother cleared his throat. "I'm never going to *not* answer a call from my sister, single in the city." His voice was hushed, muffled, as if he'd stepped out of a room full of company to sneak in a private call. "But if it's not an emergency—"

"I'm okay, but it might be. I don't know." A beat of awkward silence descended, and she cleared her throat. "I was hoping you could drive over and check on Molly? Daniel is out of town, and—"

"Liza, Steph is having a complication."

She let the words register, and her heart dropped. "With the pregnancy?"

"Yes. We found out today."

"Oh no." Her brother and his new wife had only recently announced the happy news, all smiles to have cleared the first-trimester danger zone. "Is it serious?"

"We hope not. It's rarely *super* serious, but it's also rare for it to happen at all." His voice sounded funny, off. She tried to picture him but couldn't. He was such a walking dichotomy—stiff suit-and-tie by day, lovable slob by night—you never knew what you were going to get. She didn't like that she couldn't conjure him as he was now, and wished she were there sharing some comfort, even if she didn't know her sister-in-law as well as she wanted to.

"Is there anything I can do?"

"Not much to be done at this point. But she's scared. She's upset. I can't leave her tonight, unless this Molly thing is, like . . ."

"No, no. I was just being—forget it. I'm really sorry, Luke. When you're ready to give details, I'm here, okay? Keep me posted?"

Afterward, she sat staring again at her phone, feeling bereft. There wasn't anyone else back home she could think to call—especially, given the time difference, at this hour of night. She bit her lip and rang Molly again, bracing for her friend's *didn't I tell you* rage, better at least than silence. But again it went to voicemail.

"Molly, it's me. I just can't shake what I saw. I only want to hear your voice. Can you *please* call?"

She knew even as she hung up—even as she commended herself for uncharacteristic restraint in not screaming into the phone, *Molly, holy shit! If this is some sick joke, joke's over!*—that her friend wasn't going to. Liza would have a hard time forgiving her this. Molly knew, she *knew,* how Liza's worried mind would churn. How selfish of her to l it. And when they'd both finally tried to reconnect just hours ago. Why would Molly back away from that? And how could she seem so aloof, as if Liza had witnessed a smoke alarm set off by burnt toast and not an actual masked intruder in her actual house?

Unless, of course, Molly was *not* okay.

Liza again regretted the wine. She probably wasn't thinking clearly, shouldn't do anything rash. Late-night obsessing wasn't new to her, and though she didn't usually have such a compelling reason to worry, this stuff almost always looked better in the morning.

She brushed her teeth, shut off the lights, and climbed into bed.

Her throat felt tight, her neck painfully stiff, and she tried to get comfortable on the pillow, tried to tell her muscles to ease up, to let her be.

She had a rule not to look at the clock when she was having a hard time sleeping. It only made matters worse. So she tossed and turned in the timelessness, trapped inside her mind in the dark, for an hour, maybe two, or longer—for as long as she could stand it.

Until she couldn't. Not with these thoughts running races in her mind and sleep nowhere in sight. By the time she called Max, she didn't even feel guilty about waking him. She only felt she had no other option. Without intervention, she'd go insane. And there was no one else to intervene.

"Hello?" He sounded groggy, and she hedged.

"Um. You asleep?"

"I *was.* It's one in the morning, on a weeknight."

"Right."

"What's wrong?"

Max and Molly had met only once, at a funeral for Liza's favorite uncle, not the most social occasion—but they'd been hearing about each other for years. So she told him everything. How the semi-awkward video chat had been turning warm when Nori cried; how the intruder had closed it down; how long she'd waited for the police to phone her back; how cold her friend's response had been; how the only other person in Cincinnati she could call was tied up with problems of his own; how unsettled she felt; how she didn't know what to do.

"Would it be crazy to—I don't know. Just get in the car?"

"If you're saying you have a genuine worry that she's being held hostage, then yes, it would be sort of crazy to do it alone."

"Hostage." Repeating the word only solidified its power—horror, dread, unthinkable outcomes. She tried to shake it off. "I'm so *pissed* she's left me to worry this way. By the time I got there, it'd be morning. I could have her on the phone by then, giving me some explanation as to *what the hell.* Then again, she could be . . ." Liza couldn't finish the thought.

"In trouble?" Max supplied. "Unlikely. But nothing about this is *likely.*" She could practically hear him chewing his lip. He always did when he was nervous. "I'll go with you."

She shook her head into the darkness. "I can't ask you to do that. We'd both miss work."

"You didn't ask me to. And I wouldn't say I'll *miss* it. . . ."

She managed a laugh. "You'd really get in the car? Just like that?"

"I don't know what you're supposed to think. This is kind of insane. But you're upset enough to be calling me in the middle of the night, so . . . yes. I can't let you go alone."

Liza was warming to the idea. The dark highway stretching before them, Max pulling her up and away from this awful sinking feeling, and some reassurance—or *something*—at the end.

"What will we do when we get there?" she asked.

As soon as the words were out of her mouth she knew what he was going to say. That was the thing about her and Max. The thing she liked most. It was how she used to be with Molly, only . . . different.

"Knock on the door."

Anxious as she was, she couldn't help but smile.

4

THE THOUGHT HIT DANIEL LIKE A LINE DRIVE TO THE CHEST. HIM THE SHMUCK in the cheap seats out in right field, caught staring absently into his overfilled popcorn and instantly dreading, upon impact, the slow-motion replay on the jumbotron.

There would be no more Liza after this.

The friendship's odds of survival had to be nil. He could see it on their faces, his wife's somehow managing to look both chalky and flushed in the harsh morning sun, Liza's indignant and disbelieving. She wasn't supposed to be here in his foyer, unannounced, but then again, neither was he—back early from the trip he never should have taken.

No more Liza, fearless and vicarious, envied and oblivious, opinionated and choosey, loud and yet strangely quiet. Climbing the fire escape of their old third-floor walk-up, knocking on the window only to turn right around if she didn't want whatever was for breakfast—yes to French toast or waffles, no to anything that made her "think too hard about unfertilized baby chickens." Regaling them with tales of her short-lived but aptly nicknamed beaus: Ex–Reds Player. Hipster Bartender. Ping-Pong Hustler. Frat Boy Remix. Chasing raccoons from their campsite, wielding a flaming branch that had nearly ignited the tent, with a fear-strangled battle cry he and Molly would imitate for weeks, not unkindly, laughing until their eyes teared.

He'd paid close attention to it all. Because not only was Liza his wife's most amusing friend, she was also the one who had a knack for saying whatever Molly was thinking but wouldn't dare voice. If he watched his wife's lips carefully as Liza spoke, he could recognize flickers of truth by the delighted satisfaction that would twitch at the corners before they settled themselves back into a soft line.

In that way, Liza was like a sort of reverse lie-detector test. And he knew of no other. If she vanished from their lives, so, too, would those rare glimpses of unfiltered truth.

He stepped back behind the china hutch, out of view.

Molly was unaware that he'd followed her from the breakfast table, and her voice was low, practically a hiss. "Gross overreaction" and "told you I was fine" and "just tired" and "probably nothing" and "right outside all night" and "for fuck's sake" and "not my fault" and "took it upon yourself" and "really not a good time."

Not one *sorry* or *tell me again* or *come in and show me* or *can't believe you came all this way* or *I appreciate your concern* or *I feel awful you were so worried* or *you must be exhausted* or *how long can you stay?* and *please do.*

He knew what women wanted to hear. Usually. Not that Molly believed it.

He'd been sure he was saying all the right things this morning, in fact. He'd been so eager to get home, in spite of the fact that Molly hadn't seemed sorry to see him go. He was careful to stride in all smiles and light, explaining to the slow-blinking Molly that the clients had pulled the plug on the deal last night and he'd woken before the sun to drive the two hours and change home from Louisville. He'd brandished good coffee for Molly and silly little wind-up toys for the kids and masked his sudden hesitation as best he could with bear hugs.

Yes, he *did* know the right things to say. He'd memorized his lines. *I missed you all too much to stay away one second longer than I had to.*

I had this great idea to surprise you all for breakfast—banana pancakes, anyone?

I told you I'd be back soon, Grant-man.

If I'd known you were going to wake up looking this beautiful, I'd have driven straight back after the dinner meeting flopped, Mols.

Well, okay. The last bit had been overkill. It'd been too long since he'd spoken to her that way, and she'd looked at him with bewilderment, made him feel insincere.

Fair enough, but at least he was trying. And what had Molly said then?

Not a word about Liza, and what she'd seen, and what had happened next or how it had *possibly* freaked her out enough to traverse three states in the dead of night to see for herself what the hell was going on.

Not a word about the cop outside, who naturally Daniel had approached with concern, and with relief that the address was current on the driver's license he immediately offered, and whom he chatted with for quite some time as he gathered all the details of the strange incident the night before. The officer assumed he was recapping what Daniel had already been told—what woman wouldn't speed-dial her husband, after all, first thing after a scare like that?—and Daniel didn't correct him. The cop was tired, bored, and satisfied enough with Daniel's return to start the engine with a tired wave and drive away.

The realization took a while to set in, doubling back on itself in the process: Not only had his wife had an intruder reported in their home the night before, and not only had she not called Daniel to tell him, but he'd been home for more than an hour and she *still* hadn't mentioned it. She'd been acting downright normal.

He'd hung back—sensing without quite knowing why that it might not go over well if he were to rush in, demanding answers—to let her be the one to broach the subject, never dreaming that *this* particular game of chicken was about to ensue. So he found himself watching her out of the corner of his eye, his jaw clenched, as he gave the kids too much syrup just to shut them up and refilled Molly's coffee so she could keep her back pressed into her heating pad and waited with increasing unease.

Until the doorbell rang.

Oddly enough, Daniel hadn't truly, thoroughly considered the awful possibility of a life lived apart from Molly until he walked into the foyer and saw Liza filling their doorway in the morning light and his wife standing before her, hands on hips, not about to invite her in.

A distance he might have considered. The tense volley of a negotiation, the unsteady terms of a cease-fire, sure. But only as a means to finally move forward—not as an end to everything. And *certainly* not when he was still absorbing what they all may have very nearly dodged the night before.

He was no innocent. He knew he had to take some responsibility for letting the Molly he'd fallen in love with fade. He'd known for some time that he'd neglected too much, that she didn't like the way he let certain things slide, and not just in their marriage. They'd reached a monotone he never could have imagined in the earnest inflections of their early days. He'd been increasingly consumed by longing to have things back the way they were, wrapped in uncertainty as to how to get them there.

And then that moment arrived, just days ago, the tears in her eyes, not about him and yet everything to do with him, and the old conviction had seized his soul: *He loved her still.* Had he really doubted it?

He loved her even now, as he hid in his own foyer, watching her slipping away.

Because Liza was the only person who seemed able to bring what he thought of as the Old Molly back to the surface, even if these days she never floated there for long. And so good-bye to Liza could only mean good-bye, in the worst of ways, to Molly, too.

Good-bye to fun Molly. Forgiving Molly. Occasionally irresponsible Molly. *My fire escape is always open* Molly. Ex-boyfriend-renaming

Molly, who generated the nomenclature that would actually stick when they looked back on so-and-so: *Ex-Benchwarmer. Buttster Bartender. Ding-Dong Hustler. Frat Boyzilla.* Flaming branch–dousing Molly, who'd frantically upended her can of beer midair while Liza squealed with laughter, ducking the foam.

He could end the whole charade right now—stomp into the entryway, full of pleasant surprise to see Liza there, and let them both explain her presence, see Molly stammer over how she'd just been about to tell him all of it. But he didn't know where he stood, and sensed that his position was one too easily transported to Liza's side of the door.

He'd always been too curious for his own good. But if he revealed himself now, he'd never know: How big of a hole would Molly dig? How long could she possibly justify *not* looping him in? How far gone *were* they, really?

And if she could behave so unforgivably toward Liza of all people, could he be far behind?

He'd once had a legitimate worry that he'd been second fiddle to Liza, and yet even then he'd learned not to mind.

His wife's hiss came again, encased in a hard, bitter shell. "*Now* you decide to show up!" She was talking to Liza as if she had previously and thoroughly abandoned her, which wasn't fair—even if maybe, in the geographical sense, she had. But Liza hadn't been the only one to let Molly down. Daniel knew this better than anyone, as he was the guiltiest party. And Molly, apparently, had had enough.

He couldn't tell if her tone was more embarrassed or angry or guarded or tired, maybe all of the above. But its directive, however mystifying, was clear: *Stay away. Never mind.* Worse: *Forget you know me.*

And he worried she'd inadvertently borrowed that tone from him.

Certain turning points become obvious only in retrospect. Others fly at you with the crack of a bat—no time to react, only to recoil.

Behind him, the kids had started to bicker in the kitchen. Something to do with the damn syrup again. He'd need to go back in and referee, or Molly would storm across the tile to confront his incompetence and catch him here.

Go home. Much as he didn't want this distance between Molly and Liza, the space was here now regardless, and so the thought sounded so loudly in his head he hoped it might ride the tension across the hall, harmonize with Molly's harsh words, and enter Liza's ear in a chorus she couldn't ignore.

Go home and leave us to our mess.

5

ALONE AT LAST, MOLLY SLIPPED OUT THE BACK DOOR, STEALING A GLANCE to make sure no one *appeared* to be watching—the best she could hope for at this desperate stage—and started off across the backyard toward the tree line. The warmer-than-average late-spring sun made a point of exemplifying *broad daylight* as if to make her rethink her choices. Which, of course, she was already doing—a useless exercise, as it was too late to change them.

They hadn't really been choices, though, had they? More like non-choices that had seemed secure in her hand but been swept up by an unexpected gust of wind. Now, her empty fist clenched, there was no point in chasing after the opportunities it had once held. She just wanted to tie everything else down, to salvage what she still could.

The question, of course, was how much damage the storm had already done. She'd handled things so badly with Liza. In the few moments her friend had stood bleary eyed on her doorstep this morning, Molly had watched her traverse a spectrum of emotions with surprising speed: her initial worry turning to confusion to frustration to disbelief to anger to a deep and resolute sadness. The feeling of finality trailing Liza's departure had cast itself over Molly like a shadow and stayed there.

Molly had no one to blame but herself that she hadn't been able to summon the gumption to get back on the phone with Liza last night and convince her, somehow, that all was well. She'd been too afraid that Liza, who knew her so thoroughly, would see through her: She hadn't trusted her own voice. Nor had she been able to disguise her horror at Liza's follow-up house call. She'd felt sick at the realization of how terrified she'd left her friend—and how much Liza must care for her still to have driven through the night. But no other emotion seemed capable of displacing her shame over what Liza had very nearly witnessed.

So Molly hadn't apologized, hadn't pulled Liza into a hug, hadn't so much as invited her in for coffee. Instead, a knee-jerk defiance had lashed itself out, as if Liza's concern were a silly overreaction, as if the two of them hadn't been laughing together the night before, trying to reclaim what they'd once shared. The second her friend turned on her heels, Molly wanted to chase after her, to call her back, to explain—but she couldn't. Not with Daniel there, chattering with the kids in the kitchen, mere steps away from poking his head out to see what was taking his wife so long to shoo away the paperboy, or whoever had come knocking.

If Daniel saw Liza, he'd want to know why she was there.

And when Molly tried to explain it away, it would be two against one, their skepticism versus her stoicism. Not a fair fight.

Molly had thought he would never leave. He'd been in no hurry to get to the office. After all, if not for his canceled morning meetings and his sudden, unusual zeal to rush home in the wee hours, he wouldn't have been expected back until afternoon. Once upon a time, he'd have taken the whole day off and she'd have followed suit. A gorgeous morning like this, they'd have loaded a cooler with snacks and beer and hoisted the canoe atop the SUV and driven out to Cowan Lake, or splurged and paid the fee at Morgan's livery to catch a ride upriver.

It used to be a bigger deal, to leave each other. They'd be lavishly attentive before the good-bye, dining out like it was a special occasion, and on the days apart never go to bed without a telephoned—never texted—good night. Returns home brought a compulsive closeness—clinginess, really—that could last even longer than the absence had been.

These days, they circled each other, heads down, silent partners tag-teaming a to-do list that would never be finished, and scarcely acknowledged arrivals and departures beyond a *thank God you're back; please can I get a hand.*

This morning was no exception. Molly jumped at the chance to reassign Nori's drop-off, which defaulted to her given that Nori attended preschool at the nature center where Molly worked. Today, though, crews were coming to repair flood damage to the main building, and displaced employees had the day off. After Grant bounded onto the school bus, Molly feigned a headache—easy enough, when she had one every other day—and asked Daniel as sweetly as she could to take Nori, out of his way though it was. He'd obliged *just* begrudgingly enough that she had to stop herself from rolling her eyes. And so, after a maddening rehashing of where exactly to go and what was Nori's teacher's name again, Molly had been left mercifully alone to get better acquainted with the latest of her mistakes.

She'd been so stupid, about everything. No chance would Daniel avoid hearing about last night—word of flashing lights spread fast across the semi-affluent suburbs. She'd already fielded her share of concerned texts and voicemails from neighbors, and it would be a miracle if he lasted the day at work without the same. Yet she'd been unable to bring herself to tell him—which meant she'd likely missed her chance to be the *one* to tell him.

Which was only going to make things worse.

If that were possible.

"Just a false alarm," she'd told those who asked.

She wouldn't get off so easy with Daniel.

No, she wasn't foolish enough to think she could avoid telling her husband what had happened—or *almost* happened, or *allegedly* happened. But evidently she was cowardly enough to put it off, nonsensically. How now to explain why she didn't call him right that second, let alone rush him with the news this morning?

She was so good at this—making things worse.

She did it to herself all the time.

It was almost funny, how suddenly the fear of losing him seized her. Months—years?—had passed since their relationship had felt like the forevermore *given* solidified in their vows.

She could caption this particular freeze-frame of herself the way she did the flora and fauna displays at the nature center. Left to right: bad judgment, unconvincing cover-up, blind panic. She knew she needed to improve upon the caption, but first she needed, impossibly, to reach through the glass and alter the picture.

It was like half-waking in the cold night air and reaching for the covers only to find none. Anyone with sense would get up and retrieve another blanket from the closet, but all she could do was lie here, shivering. She'd once been adept at thinking faster. But the pain that plagued her body had not spared her mind.

The path into the woods at the back edge of their property started as little more than a deer trail, newly rimmed with violets and trilliums, and she headed down it, careful not to trample the blooms. Ahead were the limestone steps, lopsided and muddy where by the end of the summer they'd be coated in moss. She'd been delighted the first time she'd found this hidden detour to the older house at the end of the long, paved drive behind hers.

"Look," she'd later told the kids. She'd always wanted to be one of those moms who made the ordinary seem magical. "Whoever lived in this house and that one must have been best friends." It wasn't true, of course. The path and house both predated their own by several decades, and she sometimes imagined what had previously occupied their little square of suburban sprawl. A makeshift baseball diamond, like the one by her father's childhood home? A sunlit garden? A flat lawn? The house on the hill had none to speak of, only several tiers of decks overlooking what had surely then been a lovelier view.

Really, it didn't matter what used to be there, only that she wished with a sudden intensity that the path had never existed at all.

She had to pause on the top step to catch her breath.

She was going to need it.

Rick answered the door keys in hand, one arm in and one arm out of a chocolate brown corduroy blazer. A Disney Channel theme song was blaring through the backlit kitchen doorway on the far side of the living room.

"Molly." His eyes lit up as they never failed to, even in a rush. Behind him, his phone buzzed at the edge of the entryway table, and he glanced at it distractedly, then back at her. "What's up?"

His hair was damp, his skin shiny from the aftershave that tingled her nostrils, tempting a sneeze, and she remembered that he was bidding on a new job this morning, a high-end one.

She might have thought him handsome once, out of his standard-issue contractor T-shirt and cargos, but not today. *Not tomorrow, either.*

"How could you?" she blurted. The phone vibrated again, and she fixed her gaze on the glowing rectangle, which was so much easier to look at, just now, than Rick was. It was so close to the edge, right there on the brink. One more buzz and it might fall to the tile and shatter.

He blinked. "How could I what?"

She swept past him into the living room, bargaining that Rosie would be zoned out to the TV in her booster, out of earshot. Usually Molly felt almost more at home here than she did in her own, but the air now seemed stale, and she realized the full impact of what she'd lost, what would never be the same.

When she whirled around to face him, tears were springing to her eyes.

"I don't even know what to say. Do you know what I had to deal with last night? This morning? Do you know what you put at risk?"

Rick stood, startled, at the closed door, his hand still clutching the knob. "I don't know what you're talking about."

"You didn't stick around to know, did you? I mean, I can understand being thrown when you saw her. But shutting the screen and running was the best you could come up with? And not a word from you since?" The words poured out, fast and hot, and a surge of anger displaced the sadness that had stilled her just seconds before.

"I am utterly lost here." He stepped toward her, reached out to touch her arm. She was shaking, all over. "Molly, my God, take a breath. Tell me what happened."

"It was an offhand comment, a joke. I mean, I shouldn't have said it—clearly! But I can't believe you actually *did it.* You thought that's what I really wanted? That was how I saw it happening, after all this time? The fact that you could think that . . ."

He was shaking his head, leaning in, trying to hold her gaze. *"Molly. You're not listening. I don't know what you're talking about!* What comment? Is this—are you messing with me?"

She shook off his hand. She wasn't just mad at him. She was furious with herself.

She had let herself love him, a little. She had so desperately needed a friend.

"Act One," she said drolly. "Make a bad call, run like the wind, leave Molly to clean up the mess. Act Two. Pretend it never happened, pretend it wasn't you, play dumb. Can you give me a preview of Act Three, so I can brace myself for the exciting conclusion?"

He looked past her, and Molly turned to see Rosie, cherubic in the kitchen doorway. She was wearing a purple butterfly-print dress that had once been Nori's, gray leggings, and suede lavender boots, and her curly pigtails bounced as she ran for Molly. The sight of her jabbed at the center of Molly's chest, and she bent to scoop the child into her arms, holding her in a long hug as she blinked away her tears.

Rosie pulled back and smiled at her, patting her arm silently. Always silently.

That is, until lately. She'd been making such progress. Nori seemed to be the key—to unlocking whatever emotional hitch had made Rosie all but mute, to helping the words flow. They'd become pros at playing the therapist's game, tramping around the nature center and occasionally sitting right here on the carpet. Brave talking, it was called.

Right.

If only the girls didn't both have cowards for parents—not cheaters in the game, but imposters, pretenders, waiting to be caught.

She supposed it had only been a matter of time. But what would become of poor Rosie's progress now?

Rick caught her eye, looking from his daughter's face to hers, acknowledging the conversation stopper as if to indicate that he was not to blame for all that was about to be left unresolved. "I'm horribly late," he said apologetically.

He looked, she had to admit, as sincere as he did confused. "Clearly this is important," he said. "But can we do this later? I'm so sorry, but I can't afford to lose another job." Rick relied on his deceased wife's parents for child care and, though he wasn't ungrateful, struggled with their disregard of boundaries—especially in how they almost relished the way his daughter had retreated into herself, as if this proof of their shared grief was a comfort. They brushed past his pleas for them to participate in Rosie's treatment, and thus he tried to minimize his daughter's time there—at no small expense to his contractor work. Molly had admired his sacrifice but now wondered if she'd been too much on his side. There were at least two sides, after all, to every story.

"By all means, go."

She kissed Rosie on the cheek and handed her over, heading for the exit without a backward glance. "Let's not do it later," she said to the door. "I think it's better to keep a little distance right now. Indefinitely."

She swung the door open and then he was behind her, gripping it, still holding Rosie. She risked a glance back and felt a rush of anger at the both of them, the way they stretched her heart.

"Whoa," he said. "Look, whatever this is about, you have to know I'd never—"

She took a step back, her hands in front of her, warding him off. "You already did," she said, the tears coming loose. She turned away so Rosie wouldn't see, and kept moving, down the stairs, down the path.

She had to admit, he did look baffled. Either he was putting on a decent show, or—

Jesus. Or what?

What if it really wasn't him? If not him, then *who*?

A cutting fear gripped her as her mind raced. No. It was him. It had to have been.

"*Molly.* This is crazy. Come back."

But as she started to sob, she was already gone.

6

"YOU SURE YOU'RE OKAY?"

Max looked as doubtful as Liza felt. Midway home to Chicago, they'd hit rain—miserable, blinding sheets of it—and though it was finally starting to lessen, she'd risked a reprimand from building security by pulling into the wet service alley alongside his high-rise apartment to drop him off. The car might have been cozy under other circumstances, the rain pattering around them, the defroster vents humming, but the return drive had been grim, and the shadows of the city only intensified the exhaustion and concern pooling beneath his eyes.

More than twelve hours ago, they'd hit the road for Ohio tingling with anticipation and, she was ashamed to think of it now, an odd excitement in their investigative, determined spirit. After the first hundred miles of going over and over the shocking turn her call with Molly had taken—recapping every detail until she forced herself to stop talking and let the poor man accompany her without subjecting him to relentless speculation—they'd actually turned on the radio and *sung*.

The drive home, of course, had been quieter. Much quieter.

"I'm as okay as I'm going to get for today. I'm so sorry. . . ."

He shook his head. "*You* don't have anything to be sorry about."

"Well, given the reception we got, I think it's safe to say our little road trip was ill conceived."

"Your *friendship* might have been ill conceived. The road trip was what any good friend would have done. And she's lucky you made me stay in the car, because I would've—"

Liza held up a hand. "Please. I'm sorry you witnessed any of it."

Maybe she should have been humiliated, but that wasn't her style. It was Molly who'd cultivated a reputation for being easily embarrassed, for retreating inside herself at even the slightest perceived missteps. She'd been the girl who left the prom early when her dress ripped on the dance floor, even after Liza procured a mending kit to fix the tear. She'd been the woman who wouldn't receive visitors in the maternity ward until her hair and makeup were photo ready. Who once withdrew her application for a job she was perfect for after discovering she'd misspelled her cover letter's salutation. Liza could tell when Molly was in retreat mode, could sense when to leave well enough alone. But today had been something else entirely.

Something more like damage control. Blind, stubborn, and against all reason.

If Liza didn't know better, she'd think she'd *wronged* her friend by witnessing the intruder.

But she didn't know better, did she? And she no longer wanted to. Nothing remained in this friendship for her. She'd denied the sad fact for too long, and now—well, now it was undeniable.

"I'm not sorry," Max said. "I'm sorry you were treated that way, but I'm not sorry I was there. I'd hate to think of you going through that by yourself."

Rarely was she reminded of what a good boyfriend Max could have been, of what she'd given up on that first date as easily as a hobby she'd barely tried—but it hit her now, the urge to follow him inside, nestle into his warmth under a thick blanket, and fall into a deep, comfortable sleep. She didn't want to be alone but would never ask to follow him in, so certain was she that he would say yes. She smiled sadly. "I more than owe you one."

"If you say so. But first, I'm sleeping straight through to tomorrow morning."

The door thudded shut behind him, and the silence in the car stretched around her. Early-afternoon traffic was made heavier by the weather, and she crawled along rain-streaked blocks for a slow half mile to the only remotely affordable monthly pass garage within walking distance of her apartment—if you counted the long side of a mile as walking distance. Max had insisted on taking the L over last night just to make the trek in the dark with her.

Liza pulled into her space, shouldered the duffel she'd packed for a *just in case* overnight that seemed laughable now, popped open her umbrella, and headed into the drizzle.

Those little inconveniences Chicagoans learned not to mind—or even to enjoy, for all their urban charm—had never warmed to Liza, just as she'd never come to summon enough enthusiasm for a Burberry scarf or a Brynn Capella handbag to justify the price tag. She missed Cincinnati, where public transportation was horribly lacking, but at least she knew how to get anywhere she wanted, on her own schedule and in control of the wheel. She'd expected a new familiarity here that never came, and had only recently started allowing herself to contemplate going back, even if it would look like failure. Even if her old friends would blink at her and ask why on earth she would choose it when she was young enough and unattached enough to go anywhere, do anything. Be anyone. So many of them had lamented to her that they'd missed their own chances before putting down roots.

Molly, for instance.

Molly had seemed somewhat jealous of the move from the start, outwardly cheering her on in the change but looking, on the day Liza left, as if she wanted to either pull her back or come along. Maybe in some way her reaction had helped propel Liza, against her own will.

Because the truth was, she had *instantly* regretted the decision, even before she'd followed through with it.

Initially, Liza had talked about moving away the way many people do: As an occasional impulse she might be better off if she followed "one day" but would likely never act upon. And then she'd seen the job opening. It was similar to her then role at a respectable Queen City Hilton, only on a glitzier scale. She applied on a whim, her thoughts momentarily obscured by pictures of a presumably more interesting place, filled with presumably more interesting people—and, if she was honest, by the picture of her best friend having baby after baby with Daniel and ceasing to call. True, at that point Molly had only one infant and still called Liza almost daily, but surely the slide was only a matter of time. And so she'd uploaded her résumé, hastily whipping up a letter of intent extolling desires she'd not truly felt, much less expressed, until moments before, never expecting a response, much less an offer.

She'd known the second she accepted that it was the wrong decision. Yet she'd convinced herself the sick feeling in her gut was only fear of change. She was Molly's opposite in that respect: Rather than retreating from a misstep, she'd stand too proud to admit she'd taken one. Still, she figured Chicago would be good for her, even if she had to drag herself there. She hadn't been happy going along as she was, watching her friends pass her up, watching chances pass her by.

Now, though, no one could say Liza hadn't given it a fair shot. And the fact that she and Molly had indeed drifted—well, perhaps it had merely been a self-fulfilling prophecy, helped along by the distance. Her oldest friend had still seemed an enticing perk of the imagined *welcome back home* package.

But the events of the past few hours had made quick work of erasing that.

She folded the umbrella without missing a step, suddenly eager to feel the drizzle on her face—to cleanse herself of the whole mess. The city smelled unusually acrid today, polluted and burnt, and she was eager to get off the streets, back into her filtered shell. A police officer was directing traffic away from the intersection ahead—more construction, maybe, or an accident. Always some inconvenience here, never business as usual. She would trudge around this last block, climb into bed, and sleep until she could convince herself she didn't care about the disastrous dawning of this day. She was already well on her way.

But she didn't make it past the corner.

The swath of gray sky where her building's roof should have been stopped her cold even before she could register the orange cones blocking her path. She clutched the bag to her, instant tears stinging her eyes even as her legs continued to propel her forward, stumbling numbly through the initial wave of shock and over a ribbon of yellow tape.

"Ma'am! You can't go through here. Whole block's closed." The poncho-clad police officer was brusque but remarkably nonchalant.

"But I live here," she said, her voice mechanical, prerecorded.

"What building?"

She slowed her steps, still moving forward, and he followed her eyes.

"Oh, God. You were out last night?"

She managed a nod.

"Just getting home?"

She nodded again.

"Ma'am, you were unaware . . . ?"

She could only stare. Firefighters and various other uniformed personnel were milling around the remains of the old warehouse, still smoldering. All five levels of the building were nearly gutted. A partial outer wall here and there, bricks clinging nobly to their mortar, charred beyond recognition and subsequently soaked through, was all that remained.

He let out a low whistle, and she finally met his eye. "Is everyone . . . I mean, are they . . . ?"

She didn't know all of her neighbors but was friendly with enough of them. She was thinking now of Sally, the single mom across the hall who was sleep training her baby and kept lamenting to Liza in the laundry room—Liza did laundry as rarely as possible, but the poor woman was *always* there when she did, no matter the time or day—that she had to stop caving in and carrying the baby into her bed but that exhaustion always won out. Liza hadn't offered much in the way of encouragement, as she, too, had been relieved every time the cries quieted down.

The cries. Surely she had cried in time. . . .

The officer put a firm hand on her shoulder. "Lucky girl, you. Wherever you were, it saved your life."

7

MOLLY'S JAW-CLENCHING NIGHT FINALLY CAUGHT UP WITH HER WHEN SHE got home from Rick's, the TMJ pain taking her face in its hands and making her go dizzy. It served her right that a feigned headache would become a real one, and she climbed back into bed with a warm, wet washcloth circling her chin from ear to ear, trying to luxuriate in the empty, quiet house.

It didn't work, of course. She would never luxuriate in *anything* as long as she lived with this pain.

She missed the comfort of a pet at times like this. Daniel was allergic, so she got her fur fixes the only way she could, by feeding every stray that followed the tree line to her back door. But it was no substitute for the real thing.

She'd grown up with a cat, a dapper tuxedo named Tux who'd curl up against her and purr when she was home sick from school. She and Liza had passed many afternoons constructing elaborate structures out of cardboard boxes for him to hide in and subsequently shred to bits.

Then, when the girls were twelve, they'd almost lost him. He'd taken a rare sojourn beyond the fenced yard and failed to return. The whole family went out searching, but to no avail, and when he'd been gone forty-eight hours Molly's parents' faces turned grim; their voices dropped to whispers about the neighborhood's growing coyote problem. The morning had arrived in a soaking, freezing downpour, and so convinced were they of his unfortunate fate that they refused to go look again.

It was Liza who ventured out with her, in the rain. She'd simply shown up on her own, sparing Molly from having to ask. And after hours of trudging through the pooling mud, it was Liza who heard the faint mews coming from a neighbor's woodpile. Tux had knocked the logs loose and become trapped in an impossibly small pocket of space where they found him curled, wet and shivering.

"My parents would have left him for dead," Molly had sobbed, clutching the cat to her chest. And Liza had looked her straight in the eyes and said, "But not you. That's what matters."

Molly hadn't harbored anger toward her folks after that. She'd simply held her head higher, as if she'd completed a rite of passage.

For a long time she'd thought of her friend just as she'd been that day: pressing on through the muck with a determined poncho-clad arm extended in front of them, shaking a bag of treats. The picture of hope.

Not unlike how she'd been this morning.

The shame at how she'd treated Liza clenched at her jaw again, and Molly pressed her cheeks with balled, angry fists, trying to rub it away.

Maybe it was better to let Liza go. They no longer shared that don't-try-to-stop-me resolve. She was embarrassed to let her friend see what she'd become.

"Girls aren't strong," Grant told Daniel the other day. He was referencing something frivolous, a cartoon character on the TV screen, but he said it so matter-of-factly—like it was common knowledge—that it sucked the air from Molly's lungs. She stood in the doorway behind him, gripping the laundry basket that contained the dirty soccer uniform he was meant to wear in a too-short hour, and met Daniel's eyes over his head. A silent challenge presented itself: Would he let it ride?

"Of course they are," Daniel said, his tone between nervous and congenial. "Why would you say that?"

"I can just tell, from watching Mom. Because of her back and her knees and everything."

And everything. Daniel's eyes flicked back to hers, then away, and she wasn't sure which of them was more humiliated.

"That isn't fair," she blurted out, and Grant turned, looking surprised to find her standing there, but not particularly sorry. "Someone having an injury they can't help doesn't mean they're not strong. I'm strong in plenty of other ways." She felt ridiculous, getting defensive with a five-year-old. But he'd cut to the bone of her fears, that her children would see her this way—weak, inadequate, limited. The way *Daniel* saw her.

"She gave birth to you," Daniel pointed out, and she'd have been grateful if she had any faith the conversation would have gone this way without her present. "That's something no boy is strong enough to do."

Grant changed the subject then, and Molly went to put the wash in, where no one would see her cry.

It haunted her, that this was the example she'd set for her son. *Girls aren't strong.* She'd done everything she could think of to try to break free of this pain trap, and she *loathed* that she was still inside of it. Shivering and full of regret, like Tux. And she'd foolishly sent away the only person who'd bothered to come looking for her.

She got to her feet and tossed the damp washcloth toward the hamper, where it landed in a sad heap a few feet off target. Leaving it—that's what Daniel would do—she crossed to the walk-in closet and stood in the doorway, surveying its his-and-her contents as if they belonged to a pair of strangers. Which, in a way, they did.

Pulling off her tee, she let it fall to the floor and stood shivering in her bra, a plain thick cotton number she wouldn't have been caught dead in ten years ago. The clothes lining her side of the rack were too compartmentalized: business casual basics she scarcely needed anymore, date-night dresses that didn't fare much better, and stretchy activewear that only reminded her of how broken she felt wearing it. What she wanted was *comfort*—something to make her feel like everything would be okay, even if it wasn't true. Her eyes fell on an old sweatshirt of Daniel's—one she'd spent many of their hours apart in back when they were dating—and she pulled it down from the top shelf and slid it over her head.

An aged, worn version of her former self peered back at her from the floor-length mirror. Wrapping herself in this soft warmth had once felt like wrapping herself in *him,* on nights when she wanted him so badly she clung to the next best thing. Then as now, it smelled of Daniel, clean shaven and cool. She used to make a show of pouting when he asked for it back, unflattering and misshapen though it was. For a while, the shirt was like a game piece—she'd talk him out of his clothes and later, when he was drowsing naked and spent, she'd pluck it triumphantly from its discarded spot on the floor and shove it into her drawer, hoping he wouldn't see.

Now she shared a closet with *all* his clothes and felt little affection for them—only annoyance when they took up more than their share of hangers. Now she slept in her own clothes whether he was home or away. But she wanted to know if she could feel that way again. As if righting things between them were as easy as putting on an old, familiar shirt. As if she couldn't get enough of him otherwise.

As if she could *never* get enough.

The way she'd been feeling lately, it embarrassed her to admit, about Rick.

She tucked a strand of hair behind her ear and stared at her reflection. She looked like one of those TV drama wives who greet their husbands with kisses and do still wear their clothes, albeit in a more adorably coifed way than Molly could ever manage. She would leave this shirt on until just before Daniel was due home, and she *would* relish the empty house. And maybe, by the time she returned it to its shelf, she'd know what to say when he walked through the door.

It had to be a good sign, at least, that she really did want to be alone. This was new, hoping Rick *wouldn't* stop by. Molly was far more accustomed to biting back the urge to speak his name, as if working him into conversations might conjure his presence—even where Daniel was concerned. Sometimes *especially* where Daniel was concerned.

Of course, she never did. She hadn't exactly meant for her friendship with Rick to be a secret. Daniel knew that Rosie and Nori had a bond but was too busy questioning whether it was wise for Nori to spend so much time with a "troubled kid" to realize the extent to which that bond had extended to Rick and Molly. Daniel could ruin things that way. His dismissals came easily and without much thought, before or after. And she hadn't wanted him to ruin her one good thing outside of work and the kids, even though she was realizing that the fact that her one good thing involved another man—however tangentially, however *innocently*—was problematic on a fundamental level.

It wasn't that she wanted Rick instead. It was just that Rick knew how to look her in the face without cringing or scoffing at her pain, without reflexively looking away from it, even without minimizing it, which was something he of all people had a right to do. It was trivial compared to what he'd been through. But Rick was firm that life was not a competition of whose tragedies were the most crushing.

Ostensibly he was the one who'd needed help, at the start. That first day, late last summer, he'd rushed down the trail through the woods, toddler Rosie in his arms, startling Molly and Nori, who weren't used to backyard visitors. Molly had been coaxing Nori through a scavenger hunt, a preschool assignment to consider what was "the same and different" between the nature center and their own backyards. So far, she'd offered to Nori the wispy remains of a dandelion head, an unripe cherry tomato, and a perfect maple leaf, but all her daughter wanted was to rip handfuls of grass from the lawn and throw them like confetti.

"Sorry for barging in," Rick had said, standing over her, smiling down. "You're about to question my parenting, because though we haven't met, I'm wondering if you can take her for a second? I didn't realize these tree cutters would come so close to the house. They're making me nervous." So that was the noise she'd been hearing. The forest was thick that time of year, making it hard to tell what all that grinding and crashing entailed, or how far away it was. She got to her feet, her scavenged rejects still clenched in her hand. The last vestiges of the carpal tunnel had left her grip weakened, and she crunched the dandelion stem until she felt the milk ooze into her palm, just to prove to herself she could.

"I'm Molly," she said, wiping the mess on her jeans and extending a hand, "and this is Nori." She looked down at her daughter, who was paying them no mind, busy examining the grass stains on the knees of her light gray leggings. Nori's little fingers slid a tentative blade of grass over her ankle, experimenting, and she looked disappointed when it didn't function like a paintbrush. Molly smiled at Rick ruefully. "About the same age, I'd say? Nori just turned three."

"Inching up on three here," he said. "I'm Rick. She's Rosie. And so sorry, but if you don't mind keeping her at a safe distance—" He was cut short by the smashing of branches and a distant masculine *whoop* that didn't sound entirely victorious.

"Go," Molly insisted, taking Rosie into her tingling arms with all the assuredness she could muster. The girl was lighter than Nori, wispier, and she blinked wide eyed at Molly with the look of someone who was trying to go with the flow. A mature look, all things considered, for a two-year-old.

By the time Rick returned, nearly an hour later, Molly was clearing the dried leaves and dead vines from the bottom of the path—now that someone was going to use it, at least once more—and watching the girls with fascination. Nori had taken the younger girl's hand and not let go. Molly had brought them a picnic blanket and a tin tea party set, and they'd been sitting for an uncharacteristically long stretch, shoulder to shoulder, passing dishes back and forth, looking like the world's most innocuous two-headed monster.

She heard the rush of steps behind her, and the string of muttered curses when Rick tripped, and turned just in time to wave off his breathless apology. "Fast friends," she whispered, pointing at the girls.

"You did *me* a favor, actually—I think Nori was getting bored with me. Though the most curious thing is that they haven't said a word to each other."

"It'd be more curious if they had," he said, crossing his arms and leaning in as if she were already his greatest confidant. "Rosie doesn't talk to anyone other than me." Molly checked that he was serious, and he responded with a brisk nod. "It's early to diagnose it, but it's called selective mutism. The doctors are reluctant to tie it to her mother's death, given her age at the time, but they won't convince me that doesn't have everything to do with it."

"Oh." What to say to that? His wife's death after a yearlong battle with cancer had been the subject of neighborhood speculation not because anyone knew the family—no one seemed to—but because you didn't need to know them to know that it was just so damn sad. She had a baby, for God's sake, and had been ill for her daughter's entire life. No wonder the father was so antisocial, coming and going down his long driveway with the windows rolled up, no acknowledgment of his neighbors aside from an aloof wave. He did seem to have a surplus of relatives around, though, whether his own or his wife's—the turnout for her wake had clogged the streets—and so the others had left them to grieve in peace. Or so they told themselves when someone ventured that perhaps they should have approached.

"I'm so sorry. That must be . . . difficult." She tried to imagine a life where this had become requisite small talk when meeting someone new—a need-to-know briefing on the tragedy and its fallout. She decided to take a chance on a little levity. "You didn't think to mention that she wouldn't talk to me when you dropped her off?" Molly teased, and his eyes snapped to hers, surprised. She persisted. "Good thing I'm not one to let a kid who ignores me give me a complex."

It was a good-natured lie. Even an infant could give her a complex, simply by crying—oh goodness, what was she doing wrong, what was she missing, and why was she so incompetent? Molly had stopped liking that once-favorite Eleanor Roosevelt quote—*No one can make you feel inferior without your consent*—awhile back. Around the time she realized that she'd taken to granting permission rather indiscriminately.

A guilty half smile crept across his face. "Would you have agreed to watch her if I had?"

"Of course." Actually, there was a decent chance she'd have talked herself out of it—or, at best, agreed but then ruined the hour by trying to overcompensate, talking too fast and loud and forcing things.

"Then we came to the right place." Rosie hadn't noticed her father yet, and he watched with interest as she reached out a spoon and stirred Nori's invisible tea. "As I said, it's early, but we're in therapy now, trying to make headway before preschool, or pre-K—" He stopped, considering. "Actually, the therapist encouraged a playmate. To expand her comfort zone." He turned to Molly, his expression infused with such hope it took her aback. She couldn't remember the last time she'd *felt* so earnestly about anything. Anyone.

"It's my fault. I've kept her holed up there on the hill, walled in by grief—mostly mine. It's heartbreaking how little she remembers, already. Though maybe for the best." He cleared his throat, and Molly's inclination was to put him at ease. He could leave himself out of it; no need to go there.

"What kind of therapy is it, exactly?" she asked.

"Behavioral. It's focused on what's called 'brave talking'—which might be bunk, who knows. But no way am I letting them medicate this kid. So it's this or nothing."

Molly had become an expert in filling that space between "this" and "nothing" with other approaches that someone, somewhere thought might be a good idea. But given her track record, she kept that to herself.

"What kind of medication would they possibly use for a kid who just doesn't speak?"

"Antianxiety stuff. A good percentage of selective mutes have an underlying anxiety disorder, so they try to treat that. But hell if I'm going to let them make a guessing game out of my kid. Who, by the way, is not anxious."

It wasn't a father's blind denial, as far as Molly could tell. Rosie seemed on first meeting—which with many kids was the worst meeting, where they only hid behind their parents—to be a charming, smiley girl. The silence, he went on to say, could become part of her identity if it wasn't corrected soon. Which would make it even harder to crack down the road.

"How can we help?" she asked. "'Brave talking' sounds like something Nori might benefit from, too." This was blatantly untrue. The idea of her daughter having any more of a filter lifted was enough to send tingles down her spine. But maybe she could use it herself.

Rick explained part of the trick was to refrain from asking yes-or-no questions. To coax her, in front of other people, to state a preference between alternatives or to suggest a next step for an activity in progress.

"So far, she won't do anything but point. I'm supposed to wait until she speaks to get her what she wants, but when I feel a scene coming on, I cave too easily. Especially because the other party present is usually my in-laws." He threw up his hands. "Maybe if you and Nori came over? Or if we could play here . . ."

Molly thought of the busloads of special needs kids who came through the nature center every week. "Do you two like to hike?"

That had been the beginning. He'd offered to barter. He was a contractor; if they had something that needed fixing, he could help. But Molly waved him off.

If he'd been walled in by grief, her own walls were built of pain, and she'd been content to hide beyond them—until the minute she could see over her flimsy, halfhearted barrier and into someone else's tougher, sturdier one.

He'd reminded her what it was like to have a friend who was on your side by default, until or unless you gave him a reluctant reason not to be. Where Daniel had somehow become more adversary than partner—someone to whom she always felt she owed an explanation for the inexplicable causes behind her aches, for the frustration behind her persistent failure to just *feel good again,* to just *be normal*—Rick was a sympathetic ear who accepted her feelings as valid without requiring a list of reasons, of treatments she had tried that hadn't worked, of diagnoses she had looked into and ruled out. When he did make suggestions, they were more thoughtful than her husband's reaching for the obvious, which came off as condescending. Rick knew something of alternative medicine from his wife's battle and didn't discount anything or make Molly feel foolish for trying.

And when it came to Rosie and Nori, they were all stronger, they discovered, as a foursome. Rick was patient almost to a fault, even on days he must have been inwardly screaming over all he'd lost. He inspired Molly to follow suit, to do better. They traipsed determinedly through the changing leaves in the fall; they rewarded small victories with hot cocoa from The Nature Shop in the winter. When Rosie started whispering on occasion into Nori's ear, when the girls bubbled over into giggles, and when Rick played the piano and all four of them sang along, Rosie forgetting herself in the music, her little voice high and thin and happy beneath her father's easy tones, Molly felt as if she was helping to restore a fraction of the life he'd breathed back into hers.

He'd set out to help his daughter, and he'd helped Molly instead.

Until last night. When everything had come undone.

And now she was hanging from the last, loose thread.

She would have *rather* hinged every inch of her affection to Daniel. For a time, Molly had tried psychosynthesis—attending weekly consultations with a practitioner who specialized in the intersection of body and mind—and in seeking connections she never found between Molly's various ailments, the clinician had broached the subject of interpersonal relationships, offering this: that the person who wants less from the relationship holds the power. Molly knew without question that as long as she struggled with pain, and as long as Daniel persisted to deny that it was both significant and beyond her control, she would be the partner in her marriage who wanted more—from herself, from motherhood, from Daniel, from *life*—and she was so uncomfortable with the implied weakness of her position, she'd never gone back after that.

The beauty in what she and Rick had was in their equal standing, in their give-and-take. And so it had been easy to convince herself that such an arrangement meant that neither of them was left wanting—for anything. She could see now that between her and Rick *she* might hold the power—and that perhaps she'd sensed that, recognized its appeal. Rick might have brought them to this new, uncomfortable moment when he'd called her bluff, but really she'd been the first one to step out of line, and though she'd done it not with actions but with words, she couldn't deny that it was on her. Rick wasn't immune to wanting. And he was no longer bound by a promise he'd made to someone else.

But she was.

The thought of losing Rick and Liza at the same time was almost too much to bear. And yet right now the only one she could think of salvaging things with was Daniel. Funny how it took a new wave of guilt to displace the old hurt that had stopped her from trying.

She pulled his shirt around her, tighter. If he held the power, maybe it did, too.

8

I CAN GIVE YOU PLENTY OF REASONS TO RECONSIDER.

Daniel had been staring at the email on his screen for a full ten minutes, trying to decide whether it was a threat or a bribe. He might have convinced himself it was neither if that sentence weren't the whole of the message, or if the subject line hadn't been left blank.

There was no space currently available in his brain to allocate to this worry. He hadn't come to the office to *work.* He'd come here to work out what to *do.* About Molly.

He'd come here, ironically, for a refuge.

"Regret coming back early yet?"

Not bothering to wait for Daniel to answer her knock on the open door, Jules carried the stack of folders right in, bringing with her an apologetic smile, a waft of the coffee she brewed fresh every afternoon, and the ridiculously on-point question. She'd been surprised to see him this morning but adjusted quickly, not prying when he told her the meetings had been a bust, canceling out today's agenda, not asking why he'd rushed home. He bit back a sardonic laugh as she plopped the pile onto his desk, and instead offered a *what can I say, I'm a glutton for punishment* sort of shrug.

His most tolerable days in the office were the ones when Daniel managed to talk *only* to Jules. The administrative assistant shared by his department had a cut-the-crap efficiency and dry sense of humor he appreciated. She seemed to favor Daniel over his counterparts who looked a little too long at the plunge of her neckline. She also, he suspected, knew everything there was to know—and then some—about his colleagues, yet kept most of the intel to herself.

Most of it.

In other words, not even Jules was safe.

"Ask me again after I get a look at what's in there," he replied.

She laughed but didn't stick around to banter. He took that as a bad sign. The screen in front of him went black—back to sleep—as she closed the door behind her, and he swiveled his chair to look out the window, ignoring the new stack of paperwork.

He'd liked the job, once. Sure, he'd always known the guys in charge were assholes, but what company didn't lack compassion at the top these days? It wasn't so hard to separate *what* he was doing—pushing numbers, his old, reliable friends—from *whom* he was doing it for. Even when he reached a level where there were fewer hierarchical buffers between him and said assholes, where he no longer just pushed the numbers but signed off on them, even presented them to prospective partners, he still compartmentalized the two, the sum of Column A and Column B being a good living for quite a few years. He wished now that it hadn't been so easy to go along, get along, wished something had prompted him to move on before he'd started noticing things that *didn't* add up. Literally.

And before his inbox had become occupied by this reminder that Daniel's wordlessly complicit role in that bad math wasn't wordless anymore.

Why *hadn't* he moved on? The company had grown quickly, and at first the enthusiasm was catching. They were innovating ways to make home furnishings less toxic, from exploring alternative dyes to reducing outgassing. It was the sort of work people felt good about being involved in—with the bragging-rights bonus of being "on trend," as evidenced by their booming consumer outreach campaigns. But the growth proved too quick to stay ahead of, and they'd been left scrambling to restructure and expand operations to meet the demand.

Right around that time, Molly had been going on about wanting to reduce her own hours. He thought it an overreaction to a difficult stage she could have waited out. Nori was *not* an easy baby, and Grant's boundless energy *was* hard to keep up with, and Molly's lingering gestational carpal tunnel *did* make her workdays at the keyboard miserable, but those things would have passed. Her unhappiness seemed surprisingly aggressive, however, and so when his department came up for expansion he pushed back. He presented a plan that made do with department-level analysts and bookkeepers in lieu of their proposed controller to review broader numbers—then made a play for the top financial seat, assuring them it wasn't too much for one person though he was fairly certain it was. They went for it, nearly doubling his salary even as they saved six pretty figures on their own bottom line.

At first he'd buckled under the load, and it didn't help that Molly, in spite of all the shifting and convincing and compromising he'd done so she could get her way, was *still* barely holding it together at home. What busy co-parent of young children had time to be encumbered by pain? She was always needing him to compensate somehow. So he'd shaved away the extra hours he should have put in here—focusing on strategy, which the board was paying closer attention to, and pulling back on oversight—and braced for the blowback.

But none came. He'd discovered the fine art, with a fancy new title and fat raise, of doing what was commonly known as a half-ass job.

Daniel wasn't used to contemplating words—less trustworthy than numbers, frustratingly unpredictable. But he'd spent a lot of time doing it lately, even before this cryptic email, even before Molly's evasive responses this morning. Take the phrase *human resources.* Was it supposed to refer to the humans who worked in that department, helping the rest of them navigate the basic benefits they'd earned? Or was it meant to refer to the employee pool at large, as if they were a breed that had been baited, caged, and brought to this place where they must be begrudgingly provided for?

Either way, the idea of having the word *human*—which surely went without saying—in your job title was still not as off-putting as the department's director himself, who barely qualified as one. The other execs—hypocritical enough to pick out the chief asshat among them—snickered that his name was, appropriately, Toby, same as the HR rep on *The Office* whom boss parody Michael Scott dubbed "the worst." But Daniel thought the name too good for the real-life Toby. The show's running gag was that there wasn't really cause to dislike Toby so intensely, whereas this guy provided plenty.

Many of his failings were readily on display: his passive-aggressive missives implying that holidays off were conditional, for instance. But now that Daniel knew those merely scratched the surface of what Toby was capable of, he wondered if the man actually *strived* to be so grating, so that no one would ever want to spend enough time looking in his direction to realize he was downright criminal.

Toby, like Daniel, had taken a hands-on approach to his own department's reorg. Toby, unlike Daniel, had had a long-term plan for doing so, something beyond the instant gratification of *get a bigger paycheck to get my wife off my case.*

In the new and improved HR, he'd delegated things like recruiting and health benefits, while keeping oversight of the retirement plans under his purview. At first Daniel assumed this was a matter of personal preference. Toby, to his chagrin, seemed to have singled him out for watercooler-type chitchat—in the lunchroom, in the john, wherever mold grew, come to think of it. And even in casual conversation Toby talked about money so much you'd never know he wasn't working toward a year-end bonus or revenue goal.

The first time Daniel's head was turned by an exorbitant expense report—exorbitant enough to draw a flag that sent it up the chain—Toby explained it away. He was courting new firms to handle their 401(k) plans—something by rights they should have had a whole committee overseeing, but no one had time for that, not with everything else in rapid-expansion flux. There was nothing wrong with the current plans, per se, but the provider's website was clumsy to navigate, and there'd been complaints.

"Shouldn't the firms be courting *us*?" Daniel asked, eyebrows raised.

"It goes both ways." Toby's smile was a bad fit for his face, like a shirt stretched too tight. "I'm trying to get them to give us a premium upgrade we're not quite big enough to qualify for. And if we get it, it'll be worth the cost of a few five-star dinners, I assure you. Think ROI."

I assure you was in the top ten of Daniel's way-more-than-ten pet peeves in the world of condescending corporate speak, and *ROI* was on his separate list of hated acronyms, though at the EOD he had to use a lot of those himself, what with all the EBITDA and YTD reports. Daniel had mocked Toby to Molly that night, but instead of laughing with him, she'd turned her disdain on Daniel, saying he should either get involved with the provider selection, given his own expertise, or report Toby's abuse of their meals and entertainment policies. Daniel, who'd grown to like coasting in the half-ass zone, wanted to do neither. Besides, Toby's selection and its implementation would be accountable to auditors—eventually. Daniel had gone to bed stewing that she'd lost her sense of humor so entirely he couldn't even complain about a colleague without ending up in the hot seat.

Still, he didn't have the good sense not to do it again. When Toby's next visit was to a Florida-based provider and included two days on a world-class golf course, Daniel marveled once more to his wife at the man's audacity—and Molly again made her displeasure clear, her moral high horse putting his to pasture. Both were gnawing at the wrong thing, but he didn't know it yet. He finally wised up about talking Toby at the dinner table when a meeting in New York City somehow ended with orchestra seats at *Hamilton*. *How often do we switch providers?* Daniel reasoned. *Let the guy have his fun, if it'll work out better for everyone else in the end.*

But when Toby finally landed on an investment group—and indeed a boutique one Daniel had thought out of their league—Daniel wished he *had* enforced some sort of approval over the director's choice. The administrative fees seemed prohibitively high, without above-average returns, as far as Daniel could see, to justify the expense.

More curiously still, Toby's own expenses didn't exactly stop. For a while, they kept Daniel focused on the wrong columns of the spreadsheets.

Until, at last, he began looking at the right ones.

The esteemed HR head had accurately calculated his subordinate humans' blind spots. The staffers were people who were passionate about the environment, or design, or public health. As such, they were not particularly bottom-line driven, nor were they the sort who moved investments from fund to fund for kicks or questioned the size of routine-sounding fees. They'd set the percentage to be deducted from their paychecks and let it be, barely glancing at the reports, trusting that the rest would take care of itself.

Trusting, in other words, that they could trust Toby.

No one had noticed that loose change was being skimmed off of investment earnings and deposited into a fund that did not in fact exist. No one had seen further evidence of certain arrangements reached between Toby and said provider—in the mysterious fees, in the continued clandestine meetings, and even in the weasel's shiny new car.

No one but Daniel. Because while the others could have been paying more attention, it wasn't their job to notice.

It was, arguably, his.

When Daniel started to see the real red flags, he hadn't *wanted* to look closer. By then, if his suspicions were true, they'd escalated to a level that would reflect badly—worse than badly—on him as well. But his curiosity wouldn't be quieted. And so, just days ago, he'd found himself running his finger over it with dread and disbelief: the residue remaining after layers of scrubbing, faint but visible, in black and red.

Daniel still wasn't sure exactly how Toby was doing it. His guess was that someone in payroll must be involved—as well as the third-party administrator grooming them for the audit. He only knew that it was happening, and this knowledge was new enough that he hadn't processed it fully. In fact, he'd been only 98 percent sure—*might* he be reading the discrepancies wrong?—until just after his discovery, when Toby, who could not lock the files down but *could* see who accessed them, preempted his conclusion with a vaguely but transparently worded invitation. To participate.

And it appeared Daniel's brusque, ignorance-feigning decline—*I don't know what you're talking about, but even if I did, I'm confident I would not be interested*—had not satisfied.

It appeared he could be given, as this morning's email proclaimed, *plenty of reasons to reconsider.*

Daniel had never had much contempt for employees who siphoned money away from greedy companies. But from their coworkers? From retirement funds, for Christ's sake? He'd never be swayed to that kind of activity—*never.* But if he were to blow the whistle now, everyone would rightly wonder how Toby had gotten this far. Hating the boardroom admonition to *get more granular* was one thing; failing to follow it was another. Exposing the fraud at the risk of his own negligent hide was something Daniel had to consider carefully, and he hated himself for that.

For all Molly's misdirected anger in his direction, on this matter she'd been right to call out his complacency from the start. She'd be horrified if she knew the worst of it. His inaction had put them at risk, and for what? A part of him wanted to blame her, for having a hand in making him so damn complacent in the first place, but that wasn't fair. If anything, the wall she'd been erecting at home should have made him eager to tackle something he could actually fix. It had become habit, assuring her things were no big deal, under control, assuming she was blowing them out of proportion.

But the Toby issue had waited this long. Daniel could stall for another day.

Molly could *not* wait. Not as of this morning.

Not as of a week ago, in fact, when kindhearted, earnest Grant had said to him—so sweetly and unthinkingly and confident he would agree—"Girls aren't strong." Then: "I can just tell, from watching Mom."

Daniel had cringed, but he might have chalked up his son's words to the realm of *things kids with no filter say* if not for the broken look on Molly's face, her sobs that night when she thought he was asleep, her defensive posture the day after that, and the next. Because he'd known: He bore responsibility for this. He had influenced his son to see Molly as less than. Because he'd treated her that way himself.

And though things between them *were* a bit chicken-or-the-egg, he had to admit: He couldn't recall her ever behaving as incapable until he'd started doubting her capabilities.

Now their children were doing it, too.

This wasn't like the nagging shame he'd been feeling at the office. Not a persistent background alert that had finally drawn his attention, but a blaring, horrifying wake-up call from the one source he'd hoped would be untouched by his shortcomings. How had he not seen it before?

Suddenly he'd desperately needed her to know that he was sorry, that things would be different now. But he didn't know how. And now this. She *hadn't even told him about an intruder in their house.* This was worse than her not thinking he'd be there for her: This was her not *wanting* him to be. Not needing him at all. Not holding out her hand for him to take.

He had two choices: confront Molly about what had happened last night, her awkward silence this morning, and the unmentionables in between, or wait and see if she took the lead. The latter seemed less promising with each hour that ticked by without her lighting up his phone with a text, a call, anything at all. Not so much as a notification that she'd added milk to their grocery list app.

He shut down his computer, switched off the lights, and, not bothering with the pretense of gathering up work to take home, hustled out without a glance at Jules. It would take nerve for anyone to stop him. He never left early. And he hadn't been expected today anyway.

Feeling like a cheat of a cliché, he walked two short blocks to the florist, where he passed over the roses and lilies and stood contemplating a bouquet of yellow tulips. "Those traditionally symbolized 'hopeless love,'" the clerk called out from behind the register.

She was young and wide eyed, and said it like it was a good thing.

Still, it was too spot on *not* to buy them.

Back on the sidewalk, he surveyed the storefronts, wanting some other gift, something more original. But he hadn't the faintest idea of what his wife might *really* like just now, aside from the many mysterious balms she'd taken to for her litany of pseudo-identifiable ailments. Nothing about a new essential oil diffuser seemed thoughtful or romantic, even if it did cost more than seemed passable.

He couldn't stop thinking about that word. *Hopeless.*

He walked back to the office parking lot, which was still full, and headed for home, uncertain what he'd do when he got there but no longer able to bear being anywhere else.

—

Molly was wearing his shirt. His old favorite. *Her* old favorite. One neither of them had touched in years.

She was lying on her back on the living room floor, perfectly still on her acupuncture mat, knees bent toward the ceiling. Once, just the sight of her lying down had stirred something within him—an impulse to join her. These days, her body radiated tension—he wasn't sure if it was true discomfort or just a constant, tentative fear of it, but she seemed to have gotten used to it and adjusted accordingly.

He never would.

Worst was the feeling that he must have contributed to how out of sorts she'd become in her own skin. He couldn't fathom how she'd ever have ended up here had he not failed her. Her growing disappointment in him was easy to recall, but its exact origin was not, and he wanted to go back, to find the precise moment where the discord had begun and do the opposite thing.

When was the last time he'd seen her reach for anything of his, much less put it on? This particular shirt had meant something to them both, once.

Did it still?

As he shut the door to the garage behind him, she opened one eye to confirm it was him—not the jumpy response one might expect from someone who'd escaped an intruder the night before—and closed it again, showing no reaction to the tulips he was holding. He stopped where he stood, waiting to see if she'd look again, feeling ridiculous. Though he'd always thought of their living room as homey rather than dull, the yellow blooms looked unconscionably bright here, too much like forced cheer—the contrast exposing them all as the frauds they were. The wall-mounted flat-screen was muted on one of those afternoon talk shows that try way too hard, and he wondered at the mindless comfort of turning on something that you were neither watching nor listening to.

Why bother?

"Home early," he announced, stating the obvious, and this time when her eyes blinked open they formed narrow slits.

"*Please* keep your voice down. Nori's napping, for once in her life."

Poor kid. He guessed she hadn't slept well last night. But then again, if the chaos had woken her, wouldn't she or Grant have mentioned it to him this morning? Was *everyone* counting him out now?

"You're wearing my shirt," he said instead, more quietly. She looked down at herself with surprise, embarrassment flashing on her face, and he still wasn't able to discern the shirt's significance or lack thereof, only that perhaps she hadn't planned for him to see her in it, either way. He waved the flowers with a rueful smile, laid them on the coffee table, and crossed to turn off the TV. She rolled gingerly off the mat and hugged her knees to her chest, looking from the tulips to Daniel with an expectation that didn't quite mask her dread. He would pretend not to notice the puffiness now evident behind her long lashes, the tell that she'd been crying.

"Got some interesting calls at the office today," he lied, sinking onto the couch a safe distance from her. No one had called him, actually. He'd left neighborhood friendships mostly to Molly, not for lack of interest, but for lack of . . . well, initiative. But he knew that a cop camped outside the house overnight wouldn't go unnoticed, so it seemed plausible. He cocked his head at her in a way he hoped conveyed more compassion than sarcasm. "Care to fill me in?"

She averted her eyes, pressing her fingers onto the acupuncture mat's bed of needlelike tips. No way that didn't hurt.

"Maybe you can explain why you haven't mentioned it yet, while you're at it," he added. He couldn't resist.

When she looked up this time, guilt pooled in her eyes. "I wanted to call you right away, but I figured you'd just worry," she began. She opened her mouth again, but nothing came out. On the mat's needles, the skin around her nail beds whitened from the pressure. Jesus, this was painful to watch. Had she taken him for such a fool that she'd not foreseen this conversation, in some shape? Did she not see that he was trying to do this as kindly as possible?

"Why don't you start from the beginning," he suggested. He sounded calm, reasonable. Not bad, considering.

She obliged, with the barest of facts: Liza on the webcam. Nori calling. What Liza claimed to have seen. The knock at the door, the flashing lights. The police coming up empty. "I should have called as soon as they left, I know." She was talking faster now, picking up steam. "But Daniel, we were *fine,* and I was exhausted. By the time the cops left, it was late, and I knew we'd be safe—there was still an officer outside. Nori was half-awake when they came upstairs, searching the house, and I had to convince her it was all a dream to get her back down." The muscles in his neck eased up, just a little. So Grant and Nori had been left out of it after all. "I guess it worked, because she hasn't said a word about it since, but—"

"But neither have you."

She shook her head. "You caught me off guard this morning. If I'd known you were coming home early—or even that that was an option—I'd have given you a heads-up. But I didn't want to tell you in front of the kids, and then it just . . . I don't know. I was waiting for the right moment and it slipped away." Conspicuously absent was any mention of Liza showing up on their doorstep.

"It *slipped away* from you to tell me there was an intruder in our house when you were here alone with the kids?" He was losing his cool, but only a saint could withstand this. He wanted to throw something, tip over a chair.

She frowned, and in her eyes the pools of remorse congealed into something colder, harder. Determination, maybe, or denial. "I'm not even sure there was. There was no sign of it, aside from whatever Liza thinks she saw. The cops looked everywhere. No forced entry, nothing. Though I can't even say whether the back doors were locked."

"You're not calling Liza a liar? Why would she make something like that up?"

"She wouldn't. I don't know, it could have been a camera glitch or something?"

He blinked. "Did the *cops* think that's possible?"

"They didn't seem to know, but they also didn't seem overly concerned. They asked if I could think of a reason we'd be targeted—"

"What did you tell them?"

She glared at him. "I told them of course not. That's ridiculous. We live modestly on a salary and a half, and we're nice people."

Her voice warbled on the word *ridiculous.*

Then again, his probably would have, too.

"Most likely, it was some random intruder," she went on, more steadily. "He got spooked and won't be back. Cop said the worse the heroin epidemic gets, the more break-ins they see. So I don't think—"

"Fine," he said. "Say it doesn't matter what happened—though I'm not sure I agree with that. It still matters that you didn't tell me!"

"We never talk to each other about *anything* real anymore," she snapped. "Why talk about this?"

He drew back as if she'd struck him. She was supposed to be answering his knock at the barrier between them, inviting him in to make this right. Yet minutes in, her tolerance for him had already waned, and here she was, lashing out instead.

Why, though, was he surprised? He couldn't even ask her how she was feeling anymore without her shooting back some sort of roundabout statement that amounted to a skeptical *Do you really want to know?* or a frustrated *What difference does it make?* Usually he'd walk away from her—something between shrugging it off and storming off—but he had to stop doing that. He had to start *staying.* Even if it was uncomfortable, or frustrating. Perhaps especially then.

"Jesus, Molly," he said. "Have we really grown that far apart? Because that's *all the way* apart."

There was hurt in the words, emotion he would have usually worked to hide, but honesty suddenly seemed in short supply between them, and he doubled down on it. She looked taken aback, and for a terrible moment they simply stared at each other.

When she answered, her voice was barely more than a whisper. "I hope not."

"Well," he said, straightening his shoulders. "So do I. That's something, isn't it?"

She squeezed her eyes shut, and liquid emotion spilled onto her cheeks. Finally. A sign of life. He lowered himself onto the floor next to her.

"You must have been scared," he said quietly. "Thank God for Liza." He watched her closely, but there was no change in her expression. Best to leave that one alone. For now. "I'm sorry I wasn't here. And I'm glad you won't be alone again tonight." She wiped at her face with her sleeve and smiled weakly. He slid the bouquet closer on the coffee table, pulled a tulip out of the bunch, and handed it to her. She hesitated, then took it, burying her nose in the bloom.

"Florist said they stand for 'hopeless love,'" he told her. She looked up at him, eyes widening, and a beat of silence hung between them. He waited.

"Don't take this the wrong way, but I'm more of a red roses kind of girl," she said finally.

Was this *criticism*? A dig, even now? He decided not to take it as one. *Someone* had to stop this between them. So instead, he just asked: "What do those stand for?"

"I don't know. Plain old ordinary love, maybe?"

He put an arm around her shoulder and pulled her to him. "Plain old ordinary love it is," he said.

And for a moment, it almost felt like it.

9

THE COVERAGE OF THE FIRE READ STOICALLY, DEVOID OF THE LIFE THAT HAD existed—and ended—within the charred walls: unknown start; rapid spread; a lawsuit already pending, it turned out, against the contractor who'd converted the warehouse, alleging that safety codes had been skirted in a couple other projects completed for the same developer. Six floors of apartments, dozens of families and couples and singles housed therein, nearly half of them rendered homeless, the rest gone, just gone, a part of the ash. No one on or above the fourth floor, where Liza's loft had been, had survived. Except Liza.

Cold as the reporting was, she was glad she could hold it in her hands. It would have seemed even more insubstantial blinking by her on a smartphone screen. And for the *Tribune* in her grasp she could thank Max, who evidently—just in case she hadn't found him charmingly reliable enough—still subscribed to the seven-day print edition.

She'd raised a halfhearted but impressed eyebrow when he dropped it in front of her first thing this morning at his glass-topped dinette, where she sat staring numbly at how different his apartment looked in the early hour and trying not to think of how she'd never see the sun light her own little kitchen again. "You read them every morning? They don't pile up?"

"Right here before work, with my coffee and avocado toast."

"You're like a character on an eighties TV show."

"Not true. I don't remember seeing a single avocado in the eighties."

"Well, they liked the color for cabinets."

The banter while he set the coffee to brew had kept her clinging to some semblance of humanity, until he'd gone to shower and she'd been left sitting here, rereading the front-page article that didn't contain a trace of it. She wanted to crush the paper, to shove it as deep into the trash can as it would go, but she couldn't keep her eyes from the spaces between the grainy type, where the real story of her own night was an unwritten footnote.

Liza Green dodged death last night in a strange turn of events that may have amounted to trading her longest friendship for her life.

Every single person affected could rewrite this story in a different way, and every one of those versions would hold more worth than the one sitting in front of her.

She'd write them if she could, one for each loss, one for each survivor. It felt inadequate, to be left imagining them through her own limited lens.

Ms. Green's neighbors were not so fortunate. Not Judy Joseph, the grandmotherly type who left peanut butter fork cookies in her mailbox at least once a month, because she "seemed a little homesick, dear" (which, of course, she was). Not Sally Tremont, the single mother who we can only hope was with her baby when the smoke and flames overtook them. Not Christopher Sebold or Kurt Brown, whose names no one in the building even knew before this morning's casualties were released, but whose songwriting most of them quite enjoyed, when it occurred at reasonable hours. Ms. Green wishes she had told them how talented she thought they were, especially the one who rehearsed sad, sweet ballads about his ex-girlfriend when his roommate wasn't home.

Max appeared in the doorway, tugging at the open collar of his gray button-down, and Liza felt comparatively childish in the flannel pajamas she'd dug out of her duffel. But they were all she had. "I really don't feel right about going to work," he began.

"Don't be silly. You already missed because of me yesterday. And I'm just going to shower and go."

He crossed to the bread box and lifted a loaf of rye into the air, an invitation. She waved it away, and he frowned. Popping two pieces into the toaster, he crossed to sit sideways next to her, grabbing his seat back as if to restrain himself. "I wish you wouldn't decide this so quickly, Liza. It's such a shock. You can take a little time—"

She shook her head. "We talked about this last night."

"I'm just not sure you should be making major life decisions *hours* after a tragedy like this. Stay here. We'll get you set up temporarily. I'll help take care of anything you don't want to deal with."

She had to smile, because she knew it was true. He'd been attempting it for years, always willing to step in where a boyfriend or a brother might. More often than not, she shrugged him off. She was perfectly capable of speaking to the car mechanic about her brake pads. Of course she could haul her new bookcases up four floors by herself. And no, she did not need a pity date to her coworker's wedding—besides, how would she ever meet someone if she looked taken?

When it mattered, though, Max's easy loyalty would leave her swimming in gratitude. Even when he was dating someone, he never neglected their friendship. The last time she'd returned from a trip home for Christmas, he'd been waiting at her doorstep with a deep dish and a six-pack, knowing how empty she always found the place in contrast to the chaos of her family, and how much she loathed the task of taking her tree down alone.

He was so good to her, she sometimes wondered what was in it for him. She'd never *fully* leaned into their friendship because a part of her, she realized now, had always viewed her time here as *status pending*—a fact she'd never dared voice.

"Chicago is better with you in it," he said.

"Oh, come on," she said ruefully. "Chicago is trying to kill me." She'd meant it as a sort of joke, but to her surprise, she burst into tears. Max startled, shaking his head vehemently. "Don't shake your head," she sobbed. "It's true. It's a miracle we're having this conversation. I should be *dead*!"

The outburst felt strangely good—the truest thing she'd said since she'd called Max trembling from the sidewalk the afternoon before. She pushed back her chair and dropped her face into her hands. He leaned down, touched his forehead to hers, and rested his hands gently on her knees.

"I'm sorry!" she cried, her voice muffled by her palms.

"You have nothing to be sorry about." The toaster popped, but neither of them moved. They sat that way for a minute or two, until her heaves slowed to sniffles. Finally, he tapped the bottom of her chin with a fingertip, willing her to raise her red eyes to his. She was surprised to find them equally watery.

"Do you think I haven't thought about it?" he said. He handed her a napkin from the pile in the center of the table, and she pressed the rough square to her cheeks. "You got unbelievably lucky, Liza. What a weird-ass way to survive, but thank God. I'd unequivocally say that you're supposed to be alive. I don't want to hear any more of this *I should be dead* talk. This isn't—what was that kind of campy movie, with a bunch of sequels?"

She gave a little laugh. *"Final Destination."*

"Right. *Chicago* isn't going to hunt you down until it gets you. Those corner-cutting contractors, though, will have hell to pay. We'll find out this was human error, not destiny."

Did it matter? The terrible outcome was the same. And the ways that it could come about suddenly seemed endless.

"It's just—you can walk out of this apartment, turn left, and be fine. Turn right and be leveled by a bus. How screwed up is that? How is anyone supposed to know which way to go?"

He blinked. "I guess we're not supposed to know. We're just supposed to live our lives."

He made it sound so simple. Someone less prone to her special kind of *almost anxiety* would have found it comforting.

She took a shaky breath, managing a sad smile. "I know you're right. And I know this isn't what you want to hear . . . but I don't see a point in rebuilding a life that wasn't making me all that happy in the first place."

He looked stung, and she rushed ahead. "It's nothing to do with you, Max. Being friends with you is the best thing I have going here. It might even be the only thing that's been keeping me here. The job was supposed to be this big step up, but I'm a smaller fish in a bigger lake. My coworkers are . . . we can't seem to find much else in common. I've been trying to ground myself in this town, and I just—didn't. I think I did it wrong, moving to the city." She tried a little laugh. "I should have found a spot outside of downtown, where I could actually afford to hang out and make friends. It's no wonder I've wasted the last couple years on a string of bad dates—they picked up the tab!"

"Come on. Some of them weren't that bad. I wouldn't say you've *wasted* the last couple *years.*" She hadn't meant the words as harsh, but she understood their effect was worsened by the fact that he hadn't been expecting them. A stab of guilt hit her—for never letting on how she'd been feeling, for being her blunt, don't-hold-back self about everything but this, for trying too long and too hard to fake her way through until things got easier. But she'd known, on some level, that Max being Max, he'd only get caught up trying to fix the unfixable.

Hell, maybe he'd have succeeded, if she'd let him. But it was too late now.

"I shouldn't have said that. I just never felt like I belonged, outside of tagging along with you. If I was waiting for a sign that it was okay to go home, this is it."

"Shouldn't you at least give two weeks' notice?"

She raised an eyebrow. He was reaching and knew it. Her boss had made it clear he found her the most capable of his whole management team, but that didn't change the fact that—as both the only woman and the only transplant from a less expensive market—she was paid the least. His repeated denials of her requests for a raise had rubbed away any sense of duty she might have felt otherwise.

"I don't want you to go," Max persisted. "You're—" He looked away, then back at her, clear eyed. "I guess you're my best friend."

"And I guess you're mine." If there was ever any doubt, the competition had dwindled after the trip to Molly's. She nudged his knees with her own. "It's not that far to visit. I'll only be staying with my brother until I can find a job and apartment—he'll want me out before the baby arrives. And he has enough room that even his guests can have guests. Compared to anything here, it's ridiculously big."

Luke hadn't hesitated when she'd called him yesterday, for which she was grateful. She didn't want to put in two weeks at work and make insincere platitudes about wishing things had turned out different. Didn't want to bide her time here on the futon, waiting for calls from insurance agents and whoever else would be involved with sweeping up the ash of this mess. She just wanted to go. Staying with Luke and Steph wouldn't be like going back to her parents' house—it wouldn't feel like a step back, only a break, an intermission to splash some water on her face and regroup. And now that she had an external reason to go, she wouldn't have to worry that it would look like city life had chewed her up and spit her out.

It would look only like what it was: like the world had tried to swallow her whole.

And she had survived.

So far.

10

IN SPITE OF THE FACT THAT MOLLY HADN'T MANAGED SLEEP AGAIN LAST night, it was nice to be busy—mindlessly, outwardly, dutifully busy. The displays along the front section of the visitor center had been moved to repair the flood damage, and the director decided to have the work crew add a membership desk while they were at it. Molly loved that just days later this rustic building she'd come to love wasn't just good as new but better—that you could almost be glad of the temporary damage, thanks to the permanent improvement. As they partially reopened to allow access to the naturalist stations and restrooms, pardon our dust, Molly's normal sections of the Nature Shop and birdwatching outposts remained closed, and so the shuffling and reorganizing fell to her while the others made themselves available to the morning crowd.

If only people were as easily put back together, relationships as easily remodeled.

She'd never stop appreciating that this was what passed for a crazy day at the office now. In her earliest years of parenthood, she'd been as frantic as working moms came, caught up immediately and swiftly in the Monday-through-Friday hamster wheel. Her friends at the office assured her that these mornings of crying in the daycare parking lot would pass, that one day she'd give up on spending her lunch breaks back at the infant room, nursing her son, and rejoin their group outings to Thai bistros and Indian buffets. But once he was weaned, she took to working through that hour in hopes of leaving on time, which for her division was early. Then Nori came along, and it wasn't so much that Molly couldn't stand to leave the kids—truthfully, some days she handed them over gladly. It was that she couldn't stand the pace of it all, the run-run-run, the *what did I forget?,* the *Mommy will be back,* the *just a minute,* the constant feeling of being two steps behind everyone else even though she seemed to be trying ten times harder, forcing herself through the motions even while enduring the pain, which she hadn't yet thought of as chronic, but which seemed to have a new source every day. She and Daniel couldn't afford for her *not* to work, but she thought she might get away with something less breakneck, a reduced salary if it came with reduced stress. The mere prospect of seeking it out, though—updating her résumé, finding a suit to fit her post-baby body, sneaking off to interviews—was enough to overwhelm her.

Then one day, she'd called in sick, thrown on the most casual clothes that could pass as professional, dropped the kids off as per usual, and come here. These days, she wouldn't beat herself up over taking a day for a little self-care, but in that overextended phase she'd felt so guilty about *not* devoting every "free" minute to her babies that she hadn't even been able to enjoy the stolen morning, in spite of the fact that she hadn't been able to resist stealing it.

As she'd sipped her lukewarm coffee right here in the visitor center, staring lethargically into the cold stone fireplace, something had happened. Something that wasn't about her, not at first. She became aware of the conversations floating in and out of the lodge. The bright-eyed school groups with their cries of "Whoa!" and "Cool!" The patient chuckle of the naturalist. The local artists restocking their wares on consignment, remarking kindly on one another's pottery and jewelry and prints. The retirees analyzing their new plantings for the herb wall. This wasn't just a nonprofit; there was a community here, a place for good, a feeling of connection, and to Molly the pull was like a rescuer's rope lowered to a ledge where she'd been stranded so long she'd lost all sense of time. By the time she'd headed home, at last refreshed from exploring the trails, she'd already spoken with a hiring manager and had regained enough strength to withstand Daniel's grumbling about the waste of taking a job that didn't even require her college degree. He'd just gotten a promotion, after all. She wasn't putting a strain on anything.

Discounted enrollment at the on-site preschool helped sell Daniel on the idea, as did her willingness to drop the pretense of expecting him to share in a certain segment of the family duties: the kids' activity calendars, shopping, cooking, laundry. They argued less as a result, though they communicated less, too.

Reducing her routine to thirty hours a week also left more time to focus on trying to heal, and to botch those efforts spectacularly. But that wasn't the nature center's fault.

Most days here weren't like this one. Ordinarily she'd have bemoaned the physicality of this work—she'd have to ice her knees tonight to control the inflammation, and to adhere one of those annoyingly sticky heating strips to her back just to remain upright until the kids' bedtime. But today she welcomed the labor, even the pain. It was better than being trapped inside her head, which remained filled with the shocked hurt on Liza's face at her front door, the confusion emanating from Rick at his, the sudden hopelessness exhaled in every breath of her husband, right down to the flowers.

For a moment, he'd looked at her the way he used to. Like he loved her. Like he finally, *finally* saw their situation for what it was—and maybe even wanted to fix it. Like if they failed, his heart might be just as broken as hers.

She'd been waiting for that look. Years. Just about given up. But now that she'd seen it, she didn't know what to do with it. The resentment she'd been collecting wanted to stiffen, to declare *any* overture from Daniel too little too late. The hope she'd rediscovered wanted to jump at the chance, at the expense of all else. And her ever-present guilt laughed cruelly at the irony—that he'd picked a fine time to about-face his betrayals, just as one of her own was about to do them in.

She was taking her time with the little table of log-shaped blocks, grimy from so many fingers and dusty from yesterday's construction. Wiping the pieces clean one at a time, she arranged them in neat little piles on the area painted to look like a forest floor, then erected a small cabin to demonstrate the possibilities. She'd just dropped a chimney onto the sloped roof when she heard her name, the last word of a question, and Brian, her favorite naturalist, responding with a friendly greeting. "Go on back—just watch your step."

Rick was climbing over the rope, unsmiling.

No. He'd texted her twice last night, wanting to clear the air from her morning visit, still claiming he had no idea what had upset her. She hadn't responded then and sure as hell didn't want to now, here. Rick was a familiar fixture to her coworkers, who found their daughters' sweet hand-in-hand hikes adorable. Here as in the neighborhood, the slightest bit of awkwardness could ruin things. Things she quite liked.

"Sorry to come here," he said quietly, "but we *need* to talk."

She glanced over her shoulder at Brian, hoping he might shake his head or call out a reminder of how much work there was to be done, but he'd never admonished her before and was unlikely to start now. There was never much hurry here, with so much of their staff made up of volunteers no one wanted to chase off. He wasn't looking anyway. He had the lid off the milk snake's aquarium and was peering in, murmuring something soothing, the cleaning supplies spread on the counter behind him.

She met her neighbor's eyes, afraid to speak, afraid that anything worth saying was something she didn't want Brian to overhear. Her expression, she hoped, said it for her. *Really? Now? You think this is appropriate?*

It can't wait, he mouthed, and his return look wasn't the kind one she was used to or the confused one from yesterday. It was angry.

She led him through the adjoining library, free today of the usual smattering of members with packed lunches or knitting projects or laptops, and opened the door to the balcony, big enough only for a small bench and the woodpile to feed the fireplace inside. The latter made the ledge a haven for spiders and so she was wary of the spot, though it afforded a pretty view of a busy row of bird feeders and the marshy edge of the lake beyond. She gestured to the bench, but neither of them made a move to sit.

"The police were at my house this morning," he said. She froze, her eyes on his, betraying her. "Wanted to know if I had any security cameras on my property that might have caught an intruder coming or going from yours."

He cocked his head expectantly, and she looked away, her mind racing. *Shit. But why? They'd come; they'd seen; they'd left. Hadn't they?* She'd thought that part, at least, was done.

"Do you?" she said finally.

"Do I? Molly, you had an intruder? While Daniel was away? And that's what you were referring to yesterday, when I couldn't make sense of it?" She didn't look up. "I've been trying to put two and two together ever since they left, and the best I can come up with is that you think it was me." Her anger came rushing back then, that surge that had carried her through the woods yesterday and pounded on his door. When she lifted her head, her eyes were blazing. "*Please* tell me I'm wrong," he snapped.

"You have a lot of nerve," she replied, defiant.

He buried his hands in his hair and pulled, fists clenched, like a frustrated child.

"Because of that joke you made? One shared, awkward laugh? You thought I'd actually act on that?" He dropped onto the bench, clasped his hands, looked up at her. "You honestly thought if I was going to—" He fumbled for the right words, and she realized that of all the less-than-perfect ways she'd seen him in these months since they'd grown close—sad, impatient, annoyed—she'd never seen him like this. Flustered. That was *her* role, perpetually. She honestly hadn't thought he was capable of it, a fact she'd both admired and found a little maddening. "If I wanted to *try to change things* between us," he said finally, "you think that's how I'd go about it? That's what you think of me?"

"What did you tell them?" she asked, her voice shaky. A disturbance erupted at the bird feeders—flapping wings, a few warning squawks. Squirrels, probably. No matter how many barriers stood in their way—how out of reach the seeds, how smooth and high the poles—they couldn't help going after things that didn't belong to them.

He blinked at her. "Nothing," he said sharply. "There isn't anything to tell."

Her breaths were coming shallow, quick. *Easy,* she commanded herself. Her one-word mantra, repeated dozens of times on any given day, hundreds on a bad one. *Easy now. Take it easy.* It did little to stop everything from feeling so damn hard.

"Molly, listen to me. It's hard to know where to begin with this talk we clearly need to have. But let's set that aside for a very important minute to establish that the person who entered your house *was not me.* Whatever you convinced yourself it was—a sick joke, some twisted come-on, a reenactment of the thing we saw—it wasn't. I promise you. Okay?"

Even cloaked in anger, he was impossibly sincere. There wasn't a soul alive who wouldn't believe him. She wanted to cry. She wanted to run, crawl under something, plug her ears. A searing acid rose into the back of her throat. If not Rick, then who? "My God, Molly, someone broke into your house and then took off, got away! The whole neighborhood should be on edge right now, and you haven't even said a word about it!"

"I assumed . . ." She took a step back, and the slabs of the wooden wall grazed her spine.

"Yeah, I'm still trying to wrap my head around that one."

"What exactly did the police say?" she managed. "Are they—making rounds? I thought they'd sort of . . . dropped it."

"He just said he was following up. That they figured the intruder had been sufficiently spooked, but thought it was worth a try to see if anyone saw anything." He shook his head, incredulous. "You have a friend who caught him on your *webcam*?"

Her mouth opened, but nothing came out.

"Would the provider have a record of the video?"

"The police seemed pretty certain there's no video record unless you make one. Privacy laws. Like with a phone call. They can access *who* you called and how long you talked, but not what was said."

"Okay . . . but a burglar just *happened* to hit your house on a night Daniel was out of town? Did you tell anyone he was leaving? Anyone at all? A repair guy, a cashier?"

Molly shook her head. She couldn't remember the last time she'd bothered with friendly chitchat in the checkout line or scheduled a service call. It was all she could do to muster the energy to be pleasant with her children, her coworkers. Her husband.

It had only come easily with Rick—every conversation like an exhale of a breath she didn't know she'd been holding.

From now on, she'd have to keep it in. Or to find another way to let it out.

"Can you think of anyone who'd target you, or Daniel, or your house, for any reason at all?"

"No." She shook her head again. "I don't know." *Could* she? It had sounded routine when the police asked it. And Daniel had been just as willing to brush the possibility aside. But hearing the words from Rick somehow made it seem real.

He glanced past her, into the building, and she turned to follow his gaze. No one was approaching. "You mentioned some debts, not long ago," he said more quietly. "How bad are they, Molly? Are they . . . on the up-and-up?"

"I don't owe the Mafia, if that's what you're asking," she said, crossing her arms in front of her.

"And Daniel. You've been upset about—some boss at his work, wasn't it? Wasn't there something you thought he should report?"

She rolled her eyes. "A regular, shirt-and-tie boss, Rick. Again, not a

Mob boss. It had to have been random. Right?" She was talking as much to herself as to him. He shrugged, and she did, too. "I guess we're all lucky my friend scared him off. I know the cop said sometimes burglars will case multiple houses, hit another one if they're successful on the first. But he wasn't, so . . . hopefully there's no reason to think he'll be back."

The worry lines in Rick's forehead softened, just a little. "I wish we could all thank your friend," he said. "She must have been so freaked out."

Molly cringed. She was too ashamed to go there.

He shook his head again. "I can't believe you didn't call me. You must have been beside yourself. Even if you'd thought it was me—" That embarrassed flush again. "I still wish you'd called. We could have had this conversation then. I could have helped, somehow. Instead it's—whatever the hell that visit yesterday morning was."

Easy. A deep breath. A little steadier. "I guess I wasn't thinking clearly," she said lamely. "I was—tired. And I'm sorry, for thinking you would've . . ." Now it was her turn to feel the blood rush into her cheeks. "But you know, the idea that it seemed possible, maybe we should take that as a sign. Take a little space." The last thing she'd wanted, up until all of this, was space from Rick. She'd only ever wanted more of him. But the fear that her bluff had been called had changed everything. Just like that.

"Look, it *was* an odd coincidence," he said, smiling sadly. "Which was the only reason it seemed possible, right?" He got to his feet. "You know what, let's *not* talk about it. Let's forget it. The important thing is, you're safe."

Was she safe? Evidently, there had been an actual intruder in her home, and she'd blown it off, practically shooed the police away. She'd behaved completely inappropriately, missed her chance to pursue this further—though it sounded as if the police were still following up on their own. All she could hope was that her own shaky assurances—and Daniel's, and Rick's—were correct. It had been random. Nothing to do with her.

It just didn't feel like an easy jump, to go from being so sure she knew who it was—and why, thanks to an *off*hand comment that got *out* of hand—to accepting that she'd never know, that it probably, with hope, didn't matter.

Maybe if she *had* called Rick that night, she could've gone along with what he was suggesting. *Let's forget it.* But she hadn't. And Daniel had brought *flowers* yesterday. He might have brought home demands, fury that she hadn't told him, slammed doors—it's how she would have responded, were she the one fielding phone calls during business hours from concerned neighbors catching her mortifyingly unawares. Instead, he'd brought sadness, longing, a mirror of her own feelings—one she hadn't looked into in a long time. And she owed him something for that. She'd looked at him and seen what it was that she owed herself.

She squared her shoulders and sucked in a brave, steadying breath. "I think we've both known that maybe we've grown too close, Rick. Neither of us wanted to step back, because of the girls. And I love spending time with you. But I think I might like it too much. I'm going to take this debacle as a sign that we should . . . take a break."

He cocked his head at her, the kind of confused-puppy look that was almost cute enough to convince you someone else had chewed the rug. "Are you saying you have feelings for me, Molly?" His measured tone didn't quite match his expression.

If only there were some way to put more distance between them on this tiny balcony. "Of course not. I just don't want it to seem—inappropriate. The amount of time we spend together."

He hiked a thumb toward the building. "No one in there looks at us strangely. Why would you?" He knew why. The instant he realized what Molly had believed he'd done, he should have run in the opposite direction. But he'd come here instead. "I'm pushing back on this *people of the opposite sex can't be friends* trope," he continued. "*All* my friends are the opposite sex these days. That's what happens when you end up a single dad, without another one in sight. Whose definition of *inappropriate* are you afraid of? Is it Daniel? Has he said something?"

She shook her head. Could he not just gracefully back away?

"Look, forget the fact that of everyone I know, I relate to you most—we've both been dealt some losing hands, but we're still at the table. I'm not one to force an issue, even when I should. My wife used to call me passive, and she was right. I'd often regret it later." He stared straight into her eyes. "But when Rosie is involved, I will force it. Our time with you and Nori is the *only* thing making a difference for her. I won't walk away from that without good reason. Which we both know this is not."

So that was it. Either he *had* been entertaining it, too—this thing between them that was more of a not-so-harmless-after-all fantasy than a wish for a different reality—but loved his daughter too much to admit it, or she was out here on the limb by herself, exposed and disgraced, but he was willing to pretend he didn't see her there. Could they—could she—really go on as they had been? Firm up everything that was right between them and leave behind the rest?

"I'm sorry," she squeaked out. She was. And she wasn't.

"We're better than this," he said firmly. "Tell me what you need from me in order to move beyond this, and I'll do it. Just don't tell me you don't want us in your life anymore. We didn't do anything to deserve that, Molly. And we never would."

She closed her eyes. The aura that preceded her migraines was instantly recognizable—a pixelated spectrum of reds and oranges at the far corners of her vision—and one was coming at her now, hot and demanding. If she didn't take a pill within minutes, she'd be rendered useless for the rest of the day. She held very still, visualizing the little packet in her purse, under the Nature Shop register. *Easy,* she told herself. *Easy.*

When she opened them again, Rick was watching her with concern. "An aura?" he asked. She dismissed the unwelcome thought that he was more astute than Daniel at reading the signs.

"It's been a long couple days," she whispered. "Just give me a little time, okay?"

He touched her arm lightly. "A little," he said. And then, at last, he was gone.

11

AS WAS HER CUSTOM, LIZA HAD BRUSHED OFF THE LAST THING MAX HAD said to her.

I just worry that maybe you're not actually okay.

But by the time she was crossing the Ohio border, she was starting to worry the same.

There had been an accident. A safe distance ahead of her—a few miles at least. The police had just arrived on the scene when she came upon the flipped SUV—two officers were crouched down at the shattered windows, while another set out flares. As recently as yesterday, she'd have simply said a silent prayer for the driver and thanked the traffic gods that she'd made it past before the lanes were closed.

But now she couldn't stop thinking about it. The tension turned her knuckles white on the wheel. She'd stopped at a rest area only moments before, which was practically a special occasion—usually she was fanatical about making good time on long drives. But she'd caught sight just in time of the retro yellow sign advertising Stuckey's—a roadside luxury they didn't have in Ohio—and remembered how much her brother liked their peanut brittle. Arriving gifts in hand didn't seem a bad idea, considering, and she figured his pregnant wife wouldn't turn down imported calories. She'd taken a few minutes to browse, picking up a pecan log and pralines, too.

But what if she hadn't?

What if she hadn't seen the red-lettered billboard in time, had kept on driving? Or what if she'd bought only the brittle, in her usual rush, without staying to wander the aisles, to let her eyes skim the bins of archaic bargain CDs, to squeeze a few stuffed animals before deciding a gift for her baby niece or nephew might be premature given the complications Luke mentioned? She'd have been miles ahead of where she was now. She might have been out in front of the accident, might not know a thing about it. *Or* she might have seen it happen. She might—it suddenly seemed more than possible—have been in it. The SUV could have lost control, the driver having a heart attack, perhaps, or a stroke, bouncing off the guardrail and barreling roof-over-wheels toward her, dragging Liza's little two-door into the crunch of metal.

Was life just one death dodge after another, while people carried on oblivious to the danger until the day it was too in-their-face to ignore, the day their home burned down in the dead of night while they were against all odds away?

The *oblivious* part seemed essential to not driving oneself crazy. Now that Liza was hyperaware of the frequency and fragility of the near misses that made up any given day, how could she ignore them? Her old habit of not-quite anxiety had been a bother, a running joke even to her, but this new kind of startling, piercing fear was something else.

The "Ohio Welcomes You" sign came into view, and she powered open the windows and let the chilly spring air whip her hair into a frenzy. Her left hand on the wheel, she raised her right through the sunroof, fingers splayed, and visualized the molecules rushing between them. She made a fist and then opened it again, trying to let go of these thoughts she didn't want to have, to let the wind sweep them away.

Her brother's house was north of Cincinnati, in the affluent municipality of Blue Ash that boasted its accolades on the welcome signs.

Thanks to an excellent school district, the area had its fair share of supersized suburban sprawl, alongside older, smaller homes that drew a hefty price tag for merely existing where they were. Luke and Steph had settled for neither, finding a best-kept-secret sort of anomaly, a historic beauty someone else had gone to the trouble of restoring in a wonderfully walkable part of town near the library, shops, pubs, an outdoor amphitheater, even a park with a picturesque duck pond.

By the time Liza arrived, her two-night sleepless stretch was catching up with her, and she was too tired to feel nervous about intruding. She'd never spent more than a day or two here, but she liked that it was a safe distance from her parents, who'd retired thirty miles north to a more secluded slice of land—conveniently inconvenient, as they accepted Liza's explanation that she planned to look for jobs in the city right away and didn't want to hassle with their commute. Much better than telling them she'd feel like a backsliding failure if she moved into their finished-basement guest suite. Blue Ash was closer than she'd like to Molly, but it'd likely be a while before her friend realized she was here. She certainly wasn't about to tell her.

Liza pulled parallel to the curb in an open spot a half block away and caught sight of Steph sitting alone, earbuds in and eyes closed, on her gently swaying front porch swing in what looked like a page from a Pottery Barn catalog, all throw pillows and hanging lanterns.

Until Luke brought her to Thanksgiving dinner a couple of years ago, Liza had known Steph only as her ex-boyfriend's ex-girlfriend, by name and photo alone. The two had never spoken, and Liza harbored no grudges toward that particular ex, nor had she known if Steph realized their second-degree connection. Still, Liz had been weirded out enough to keep a polite distance all the way up to the drunken bachelorette party, when she'd found herself sharing a tiny wine bar bathroom with her future sister-in-law, both of them seeking a momentary escape from the high-pitched shrieks of their increasingly rowdy group outside.

"Don't let yourself get suckered into this," Steph had muttered, crumpling the cheap wisp of a veil someone had coerced onto her head and jamming it into her clutch. "I love your brother—and I plan to love him forever—but I fucking hate weddings."

She'd turned to Liza with a rueful smile. "Are we ever going to talk about that dud we both dated?"

Liza's eyebrows had lifted. "No?"

"Perfect."

Steph endeared herself to Liza pretty quickly after that, in spite of the fact that everything about the woman was ridiculously photogenic—she was one of those people who could make even yoga pants and a messy ponytail look enviably stylish and who treated bad days with humor and wine. Liza had yet to see her effortless confidence shaken. It was easy to see why Luke was crazy about her.

Grabbing her purse and duffel from the passenger seat, Liza locked the car and headed out. Steph's eyes opened at the thud of the car door, and she called into the house through the open window. Luke bounded onto the porch and down the stairs to catch Liza in a bear hug on the sidewalk.

"Damn, it's good to see you," he murmured, squeezing her tight, and she knew then, as she steeled herself against a surprise torrent of emotion, that her brother had been just as rattled by her near miss as she was. With Steph, his affection was plain, but when it came to Liza, Luke was too laid-back—too cool, really—for sentiments, though they were implied. He stepped back and held her at arm's length, taking her in. "Can I help get the rest of your stuff?"

She smiled weakly through her shrug. "This is it," she said, lifting the sparsely filled bags out to her sides. "All that's left."

The realization shuddered across his face, and she burst into tears.

—

"Tell me again how you managed to be away in the middle of the night," Luke said.

The *again* was a courtesy word. She'd simply told them she'd gotten lucky in being somewhere *other* than her bed, not how or why. It had seemed too bizarre to explain on the phone and still did here, on the nicer side of ordinary. Luke had led her to the kitchen table, presented her with a glass of pinot grigio and a plate of cheese, and sat down opposite her with a beer. At the counter, Steph was tossing strawberries and walnuts into a bowl of greens. Luke and Liza's parents were coming for dinner, to see for themselves that she was unsinged by the fire. She didn't know how she'd keep her eyes open for the duration. The wine would only put her to sleep, but all the coffee she'd downed today was giving her the shakes. She sipped from the glass numbly.

"Remember how I called that night to ask you to check on Molly?"

Steph looked at Luke in surprise. "You didn't tell me that."

He glanced nervously at Steph and back to Liza, a silent plea that his sister not mention the pregnancy complication just now.

"I decided to do it myself," Liza continued.

Two pairs of confused eyes turned on her. "You were in *Cincinnati*?"

"For all of five minutes." It was a slight exaggeration, so as not to hurt their feelings that she hadn't called. She'd treated Max to a stack of cinnamon-sugar-sprinkled goodness at the Original Pancake House, where they'd fueled up on Kona coffee and mutual disbelief before heading home in a well-fed, if otherwise sheepish, silence.

She told them the rest, the strange mess of it. By the time she was done, Steph was seated at the table with them, downing seltzer as if it were something more interesting and looking longingly at the wine.

"What the *hell*?" Luke said, for about the tenth time. He shook his head. "I wouldn't have said so before, Sis, but something hasn't been right with your pal Molly these past few years. I thought she'd just succumbed to the evils of suburbia or something, but this . . ." He shook his head.

It wasn't a fair assessment, really. Luke had never been much of a Molly fan, something Liza had chalked up to him being annoyed by his kid sister and her ever-present friend until the adult day a few years ago that he'd surprised her by muttering, "I swear, that girl doesn't know who she is without you around. God help her when you leave."

Steph shot him a look. "Cool it with 'the evils of suburbia.' No worse cliché than a hipster dad-to-be in denial." He opened his mouth to object, but she pressed on. "And speaking of something not being right, I can't believe you denied your worried sister a favor on my account. You're lucky it happened to have saved her life."

"No, he was right," Liza said quickly. "I wouldn't have called if I'd realized what . . . what you were in the middle of. Besides, it's pretty clear Molly didn't want to be checked on."

She'd always been quick to forgive Molly, maybe even too quick, but Molly had tolerated Liza's own shortcomings so well in return that it never seemed a concession. Liza knew that she was a walking inconsistency, neurotically anxious by night and thoroughly noncommittal, even nonchalant, by day. It was as if everything that might have caused concern in the moment—a scuff-up at work, an unanswered email, a dirty look—rolled right off and collected at her feet, waiting to climb back up to her brain later, when she was trying to sleep. Molly had always embraced her curiously split persona, making Liza like herself in moments she wouldn't have otherwise. It was odd to view their friendship from this curious distance, as if it were a thing of the past. Before yesterday, she might have persisted, calling her friend again to at the very least serve up the piece of her mind she'd been too dumbfounded to unleash on Molly's doorstep.

But now Molly seemed the least of her worries. Why expend precious energy grappling with the problems of someone who didn't want her there?

Steph crossed her arms in front of her. "I'm not some fragile being," she said, bumping her shoulder good-naturedly against her husband's. "I'd have been fine on my own for an hour."

Liza took a chance. "Do you mind if I ask . . . What's the complication, exactly?"

Steph clunked her seltzer onto the table matter-of-factly. "It's called an incarcerated uterus."

Liza pulled a face. "Incarcerated?"

"Sounds scandalous, doesn't it?" Steph chirped. But her eyes were anxious, sad.

Luke, looking the picture of discomfort, dropped a protective hand onto her shoulder.

"Honey, you don't have to—"

"Essentially the baby is caught in my pelvis," she explained, ignoring him. "As your uterus expands, it's supposed to pop up, then out. Mine is starting to grow, but hasn't lifted, so it's creating problems." She turned to her husband. "Women can have these conversations without getting freaked out by our anatomies."

"That's not why I—"

"She's going to be living with us. There's no reason to hide what's going on. That's just going to stress me out worse."

The last bit did the trick. He fell silent, but Liza was wishing she hadn't asked. Causing any kind of tension between them was the last thing she wanted. Still, they'd come this far. She wanted to know. "What kind of problems?"

"It puts pressure on her bladder, for one thing," Luke said, sitting up straighter, more comfortable with this scientific tact. "That's how she was diagnosed."

"You know how sometimes you wake up and you *really* have to go?" Steph asked. Liza nodded. "Well, I ran to the bathroom to pee, and nothing came out. Weirdest moment ever. At first I thought it was some weird UTI, or—I don't even know."

Liza cringed. "What did you do?"

"I thought maybe I just needed to move the baby around a little, so I hopped on the elliptical machine for a few minutes and then tried again. It worked, thank God—turns out some people need a catheter. But then I Googled the symptom. Bad idea because—"

Luke cut her off with a shake of his head. "There are these yoga poses she's supposed to do, and she's already on it," he said firmly. "They'll help the baby lift up and out. Everything is going to be fine."

"It's a rare cause of second-trimester miscarriage," Steph finished.

A small cry escaped Liza, an involuntary hand flying to her mouth.

Luke frowned at his wife. "That won't happen," he said, his voice eerily calm. "We're not even going to say the words."

Steph met her eyes, and Liza understood: Steph didn't want to be alone with her fear, but Luke didn't want to acknowledge it. This was the same work-around her brother had given her over the years, every time she'd tried to talk to him about the slightest worry. Mr. Positivity, her mother called Luke affectionately.

Cloying as his approach could be, it was not ineffective. Still, sometimes you wanted to have a real conversation about your not-entirely-positive feelings.

Liza leaned in. "I'm so sorry," she said. "If there's anything I can do to help, or you want to talk—anytime. I'll even do the yoga poses with you. What are they?"

Steph blinked back tears. "They're ridiculous," she said, and Liza laughed.

"I specialize in ridiculous," she assured her.

She wished it weren't so true.

After her parents had come and gone—a visit marked by her many assurances that she was "fine, as you can see," and, more usefully, by her mother's care package of toiletries and clothes that, while not exactly her taste, she could hardly turn away—after she'd helped with the dishes and cut the tags off the jersey-knit pajamas, after she'd sprawled on a yoga mat next to Steph while they positioned themselves pelvis up for an unconscionably long time (*up and out,* Liza silently willed the baby, *you can do it, up and out*), she retreated to the sleek gray-toned guest room in the back corner of the second floor and marveled at the silence. She didn't miss the Chicago street traffic, but she'd become accustomed to tolerating it, like a runny nose that won't go away. Amid the honking and idling and shouting had always been sirens, she realized now, and yet she'd scarcely even registered them with curiosity about what the emergency was.

How flippant she'd been; how dismissive *everyone* was. Never again would she encounter someone in a hurry and ask, *Where's the fire?*

Lights out, covers up, she tried to sink into the exhaustion that had plagued her all day. Her mind was a movie reel—charred brick walls and flames in the darkness and Max's face, sadder than she'd ever seen it. She couldn't switch it off, couldn't even find the mute button.

In the past, the worries that had proven unshakable to Liza had ultimately meant something. Her grandmother *was* going to die in that hospital bed—against her doctor's assurances that she was fine, on the very day she was scheduled to be discharged. Her best friend *was* more crippled by her pain than she'd initially let on. The move to Chicago was *not* going as planned, not even close.

Yet this new set of endlessly spooling worries related mostly to the past—didn't they? She would have to learn to separate anxiety from intuition if she wanted to stay sane.

An owl hooted outside her window, a soft song in the cool night. Her eyes blinked open and she held her muscles rigid. Had she imagined it?

Who. Who-whoooo, who. A second set of hoots repeated, then a third. She strained to hear it again, trying to remember if she'd ever actually heard one before. It felt special, just for her—so close and so clear. Sacred.

Liza burrowed once more into her pillow—which was not like the pillows she'd cast off to guests, in the custom of her own parents, flattened and yellowed and lumpy beneath the clean cotton cases, but billowy and soft, as if she were in a hotel. She felt welcome, if not at home. Perhaps the wide-eyed bird was standing guard, a sentry hidden in the branches. A nice idea. She could use the protection.

But wait. Wasn't there something about a hooting owl being an omen?

She would not reach for her smartphone, right there on the bedside table. She would bask in how the moment had made her *feel*—the novelty of it. Why bring the internet into this?

She would go at last to sleep.

But the question would not leave her now that she'd dared to think it. Just a peek. She was probably wrong. She'd sleep better knowing so. She palmed the device and squinted as its garish glow responded to her touch, pecked in her search terms with an index finger.

Her nocturnal visitor, it turned out, could be interpreted many ways, depending on who you asked. In some cultures, owls signified wisdom. In others, yes, protection.

Maybe she could ignore the ones that felt an owl foretold death.

But the search results favored bad omens, even via sources that believed owls sacred. There existed instructions for attempting to hoot back, to gauge the severity of the impending doom. The death in question *could,* it seemed, be symbolic rather than literal.

Three nights ago she'd been mindlessly going about her life, and tonight she was contemplating hooting out a window. It should have been her clue to pack it in, stop looking, before she got to the hysterical pregnancy board thread where a woman swore that every member of her family was terrified her baby would die now that she'd heard a set of three owl hoots.

OMG, someone had written. *X3 = death of a newborn. Not to freak you out, but I've heard that, too!* Others had chimed in, sending premature sympathy.

Liza stared down the dark shape of the window, willing the creature beyond it to sound a fourth time. If only she weren't sure she'd heard three.

Had death followed her here? Luke and Steph's baby was nowhere near being a newborn—Steph wasn't even showing yet—but there was already a problem, a risk, and now here was Liza, sweeping in with nothing but the contents of her bag and bad karma on her back. She felt a strong, irrational urge to leave, to get as far as she could from everyone she loved.

This was crazy. She told herself that in the morning she'd see this for the irrational bout of late-night anxiety it was. She'd smile, again, over the surprising sound of the owl, just passing through. And she'd stay.

Of course she'd stay.

Where else would she go?

12

CLARITY—DAMN IT TO HELL—HAD A WAY OF COMING IN THE MIDDLE OF the night. Molly sat with the invoices spread on the coffee table in front of her, every moan of the refrigerator or creak of the kitchen floor jerking her head reflexively over her shoulder. She wasn't sure what would be more terrifying at this point: the masked man's return or the sight of her rumpled husband looking for the missing occupant of his bed.

Right here, at the very table where Liza had witnessed the triggering of Molly's undoing, would not have been her choice of places to face facts, to do what she'd resisted before.

To view all of her failures at once, in the exact spot they might have added up to another.

But it was the only place in the house she could risk turning on a light without discovery.

In the dining room or the kitchen, Daniel could come up on her too quickly. And there was no plausible reason for her to be in the stuffy, never-used guest room or down in the basement, which she avoided because they could never seem to keep the mice out for long. Here, at least, she'd have the buffer of the galley kitchen, should anyone wander downstairs, to buy her precious seconds to sweep the evidence into a pile or at least to hide the slips beneath the photo albums she'd set on the table's edge as cover. Here she could say she couldn't sleep, that her back was acting up, that she'd come down to turn on the TV and gotten caught up reminiscing instead.

As usual, her ready excuse was only a half lie.

There was plenty here to reminisce over. Because in her quest to end one pain after the next, when the round-robin referrals from one specialist to another had done nothing but spin her around a circuitous track, Molly had taken matters into her own hands and tried . . . a few things.

At first she told Daniel about them all—the theory, the approach, and, yes, the cost. The healing massage, the herbal supplements, the Reiki, the meridian point tapping, the gel supports and orthopedic braces. But as his skepticism became clear, she began keeping them to herself. What did she care if he thought her anti-inflammatory diet was a waste of effort, if he wrinkled his nose at her essential oil diffusers, if he smirked at the pouch of crystals she strung around her neck? He was entitled to his opinion, and she was entitled to hers—which was *not,* contrary to his deaf assumptions, that all these things worked. She only believed that they were worth a try. As for the dollar signs attached to each one—well, those weren't so hard to rationalize. One might grumble over the cost of a doctor's visit in these days of high deductibles, but no one questioned that *they* were necessary. Was this so different? In fact, compared to the orthopedists and neurologists and otolaryngologists she'd already been through, an alternative treatment could save her a bundle, if she could just hit on one that worked.

The little ones added up, but slowly enough for her to delay doing the math. And the big ones? As time wore her down, even those seemed a small price to pay to be free from the grips of this unrelenting captor.

Molly had never struggled with anything like addiction before. But she recognized that this was something like it—though being aware of it and putting an end to this chain of *if-not-this-how-about-that* did not go hand in hand. Even failures that should have been shrugged away cut deep. Reading hours of reviews of a new miracle cream that was bringing thousands of people relief, only to have it break her out in a terrible rash, was disheartening enough to feel like a devastating setback. She could only boost her spirits with some other brand of prepackaged hope.

Daniel had accused her once of "being taken in by quacks." Pretty high-and-mighty coming from someone who'd privately questioned whether his employer's entire nontoxic product line was even necessary ("It's not as if people *eat* their furniture.") and yet had no qualms about collecting his paychecks there.

Somehow she'd lost her ability to laugh things off. The difference, she supposed, was that she used to get some help doing it. Early on, a lot of it had come from Liza. The time Molly trailed tampons down the high school halls through a rip in her backpack, she'd played sick for two days until Liza drew her out with a hilarious reenactment, skipping down the sidewalk in front of her house dropping Snickers and Midol behind her. Later Daniel had taken the baton and, for a while, carried it well. Even a shared bout of food poisoning in a Miami hotel room had, once they could hold down Gatorade, left them giggling at their misfortune until skipping the cruise they'd planned on actually seemed romantic.

But now, as her private attempts at self-healing fell short, she had no one with whom to share these disappointments, these foibles. Except, occasionally, for Rick.

Even so. It wasn't the failures that had caught up to her. It was the cost of them.

Alternative health was mostly uncovered by their insurance, and it didn't come cheap.

She'd known it was wrong, opening the credit line Daniel didn't know about. When she found herself maxed out and shamefully dodging phone calls and burying payments—thank goodness they'd forgone a landline and kept separate bank accounts in addition to their joint ones—she'd also known what a bad idea it would be to open another.

She'd done it anyway, steep interest rate be damned, and hit that limit, too. She tapped retirement funds she wasn't supposed to touch to slow the bleed, but the problem was, she couldn't bring herself to ebb the spending, either. With your well-being slipping away from you, how could you put a price on getting your life back?

Enter a worse idea.

She'd seen the man before, around the meditation center. They got to chatting one day in the parking lot, and when he alluded to a future encounter she fessed up that she wouldn't be back. His kind concern and her rock-bottom desperation made her suddenly tearful, explaining herself for no real reason. Her TMJ was at its worst then—her jaw so tight she could barely chew, her ears' incessant fluting driving her mad—and the classes still held hope for some relief. She worried she hadn't learned enough to maintain the discipline on her own but could no longer afford it.

That's when he volunteered that alternative treatments also had alternative payment options. Of course they did. If good people like Molly couldn't trust the medical system of all things to take care of them, why would the credit racket be any different? She *could* make that call she'd been planning to the debt relief help line, but that wouldn't buy her more than time. He worked with a place that specialized in helping sufferers like her fund wellness *without* adding to the stress they were already enduring. Founded by a few generous advocates who preferred to remain anonymous, this godsend of a company could lend her what she needed to pay off the five thousand here and the seven thousand there and all the rest, and then she'd owe only them. One bill, instead of so many to juggle, and he could guarantee their interest rate was lower than the credit cards'. All she had to do was join and let them help. Let go of that bag of rocks she'd been dragging around and let them carry it for a while.

YWBF, they were called: Your Way Back Financial. Even their logo held promise: a spiral reminiscent of the sun, rimmed by arrows pointing outward. Their office was inconveniently located, but they could bring the paperwork to her—they did it all the time. She could find a whole page of grateful testimonials on their website—but what luck, here comes a client now. *Samantha, are you in a hurry? Do you by chance have a few minutes to tell Molly here about your experience with us?*

The picture of reclaimed health, Samantha had been an especially nice touch.

It was too late to lament now what a fool Molly had been, that "if it sounds too good to be true . . ." had become an adage for a reason.

Because Molly had signed. She had practically cried with gratitude when she paid the other bills—punching in the totals as fast as her fingers could fly, getting it over with, putting it behind her, not even stopping for a last look at how she'd gotten here and what she might do to avoid returning in the future, because things would be different now, simpler. Streamlined.

But she was looking back now.

She couldn't afford not to anymore.

The interest rate *had* been a lower number. The language very cleverly buried the startling fact that it would not, however, be applied monthly. These invoices were coming weekly. She'd actually ignored the first few, tossing them unopened into a drawer, so certain was she that they were duplicates. She'd ignored, too, the "reminder" calls and messages, so close together. "Hold your horses," she'd grumbled. "What happened to lowering my stress?" At this interest rate, she hadn't concerned herself with the fact that she had no intention of paying for a while. She'd deal later; the penalty would be manageable. And she needed a break from all this. She hated anything to do with money, typically leaving those matters to Daniel.

Finally, last month, she'd torn open an envelope, taken in the total, and thought it had to be a mistake. She'd called. They assured her it was not. She hung up, staving off panic, and did her own math, applying the interest rate weekly, and still her total didn't near theirs. She called back, triumphant, an error after all. But no. This loan was intended as short term. Evidently, they'd assumed bags of money were going to rain into her lawn and magically supply the funds they already knew she didn't have. And in the absence of such a rainstorm, penalties were being applied. More fees.

She drained what was left of her retirement funds to pay what she could. It barely sandbagged the rising floodwaters. She'd started to wonder if this was even legal, but she *had* signed the contract. She'd never felt so stupid.

In the moments when she and Daniel still talked of the future, there was a dream of the life they'd settle into once the kids were gone. She'd contributed aggressively to long-term funds in her days of a full-time, white-collar salary, and when she scaled back it was a bone of contention with Daniel that she wouldn't be able to sustain that rate. He'd helped her roll what she had into an IRA—but, still smarting from his reaction to her career shift, she insisted she could take it from there. Didn't need his help, thanks anyway.

She wished now that she hadn't been so convincing. If he'd had access to her monthly statements, he might have saved her from herself. As it was, hiding her missteps was for the most part as simple as beating him to the mailbox. She continued to contribute to the joint accounts, as always, and ignored the rest.

Now Rick's voice echoed in her mind. He'd been the only one who knew anything about her debts. *Are they . . . on the up-and-up?*

She'd scoffed at the question. But should she have?

Did it stand to reason that alternative loans might have alternative collection methods when you failed to pay up?

The idea of having to tell Daniel how she'd not just violated his trust but also squandered their future and *by the way possibly endangered their family's security* was almost scarier than the prospect of trying to find a solution on her own.

Almost scarier than the idea that if it was they who'd come for her, then they'd be back.

No. This was not the seedy side of Las Vegas; it was the suburbs of

Cincinnati. If she couldn't pay, she'd be dealing with collection agencies. Not henchmen. She had to keep her head.

She would cling to the theory that the intruder had been random.

But she was also going to have to solve this cash-flow problem, regardless. She'd been living in a state of denial about how bad things had gotten, but she was facing it now.

Well. Technically, she was only facing its paper trail. But she had to start somewhere.

"Mom?"

She whirled around. Grant stood barefoot and pajama clad in the kitchen, looking somehow smaller than he did by day.

"Sweetheart." She glanced uneasily back at the invoices. "What are you doing up?"

Grant was a restless sleeper, prone to waking at random and coming to stand at her bedside until an uneasy feeling would compel her to open her eyes. She expected that zombie-like, mournful stare now, a mumbled excuse about wanting to be tucked back in, but instead he surprised her by running at her and leaping into her lap, sending papers fluttering off the table, skimming the carpet, and sliding under the sectional.

"Oh no, no!" she hissed. "Damn it, Grant!"

He recoiled, and she regretted her words, her tone, the fact that all the worst parts of her seemed to have become perpetually spring-loaded. It wasn't his fault the mess she'd made was so precarious, so easily scattered. And he'd only wanted a hug.

"I'm sorry," she said, sinking to the floor and opening her arms. "I didn't mean to snap. I was only startled." He hesitated, then let her pull him close. He smelled of bedtime—tear-free shampoo and bubblegum toothpaste and slightly sweaty sheets.

"Are you ow-y, Mommy?" She hated not knowing whether the question was a guess at the source of her insomnia or of her quick temper. Neither boded well for her track record.

"I'm okay," she said, tipping his face up and smiling into it. "What about *you*?"

He buried his head in her torso again, which was just as well. Involuntary tears were welling at the way he'd looked at her, like *she* was the frightened child. "You weren't in your room," Grant said. She was glad he'd come looking for her rather than waking Daniel, alerting him to her absence in the process. Even if it *was* an extension of the mind-boggling phenomenon by which the kids would seek her out—in the shower, in the garden, in the laundry room—to request a drink or a snack, only for her to comply and find their equally capable father right there in the kitchen all along. "Being ow-y makes you sad," he said.

She shook her head, dismayed at her failure to hide it even as she cringed anew at the still-fresh memory of his less sensitive take, just days ago: *Girls aren't strong.* "Don't worry about Mommy," she said. "Mommies should worry about their kids, not the other way around."

"But . . ."

"It makes *you* sad, too?" She held her breath. She'd feared this moment, tried to avoid it. He didn't answer. Maybe she was making it out to be worse than it was. "You wish Mommy was less cranky because of it? That's my fault. I can do better."

He shook his head.

"There's a race," he said. "At school. A fun raiser."

"Fund-raiser?" He nodded. "That's when people do something to raise money for a good cause. *Fund,* with a *d,* is another word for money. Though they do try to make them fun." She looked around at the windblown receipts and felt an inappropriate urge to laugh. Maybe she should throw one for herself. If only she were a sympathetic cause.

"All my friends are doing it."

"All you have to do is ask, buddy. How far is it?"

"Five. And there's a letter. . . ."

"K? A five K?" He nodded, and she considered it. "That *is* pretty far, for kindergarten legs. You'll need to practice." This would default to Daniel. She was under no-impact-exercise instructions from the sports medicine doctor she loathed to visit, so conspicuous did she feel alongside actual athletes, the sole patient whose body had just *decided* to give out. Even a short jaunt across the yard, if she didn't stride just right, could leave her arthritic knees protesting for days. But what parent didn't have to run a little?

"You have to run with a grown-up," Grant said. "You're a team."

"Well, Daddy has been saying he wants to get in better shape. I'm sure he'd be happy to." She began gathering the receipts into a pile. It was time to get Grant back to bed, and she couldn't risk leaving this out.

"He can't. He says he has a big persuasion that day."

She bit back a smile. "A *presentation*?" Grant nodded, and she tried to think of what that might be. "When's the race?"

He told her, and then she understood. The start of the fiscal. The budget proposals. Every year, Daniel would get so keyed up about them he couldn't hold a conversation about anything else for days beforehand. It was the one time of the year that he behaved as if his job was actually on the line. They had to like what he had to say. And he had to be there to say it.

"Ah. He does have something important that day."

Grant nodded. "And you're too ow-y." One of the bigger invoices—cataloging a laundry list of mistakes resulting from an ill-considered trip to Urgent Care—sliced through the tip of her ring finger and she winced, reflexively putting it in her mouth, tasting blood.

"Well, usually you can walk these races. I can walk it."

"Mom!" He looked mortified. "It's a *race.* Our team cannot *walk.*"

"Plenty of people do."

He shook his head firmly. "I'd rather sit. Do you think Granny or Gramps would run with me?"

She shook her head, trying not to dwell on the fact that her son thought senior citizens more likely to complete a race than she was. And that he was not entirely off base. Her parents were pretty fit, recent retirees, but as such were at this moment in an RV somewhere, exploring the West Coast. Daniel's mom and dad, who were at least in driving distance, were not exactly in poor health but were more into quilting and astronomy, respectively.

"I don't think so," she said gently.

"Everyone else has someone to run with," he said, his bottom lip jutting out. There was no guilt trip in his words, merely a matter-of-factness. He was a good sport, usually. Sometimes he'd catch her sitting with a certain reluctance to move and come over, set a gentle hand on her arm, and ask, "Ice or heat?" And get it for her. Unbidden.

She was just as tired of this as everyone else was. Every wistful look from her husband, her children, her friends, even her parents—who kept their visits short and asked conspicuously few questions about her state, having *earned* their newfound freedom—chipped away at her sense of self. They thought she was tiresome, but they had no idea how much she held back. Even at the risk of—well, as it turned out, damn near everything.

"Maybe I could try," she heard herself say. What was she *doing*? The training alone would do her in. All that pounding on her joints—it would start with her knees, then reach her back, her neck, her jaw, her mind. It would be too much.

Unless she didn't train. Unless she just . . . showed up on race day and had a bucket of ice waiting at home.

"Really?" He had the good sense to look not unkindly skeptical, and her heart swelled.

Never mind that she couldn't tolerate anti-inflammatories anymore, that even a single over-the-counter pill would leave her so nauseated she feared her stomach must be bleeding. Maybe the only way through this pain was to just contend with it without letting it slow her down. She'd had this conversation with herself before—after she'd been told she didn't meet the criteria for fibromyalgia and had been filled with such relief it had felt like a second chance—but it hadn't stuck. Maybe this time, though, things could be different.

"Well, I'm a lot younger than Granny," she teased him, as if there were no other reason she couldn't follow through. Excitement sprung to his eyes, and she realized she hadn't seen enough of it there lately. Usually he looked more . . . resigned, maybe?

Not a good look for a five-year-old.

She ran her fingers under the edge of the couch to make sure none of the receipts had escaped her reach, and shoved the crumpled stack into a file folder, which she tucked into one of the oversized photo albums. This was a problem she still didn't know how to solve. But maybe there was another one that deserved her attention first.

"Do I get a ribbon, too?" she asked, and he looked worried.

"I think they're just for the kids. . . . But I can make you one?"

"Deal."

He flung his arms around her neck, and she got to her feet, carrying him in a way she hadn't pushed herself to do in months.

So what if it would hurt later.

13

LIZA COULDN'T REMEMBER THE LAST TIME SHE'D SLEPT SO LATE. THEN again, she couldn't recall ever having slept so little as in the days prior. The phone woke her after ten, the house quiet, Luke and Steph gone to work. They'd offered to stay home, but she insisted she'd be fine, reminded them she had shopping to do and a résumé to re-create. She didn't mention that actual forward motion seemed beyond her, that she still felt outside her body, as if observing this disaster's fallout from a vantage point several degrees removed.

"Good morning. This is Amelia, from Front Door Insurance—I've been assigned to handle your renter's claim."

"Oh. Right." She'd never been one to tempt fate—she even bought insurance on car rentals, even though she knew that was supposedly a redundant expense. She told herself it was *not* because the reps at the counter were so insistent; it was simply a small price to pay for one fewer worry.

"The report your agent submitted says this fire was a total loss for you—is that correct?" This woman—this *Amelia*—sounded too matter-of-fact, like she talked to survivors of fatal infernos every day.

Then again, maybe she did.

"Pretty much."

"I'm so sorry. Fortunately, you're one of the lucky ones. You wouldn't believe how many people forgo renter's insurance. We'll get you taken care of."

Liza blinked into the morning light. She wouldn't have even had the presence of mind to call her insurance agent if not for Max, who'd taken charge while she sat teary eyed and shivering. She'd been so shaken by the understanding that she was lucky to be alive that it hadn't occurred to her how lucky she was to be *insured.*

"Let's start with where you are now. Do you have a place to stay?"

She licked her lips. Her mouth was uncomfortably dry. "I've arranged to stay with my brother and his wife."

"So you won't be needing—"

"What if I *hadn't* had renter's insurance?"

The claims rep hesitated, as if reluctant to go off script. "Well, then a total loss would be just that, I'm afraid. Your deductible is five hundred dollars, but that's all this will cost you. Now, will you require temporary housing assistance? If you need to be set up in a hotel or a furnished sublet until you find a new place, that's something we can do."

Liza squinted at the phone, surprised. "That would be covered?"

"Absolutely. Sort of like a rental car allowance while yours is in the shop. I could make recommendations if you'd like—how close to your original apartment were you hoping to stay? Are there other areas of Chicago that would be suitable?"

"I'm in Cincinnati, actually. I mean, my brother's in Cincinnati."

"I see. Okay. When do you plan to head back?"

Liza swung her legs over the side of the bed and reached out to pull the sheer curtain away from the window. The sunlight-dappled branches of an old, thick tree sprawled across the frame, and her eyes followed their lines, looking for some sign of the owl she'd heard the night before—a nest, a feather. But she found none. The tree was not yet budding; it offered no cover.

"I'm not sure I do. I'm, um . . ."

She should have said a firmer no, set the woman straight. It was just that it hadn't occurred to her someone might have paid for her to stay somewhere other than on Max's futon in Chicago, figure things out there. If Max knew, he'd say this was *just what he meant* about not making snap decisions. But it was too late now. Wasn't it?

And she wanted to be here instead.

Didn't she?

"I'm from here," she said finally. "Originally. I'd been thinking of moving back."

In the swath of blue sky showing between the branches, an airliner was crossing a maze of vapor trails, leaving one of its own. She imagined the passengers looking down at Luke's tiny roof, perhaps, or engrossed in something else, something they could put their hands around. You could get from one city to another, even hundreds of miles away, just like that. You could decide at any point to go back or not to go back. Surely it wasn't so unusual? She let the curtain drop.

"I see," the woman said again. "Well, certainly no one plans for something like this. Take a few days to get it sorted. We can assist with the transition, regardless of what you decide. Have you begun replacing any items yet? Clothing, smaller necessities?"

"Just a few things my mom brought me. I haven't had a chance . . ."

"Save the receipts. Probably best for you to foot the bill, though I understand your family is trying to help. We'll get you reimbursed—we'll get to that. First we need to do our best to catalog what you've lost." The sound of typing was faint across the phone line as Liza conjured a picture of her old living room. The futon, the flat-screen TV, that vintage Tiffany lamp . . . The idea of making a lifeless list of it all when others were mourning the loss of entire families made her feel sick.

"What about the cause?" Liza asked. "Of the fire, I mean."

"The cause? That wouldn't play into a renter's claim."

"It doesn't *matter* what caused it?" She hadn't meant to snap. She drew in a steadying breath.

"If you were the property owner, that would be different, but your coverage is the same regardless."

"But someone is investigating? The paper mentioned possible safety code violations. Negligence."

"That would be up to whoever insured the building commercially to investigate. And the fire marshal and whatnot. But again, that's not something we get involved with."

"What about me?"

"I'm sorry?"

"*You* don't get involved, but will the tenants be involved?"

"I can't imagine why. Unless a tenant was at fault somehow."

She couldn't imagine *why*? People had *died.*

"How long can it take to determine who *was* at fault? Not a tenant, but say a contractor."

"Liability, that sort of litigation? A long time."

"Months?"

A heavy sigh. "Unless it's clear cut, maybe years."

Liza's temples throbbed. It was hard to imagine going even one more *day* without knowing why this had happened. Surely others were just as motivated to find answers—especially those who'd lost more than just *things.* People, for God's sake. If someone was responsible, then that person should have to face them.

"Who would I call, about that sort of thing?" She didn't sound at all like the proud survivor her family had made her out to be around the dinner table last night.

"I'm not sure—all I know is it isn't me. I understand this is upsetting, and I do want to help. The best way I can do that is to focus on this claim." The keyboard clicked again in the background, and Liza imagined the notes she must be keying in. *Total basket case. Please reassign.* "Making this list could take a while—if this isn't a good time, we can set another one?"

How much, Liza wondered, *for the family photos I promised Mom I'd digitize, but never got around to? The souvenirs from the semester I spent in Italy? That cheesy under-the-arch prom picture of me and Matt—the only one I didn't tear up when we broke up the next month, the only one I had left to cry over when he was killed in that motorcycle crash the next year?*

Liza considered the bizarre blank of the empty day in front of her. She had nowhere to be, no witnesses to attest to whether she accomplished anything or nothing at all. "Can we do this tomorrow, actually?" A day would help—just one. A day to process this, to remove herself from the absolute tackiness of getting reimbursed for her life while others had lost theirs. Now that she was fully awake, the pulsing in her head was reminding her that she'd usually had several cups of caffeine by this hour. And that she might need it more than she wanted to admit she did. Among other things.

"Certainly. In the meantime—"

"Save receipts," Liza said dutifully. "Thank you."

Amelia was saying something else when Liza disconnected the call, but she couldn't bring herself to care what.

—

Liza didn't know what drew her to make the short drive down the interstate and east on Red Bank Road to the small complex of Lunken Airport. It might have been that she and Molly used to meet here after work, power walking their frustrations away on the five-mile trail that wound around the municipal airfield and along the adjacent golf course. It might have been that back when she'd felt restless in Cincinnati, she'd liked to watch the takeoffs, to crane her neck for glimpses of the colorful small aircraft inside the hangars, to imagine the freedom-fueled lifestyles of their owners—who might stop off for a quick jaunt into the sky the way others kill an hour at the mall or clear their head at the gym. Or it might have been the weather, the sun a beacon in a cloudless blue, one of those warm spring days that carried the promise of summer.

After hanging up with the insurance agent, she'd sat alone at the kitchen table with Luke's laptop, sipping reheated coffee, browsing the Chicago news sites, and then searching every keyword combination she could think of. There was, incredibly, *no* further news about the fire or its aftermath—not an update, not a what-we-know recap, not a blip. All she found was a GoFundMe page raising funeral expenses for a tenant who didn't look familiar, and a blog post soliciting prayers for another in a burn unit. She forked over fifty dollars for the first and felt a wave of shame over the latter. Liza's relationship with God was complicated. She'd never been able to decide what to believe, but she envied those who had. Especially now, when faith might have offered comfort.

She couldn't shut out that Amelia woman's voice: *That's not something we get involved with.* So compartmentalized. The idea of having no vested interest in how the fire had started or why—well, Liza supposed she envied that, too. As it was, the fact that her own life-changing headline was so easily buried in the steady stream of other Chicago news seemed a fitting end to her time there. One that left her longing for something she couldn't put her finger on, until she couldn't stand to stare at the screen anymore. Until she needed to get out.

And found herself here. Maybe she was after the reassurance, the miraculous normalcy of a place where flimsy things took flight, glided through the danger zone, and came safely back down.

She parked at the far end of the trail, near the ballfields, and began a tentative stroll, though she wasn't dressed well for it, the most suitable outfit her mother had brought consisting of jeans that would start to chafe and a light sweater that would prove too warm for the day. It was useful, at least, that her only surviving shoes were sneakers. Lunken managed to be both the same as she remembered it and different. Smart new signs directed traffic, with maps showing how the loop now connected to another trail network, and there were more bikes than there used to be—the athletic crowd on its lunch break—whizzing past her with a brisk, "On your left!" A large sign advertised an air shuttle offering regular service to Chicago and a few other select cities.

Liza could almost hear Max. *Let me get this straight,* he'd say. *So far, on your first full day in Cincinnati you've gotten an offer for expenses-paid housing in Chicago and then, immediately upon leaving the house, stumbled upon the fastest way back?*

She wouldn't take either as a sign. Only as a test. One she intended to pass.

She and Molly had always been walkers—as teenagers, they'd gone out late at night, long after dark, pulling sweatshirts over their pajamas and each starting out from her own house until they met in the middle. In the glow of the streetlights and the shadows in between, they'd talk about their crushes, their fears, their dreams for the future. It was something girls would no longer be allowed in the age of helicopter parenting and social media shaming—heaven forbid something should happen, the parents would be skewered alive—and too bad. She'd missed those intimate walks once she and Molly took to pounding this sunny pavement instead, trading in their flannel pants for designer exercise gear. Not that their conversations hadn't still been earnest, but even then their friendship had been changing. She couldn't think of an example of anything that was actually improved by becoming more conventional.

As she made her way past a sea of parked golf carts and down to the chain-link fence enclosing the airport grounds, a small jet was taxiing to the runway, and Liza thought of Molly's nervous recounting of Daniel's departure that last night on the phone, about the way Grant had begged his father not to leave.

You're never coming back, never!

She had a sudden vision of someone chasing after the plane, arms waving, saying the same. She shivered, looked away as the jet aligned on the strip and began to pick up speed. Maybe Grant had rightly sensed impending doom, just not where it was coming from. Had things played out differently, she might have found a way to ask him, might even be staying with Molly instead of Luke now.

Then again, had things played out differently, she wouldn't be anywhere at all.

The trail veered uphill to its most isolated stretch, parallel to the river, and Liza took deep breaths of the warm air to calm herself—in through the nose, out through the mouth—and gave herself over to the rhythm of ambient noise, propellers and distant motors, and a chorus of insects strumming to life where wildflowers and weeds would soon rim the path. In Chicago, her favored trail had the open water of Lake Michigan going for it but left little opportunity to tune out the urban center towering on the opposite side. Here she might have pretended she was just about anywhere—in any field under the endless sky—but for once, in spite of everything, was where she wanted to be. More or less. *Home.* One day soon, she would be glad of it, if she could stop thinking so much of how and why she'd found herself back where she started.

She rounded the final bend, where the dusty farmers market assembled, pulling at her sweater, which had grown as sticky as she'd known it would. In a triangle of newly painted crosswalks and parking lots, she was delighted to find the original art deco terminal looked just as it always had, a monument to the brief era before airports had morphed into endless corridors barricaded behind winding security lines. This one, which had neither a metal detector nor a ticket window that she'd ever seen, was mostly patronized by people in need of a public restroom or a cold drink, the word *terminal* accurate only in the sense that hangars filled with private and corporate aircraft were beyond its walls. She'd forgotten there was a restaurant here, and the nostalgic Sky Galley sign beckoned her. She hadn't managed anything at breakfast, and the miles she'd clocked were starting to make her lightheaded. Business at the trail was winding down with the lunch hour, bikers loading their car racks, dog walkers pouring water into collapsible bowls, a stroller-toting group of moms converting a bench to a diaper-changing station. Maybe she could snag a table on the patio. Funny enough, she'd come to watch the planes but had scarcely noticed them once she'd gotten going, lost in her thoughts.

She climbed the concrete stairs and pulled open the heavy metal door, blinking as her eyes adjusted to the dimness inside. An aviation-themed gift shop was dark in front of her, a "Closed" sign flipped on the glass door, but the restaurant was open to her left, and she stepped past a chalkboard easel—"Now Hiring: Shift Manager"—to poke her head in. Making her way through the narrow galley of the bar to the hostess station, she saw that only a few tables were occupied. Receipts peeked out of black folios on several others waiting to be cleared.

"Be with you in a moment," a waitress said, breezing past with a tray.

"I'm not in a hurry!" Liza called after her. "Take your time."

The woman disappeared into the kitchen, where she apparently intended to take Liza up on her offer. By the time she reappeared moments later, she'd smoothed her frizz of a ponytail and smelled of cigarette smoke. "Anywhere you like," she said, menu in hand, as if this were a fair trade for the wait. "And thanks for the breather. We're beyond short staffed."

"Got anything on the patio?"

"You'll have it to yourself."

A handful of metal tables huddled behind the restaurant in full view of the airfield, and Liza chose one of only two in the shade, giving the menu a cursory glance before ordering a water and a chicken Caesar wrap, substituting fries for the Saratoga chips. The beer list was decent. Maybe she'd stick around for one once she put something in her stomach. A helicopter was making quick work of takeoff, and she watched it hover there, enjoying the man-made breeze even as it carried the faint scent of fuel.

For the hour around the loop, she'd resisted the weight of her phone in her pocket, the urge to check again for some update. She took it out now—a habit, anyway, when dining alone—but she'd drawn out the suspense for nothing. Few of the headlines had changed since this morning, though she did have a text from Max: *How you holding up?*

What to say? How was one supposed to hold up when half of her neighbors were dead, the other half injured, homeless, or both, and all rendered yesterday's news? She scrolled past today's tragedies again, and the headlines called out to her, begging to be reconsidered. "Undetected Gas Leak Kills Five" might have been "If Only Someone Had Noticed the Smell." Or perhaps "She Noticed the Smell, and He Assured Her It Was Nothing." Or maybe "Undetected Gas Leak Almost Killed Six, but One Got Invited to a Slumber Party."

"Are you okay?" She looked up, startled, to find a man in a starched pilot's uniform seated at the adjacent table. His eyes held hers as he plunked his straw into a glass of water and twisted the paper in his fingers. She hadn't noticed anyone coming or going, yet not only was he here, sharing the shrinking shade, but so was her lunch order, perched with a roll of silverware on the table's edge.

"I don't want to overstep," he continued, "but you look upset."

She shook her head quickly, setting her phone aside and pulling the plate in front of her, unrolling the napkin into her lap. She could feel his expectant stare. At major airports, the pilots appeared rushed, overworked, headed somewhere important, usually in pairs. This one seemed buoyant, energetic, fit. He took off his cap and laid it next to his water. He looked, when it came down to it, damn sure of himself. Of life.

"Ever have a near-death experience?" she blurted out.

He sat back in his seat, surprised, and she flushed. "A close call, I mean." She pointed at the sky, indicating her meaning. *Up there.*

His expression shifted toward amusement. "Probably," he said, with a small shrug. He had a shock of auburn hair and an easy, open smile, and she guessed he was about her age, maybe a few years older. He cocked his head at her, as if debating whether to say more. "Are you about to be one of my passengers?"

She shook her head, and his posture relaxed. "Okay, then. Seven things generally have to go wrong for the plane to go down. Does that make you feel any better?"

She blinked. "Well . . . no. I'm not sure I believe that's true."

He laughed again. "Which one of us is the pilot?"

"But what about a—" She looked around. No one else was here. The word was forbidden in airports—did this one count? "Bomb?" she whispered.

Homeland Security did not appear.

"You went there," he said, eyebrows raised.

"It's six fewer than seven things," she said.

"Well, I don't know. First, a bomb could go off anywhere. Second, seven things might have to go wrong for a bomb to *make* it onto a plane."

"Okay," she said, pointing a skeptical French fry in his direction and taking a bite. It was slightly undercooked but satisfyingly salty, and she washed it down with the rest of her water. "What are the seven things?"

"Well, they're not always the *same* seven." He nodded at her fry. "Those any good? My past few orders were undercooked."

The waitress reappeared with a pitcher and refilled her water glass. Liza was suddenly as ravenous as she was thirsty, and she took a big bite of her wrap as the ponytail swung toward the pilot.

"The usual, Henry?" the waitress asked him.

"I'll change it up and have that wrap, too," he said. "It looks good. With the—" He glanced at Liza, and she swallowed the bite and mouthed, *Saratoga chips.* He smiled at the server. "Just as it comes, thanks." She disappeared inside, and he laughed. "Undercooked, I take it."

"Seven things must have gone wrong with the fryer." She held out a fry, and he took it, chewing thoughtfully.

"Probably just one," he conceded. "That theory applies to disaster. An undercooked fry doesn't really qualify."

"Having worked in the hospitality business, I can assure you not all customers agree."

He laughed again, full and hearty, and she went on devouring the wrap, not really caring that he was watching. She didn't mind the company but wasn't about to put her lunch on hold now that the walk had coaxed her appetite back. "Let's back up," he said, gesturing toward a puddle jumper coming in for a landing. They watched as it hopped onto the runway, then rolled to a stop not far from them. "The general idea is that for something *major* to go wrong, a lot of little things have to go wrong, in sequence. The only constant is human error. It usually plays a role."

She frowned, turning back to him. "So when you hear about a near miss, that just means someone stepped in or something stopped the momentum before the seventh thing?"

"Exactly. You asked about close calls, but those don't just happen, either."

"You don't believe in luck?"

He shrugged. "A winning lottery ticket is pretty lucky. But a plane that doesn't crash after something went wrong just has a well-trained pilot." There was something maddeningly charming about how certain he was. Or maybe she just liked that he'd given the theory so much thought. It made her feel less crazy for having asked in the first place.

"You're agreeing with me, then," she pointed out, sounding more coy than she'd intended. Sometimes her inner flirt couldn't help herself. "Disaster could always be right around the corner."

"Ideally, around seven corners. But usually at least three or four of them. I don't think you should worry so much, is all." It was a nice distraction, talking about this without really talking about it. Voicing her concerns without addressing what had caused them. She'd do better to stay out, like this, making idle chitchat instead of holing up with her thoughts, where even a hooting owl could give her an anxiety attack.

The waitress returned with her check and his food, and Liza plunked a credit card on the table and smiled at her. "I saw that you're hiring a manager. Do you think they'd consider someone whose experience is mostly in hotels?"

"I think they'd consider just about anyone at this point. And that I should probably not be so blunt with someone who could end up being my boss. Would you like an application?"

"Please." Liza turned back to the pilot as the server disappeared inside. "Look, if that's what makes you feel better when you're up there, I won't dissuade you."

His eyes held a hint of mischief. "If you're looking for a job, I could use another crew member, but you might have to chill out seven notches." She crumpled up her napkin and tossed it at him, and he ducked dramatically. He held out a Saratoga chip as a peace offering, and she popped it in her mouth.

"A little *too* crunchy, Henry," she said, trying out his name, and he tossed the napkin back. She caught it midair.

"You know," he said, then stopped short. "I'm sorry. I didn't catch your name."

"Liza."

He smiled as if this affirmed some suspicion he'd had—like he'd known it all along and just wanted to see if she did, too. "You know, Liza, most people are *looking* for a statistic that will make them feel better—the probability of a positive outcome—not arguing against it. Why aren't you?"

The server reappeared, credit card and application in hand, and Liza picked up her purse and got to her feet, trying to pretend it wasn't an excellent question.

14

DANIEL HADN'T TRAVELED MUCH FOR WORK UNTIL RECENTLY—BUT WHEN he did, he usually flew out of the international hub, like most everybody else, allotting extra time to deal with the excruciatingly slow long-term parking shuttle, with the unpredictable bridge construction, with the remote possibility of being pulled out of the security line for a pat-down. He'd have traded it in a heartbeat for this—the VIP jet out of Lunken, with practically door-to-door service—if it didn't mean he also had to wonder what he'd done to deserve it.

Or what he'd be expected to do in return.

I can give you plenty of reasons to reconsider, Toby had written. Daniel hadn't replied and had managed not to cross his path since. But Daniel also knew that Toby had booked this flight—this whole trip, in fact, of which the purpose was murky—and Daniel clung to an uneasy hope that it had nothing to do with either reasons or reconsidering.

He'd been weighing his options. He did not, he'd decided, want to investigate further—to look into who else might be involved in Toby's scheme and to what extent. The less he knew, the better. The ship of feigning complete ignorance seemed to be sailing, but he wasn't quite ready to see it off. Maybe he *could* still continue as if he knew nothing or even start looking for employment elsewhere, get out while the getting was good.

Or he could bring his suspicions quietly to his superiors now and hope they'd go easy on him, spare his job, though he hadn't given them much reason to. He was still working out the best way to plead his case, should he choose this route. But he was also considering another: one that turned this on Toby, giving him a chance to put the cookies back in the jar, no one the wiser. If he succeeded, both men could ostensibly proceed without consequence—though if anyone were to discover what had happened after the fact, Daniel would then be involved at a level he could lose more than just a job over.

He might have reached a decision by now if he weren't preoccupied with so much else.

The fact, for instance, that this did not seem a good time to leave Molly home alone. A week had passed since the incident with the intruder, and in that time they'd been more careful with each other—hesitant, yes, even a bit awkward, but nevertheless kind. Which seemed a sign that he might have gotten through to her—that they might be on the verge of some kind of progress, something other than standing still.

Then again, maybe stepping away when by some miracle neither of them wanted him to would be for the best. Absence and growing fondness and all that.

There was something else, too. Some assigned reading. From her neighbor friend, the one who might as well be starring in his own prime-time drama for the housewives to coo and cry over. Rick was his name, and Daniel had taken note of how seldom his wife said it, of how cautious she was to avoid it, though Daniel knew from his daughter's chatter that the pair from the house in the woods had become a regular fixture in her days. "We're letting Rosie get used to us so she'll learn it's okay to talk to strangers," Nori had explained sweetly. How was that for a message that could backfire? But when he tried to bring it up to Molly, she refused to discuss it. When it came to Grant and especially Nori—where Daniel could claim no gender-specific expertise worth consulting—he was vice parent at best, and Madam President never hesitated to use her veto.

Previously Rick and Daniel had talked only in passing, trading the kinds of fascinating observations about crabgrass and leaf blowers that made him pine for his and Molly's old Clifton apartment, where his maintenance efforts began and ended with a call to the landlord and even the hallway pleasantries were more interesting, about an indie flick playing at the Esquire or the new latte on special at Sitwell's. Yet Rick had come by the office, found Daniel somehow, gifted him a book on managing a loved one's pain. It had the word *mindfulness* in the subtitle. Said he'd bought it when his wife was diagnosed. He'd seemed to think he was doing the couple a great service by passing this guide along, leading Daniel to wonder what had brought this on now and not before. Unsure whether to thank him or deck him, Daniel had done neither, only nodded and stared blankly at this physical, written-out acknowledgment of what he didn't want to acknowledge. That Molly was not okay.

Still, he'd brought it with him. It was worth a look.

He might have walked right past Liza if not for the dress she was wearing. Molly had an identical one, purchased just last week on sale at the Kenwood mall for a family photo shoot his parents had scheduled, so it turned his head and then, once he realized who was wearing it, made him marvel that the once sister-close friends were still so obliviously in tune.

He'd practically had to surgically separate the pair in order to marry Molly, though it wasn't that Liza was a clinger. She'd have kept a respectful distance had Molly not constantly pulled her back in. If Daniel took Molly alone to a great concert, she'd remark, more than once, how much Liza would have enjoyed it, too. If they found a solid new restaurant, Molly would be texting Liza highlights from the menu right at the table. To his wife's credit, she never actually said the words *it's not the same without Liza,* but she didn't have to. Daniel had succumbed and, even after they were married, took to making plans for three, four if Liza was seeing someone who'd been around for longer than five minutes.

After she'd moved to Chicago, it was as if Daniel and Molly had an unspoken agreement not to outwardly lament her absence. It took some time, but the point did come where his wife began to enjoy things even *he* knew Liza would love without that wistful look in her eye. Molly was fine without Liza. Of course she was.

But she wasn't quite the same. And for that reason, Daniel had missed Liza, too.

Now he couldn't even remember the last time he'd seen his wife's best friend—aside from watching, out of sight, as Molly closed their door in her face.

She was perched on a chair outside the Sky Galley holding a thin stack of good letterhead—résumés?—in a pose of nervous anticipation, and her presence registered with an odd mixture of happiness and alarm. How had she maintained the superhuman ability to track *both* of them down at the moments they least wanted anyone to observe? And why was she in Cincinnati at all, much less at the tiny regional airport he was only today flying out of for the first time? Last week's cold reception from Molly would have been enough to send even the kindest, most patient of souls riding a giant wave of good riddance back to Chicago. And Liza possessed a perfectly average amount of kindness and patience.

Was she still here, or was she back? And did Molly know?

"Liza." He fixed a smile and made his approach. Her expression flickered from surprise to that of someone seeking an escape hatch and then quickly to something purporting to be warmer. She stood for a one-armed hug while holding the paperwork at a crumple-safe distance.

"How about that," he said. "What are you doing here?"

"Interviewing, believe it or not." She looked over her shoulder toward the restaurant door, but no one was there. "I know it's a step down," she murmured confidentially. "But the place has charm."

"You're thinking of moving back?" He raised his eyebrows. "That would be great. But why? Everything okay with your parents?"

"They're fine." She hesitated. "Other than freaking out on my behalf. My apartment building in Chicago—there was a fire."

"Oh, God. It was bad?"

She scrunched up her face and nodded.

"I'm so sorry. Tell me you had renter's insurance."

"I did. I just—I wasn't sure I wanted to start over there. My heart wasn't in it anymore."

He nodded. "You know . . . Don't take this the wrong way, but I sort of had the impression you liked the idea of relocating to Chicago more than the reality of relocating to Chicago."

"That would be accurate. Although I thought I'd put up a better front than that."

"Well, Molly will be over the moon. She doesn't know yet? I assume she would've said something. . . ." He kept his eyes as blank as he could, his voice as even.

She shook her head. "It's been kind of . . . sudden." He noticed she did not add that she'd been meaning to call. Would she assume Molly had told him about her showing up at their door that morning? And if not, would she tell him herself?

"Guess so. Well, I'm so glad you're okay." She paled a little at that, looked away. "What can we do to help? Where are you staying?"

"With my brother. I'm set, thanks. Working on it, anyway."

Her voice warbled in a very un-Liza way, and he faltered. "Listen, I owe you a huge thank-you. That call you made about the man you saw enter our house—I don't even want to think about what might've happened if you hadn't been watching."

At that, her eyes dimmed. "I just did what anyone would've done." She didn't share in his relief—not that he blamed her. But she didn't ask after Molly, either.

Maybe it was a good thing, him running into her like this.

Maybe he could turn it into a chance at something.

"Such heroic modesty."

She smiled a little. "I learned it from you." It was an inside joke, a reference to how he'd met Molly on a night when she'd been caught alone in the wrong place at the wrong time. Or the right place at the right time, depending on how you looked at it. Because he'd come across her when she needed him. And that had been the beginning.

"I think you have me beat. As soon as you're sorted, you've got to come to dinner. Wait until you see the kids—I'm only leaving for two days, and they'll be even bigger by the time I'm back." He'd calculated the angle. She could act too busy to see Molly, but she could hardly avoid feigning interest in the kids. Liza was blunt, in a #nofilter sort of way, but she wasn't *rude,* unless people deserved it. Which Molly maybe did, but Daniel did not.

As far as she knew, anyway.

At best, having Liza here—on the off chance that she and Molly could patch things up somehow, chalk it up to a weird situation all the way around—could be the boost his wife needed, a way to reconnect with who she'd been before the past few years wore her down. Maybe that was too optimistic—reconciliation might not be possible without a level of effort both women were unlikely to muster. But at worst, Liza could be a liability—someone who could, at any moment she felt like it, tug this whole intruder ordeal back up to the surface even if they managed to make peace with it. And he didn't want that hanging over them indefinitely.

"Are you Liza?" A woman in black pants and a white button-down stood in the restaurant doorway, unsmiling, and Liza nodded. "Sorry to keep you waiting."

"No problem at all." She turned back to him. "I'd love that. Thanks, Daniel. Are you flying out of here?" He gave her a *crazy, huh?* nod. "Well, have a safe flight."

She turned and shook the white shirt's hand, the interview practically under way right here in the doorway—but he'd come too close to let her slip away without committing. "How about next Saturday?" he called, biting back a cringe at his evident inability to take a cue.

Liza shot an annoyed glance at him, then checked herself. "Maybe. I'll let you know."

"Don't tell me your calendar's already full!" His voice sounded bizarrely jolly, and she looked at him oddly. Damn it, he'd overplayed this. She'd suspect, now, that he knew *something,* if not everything. That he was trying to get her and Molly to kiss and make up. Even if that was an oversimplification . . . He was just so tired of guessing at what Molly wasn't saying. And Liza's reverse lie detector hadn't failed him yet.

"Fine," she relented, her smile tight.

"Great! Let's say seven. Bring Luke and his wife, or a date, whoever you'd like. We'll make it a welcome back party." He hurried off before she could change her mind. He wasn't sure why the hell he'd offered that last part. More people around the table would make a *real* conversation between her and Molly less likely. It just—slipped out. He wasn't used to seeing her like this. Something about her had turned stricken, timid. *Welcome back* seemed like the thing to say.

Molly was going to be secretly, unable-to-tell-him-so furious.

—

What little novelty Daniel allowed himself to enjoy in flying out of Lunken evaporated the instant Toby slid into the aisle seat next to him and started breathing the same recycled air. Just his luck.

"First time on the air shuttle?" Toby asked brightly, and Daniel nodded. He tucked his laptop bag under the seat in front of him and leaned back. "Thought so. *Well.* You're in for a treat. I mean, not only can you literally show up fifteen minutes before takeoff and stroll right on, but the flight only takes an hour. With the time difference, you land at the same exact time you took off. It's like some science-fiction warp or something." Toby ran a finger down the leather seat back in front of him. "How the other half lives. A guy could get used to it."

Daniel nodded again, wary. The shuttle *was* nice, especially for anyone who spent as much time hauling strollers and boosters around as Daniel did. The simple act of leaving the house as a family sometimes seemed so complicated he wished they didn't bother. But nothing would ever feel first class with this sorry excuse seated next to him. Daniel reached into his bag and removed the book Rick had given him. He placed it cover side down in his lap—not wanting to open the subject for discussion, especially with this audience—and folded his hands on top of it, hoping Toby might take the hint and get some reading material of his own.

"How's your wife?" Toby asked. The exact wrong question.

He cleared his throat. "Fine, thanks. Never too excited to see me go, of course." It seemed a conversational enough thing to say—and for once, maybe even true.

"I guess not. Especially not now."

The hairs on the back of Daniel's neck bristled to attention, and he glanced sidelong at the man. Toby was no more than five-foot-six, and his hair was trimmed in a deceptively boyish cut with the uneven look of someone whose mother still did the honors. He had no right to be looking at Daniel the way he was now—with a challenge in his eyes.

"What do you mean?" Daniel asked, trying not to sound uneasy.

"Well, with the incident the last time you were gone. Just last week, wasn't it?"

Daniel looked at him sharply. "How do you know about that?"

"Did I not mention that my sister lives in your neighborhood? Cathy McCreedy is her married name. You might know her as the original Chatty Cathy." Toby rolled his eyes, and Daniel had a vision then, of a fussy woman who did, come to think of it, look a bit like Toby, walking a hefty Rottweiler mix on an intimidating chain harness at all hours, stopping to talk with everyone she passed. Daniel avoided her like the plague. "Makes it her business to know *everything*. She isn't above chatting up a cop at the curb, if you know what I mean. And she relays it all to me, as if I care about all these people I don't know." He laughed easily. "But I figured out a while back that one of them was you. Could have sworn I mentioned it?"

Daniel shook his head. This just kept getting better. Now Toby was keeping tabs with his own neighborhood spy.

"Well. How terrifying for your wife. For all of you. An intruder, Cathy said. Or a false report of one? She wasn't sure. Do the police have any idea what happened?"

They were interrupted by the intercom announcement to turn their attention to the flight attendant's safety demonstration. She was tall, blond, the perfect updated picture of a retro stewardess. Guys like Toby probably never left the poor woman alone. Daniel cleared his throat and spoke in the lowest audible tone he could muster. "Probably just some random thing. We were lucky he was spotted and got scared off."

Toby turned to him, eyes merry. "Is that your party line, or is that what you really believe?"

Daniel inched closer to the window, taken aback. God, it was hot in here. He reached up and twisted the overhead vent, but it was already open as far as it would go. For such a small plane, the loudspeakers didn't work very well, either. Or maybe Daniel just couldn't make out the finer points of the droning-on demonstration over the sirens of alarm blaring in his ears. A ringing—tinnitus, it was called—was among Molly's litany of complaints in recent months, and it *had* sounded like an awful thing to endure. She couldn't stand silence, was always turning on the radio or cranking the white noise of the baby monitor next to her pillow to drown it out. He'd resented her efforts, though, craving the quiet that apparently he didn't get to have, either. The alarm bells now felt like payback for his lack of sympathy, and he could only hope they were temporary.

"None of my business, I'm sure," Toby whispered. "I just know people do better work when they're happy at home."

"Just seems a little personal," Daniel said, opening the book in his lap to a random page and staring at it blankly. Who did this guy think he was? "I try to keep my home life separate."

"The two have a way of bleeding together whether we want them to or not," Toby said easily. "Plenty of people know the basic details of my personal situation, even though I don't talk about it." Daniel kept his eyes down. "I know your wife has medical issues, and that you have two small kids. And your house is the cedar with the window boxes, right?" A chill ran through Daniel, even as he told himself these details could ostensibly be gleaned from his employee file, from the benefits records HR kept, and from Toby visiting his nosy sister.

"How about the other way around?" Toby persisted. "Do you talk about work much at home?"

"About as much as anyone, I guess."

"What are your wife's feelings on your job these days?"

Daniel's breathing stilled. Until that moment, he'd thought maybe he was imagining the crossing of the line. But the last time they'd talked, Toby had assumed—rightly—that Daniel was on to him. Daniel's attempt at buying time by playing dumb had fallen short. And now Toby wanted to know whether he'd talked to anyone else.

Only he wasn't asking about their coworkers. He was asking about Daniel's *wife.*

"I take it from your silence they're not overwhelmingly positive. That's too bad."

Do not engage, he ordered himself. "She's not a huge fan of the increased travel," he ventured, trying to make the gripe sound ordinary.

"Ah. Well, maybe she'd feel differently if she knew you weren't really away for business on that particular night." Toby's eyes were bright, and he leaned closer. "Unless I've missed something? Some . . . secret assignment?"

The flight attendant hung up her mic and took her seat, and the plane made a brisk turn onto the runway. But as it began to accelerate, Daniel was already flying above himself, horrified at the scene below—at how easily he was reduced in his mind's eye to the diminutive stature of the terrible man seated next to him.

"You've missed plenty," Daniel tried, his mouth dry, and Toby laughed.

"I didn't know you had it in you," he said, delighted. "I hope she's a real looker, worth the risk. Anyone I know?" He held up a hand. "Wait. Don't answer that. We might be friends, but I *am* HR. And we're a family company."

It was Daniel's turn to laugh. He couldn't help himself. "If that's true, I feel sorry for your family."

"Tsk-tsk. Those in glass houses . . ."

"And where were you that night?" Daniel growled. He hadn't known he was about to ask, but now that the question was out, it seemed disturbingly relevant.

"I beg your pardon?" Toby was the one averting his eyes now, glancing down the aisle as if expecting a cart of refreshments, though the crew was strapped in for takeoff. Daniel felt the break from gravity, the pop of his ears.

"You heard me. If you know so much about me and my family, and about what did or didn't happen that night, where were you?"

"What kind of question is that?"

"I could ask you the same about this entire conversation."

He laughed, hard enough for his whole body to shake heartily, and slapped Daniel on the shoulder. "Lighten up, Perkins. I think you misunderstand me. I'm trying to help."

Daniel fixed his stare out the window, struggling to contain his mounting rage.

"If I figured it out, don't you think the police will, too?" Toby asked. "I mean, don't they *always* verify where the husband was if something bad happens at home?" Daniel shook his head. He'd told himself they had no reason to. *I hope she's a real looker,* Toby had said. *Worth the risk.* It wasn't like that—that simple, that base. But it was also never going to happen again. The idea of having to explain . . .

"I have connections through our booking agent," Toby went on. "I can make sure that they'll confirm, no matter who asks, that on the night in question, you checked into a hotel room in—wherever you said you were." He smiled. "Backdated itinerary, too, if you need it. Like I said, I'm trying to help."

They were interrupted by another announcement, this time some requisite who-cares tidbits about their projected trajectory and cruising altitude, and that beverage service would begin shortly, with a cash bar available. When it was over, the compartment seemed full with the sounds of the engines, the propellers, the wind.

"I mean, forget the cops," Toby said, his voice thoughtful. "If Molly were to find out that you were fritting around when she was going through such a terrifying ordeal? That you were maybe even in town? If she's like most women I know, she'd blow a gasket over how you could have been *there for her*. I mean, hell, she might have a point. Maybe if you'd been there, the whole incident wouldn't have happened at all."

Daniel turned on him, dumbfounded and furious, but before he could unclench his teeth to reply, Toby laughed again, right in his face this time.

"Just *imagine*. Even if the police have dropped this—what if someone were to tip them off? If they started investigating you, why you lied . . ." His voice was low, but not low enough to veil the threat, and Daniel sank into his seat, the plane's cramped interior closing in around him.

"What are you getting at, Toby?" A man with no moral compass could swivel on a dime, with nothing to pull him back to north, meaning Toby would always be one turn ahead of him. Might as well get this over with. "What is it you want?"

"Well, it seems we both know—or think we know—something undesirable about the other," Toby said. "Silence seems a fair trade. At least for starters."

"You have me wrong," Daniel whispered. "I'm not like you. We aren't even on the same playing field."

"Aren't we? Don't forget I see all the paperwork that comes through—the job openings posted, filled or retracted, the promotions, the salaries. I know exactly how you manipulated your position, at the expense of what was best for the company—and its employees. You made it very easy for someone to take advantage." He tsked, shaking his head. "Greedy as *you* were, I think it's a little hypocritical for you to begrudge someone else a modest salary increase. You know how tight they are at the top. Guys like us, we have to get creative."

Daniel cursed himself. He should have decided on his next move more quickly, long before he'd been stupid enough to get on this plane—to do as he was told without even knowing why, just like every other bonobo in a suit.

"There is no *guys like us,*" he growled.

Toby shrugged. "If I *were* like you, I'd be carrying around some guilt right now. Over a lot of things. Might be nice to know my secrets were safe, if I were like you." He leaned closer. "Might be nice to know my *family* was safe."

Daniel's throat went dry.

"From your secrets, I mean." Toby grinned. "Tell you what," he said as the drink cart came into view. "Bloody Marys are on me." Daniel opened his mouth to decline, but something in Toby's eyes stopped him.

"It's like I told you, Perkins. It's the damnedest thing. You land *at the same time* you took off. It's like the hour in the sky never happened at all."

15

ROSIE AND NORI RAN AHEAD TO THE SPLIT IN THE TRAIL—MORE OF A SIDEways T than a fork—and looked expectantly back at Molly and Rick. The kids knew the drill by now, that any place with options could be *the* destination for the day's "brave talking," and Molly smiled and nodded, resisting the urge to quicken her step to catch up. It was best not to make too big a deal of these decision points, though everyone knew them to be the reason for the outings in the first place.

Rick had broken their silence this morning with a text message inviting them to meet after Nori's preschool let out and, after much deliberation and many half-typed, never-sent alternate responses, Molly consented. She had no real excuse not to, as Daniel was away for work again and Grant was staying after school for the "running club" of kids training for the 5K—something Molly was holding out hope he'd discover he didn't enjoy after all. Convincing herself that she might still have an out—that she'd gauge how Grant's enthusiasm weathered the next couple weeks—was the only thing staving her panic at what she'd agreed to. Best to keep her mind on something else, and it might as well be Rosie. Molly wasn't sure she was ready to be here with Rick yet, but she understood consistency was important for the girl. She knew about forward momentum, about how things could grind to a halt if you let it falter.

She knew about pushing, about being pushed.

Rick dropped back as she approached the girls. Nothing at these junctures could come from him, and just as well. Molly didn't have to think much about what to say to him, how to act, whether they could—or should—return to the way things had been. These excursions weren't about them.

Or at least that's what she'd been telling herself all along.

"How about you pick what's next for us today, little Miss Rosie," she said lightly. "If we keep going straight, we can visit the pretty fountain outside Krippendorf Lodge." She jangled her pocket. "I've brought pennies to throw in."

Nori bounced on her tiptoes, and her coiled pigtails transformed into little brunette springs. "We could make *wishes,* Rosie!" she whispered.

Molly nodded. "Or, if we go left, we can make our wishes in the fairy garden by the herb wall. Have you seen that before?" Rosie shook her head, her lips pressed together tightly. Molly always started feeling nervous at this point—about how much coaxing might be required and whether she was doing it right. "Well, they've just come out of their winter's hibernation. There are tiny doorways. Tiny houses. Some you can find right away, but some you have to look for. Like the forest's little secrets."

She smiled and fell into what she hoped was the kind of silence that would invite the girl to respond. Early on, Rosie had tried the same work-arounds that had thwarted her dad's efforts at home—pointing, leading them by the hand in the direction she wanted to go—but the rest of the group stood their ground, literally, until Rosie learned that responding verbally was the only way to get results. Molly had gambled when she'd conceived of these outings that the temptation would be strong, and she'd been more or less right. Nature called to everyone, especially children, and they'd been making slow, steady progress with the ritual.

The key was to be nonchalant about the waiting. Quiet was relative here, which helped things feel less stilted. A mishmash of gravel and dead leaves scuffled beneath Nori's fidgeting feet; birdsong harmonized around them. A gust of wind rustled the young leaves above, and Rick tipped his head back to look up—anywhere but at Rosie. And just like that, a question burned in the girl's eyes, eager to be set free.

Go ahead, Molly willed her silently. *Ask it. Ask if the fairies are real. Ask who put them there. Ask me anything at all. You can do it. You know us—we're your friends.* Usually the best they could hope for was a clipped, timid response, a polite *fountain* or *fairies* with perhaps a *please* or a *maybe* tacked on. But the words had been coming more readily, with less delay.

Ironically, given that Molly had come to specialize in failure with her own healing attempts, Rick was more surprised at Rosie's progress than Molly was. With this, he was the one at wit's end and she objective and fresh eyed—a welcome switch. Her faith in the nature center was her one faith that remained unshaken; though physical relief eluded her, the invisible forces that had drawn her here kept pulling. She'd seen the good work done with the small groups bussed in from special education centers. She'd shared the reclaimed joy of the retirees newly freed from cubicle walls. Rosie was starting from such a young, innocent place—she'd experienced a terrible loss, but she had a wonderful father, and Molly felt confident she was going to be okay, one way or the other.

That made one of them.

Molly's strategy focused on points of interest on the grounds—the options were plenty, as the place had begun as a private estate, full of historical landmarks, and grown outward. Miles of hiking trails wrapped around outbuildings and overlooks, a lake, ponds, boardwalks, bridges, the children's area, and of course the visitor center, the preschool, and the more isolated buildings for research and study. Early in her time here, she'd made it a point to come to know these trails as if they were her own—there was satisfaction in feeling at home somewhere that was so outside of her, that belonged to everyone—and the prospect of putting her expertise to good and selfless use had inspired an optimism she'd feared she was no longer capable of.

"If it works," Rick had cautioned her, "we can't make it a big deal. No cheering. Her therapist says it'll just add pressure for next time."

"So how do we act?"

"We're supposed to use something called 'labeled praise.' Not, 'good job,' but 'I love how you told us which way you wanted to go.'"

Simple enough. Molly could have used a little labeled praise herself. *I liked how you gave acupuncture a try even though you have always been terrified by needles.* Or, *I liked how you did your physical therapy exercises three times yesterday instead of the required two, even though the thought of more leg lifts made you want to scream.*

It turned out to be hard not to cheer for Rosie's progress. The first two outings had indeed left them retreating to the parking lot in defeat when no decision was made. But the disappointment of leaving the riches of the forest unseen had gotten the best of the little girl.

"Frog pond," she'd whispered on the third day, with little prompting. She'd been psyching herself up even before Rick had brought her, Molly could tell.

Now Rosie leaned closer, and Molly crouched to her level.

She said something so softly that Molly couldn't make it out. She detected a long "oh." *Go? Show?*

"Sorry, Rosie, I didn't hear you. Can you say it again?"

The little girl cleared her throat. "Can we do both?" she said, clear as the sky, and Molly's hands shot triumphantly in the air before she caught herself and clasped them behind her. "We sure can," she said, soundlessly applauding in the air behind her back, where only Rick could see. "Where to first?"

Rosie looked to Nori, and Molly tried to catch her daughter's eye, to shake her head that she shouldn't answer for her friend, but Nori was bouncing again, too excited to stick to the rules. "Pennies?" she squealed, and Rosie nodded eagerly. Nori took her by the hand. "I bet we can get there in twenty steps. Want to count?" Rosie nodded again, and the two began marching ahead, "One, two, three . . ." Molly heard only Nori's voice but dared to hope Rosie was whispering along.

"Sorry," Molly said, turning to Rick. She hadn't delivered the labeled praise, which was supposed to happen right away. "I wanted to see if she'd answer twice. She's having a good day."

"Sorry?" He laughed. "For what? It isn't a 'good day'—it's the best one yet!" He scooped her into a bear hug and swung her in a circle, the branches whirling around them, and she stiffened, swallowing a gasp of surprise. They should be keeping boundaries, especially after . . . but he was letting go, doing a goofy dance, letting out a *whoop* now that Rosie was too far ahead to hear, and Molly couldn't help but laugh. Who could blame him for being excited, for forgetting himself? The child was all he had left of his wife.

"We should catch up," Molly said, starting down the path, putting a few steps of distance between them. "Before they wind up *in* the fountain."

But he crossed the distance easily, falling into step beside her. "Hold back some pennies for us," he said. "Your progress with her has given me something more to wish for."

She allowed herself a glance sideways, and he was looking at her with gratitude, admiration, and . . . something else. Had he always looked at her this way, or was it new, an overcorrection after their rift? She felt herself blushing and returned her eyes to the path ahead.

"*She's* given it to you, not me," she said.

"I don't know where we'd be without you and Nori. You two have made a world of difference."

That's when Molly realized. It didn't matter what he meant by it. It mattered that right up until the night she thought he'd stepped across the line, she'd have *glowed* to hear him say those words. She'd have hung her whole day's happiness on them. And she wouldn't have let herself think about what that might be a sign of or what it could lead to.

The last time they had Rosie at one of these brave-talking crossroads, Rosie's eventual whispered response wasn't—if Molly was being honest—what had made the excursion worth the trouble. The reward had been in the way Rick beamed at her.

When had things started to change between them, and how had she not seen? Had the protective coating she'd built up around her pain made her so fireproof, she'd been impervious to the danger of what she'd been playing with? Her own false accusation seemed to have stripped off the protective gear and left her standing shockingly close to the flame.

Even on days when she'd feared Daniel might leave her, even on days when she'd wondered if he already had, and even on days when she worried she might actually want him to, Molly had never sympathized with *anyone's* temptation toward adultery. Not okay, no way, never her. Only now did she have the good sense to feel scalded by the self-deception that had carried her this far. She'd told herself she'd merely been distracting herself from her own problems, taking vicarious joy in the kind of progress that eluded her. She'd reminded herself the fear of getting caught for her other transgressions—the financial ones—was already more than she could handle.

"How did you know this would work?" He shook his head. "You seemed so sure, from the start."

His tone was intimate. Too intimate? *It's just a conversation,* she told herself. *No different from all the others you've had over the course of your friendship.*

Friendship. That's all.

"I don't know if Rosie experiences actual fear when it comes to talking, but I do. Not about talking, I mean, but about everything else. Fear the pain will get worse, fear I won't be able to stop it, fear that it's defining me in ways I don't want it to." *Fear I've committed to a race I can't run. Fear I've let things fall apart irreparably—with Liza, with*

Daniel. Fear I've stepped into something with you I never intended. Fear the intruder was not random. Fear my mistakes have caught up with us all. "Out here is the one place fear doesn't seem to follow me."

He paused, considering. "Explain."

She shrugged. "I can't. I never hiked alone much before I started working here, but now I'll spend my lunch breaks off in the woods, and it's occurred to me that maybe I *should* be afraid. Especially with my issues, there are plenty of ways I could hurt myself pretty easily. Loose boards on the footbridges, slippery rocks on the creek—even as crowded as this place gets, there are plenty of spots you could go down and not have anyone come along for an hour or two." She caught sight of a thin silver snake winding through the undergrowth to their left and gestured to it. "Also, much as I love nature, I don't love those."

"But you're not afraid out here."

"It's the least afraid I feel in a day. It's the most at peace."

He brushed her arm, so gently she might've missed it had it not sent a jolt directly to the longing center of her brain. "Well, that just makes me sad that you're afraid the rest of the time."

He was such an uncommonly good listener, was the thing.

Peals of delight came from up ahead—louder than Nori alone could muster—and Molly smiled at the thought of Rosie joining in when no one was watching. Rick caught her grin and returned it. "Why don't you and the kids come by for dinner? It must be unnerving having Daniel gone again so soon after . . ." He cleared his throat. "It's nice weather, and it seems like a waste to fire up the grill just for me and Rosie."

She wanted to say yes.

Which meant she had to say no.

If Nori hadn't thrown a tantrum the second Rick and Rosie pulled away—screaming "I want to go to Rosie's house!" and hurling a fistful of leftover pennies across the parking lot—Molly might have made it to her car.

As it was, she was crab walking across the spot Rick's SUV had vacated, picking up the copper coins while her daughter stomped and sobbed, when she heard her name.

"Molly Perkins?"

The man seemed to be trying too hard *not* to look out of place. He was wearing a stiff, clean Panama hat and a short-sleeved khaki button-down still creased from the package. With one hand he grasped a thick walking stick too large to be more help than hindrance, and with the other he caressed a pair of binoculars that hung from his neck. He was older than her by a couple of decades, and carried his short stature with a formality that might have been charming if something about him didn't instantly strike her as off.

The fact that he knew her name, for instance.

"Yes?"

"I think we might have met once. Through a mutual friend. At a TM intro session?"

TM. Shorthand for Transcendental Meditation. There was exactly one person Molly remembered from that session, and he was no friend of hers—or of anyone in her position. If only she hadn't discovered that too late.

"I'm sorry, I don't recall." Nori had stopped fussing—she'd push her limits with wild abandon when it was just the two of them but had an intrinsic wariness of witnesses to her antics—and was sniffing loudly, staring slack jawed at the man. Molly opened the car door to the backseat and gestured for her daughter to climb in. Mercifully, Nori obeyed.

"Fancy running into you," he said easily. "I thought I'd missed out when they said your shift had ended, but I can see why you'd stay late. It's a very therapeutic place, isn't it?"

She leaned down to strap Nori into her harness, blocking her from view as much as she could while absorbing the dread that hit her with his words. Of course they knew she worked here. She'd filled out her place of employment on one form after the next.

"Not a bad deal for the membership fee, either," he continued. "*If* you can spare it."

She pushed the remote start button on her keychain and checked that the air-conditioning was on before shutting the door, turning to face him. *Please. Let the car muffle this conversation enough that Nori can't make sense of it.*

"I'm afraid we're running late," she said as politely as she could. It *was* time to pick up Grant.

"Then I'll get to the point," he said. "Our mutual friend is well versed, as you know, in helping with challenges like yours. It's so sad when patients' families do not understand their need to seek treatment outside traditional channels, and he prides himself on being discreet. I think you'll agree he's held up that end of the bargain quite well."

She couldn't contest this, chilling though it was, and she found herself nodding.

"Always happy to meet a satisfied customer." A smile stretched across his mouth but did not reach his eyes. "At a certain point, however, you understand that discretion isn't free. And neither are loans. Payments *need* to be made."

If only Rick hadn't left.

"We tried to make this clear before—perhaps you didn't get the message?"

She drew a shaky breath, but the exhale wasn't enough to release her terror as his words sank in. Suddenly she very much wanted the masked intruder to have been Rick, at any cost to her marriage, their friendship, her reputation—at least with that, she knew what she was dealing with. But surely that wasn't what this man was referring to? They *had* left an awful lot of messages.

"I'm sure you won't need another of these reminder visits, yes?" He tipped his hat. "Wouldn't want to have to involve anyone you'd rather leave out of things. It's lucky when we happen to spot someone out and about, but we do make house calls, too." With that, he headed off toward the butterfly garden, the walking stick punching the gravel with every other step.

She scrambled into the driver's seat and backed out without bothering to watch him go, lest he decide to add to his parting words.

Less than an hour ago, she'd boasted that this was the one place she never felt afraid.

As usual, she'd jinxed everything.

16

LIZA HAD NEVER FELT SO OUT OF PLACE, OR SO GRATEFUL TO BE OUT OF place, as she did waiting for Steph in the waiting room of the hospital's Perinatal Center. While the brochure on the table said the unit handled "routine" care for "normal" pregnancies, everyone here seemed to be fighting some invisible foe on behalf of the life growing inside of them. You could tell from the set jaws and bitten lips, from the tearstained faces and determined stares, from the loved ones who'd come along—protective husbands and anxious grandparents-to-be—and the way they moved from the door to the check-in counter to their seats to the clipboard-bearing nurse clasping each other's hands, a white-knuckled tethering to the empty promise that *everything is going to be okay.* It was an assurance, if you thought about it, that no one had the power to make and yet everyone had the gall to. False comfort may have seemed kind to those offering it, but from where Liza was sitting, it seemed equally possible that it was cruel. Delaying the facing of facts.

She hadn't held Steph's hand. Steph's family was in New York, where she was from, and Luke had a meeting he couldn't get out of today, so—when her condition had not resolved on its own after a week of careful observation and diligent at-home positioning and her doctor had referred her here—Liza had offered to come along for support. Steph accepted at Luke's urging more than of her own accord, and Liza worried that her presence wasn't really welcome, was making things less comfortable instead of the other way around. They'd sat quietly until Steph's name was called. That was nearly an hour ago, and plenty of other patients had come and gone. Only one of them had left smiling.

Liza had brought along busywork, insurance claim forms and the new-hire paperwork she was to bring to her first day at Sky Galley tomorrow. She'd been hired with little fanfare on either side of the table, aside from a mutual eagerness for her to start as soon as possible, and it was nice to feel she'd accomplished *something* that counted as getting back on her feet. If pressed to admit it, she was also looking forward to the possibility of running into the red-haired pilot again. She kept catching herself thinking over his theory, preparing more counterarguments she had no way to give. The business of proving to herself that disaster was in fact random kept her oddly but mercifully focused on stating the case rather than imagining the implications.

The worst of her imagination was harder to ignore here, where fear was taking up its fair share of the waiting room. She wasn't making much progress on the forms, either. How could anyone concentrate in the midst of so much tension? She didn't like it here, breathing in the uncertainty, heartbreak, and loss hovering just a breath away. At least Steph wasn't supposed to be getting any *news* today, just more monitoring, with the expertise of someone who'd encountered this rare complication more often. But if that was really the case, then what was taking so long?

The door banged open and Steph appeared in the frame, looking no more happy than anyone else had, plus something else. Embarrassed? "Let's go," she mumbled, breezing past Liza and through the door to the corridor, and Liza rushed to gather her papers and chase after her, catching up only at the elevator. As they stepped inside, she realized Steph was crying.

"What's happened? Did they—"

"Not here!" Steph hissed, sniffing hard, though they were the only two in the space, which smelled of stale coffee and antiseptic. "In the car."

The walk through the vast lobby was excruciating. Slow.

"I'm sorry," Liza blurted out as the revolving door deposited them on the pavement. The car wasn't far, but she couldn't stand the silence anymore. "I feel bad you're stuck with me here. I know what it's like when the person you really want can't be along."

"Do you?" Steph snapped, then caught herself at the stricken look on Liza's face. "I'm sorry. That was wrong of me. I don't want Luke here anyway. Thank God he wasn't, actually." She shuddered, her tears still flowing, and Liza didn't risk another word until they were shut inside her little car—she'd driven, just in case of . . . something—with the engine running, the vents revving to clear the stuffy air.

"I thought I'd come to terms with setting aside my dignity for anything related to feminine care," Steph said, wiping at her eyes with a tissue, drawing a shaky breath. "But that? That was humiliating."

"What did they do?"

"They tried to move things in the right direction, literally. They reached up there . . . they had me on my hands and knees. . . ." She shook her head, and Liza tried to mask her horror, to maintain a *happens to the best of us* front. "Hurt like a *motherfucker*!" Steph yelled suddenly, pounding the dashboard, and started to cry again.

Liza placed a tentative hand on her shaking shoulder. "I'm so sorry. . . ."

"The worst part is that it didn't work." She looked miserably at Liza. "If I can't resolve this on my own in the next week, they want to *really* get in there and fix it. I'd have to get an epidural. And . . . there are risks. I could miscarry."

Liza recoiled, in spite of herself. "Wait. They want to do this so that you don't miscarry, but in the process, you could miscarry?"

Steph nodded, cupping a hand over her mouth to muffle another sob, and Liza leaned back into the headrest and stared straight out the windshield, as if that might afford her sister-in-law some privacy. But the next thing she knew, salty emotion was streaming down her own cheeks, unstoppable. How could Steph bear it, holding out while she and the baby were both at risk, not knowing whether it was even okay to be happy? How could Luke? How did anyone?

They passed a few minutes like that in what might have been solidarity, but when Liza finally swiped her cardigan sleeve across her cheeks and glanced over at her sister-in-law, Steph was taking her in with a mixture of concern and pity. Just as they were not close enough to hold hands in the waiting room, it was hardly proportionate for Liza to wail along with her afterward.

"Some comfort you are," Steph teased finally, awkwardly.

"I apologize. I don't know what's gotten into me." She thought of her brother, who would not be touched at this show of emotion. She was his stand-in, and if *he* were here instead, he certainly wouldn't be carrying on as if the outcome was too terrible to imagine.

"Just—tell me something good," Steph said. "Something to get my mind off all this."

Liza blinked at her, considering. When in doubt, might as well reach for the kind of retelling she was known for. Never mind that it was also what she'd been purposely avoiding for months. "Well. I think I flirted with a pilot at lunch the other day. . . ."

Steph took a deep, steadying breath and nodded. *That'll do.* "You think he was a pilot, or you think you were flirting?"

"He was in uniform, and he was at Sky Galley, so I'm positive about the pilot part. Also, he ate one of my French fries. Which seemed natural in context but, looking back . . . maybe flirty?"

"Too bad you're going to be a manager. I'm guessing they frown upon feeding customers off your own plate," Steph teased. She reached into her purse for a compact and flipped open the mirror. "Wait." She turned back to Liza, her mascara-smeared eyes wide. "Don't tell me that's why you applied! Is he *that* good-looking?"

"I applied because I'm guessing you guys don't want me living with you indefinitely," Liza said, shooting her a look. "But . . . he was interesting. I'm not sure I've ever had a conversation like the one we had." She shook her head. "Anyway. It doesn't matter, because I'm on hiatus from dating. And this hardly seems like a good time to go back into production."

"Why not? I mean, I understand why you wouldn't go looking, but if you happen to meet someone . . ."

The same had occurred to Liza, but she'd dismissed it as old habit. "I can't shake this new sense that life's too short," Liza said, and she could see from the look on Steph's face that it was the exact wrong thing to say. She scrambled forward. "I only mean—I don't want to waste time just . . . mucking around."

Steph got to work on her makeup as Liza put the car in reverse and eased out of the space. "Really great things begin by mucking around," she countered. "It's not like the second I met Luke I knew we were going to be serious. I mean, you've met Luke, right?"

Liza laughed. Somehow, right up until this crisis, she'd *still* hardly thought of Luke and Steph as serious. She'd seen it in her brother's eyes, though, how it would wreck him just as deeply as it would wreck his wife if anything happened to their baby.

"You're right that life is too short," Steph said, clearing her throat to still the quiver in her voice. "So why put limits on it? Take it from someone with an incarcerated organ: *You are free.* For now. You'll have plenty of other opportunities to be confined by rules."

That was true enough. So why didn't she *feel* free? Just as she was now cursing herself for not having better records of all the things she'd acquired before the fire—it seemed an impossible task to calculate the value of possessions *after* they'd been lost—maybe she should have paid more attention to the social and emotional load she'd accumulated along the way. Keeping a closer tally of the deposits and withdrawals might have made more sense than getting overwhelmed and closing the male relationship account entirely. She didn't know if it was the pilot himself or his oddball theory that was causing him to linger in her mind, but maybe it wouldn't be such a terrible transgression to let herself find out.

"I think I'm supposed to be giving you pep talks instead of the other way around," Liza said, easing into traffic. "But that wasn't a bad one, thanks."

"Do you think you'll run into him again? I mean, without going out of your way?"

"He seemed like a regular. I think it's a decent bet."

Steph smiled. "Luke is a regular everywhere he goes. I used to think it was boring, that he always went to the same places, but now I like it. When you go out with him it's like he's in his own version of *The Truman Show*—the idyllic part before it got creepy. He turns these regular little moments of ordering food or whatever into real connections."

Liza bit back a sarcastic comment about how he'd been striving to star in "The Luke Show" since he was born. The admiration in her sister-in-law's voice was clear.

"Well, this guy didn't exactly remind me of Luke," she said. "My brother is the master of small talk, without question. But this was kind of . . . the opposite of small talk." She took her eyes off the road long enough to see Steph's satisfied grin.

"He set you up for a recurring role!" she said. "Might as well stick around for the next scene."

—

Liza didn't realize how much she was missing Max until he flashed on her cell phone screen, the incoming call set to a snap of him decked out at a Cubs game, ball cap, foam finger, and all. Sitting next to him along the third-base line the night his turn at his corporate seats rolled around, she hadn't been able to decide if he looked like an embarrassingly unabashed tourist or an over-the-top local. But that was vintage Max. When he called, she was sprawled on the couch half-watching a reality show she couldn't believe was still on the air—Luke and Steph nowhere to be seen—and she carried the phone out to the front porch swing so she could sit with him somewhere more authentic. Somewhere good.

"Hey, Cincinnati." This was her new nickname, apparently. If he was trying to make her dislike the association, she had to admit it was working.

"Hey yourself, Cubs fan."

"If you're rubbing in the Reds' victory from last night, that's just mean."

Even when Liza was *at* a game, she had trouble paying attention to the score—a fact Max knew all too well. "Well, if I'd known about it, I'd have rubbed it in harder."

"You're kind of a disappointment to both franchises," he joked.

"Yeah, well, they can join the club."

She filled him in on Steph's awkward doctor's visit and the bang-up job she'd done of standing in for Luke, and he said the right things, how he was sure Steph appreciated that she was there at all—until Liza mentioned that once she started work, she might not be more available than Luke anyway.

"You got a job?" His disappointment was clear even as he politely asked for the details. She gave him the short version, weird as it sounded to describe the little old airport with the restaurant inside.

"It's kind of a cult classic," she told him. She knew of nothing like it in Chicago, or anywhere else she'd been. It was just—one of Cincinnati's cooler quirks.

"I guess this is real, then," he said finally, his tone more concessionary than sad, as if they'd reached the end of a running joke. "That you're not coming back."

"Guess so. For now, at least." She didn't know why she tacked on that last part. The job was just for now, but the move was not.

"Have you seen Molly yet?"

Liza allowed herself a breath to wish it weren't such a loaded question. That of course she'd seen her, and why wouldn't she? Even though, all things considered, she was hoping to avoid her at all costs. "As a matter of fact, I ran into her husband at my job interview."

"At the tiny airport? We *are* talking about a midsized city, right? Are you sure you haven't accidentally moved to some smaller town? Shmincinnati? Vincimmati?"

She laughed. "It wasn't the happiest coincidence. And get this: He invited me to dinner. To *thank me.* For being so *helpful* in notifying the authorities."

Max snorted. "Did he offer you gas money, too? Because they owe you some."

"I'm not sure he knows about her slamming the door in my face."

"But he was home—we saw his car. You heard him in the kitchen, talking to the kids."

"Yeah, well. Assuming he rushed back because of what happened—in spite of her acting so weird about it—he was probably pretty preoccupied at that point. And Molly has never hesitated to censor stories to paint herself in a better light." Liza had once admired Molly's affinity for selective omission. It came in handy when they were teenagers on the brink of getting caught doing something they weren't supposed to be. "Besides, Daniel and I get along pretty well. If he'd known I was there, he'd have come out to see me."

She didn't mention that he'd seemed a bit off at the airport—forcing the issue of the invitation even as she'd been trying to make a good first impression on the hiring manager. Then again, overcompensation had occasionally been Daniel's MO. Early in his relationship with Molly, he'd seemed almost *too* willing to include Liza, as if he was indebted to her for graciously lending out her friend for him to date. And when he and Molly did argue, he'd repent with what Molly referred to as a "grand gesture," some over-the-top romantic night out. Molly had gushed over those prearranged overtures, but Liza couldn't help suspecting they were shortcuts, faster and easier than doing the real work of making up.

Molly hadn't mentioned one in a long while, though. Then again, she hadn't mentioned any real disagreements, only vague discontent. It seemed as if the couple had grown to favor wearing things down over having them out. Not that Liza really knew.

"Well, you and Molly have always gotten along, too, but look what happened there."

"True."

"Sounds like great dinner table conversation to me!"

"Ha. Yeah, well, I'm not going. I figured I'd wait until it gets closer, and then make up some excuse."

He was quiet for a moment. "You know, I totally get why you wouldn't go. But—maybe you should? If you're really moving back, you can't avoid her forever, and she *is* your oldest friend. Maybe it's worth at least trying to clear the air. Maybe there's some whole thing you don't know about. Who knows?"

"There *better* be some whole thing I don't know about. Otherwise, she's completely lost her mind. But still, no thanks. I'm just—I don't think I'm up to that yet. If at all." People seemed to hold on to this notion that the oldest friends remained the best friends, but was it really true? She wasn't sure she wanted to reconnect with this version of Molly, who seemed to spend a lot of time feeling sorry for herself. "Just because I've known her since we were kids doesn't mean we have to stay friends. People change."

"When is this reunion supposed to take place?"

"Not this Saturday, but the next one."

"Well, I have that weekend open. What if I go with you? Then you won't be outnumbered."

Liza started to laugh, but the semi-offended silence on the other end of the line made it clear he wasn't kidding. "That's a sweet offer, but completely unnecessary. I can take care of myself."

"You have made that abundantly clear over the years. As if you know that it's one of your most lovable qualities. We get it, already."

"Har-har."

"All I'm saying is, that doesn't mean you can't let someone help you once in a while."

"I do! In fact, in this exact case, I already brought you into it, and look what happened."

"Exactly. I drove ten, twelve hours through the middle of the night for nothing, too! You're not the only one she owes an explanation. Plus, if you need backup, I have genuine selfish irritation to fuel my already unwavering support of you in any and all battles."

His support really was unwavering, and it pulled at her, made her wish she could wrap him in an impulsive hug. Further proof that *new* friends could be the best friends. "I really was just going to bail. . . ."

"But putting her on the spot would be more fun! Plus, you know . . ." His tone was softer now. "Best-case scenario, you get your friend back. And you get to see me. Win-win."

"I do catch myself wishing you were here," she said finally, her smile showing in her voice in spite of herself. It would have been so much easier to block out her bad memories of Chicago, to sweep away the charred remains of the mistakes she'd made there, to leave all of it behind, if Max hadn't been there when no one else was. But he had been. And she had to be grateful that at least *someone* didn't want to let her go so easily.

"I miss you, too, Liza. What's your brother's address?"

17

MOLLY WAS TWENTY MINUTES INTO THE CONTRACT CONSULTATION SHE'D booked, which meant she had only forty minutes left to get the answers she needed. She couldn't even afford the cost of this meeting, let alone another one. Yet so far, most of the questions had been directed at her.

"I'm guessing I can skip the part where I remind you it's best to consult an attorney *before* you sign a document?" The woman behind the mahogany desk exuded elegance, save for her mouth, which was wiped clear of lipstick and set in a grim line. The clock was running down on a half-eaten salad forgotten on the far side of her keyboard.

"Good guess," Molly said.

The attorney sat back in her chair, still holding the contract, turning a page forward, then back. "This one is . . . I'd need more than an hour to be thorough. But predatory lenders, a lot of them have a business model reliant upon trapping people in a debt cycle, where things multiply so rapidly you can never get on top of them. The sugar frosting is spread so thick on the contract language you can't taste what's underneath. That's by design. And that's what we have here."

Molly hadn't slept last night. Before he'd left, Daniel had installed simple motion detectors on the back-facing doors and windows, but after the visit from the man in the hat they'd done little to put her at ease. She told herself she wasn't *really* afraid of the lenders coming for her, didn't *really* wonder if maybe they already had. But the worry over the "reminder" that felt more like a warning had kept her up anyway.

"So I'm trapped?"

"Not necessarily, if they're not reputable. There are regulatory commissions that look into violations." She tapped the YWBF letterhead, and Molly had to admire her restraint at not pointing out what a shyster name Your Way Back Financial was. Not to mention its logo. The arrows should point *in*to the spiral: not a sun, but a drain. "I've never heard of this company. But if there's something here of interest, someone who specializes in this sort of thing might take you on pro bono. Or there could be class action potential."

"Are you—"

She held up a hand. "I'm taking the summer off with my kids. Lightening my caseload. That's why this hour was even open."

Molly nodded, trying to convey a mom-to-mom understanding that might soften this woman toward her. She was highly rated in client reviews on the local site where Molly had found her listing. YWBF, however, appeared almost nowhere beyond its own home page. In her initial fact-finding, she'd assumed that was because the company was relatively new. But now . . . "I was hoping you could at least tell me if they're legit. Before I bankrupt myself paying off scammers."

The attorney sighed. "Unfortunately, the answer to that question isn't as simple as reading a document. There are plenty of payday lenders in business who I don't think should be, but they *are* technically operating within the law. Others, especially online, are just biding time until someone goes through the hassle of holding them accountable."

She turned another page, skimmed some more. "You say they never mentioned collateral? That surprises me. As a general rule, legit lenders don't approve a loan they don't feel you can repay, unless it's smaller and shorter term than this. You see a lot of those in low-income neighborhoods."

Molly bit her lip. She felt like she should apologize for the fact that she should have known better. But she didn't owe this woman that apology. She owed it to herself.

"Is there any chance of a loophole I might use to get out of it? Not to shirk what I already owe, but to break that cycle you talked about?"

"There's always a chance of one. But judging from the length of this thing alone, I wouldn't hedge your bets on it. Whoever drew this up knew what they were doing." Molly had more questions, but she was struggling to form them into words. "What does your husband do?" the attorney asked.

Molly looked away. "He's a financial officer," she said softly. The attorney set the papers gently on the desk and turned her focus to Molly. Seeing her, for the first time. She didn't need to verify that Molly's definitely-knew-better husband was still in the dark. Or that the time to loop Daniel in without severe repercussions had arrived and gone.

The attorney opened a filing cabinet and rummaged through. "Let me give you some resources. . . ."

Molly shook her head. "Thanks, but I don't think I'm going to pursue it. This is—well. It's embarrassing. I'll figure something out."

She'd have to try harder to come up with the money. She could sell off some of her other bad investments, maybe—she must have a couple thousand dollars' worth of unused herbal supplements and even prescriptions. There wasn't much else of resale value she could unload without Daniel's notice, but maybe she could pick up extra work. The nature center ran private parties at Krippendorf Lodge—if she could score some shifts, she might bank tips. An hourly wage wouldn't come close to cutting it.

The woman slid a stack of brochures across the table, ignoring her decline. "Take them," she said. "You may change your mind. I hate to see anyone taken advantage of."

"Thank you for your time." Molly stood, politely gathering up the handouts and heading for the door. She'd toss them in the first trash can she saw. The last thing she needed was something else to hide from her husband.

"Mrs. Perkins?" Molly turned. "I know this is a hard situation, but—please be careful. These lenders may just be opportunists, but if they're truly unscrupulous, the stakes could be higher than you think. You don't want to mess with anything that could be dangerous. Consider the proper channels. At the very least, have a talk with your husband."

Molly thought again of the man in the hat. If his job had been to scare her, it had worked to a point, but aside from the unsettling fact of him tracking her down, he hadn't been *physically* threatening. A messenger, but nothing more.

Just because an unconventional lender had unconventional methods of checking in with their clients didn't necessarily mean they were dangerous. Did it?

She'd find a way to make a few decent payments and see if she could renegotiate the terms moving forward. She knew she'd been taken for a fool, but still, they'd seemed so earnest at the start. Maybe if she could get back in their good graces, explain how she'd come to ignore the earliest invoices until things had already escalated, everything would be okay.

"Thank you," Molly said again, and hurried away. She wasn't about to make yet another promise she already knew she was going to break.

Something must have happened in Chicago. Daniel came back . . . different. He'd been home only a few hours and—though he'd won her over by stopping outside of Lunken to bring them a mom-and-pop feast from the Hitching Post—by bedtime Molly was certain she wasn't imagining it. Somehow he seemed preoccupied and attentive at the same time. His eyes darted from the fried chicken to his phone to the door as if he was expecting an arrival or a call, and yet he behaved in a way that could only be described as *doting,* ignoring the kids' barrage of chitchat to talk to her across the table when usually she was the one who couldn't get a word in. He even—while taking the dish towel from her hands and telling her to sit, no less—used the word *mindful.* As in, "I want to be more mindful of how you are feeling from day to day." The Daniel who'd been occupying their marriage these past years was decidedly not mindful, nor would he think to utter those syllables in that order.

Also, in a *how long has it been?* twist, he'd come up to bed at the same time as her.

If she didn't know better, she'd suspect he was on to her, and messing with her head until she buckled and told him everything. But his smiles were genuine. This seemed to be more about him—and if he too was harboring some guilty conscience, she wasn't sure she wanted to know why.

No, she was sure: She did *not* want to know.

If it had to do with work—with the quandaries some of his more loathed colleagues sometimes put him in, expensing plane tickets for their wives or anything else not by the book—she'd nagged her last nag on that matter. If there was one thing she couldn't stand, it was a hypocrite, and suddenly, to her chagrin, she hardly had room to talk about keeping things on the up-and-up. Nor was she feeling charitable about him sticking out his neck and putting his own job on the line at this particular financially delicate moment.

And if things *hadn't* come to a head in Chicago that way? If this different Daniel was the result of some spousal indiscretion that was now weighing on him? If some other occupant of his hotel bed had sent him scurrying back to Molly's? She wouldn't be entirely surprised, she supposed. But she'd prefer the ignorance-is-bliss path there, too, given the strikingly similar questions it raised of high horses and poor timing.

He was behind the ajar master bathroom door now, brushing his teeth and unpacking his toiletry bag. She lay curled on the bed, clad in a soft sleeping tee and flannel pants, holding a book she wasn't really reading and thinking how cozy it could be to simply lie and listen to the sounds of a companion puttering about. Her last year of college she and Liza had shared a house crammed full of six girls, and when she'd tried to live alone after graduation the worst part was not the bigger rent checks or the sole responsibility, but that unfamiliar combination of quiet and stillness. She'd begged out of her lease so she could squeeze into Liza's "I guess I'm not using it . . ." loft, a space that didn't even have a door. A year later, she'd jumped straight to cohabitation with Daniel, and Liza, to her credit, had seemed neither perturbed nor relieved—perhaps in part because they all still lived on the same block. Liza and Daniel had been cut from the same happy-to-take-the-lead cloth, and Molly had found them both so comforting. But somewhere along the line she'd let the quiet and stillness close in again, even when her husband was right there, even when her best friend was just a phone call or an afternoon's drive away.

Unfathomable that now Molly was actually longing for *that* time: the miserably lonely time, right up until last week, when she'd have shut off the light and burrowed resentfully into her pillow before Daniel could join her. At least then she hadn't had this underlying mounting horror at all she'd put at risk.

Admitting to the way she'd allowed herself to *almost* feel about Rick, confronting the desperate choices that had bled her savings, regretting anew her quick dismissal of the police as the lawyer's warning echoed in her mind . . . It all weighed on her in a way that assured her she was not, as she'd feared, at rock bottom. There was still far to fall.

Daniel switched off the bathroom light and wheeled his carry-on into the bedroom. He was shirtless and barefoot, wearing only Superman-print pajama pants Grant had given him for Father's Day, and he swept the remaining contents of the bag into the hamper before tossing it into the closet.

"How was flying out of Lunken?" she asked. Better to keep the conversation away from her. And he'd told her precious little about the trip. She still didn't even understand what exactly he'd gone away to do.

"Well, I had to sit next to Mr. Human Resources. Other than that, it was pretty sweet. Like time travel—you land at the same time you took off." He brightened. "I can't believe I forgot to tell you. You'll never guess who I ran into."

She let the book fall closed. "Who?"

"Liza. She's moving back."

"Moving back?" Molly blinked at him, stunned. That the catastrophe of how she'd botched things with her oldest friend had been overshadowed by so many related catastrophes was telling. She'd been promising herself she'd reach out to Liza and make amends, just as soon as she'd dealt with the rest. Liza was the type who needed time to cool off anyway, and was far enough away that putting things on pause hardly felt out of the ordinary, even if the pausing itself had been rather . . . hostile.

"Don't take it personally that she hasn't called yet," he said, switching off the overhead light by the chain, leaving the ceiling fan whirring, and climbing in next to her. "I think she's still in shock. Her apartment burned down, and she lost everything."

"Oh my God." Molly clasped a hand over her mouth. "Was she at home? Is she okay?"

"I don't know details, but she's okay. She's staying with Luke and his wife—I can never remember her name." Daniel could never remember anyone's name. He was constantly asking Molly to remind him of exactly who the neighbors were, even that annoying Cathy woman who walked by multiple times a day with that formidable dog. Molly had grown to resent this as one more way she was supposed to be the keeper of important information—sign-up deadlines, school holidays, doctors' appointments. "She was at Lunken for a job interview."

Molly tried to make sense of it. "To manage the airport facility?" What an odd job for Liza. She'd been running glitzy hotel ballrooms like a professional homecoming queen for years.

"No, the Sky Galley."

That little restaurant? Oh, Liza. She must be scrambling. And living with Luke and Steph with a baby on the way couldn't be ideal. Guilty tears welled in Molly's eyes. She remembered the dawn of recognition on Daniel's face last week, when she'd *seen* him realize just how bad things had grown in their marriage, and she felt it toward Liza now. They'd once leaned on each other, first and fiercely, in times of crisis—yet here she was, learning her friend's life-altering moments secondhand. And it was her own fault.

"I invited her to dinner, next Saturday."

Just like that, the tears dried up.

"You *what*?" she cried, and he looked at her in surprise. *Easy,* came her mantra. There was no ostensible reason, in Daniel's eyes, why she would not want to have her best friend to dinner. If anything, waiting until next Saturday was ludicrous. In a world where Liza didn't have reason to hate her, Molly would be bounding out of bed this instant to call her and demand details.

Then again, in that world, she'd already know them.

"All I mean is," she said more calmly, "she hasn't even called me yet. She must be so overwhelmed. We'll set something up when she's had a little time to cope."

He looked at her strangely. "It seemed like the thing to do. And she was eager enough. To see the kids, especially." She bit her lip. Could that be true? Liza would have felt cornered, with no way to decline politely. Kind of like Molly felt now. "Look, if you don't want to cook, we'll get some nice takeout. I just figured it's been a while since we've hosted something grown-up. We used to throw pretty solid dinner parties, you know."

And Liza had been a fixture at all of them. Could this be a good thing, that Daniel had been the one to put her on the spot? If Liza was back for good, then letting her fade off was too awkward to contemplate. For one thing, it wouldn't go unnoticed by their families and mutual friends. Some reason would need to be given for a rift, and Liza wouldn't give a pretty one. There was also this: A part of Molly was *glad* Liza was returning. Her other friendships were flimsy things that bobbed untethered on the surface, with the lone exception of Rick—who'd reached, perhaps, *too* deep. What she and Liza had was, regardless of how things were between them now, anchored to the bottom. Or at least it was supposed to be.

"We did used to be pretty fun," she said, smiling weakly.

"It'll be nice to have her back, won't it? She made us funner, I think." Although he said *us* rather than *you,* Molly feared that was what he'd really meant, and an old irritation flickered. She ignored it, managing a smile.

"It never was the same here without her."

"I told her to bring whoever she wants. Maybe check in with her next week?"

Molly relented with a nod, and a beat of silence settled between them.

"I'm glad you're home," she blurted out, surprising herself. But what she was feeling *was* more than being loath to be alone. She suddenly had the nonsensical urge for her husband to swoop in and reclaim her: from Rick, from the lenders, from the pain itself—anything that dared stand in their way.

"Me too," he said, looking equally surprised—by his own reaction or by hers she couldn't say. He reached out a finger and ran it down the bare part of her arm, and there it was: that old feeling of security.

It had been a long time since she'd thought of Daniel this way—as someone capable of doing the saving. But that was how they'd met, in a scene out of a storybook—or an early-aughts film adaptation of one. She'd driven a little red hatchback in those days, a tin can of a car that burned oil so fast she had to add a quart every other time she filled the gas tank. She was amazed by the attention she could draw simply by being a woman confidently unscrewing and pouring things under the raised hood of her very own vehicle all by her sweet little self.

It wasn't always wanted attention, though. Least of all on the night she failed to latch the hood and subsequently locked her keys in her running car when she got out to secure it. She had to stay with the vehicle while waiting for roadside assistance, lest anyone smash a window and drive off with the thing, and was wishing she'd parked in a more visible area when the trouble started.

Replaying that moment was a funny thing. Both the casting and the cinematography varied based on her shifting view of the present-day version of her husband. Sometimes she pictured Daniel swooping in like George McFly in *Back to the Future,* awkward but determined: *Hey, you. Get your damn hands off her!* When things were especially good between them, or when she was missing the days when they had been, it was more of a sexy, emotionally charged step outside his comfort zone, à la Bradley Cooper in *Silver Linings Playbook.*

She couldn't recall if she'd ever thought of him as more of a Clark Kent type, back in the early days when even his missteps seemed adorable, well intended. She thought not. Equating your husband to a caped superhero seemed like something not easily forgotten.

"Can we talk more about that '*we used to be fun*' thing?" he asked gently. His eyes were searching hers, but for once, the judgment was gone.

Or maybe she'd been imagining it all along. Projecting what she feared he thought of her or—she hated to think of it—what perhaps he should.

"Okay." She looked down at the rumpled sheets, suddenly shy.

"We've both been so focused on the kids, we've neglected things. *I've* neglected things. I think most couples go through this phase, but on top of the usual stuff, you've been dealing with a lot, and . . . I flubbed it. I haven't been there for you the way I should have been."

It was like someone had given him notes on what to say. Liza, at Lunken? Would she have somehow rebounded from Molly's inexcusable cold-shouldering with an admonishment on her behalf? Unlikely. But so, too, was the idea of him coming to this on his own, out of nowhere.

"I can't go back and change it. But I want you to know I'm sorry. And I'm hoping maybe we can—turn a page?"

She met his eyes. She should say yes, but . . . She should also tell him, all of it. Now. Maybe not the Rick part, but the money part. The lost savings, the bad decisions, the messenger's appearance, the lawyer's advice—this was her chance to lay it out. He was accepting some responsibility for where they'd landed, so maybe, crazy as it seemed, he wouldn't lay the blame for the bigger mess she'd made *entirely* on her.

Then again, she deserved this apology. She'd *earned* it. In fact, an apology might not cut it. Daniel was the one, at the risk of sounding childish, who started it. He'd made her feel as if she couldn't turn to him. As if she were exaggerating her pain, failing them all by not doing a better job of sucking things up on her own. He might not have put her through hell, exactly, but she'd been in it, and he had *not* walked through with her. No. He'd gawked at her like a displeased spectator, waiting for her to pull her act together for the win. For *years.* And now that he was finally owning up to the damage he'd done, she was going to deflect all the hurt and blame right back on herself at the risk of resuming that scorching walk on her own?

"I want to suggest some things," he continued. "But I'm not sure how to do it without sounding cliché. Like, what if we go away, just the two of us? Someplace with a great view and room service. Someplace we can stay in bed all day if we want to." She raised an eyebrow, and he offered a sheepish laugh. "See? It sounds like a page from the midlife crisis playbook. But maybe there's a reason it's in there."

She missed their sex life, too. She'd never been one to beg off with a yawn until her rotating wheel of discomfort had ruined her enjoyment of just about everything. Nothing on her knees, which had become too volatile. Nothing that put pressure on her slipped disk, either. And then, there was the popping in her jaw, of which they dared not speak. . . . Maybe the bad wouldn't have so easily canceled out the good if either of them had been kinder, about any of it.

And now? They couldn't afford a trip like he was proposing, even if she wanted to.

"We don't need to make a big thing of it," she said. "We can just, you know, get a babysitter, plan a date night. Be intimate more." It sounded laughably simple, yet these were things they didn't do.

She didn't know, though, if halfway wanting to was enough. Somewhere along the line, she'd lost hold of the connecting thread that allowed her to lay herself bare for him. She hadn't found a way to maintain the physical weave of their relationship when the emotional one was so frayed, nor could she make out how to pick the thread back up, though she missed the feel of it in her hand, the sensation of giving it a tug and knowing she'd feel the reciprocal pull on the other end.

Daniel rarely initiated anything anymore, which had occasionally made her wonder, with more sadness than hurt, if he was getting those needs met elsewhere. Not that her conscience was entirely clear. She couldn't claim, for instance, that she hadn't wondered what Rick would be like in bed. Not in a serious way, though, as one might shop for a new laptop or a smartphone. It was more like gazing through the display case at Tiffany's, knowing everything was out of her price range but drawn by the idea that for someone else it could be real.

"When did we get so damn middle-aged?" he said, trying to laugh. She resisted, though. She would not relegate their marriage to the *ordinary rut* column when plenty of out-of-the-ordinary things had brought them to this point.

Still. She had no desire to be the sort of woman who caught herself thinking things like *there's more to life than being fun,* defending changes she wished she'd never undergone.

"Try me," she said, aiming to sound more mischievous than annoyed. "For instance, do you know where we can get weed?" When they'd started dating, they'd spend an occasional lazy Sunday getting high and taking their time in bed, their sensations heightened. They hadn't even spoken of it since becoming parents, but if he wanted to spruce things up, that was the kind of tension release that appealed. Less pressure than a negligee or some sticky new cream. Just—something to take the edge off.

He laughed, more genuinely. "I do wish they'd get around to legalizing it. Short of that, I wouldn't know where to begin."

"You could start with me," she said. Might as well see how he'd react to certain boundaries being pushed. Boundaries she'd already broken.

He looked amused. "*You* have a hookup?"

"I have the goods." He gaped at her, and she heaved her upward-facing shoulder in a guilty half shrug. "Don't look at me like that. I've tried *everything* to combat the pain. But it turned out I didn't like doing it alone. It's different when it's not social. Made me nervous."

"Wow." He fell silent for a minute, and she figured he was thinking, as she was, of all the other prescriptions she'd filled and abandoned—the lawful ones. Her body tended to be so sensitive to medications that she usually didn't like them, though she went on wishing for a magic pill. She supposed she should be grateful she hadn't found one; otherwise she could have ended up on a slippery slope to dependence. "I'm sorry it came to that, Mol. I'm sorry I didn't realize."

If she responded sincerely, she'd cry. She offered another shrug. Better if he looked back on her indiscretions, if everything came out in the open, and thought they hadn't been *all* bad. "Maybe fun would be a better cure," she said.

He grinned. "You're on, Mrs. Perkins. This weekend, after the kids are down. You bring the contraband; I'll bring every munchie you could dream of. Snickers. Doritos."

Would he still be so eager to rekindle their spark, even fleetingly, if he knew all the ways she'd betrayed his trust, all the things she'd done? If it turned out Daniel would be willing to save her again, would she still want him to?

She supposed she'd better figure it out.

18

LIZA WAS GOING ON A HIATUS FROM HER HIATUS.

In other words, a date.

Her problem with men had never been getting them to ask her out. It took exactly one day on the job to run into Henry, to whom she delivered a courtesy side of French fries just on the right side of crisp, and exactly one minute after that for him to invite her to dinner someplace "even fancier." She'd been waiting for it, even fishing for it, but still she hesitated as if teetering on some point of no return. The airport was small enough that this could be akin to dating a coworker. Although the risk, she supposed, was his; should things go south, he'd just have to find someplace less convenient to eat.

"Do seven things have to go wrong for you to have a disastrous date?" she'd teased. "I'm a little rusty, so if the bar is much lower, I'm not sure I'm up to the challenge."

He'd answered with a look of exaggerated nervousness that made her laugh.

More often, her dates were near-certain one-offs, easy come and easy go and might as well have fun along the way. She'd thought of it as a good thing when her attitude toward them changed some months ago, when she'd stopped so readily settling for so little—only now she'd swung too far the other way, to a place where every decision seemed *too* big. Earlier today, she'd been tripped up at the grocery store when Steph asked her to run in for a premade salad on her way home. There were, Liza counted, forty-two different kinds of prewashed, bagged salad. Forty-two! And that was not counting a middle row where the inventory had been replaced by recall notices warning of a listeria outbreak. Had all the rest of these brands really avoided the same crop of romaine, or radish, or whatever the culprit? What if contamination in the others just hadn't been discovered yet? What if she picked the wrong one and Steph—being pregnant and susceptible—was affected worst of all? She'd stood frozen, while other shoppers reached around her and mumbled their *excuse mes* without a second thought beyond the sale price. Ultimately she went home empty-handed, pretending to have forgotten to stop. Let Luke choose on his way home instead. His odds would be the same, but at least she wouldn't be the one responsible if not in their favor.

Thus, on the specifics of the date, she voiced no opinion. Let Henry pick; it would tell her something anyway about who he was and, perhaps, what his expectations were. She was so eager, in fact, to defer that she thought fleetingly of how nice it would be for this relationship to take hold just now, and of how disastrous, for the flip sides of all the same reasons.

Liza had restocked only on lounge clothes and androgynous restaurant manager wear, so Steph let her raid her closet for the occasion.

"It's the least I can do!" her sister-in-law gushed, breezing through the guest room door with a selection of hangered dresses over her arm. "I mean, you took my advice! Luke *never* listens to me."

"Oh, please," his voice shot back across the hall. "She can see I obey you like a Labrador." The two of them seemed to be trying too hard since Steph's appointment to keep things light between them—between all three of them, really. Luke didn't even gripe at having to stop for the salad Liza had "forgotten," but somehow even his grace was another reminder of the tiny life at stake inside Steph. Liza was glad of the excuse to get out, even if she was a bit nervous for what Henry had in store. Her first dates in Chicago often meant brief wine bar meet-ups that might or might not continue past a single glass, or at their most committal perhaps a *be forewarned that this takes a while to bake* deep-dish pizza and a draft beer. But Henry had made reservations for a seasonal wine tasting followed by a three-course food pairing at a winery in Kenwood, so she'd be locked in for a few hours at least.

"This guy is full of good signs," Steph assured her. "First, he's a reliable regular. Second, he's clearly not afraid it's not going to go well. Can't wait to find out what's third!" How quickly her married friends forgot the potential negatives of spending an evening with a stranger. In spite of their long-standing agreement never to discuss their mutual ex-boyfriend, she resisted the urge to bring him up to Steph now, to remind her of how storybook those dates *weren't.* The "let's just catch the first half" stops at sports bars that turned into hours-long marathons of watered-down pitchers and drunken darts, for instance. Then again, maybe his dates with Liza had reflected his attitude toward her. Maybe Steph had been treated to trendy cafés and riverboat cruises. Better not to know.

Liza had unintentionally lost a few pounds these past couple of on-edge weeks, and a satisfied smile spread across her face at the way Steph's silky black A-line draped over her frame. If only she'd thought to get some heels. Steph wasn't her shoe size, so the plain-Jane flats Liza had bought for her interview would have to do.

"They look fine," Steph assured her. "Besides, he knows about the fire, right?"

Liza pursed her lips conspicuously.

"Well, I guess you don't have to worry that you won't have anything to talk about. You'll be his most interesting date ever. A survivor."

The word jarred Liza. She kept forgetting that was how she was supposed to see herself.

The tasting room was crowded, a yuppyish clientele who made Liza think wistfully of the more diverse mix at any given place in the Loop—but then again, in that whole vast city she'd never met anyone like Henry. They stood next to their wine flights at a small high-top that no fewer than two other couples were sharing, but his energy drew a circle around them, in spite of the fact that it was too loud to carry on much of a conversation. She leaned in to catch the words he shouted over the din, asking how her first week at work had been (fine, if not terribly interesting) and telling her about his (drunken passengers and all).

She'd never enjoyed how even the most engaging first encounters had to be followed by a requisite debriefing that put the initial spark in a holding chamber, where it would either bloom or be extinguished. But so far, chatting with Henry felt more like catching up with someone she already knew on some level. Someone she was very glad to see again.

"Should we get the awkward stats out of the way before they call our table?" he called, his grin mischievous. A woman in a fuchsia shirt that bared her shoulders plunged into him from behind, but he seemed impervious, intent on Liza even as the wine in his hand sloshed dangerously close to the rim.

"Such as?" Liza pulled him forward by the arm, and their circle tightened. He was taller than she'd realized—until now, she'd only seen him seated at Sky Galley—and she smiled up at him. His hair seemed redder in this lighting, not the carrot of many so-called redheads but a more striking cousin to brunette.

He grinned back. "Exes. Timetables. Regrets."

She nodded, game, and ticked off her fingers, touching on the basic points—the move to Chicago, the lack of anyone serious in her time there, the decision to come back. She left off the reason—even if they were getting things out of the way, this didn't seem the time.

"Regrets?"

She shrugged. "I disbelieve people who say they don't have any."

"Smart." He took his turn. His last serious relationship was long distance, which almost worked because she was on his route but petered out six months ago. He'd begun his career flying regional jets into Canada, but his French—not required but strongly preferred—was so terrible he bowed out before they could come up with some other excuse to fire him. He liked flying the shuttles out of Lunken, wanted nothing to do with the big airlines.

"Regrets?"

"Since I can't claim none . . ." He smiled. "That I chose a career where it's impractical to have a dog. I'd love something big and goofy, a retriever or a husky."

He seemed the perfect human counterpart to just such a dog, relaxed and happy. So this was what it felt like, to be out with a man again. Not one who'd been chosen through an app but by way of that old-fashioned sequence of chance meeting, chemistry, and the testing of waters. The wine was mellow, easy drinking, better than she would have chosen for herself, and she felt warmed by the buzz that was traveling straight through her empty stomach to her brain.

When they were finally seated in a sleek booth at the window, the dining room's ambience was a grateful sigh. It was so much nicer here, in a quiet, dim corner away from the hyped chatter of the barflies. She and Henry exchanged a look that was both expectant and a little shy—now the real date could begin.

"So," he said, once fresh flights were arranged in front of them and they'd ordered a flatbread to share. "Have they followed you here?"

"Who?"

"Your spies." He leaned over the table conspiratorially. "Don't fire them, but I'm afraid they weren't terribly subtle about watching out the window when I picked you up."

She was glad of the dim lighting; maybe he wouldn't make out the color flooding her cheeks. "Oh, *them*. They have a lot of nerve, don't they? Monitoring comings and goings from their house as if it's any of their business."

"So it wasn't your house, then." He looked relieved, and she frowned. Had he thought her too independent?

"I'm staying with my brother and his wife. Temporarily."

"Excellent."

She raised an eyebrow. "It is?"

"Well, I'm as progressive as the next guy, but I was sort of hoping all those maternity circulars on the porch didn't belong to you."

She burst out laughing. "Yes, soon they'll want their guest room back. But I haven't been there long. The day I met you was actually my first full day back in town."

"Lucky me." He smiled. "Of all the crazy airfields in this mixed-up world, you decided to lunch at mine."

She laughed. "Okay, let's hear it. Tell me your craziest airfield story."

"Take your pick. We've had streakers jump the fence and head down the runway—you have the best view of that from the cockpit, by the way." His eyes crinkled with mischief. But it was occurring to her that not everything encompassed by *crazy* was quite so frivolous, and her smile faltered.

"Nothing bad, though?"

"I wouldn't call that guy's form *good*. . . ."

She rolled her eyes, trying to stay with him on the lighter side of the moment, and he grinned. "You know what I mean." She persisted. "All those small planes and helicopters taking off and landing . . . Anyone ever miss the runway? Clip the building?" She supposed she should be glad the possibility hadn't occurred to her before. She might not have pursued the job if it had. Might not have seen Henry again. Still . . .

"I've heard of close calls in bad weather, but the guys in the tower are pretty ace. The worst emergency I ever saw was a runner who had a heart attack on the trail. Never did hear how that turned out."

Liza grimaced, knowing its far points were over a mile from the access roads.

His face turned thoughtful. "There *were* a couple of bad accidents with cars leaving the parking lot in front of the terminal—people drive way too fast on Wilmer. But they finally added the traffic light to avoid that." She liked the way he answered the question so thoroughly, in spite of the fact that he probably thought the question itself was overblown. He flashed her a smile. "That's statistically accurate, by the way."

"I know, air travel is safer than car travel. I tell myself that every time I'm in the air."

He leaned closer. "If you're asking because you're worried about me, I'll take that as a sign that you like me." She laughed, and he drew back with suspicion. "Wait. You're worried about yourself, aren't you? You think something's going to fall out of the sky and land on you during your shift."

She splayed a hand across her heart. "Who, me?"

"You were probably in more danger in Chicago. Of that, or something else wild. Terrorist attacks, mass shootings . . ."

She must have cringed, because he stopped short. "Sorry. Didn't mean to make light of it."

"It's okay," she said. "You're right . . . I *was* in more danger in Chicago." She took a swig of her wine—an uncomfortably large swig—and began to cough.

He was looking at her with concern. She should have known better than to let the conversation go here, yet she could hardly blame him that it had. She'd started it, after all.

"What was it," he asked carefully, "that made you come back?"

She'd found a place to go, whenever she had to discuss the fire with her claims rep or during her mother's check-in calls—to a perch in the corner of her mind where she could watch the conversation as if she weren't the one participating in it. She went there now.

"There was a fire," she began. "It gutted my building, everything in it. Every*one* in it, above a certain floor." Her voice sounded flat, not especially lucky. Even though it was.

By the time she'd finished telling him the rest, he seemed to be taking stock of her anew, though not unkindly. "That's why you're so fixated. On the odds of things going wrong."

"I wouldn't say I'm *fixated,*" she said, trying not to sound defensive. Never mind that hours ago she'd found it prohibitively risky to decide on something as mundane as a bag of lettuce. At least he seemed content to skip to the now of things rather than harping on details. Like where she'd been that night, if not at home.

"Well, it's understandable you'd be freaked out," he said.

"Temporarily," she said, for the second time. "At least, I hope so."

"Cut yourself a break. You've made pretty impressive headway in a short time. Not only did you get the first job you applied for, but you met *me.*"

His eyes held hers until she couldn't help but smile—even as a part of her held back. *Was* it impressive headway to be jumping on the first things she came across? She liked Henry, more by the minute. And the job was a practical fit for now, more so than one that would overwhelm her while she was still regaining her land legs. But was anyone really so fortunate to come across actual good options without even trying? "Two birds with one stone," she said drolly.

Their server brought the flatbread and a pair of small plates and was gone again.

"Did you know Tom Petty's house burned down?" Henry asked. "Arson. He was inside, his family, too. He wrote 'I Won't Back Down' after that."

"Seriously?" She loved that song—had even considered it something of an anthem at one point, though at the time she'd had little more than typical teenage squabbles to back down *from.* That was during the phase when Molly had gone around spouting lines from that Eleanor Roosevelt book. Liza had admired that spirit, but for her real empowerment came with the windows down and the radio up. *Well, I know what's right / I got just one life. . . .*

Somewhere along the line, she'd lost sight of what had felt right. She wouldn't again.

"I can't imagine what that would feel like," he said, more serious now. "To lose everything you own. I'm really sorry."

She drained the dregs of her Cabernet and moved on to the Shiraz. Should she tell him? How ashamed she felt that she was still struggling with it at all? How she still had awful visions of her neighbors who hadn't made it? The emotion crept up her throat, reminding her why she'd swallowed it in the first place. So she latched on to his words instead and sang them back at him. "*You don't know how it feels. . . .*"

He laughed. "See? There's a Tom Petty song for everything."

Their eyes locked again, and though his were smiling, they also seemed to be waiting. For her to go on and tell him. She cleared her throat.

"It feels . . . *I* feel grateful, of course. But a little precarious, too." She steeled herself with another sip while she contemplated the highest degree of honesty that wouldn't scare him off. "I've always felt in charge of my life, even when it wasn't going well. Now, though, I can't shake this sense that none of us are really in control of anything, or ever have been." She smiled at him. "I realize that you and your 'seven things' theory disagree."

"I might not have gone on about that the way I did had I known why you were asking."

She shrugged. "I'm glad you did. It's—a different way of looking at things. Even if I'm not sure I buy into it."

"I take it you're not big on fate. Or God having a plan," he said. He wasn't laughing at her. Nor was he brushing this off as some kind of fleeting survivor's guilt or overreaction, the way she knew always-positive Luke would. He was considering it.

"I don't know. Which I guess means I'm not."

She'd talked openly enough with Max and with her family . . . but somehow it was Henry who made her feel less alone. Maybe it was because he wasn't trying to put Liza back in some safer box. He'd never had her in one in the first place.

"Well, I think it's natural to be spooked. But that doesn't mean you have to give in to the idea of having no control." He slid a piece of the flatbread onto his plate. The drizzled pesto gleamed. "This might sound nuts, but there's this thing we did, in pilot's training. The military does it, too. It's called pre-mortem thinking."

"As in the opposite of post-mortem thinking?"

"Yep. So, instead of waiting for something to go wrong and then assessing the cause so that it doesn't happen again, you prepare yourself for various not-good scenarios. You have a plan, train your brain, because in a panicked situation you might not be thinking clearly. When you've thought ahead, though, when you've practiced, instinct takes over."

"You know, this is going to sound more nuts, but I *have* found myself sort of collecting disaster scenarios. I see these bizarre news stories, and I . . ." She had to stop. She really was going to sound crazy. She'd been amassing a sort of list, of all the ways something can take a horrible turn. She'd linger over the articles, and sometimes she found herself imagining the *real* stories behind them, just as her own had been so far outside of anything that was printed about the fire. She'd even rewritten a few based on nothing beyond her own concocted backstories.

Like the one about the man whose car had gone into the river and who'd led such a lonely life it took days for him to be reported missing.

An incident occurred on the Brent Spence Bridge when Jim Duff was essentially doing the same thing he did every evening, which amounted to trying not to question his life choices. . . .

Or about the fatal incident involving a customer who'd taken her new designer puppy shopping for pet supplies from a high-end discount warehouse.

With the culpable forklift obscured by the ceiling-high shelving, the puppy's instincts were superior to his owner's. Thus, he lived to be adopted by an elderly couple who had no concept of his breed, or how much she'd paid for him, and who did not obsess over what kind of food might keep his coat shiny. . . .

It was her way of trying to give the victims some life beyond cold black and white type. She wasn't sure it qualified as healing, the way every imagined story chipped away a bit at her own. But it was something. A heightened vigilance, an empathy. Something that perhaps she'd been lacking before. Why else would she feel compelled to do it?

She straightened, tried to smile. "So I should practice—what? How I'd dodge falling pianos?"

"Not exactly." To her relief, he looked more interested than alarmed. "But it might make you feel better about things if you think through some scenarios. For instance, your bedroom at your brother's house. Is it on the second floor?" She nodded. "Okay, so give some thought to, if there was a fire, how would you get out?"

Liza bit the inside of her cheek. "I've thought about it plenty. Usually when I should be sleeping."

"So what's the plan? If you don't mind my asking."

"If I can make it one door down to the bathroom, that window opens onto the roof of the porch. I can climb out there, then hang and drop down."

He took a bite of the flatbread, nodding slowly, and she slid a piece onto her own plate. "Or," he said, "you could buy some of those fire safety ladders. The little kits that attach to windowsills? Then you don't even have to worry about making it one door down." He shrugged. "You might rest easier, is all. *Pre-mortem thinking.*"

"How does this play into your seven things theory?"

"It helps eliminate human error." She thought immediately of Steph, twisted into her upside-down poses. Hope yoga, they'd started calling it. Liza hoped that whoever would be doing Steph's procedure next week—if it came to that—had been doing a lot of pre-mortem. It was only fair for the person on the other end to shoulder as much of the worry.

"Has it ever happened for you?" she asked. "Instinct taking over?"

"All the time. Usually I don't realize it until later, though. When your thinking is cloudy, sometimes you don't realize it because, well, your thinking is cloudy."

Liza laughed. "Why was your thinking cloudy?"

"Stress and lack of sleep," he said without hesitation. "Biggest enemies of pilots and drivers of all kinds. Of anyone trying to concentrate, really."

It was a level of analysis she'd been lacking. She'd been doing pre-mortem thinking, all right, but the wrong kind—focused more on problems than solutions. As a result, she had stress and lack of sleep in droves.

"But you can't prep for everything," she challenged. "It wasn't preparation that got me out of the fire—it was dumb luck. And a little rope ladder wouldn't have helped me on the fourth floor."

"Not everything," he agreed. "But some things. It might help you get some of that sense of control back, that's all."

This was not a thing she was supposed to like—this masculine urge to fix things. *Don't bother to complain to them about your day if you don't want them to try to fix it,* her mother always said. That boys-will-be-boys attitude infuriated Liza, who thought it perfectly reasonable to expect a boyfriend to *listen* and *sympathize* if she wanted to commiserate about her day.

But letting Henry be Henry didn't seem so bad. Max would roll his eyes at this analogy, cracking puns about preparing for takeoff or reaching their cruising altitude. But Liza was tired of making jokes out of everything. And there was something about this man, some undercurrent that drew her to him.

"It would be easier for me to stick with my approach if you'd make less sense," she said.

"And it would be easier for me to stick with mine if I wasn't distracted by thinking a little too much about Sky Galley," he said, grinning. "If you're coming around to my way of thinking, I should fess up that I might be coming around to yours. I actually got nervous in turbulence the other day."

She raised an eyebrow. "That doesn't seem like a positive effect for me to be having."

"It's been a while since I had anyone in particular I cared about getting home to see," he said. "And I'd call that positive. So maybe we should meet in the middle, theory-wise."

Liza relaxed into the booth, a slow smile spreading at last across her face as she took a bite of the flatbread. The crust was flakey, the pesto salty, the cheese creamy. "Did you prepare for *this*? For what you'd say tonight?" she teased.

He watched her for a moment before he answered. "I'm fairly certain I was wholly unprepared for you," he said, catching her off guard. "Yet somehow, I'm okay with that. Even if it is contradictory to my training."

She took another bite, as if this moment were on par with all her dinner conversations and not potentially marking the start of something, a silent agreement to forge ahead, together. "Is that a good thing?"

He smiled. "I look forward to finding out."

19

DANIEL KNEW THE SUPERSTITION, THAT BAD THINGS ARRIVE IN THREES. HE could remember his mother waiting for weeks, after attending two funerals inside a month, certain that a third person would pass. But Daniel's run of bad luck required no patience to count it up neatly.

As if he'd needed an additional sign that things were beyond bad.

It started Sunday—on the letdown end of a weekend that had held so much promise. He and Molly had finally lightened up a little the night before, after the kids were in bed—smoked some of that weed he could scarcely believe she had, put a dent in a good bottle of vodka, made love like teenagers while a rented movie watched itself on the big-screen. On paper, it was the most fun they'd had together in years, though the reality of it was something else. They were both so hyperaware of how long it had been, of how this was no longer second nature. Of how so-called fun had come to require effort, intent. It felt like—like being watched by a skeptical third party in a private moment.

And indeed, come morning, little seemed to have changed. In fact, the dutiful woman serving French toast to his children seemed so incongruous with the unfastened one of the night before that he worried she'd simply been going through the motions for his sake.

He didn't want that. He wanted nothing from Molly that wasn't genuine. Couldn't she see that?

Small steps, the book had said. *Mindful* ones. He could accept responsibility for his part in all this. But it still stung to see her thought process scrawled across her face: *Gosh, he's being sweet. . . . But he was such a hopeless asshole before.*

Like he didn't know.

He was out back later on, taking out his frustrations on the grimy grate of the grill that had lain dormant all winter, when Molly came out the back door, a curious look on her face.

"You mentioned Mr. Human Resources the other day," she said. "Does he live around here?"

Daniel kept his eyes on the metal brush in his hand, working it with renewed gusto. "Why do you ask?"

"I think I saw him out front, when I was opening the blinds in Grant's room. It definitely looked like *someone* from your work functions—I'm pretty sure I have the right guy. . . . Walking by real slow. Kind of gawking at the house."

*God*damn *it.* He never should have made Toby memorable for Molly, going on about the golf trips and the *Hamilton* tickets. But what the hell was Toby *doing*? They had a deal.

He glanced up and saw her looking at him expectantly. "He doesn't, but he did mention his sister lives in the neighborhood. With the dog that looks like it wants to chew my face off?"

"Cathy is his sister?" Molly laughed. "I should have known. A family of irritants."

As soon as Molly was back inside, Daniel ran around to the front and stood, chest heaving, at the mailbox, looking in all directions. But there was no sign of Toby.

Ever since Daniel had been sober and back on the ground, he'd been rethinking the reluctant promise he'd made two Bloody Marys in on that should-have-known-better flight. So he'd faked a few business trips over the years. It wasn't really about finding some new slice.

It was more about getting a break from the one he had—and though he wasn't proud of it, he knew Molly had been just as grateful for the reprieves. What if he just walked away from the company—let Toby and himself *both* off the hook? Sure, the man would be pissed that he'd soon have a new Daniel to navigate, but pissed enough to follow through with his threats? More likely he'd just slink back to his lair and bide his time. Daniel didn't need this job in a daily bread, paycheck-to-paycheck way. He had enough saved up to skate by for a few months, and maybe Molly could take on some extra hours until he found something new.

He wouldn't feel good about leaving his coworkers at Toby's mercy, but that, too, he could rationalize. Toby wasn't *that* smart. He'd get caught eventually, and the employees would get their funds back. Just because Daniel wouldn't be the one to do the right thing didn't mean the right thing wouldn't eventually be done.

But if Daniel was already rethinking their agreement terms, it stood to reason that Toby could be, too. What was he *doing* here?

Daniel wanted to believe he was only visiting his sister. It was Sunday, after all. A day for family.

Indeed, this was what Toby would claim when Daniel stormed red faced into HR Monday morning—but he wouldn't bother to hide his amusement at seeing Daniel squirm.

And so it was Toby's smug face that floated through Daniel's mind when the police arrived on his doorstop that evening.

The second shot of the bad-luck hat trick.

They came in a pair: the one who'd spoken to Daniel from his parked cruiser and someone more seasoned-looking and perhaps more important. But even as Daniel's panic rose, they made it clear they were here for Molly, and his worries pivoted. What if she'd gotten Saturday's party supplies from an *actual* dealer and not, as he'd assumed, some hippy-dippy yoga instructor?

Daniel stood tall, arm around Molly's shoulder, while the police explained that they were "just checking in," "just once more," while she assured them there was nothing she hadn't already relayed and nothing new to tell. She hesitated, though, looked sidelong at Daniel as if she wished he weren't there, and his blood ran cold.

When the officers turned to him, it really did seem an afterthought in due diligence. "We realize you were away that night, Mr. Perkins, but anything else out of the ordinary?" And he couldn't help thinking back to that first morning home and wondering anew how the hell Molly ever contemplated not telling him about this, even for a second, as if it would never come up again. He shook his head, all innocent and mystified, and finally they left.

But he didn't feel better. Because Molly left then, too. Apparently they had an urgent bread shortage that must be addressed immediately. One that caused trembling hands and an unnaturally high, tight voice.

He supposed it was natural to be nervous talking to law enforcement. But he couldn't help wondering whether she was running after them to ask something out of his earshot. Or hiding, perhaps, in case they returned. Or maybe, at best, just collecting herself.

Either way, she left Daniel alone with the kids, on edge.

A sitting duck for the rest of the trifecta.

It was an innocuous enough thing, trying to help Nori with her ponytail. Not his specialty, though, and the elastic flung off his pointer and clocked some impressive yardage before skidding under the couch. When his fingers hit paper, he figured it was a discarded coloring book page or maybe one of those blow-in cards that rain from magazines. He had the thing half-crumpled before the numbers at the bottom caught his eye.

What a lot of them, all in a row.

And at the top, Molly's name. Only: Molly didn't have this kind of money.

Which was obvious, he supposed, by the red stamp beneath the total. *PAST DUE.* It was followed by an impatient line of dates indicating that prior notices had gone ignored and a bold-print final warning that collections would be notified. *Way* past due. It was dated just a few months ago.

The fantasy he'd had of walking away from his job, and his problems there with it, vanished, just like that.

Daniel had already known he was in deep shit.

What he hadn't realized was that apparently Molly was, too.

He needed to know the origin of this notice. He needed to know if there were others like it. He'd have to ask, eventually, but in the precarious state of things between them it would be delicate. Better to do some digging first. He had account balances to check, calls to make.

Choices to regret.

20

"A PIECE OF UNSOLICITED ADVICE," MOLLY HAD ONCE OFFERED LIZA, BACK when she'd bothered with attempts to match Liza's single-woman-in-the-city stories with her own dispatches from suburbia. "If you're ever invited to a dinner party where there will be children present, don't go."

Funny that she was now hosting one, with Liza as the guest of honor. In Molly's defense, it wasn't her idea. And in Daniel's, he didn't really know better—and not just because he was oblivious to her rift with Liza.

Daniel did not see these gatherings for what they were. The years had proven that no amount of subtle hint dropping or even out-and-out raging could change it: Whenever the rare delicacy of adult company was on the table, he helped himself to seconds, neglecting to notice that this meant Molly didn't get her share. It was always Molly, never Daniel, who couldn't get through a conversation without stopping an obnoxious number of times to reprimand Grant and Nori for things they knew better than to do. It was always Molly, never Daniel, who intervened when they were devouring the entire dessert tray. And it was always Molly, never Daniel, who'd excuse herself for "a minute" to put them to bed, only to spend an hour wrangling her (and, ahem, his) overtired offspring while he carried on downstairs, laughing away, refilling his drink, as if they had some unspoken arrangement that he need not concern himself. Which they did not.

When Grant and Nori were babies, Molly had been convinced she was simply *doing it wrong,* this melding of the children into aspects of life she'd once enjoyed. But now she'd been to enough such nights hosted elsewhere to know it wasn't just her. Some parents simply hid the futility of it all better than others, but the signs were there: in the gulps of wine downed too quickly in remote kitchen corners, in the tearful *it's not fair—he started it* time-outs making rounds from one child to the next, in the unserved crudités splatting onto polished floors. The childless guests endured it only out of politeness, and the parents went home wishing they hadn't bowed to guilt at the thought of leaving their children with a sitter after a long week of daycare. Why any of them bothered to continue trying was beyond her.

Still, in this case, she was glad Daniel had included Grant and Nori in his invite to Liza. She was counting on their chaos to serve as a *can't help it* excuse to remain *busy busy busy* during this reluctant reunion, even as she took steps to keep said chaos in check. Molly had fed the kids an early, easy chicken nugget dinner so they could simply singsong *hiiii!* to their aunt Liza and flit around, showing her things—Star Wars ships and princess dresses were already in the queue—without plaguing the meal with questions about the tiny green specks in the meat sauce, and when dessert would be ready because *I took three more bites, see?* But you'd never know they'd eaten by the way they wouldn't keep their fingers out of the cheese tray—an impulse exacerbated by the fact that Liza was, so far, twenty minutes late. Was it possible she wouldn't show? Molly had sent the most neutral possible *Daniel filled me in—wow, lots to catch up on* text confirming the time and gotten an affirmative, though short, *Yes, see you then.* She pulled it up now to read it again, as if Liza's feelings toward her might appear between the lines, as she swatted intermittently at her children's fingers, each time rearranging the cubes so the missing pieces were not so obvious, realigning the crackers so they'd look ready for company.

That Liza now fell under this Best Behavior category of visitors felt foreign, wrong. How had Molly allowed this gaffe of hers to wield so much power over where they stood? This was Liza, who had rolled out her unicorn sleeping bag next to Molly's at slumber parties for years, the life of the party who would secretly lie awake, unable to sleep alone someplace unfamiliar, until Molly silently offered up her headphones and Discman in the dark. Liza, who'd cried with unabashed gusto during her toast at Molly's wedding. Liza, who'd gotten so black-out drunk the first time Molly visited her in Chicago that Molly was positive she didn't remember shouting at passersby on the walk home from the after-hours bars that the whole move had been a mistake, all the while scarfing down a too-many-toppings-to-hold hot dog. Molly had been struck by the fact that no one yelled back, *Go home, then!* Even in that state and at that hour, Liza fell on the honest side of outspokenness, soliciting only looks of sympathy, and Molly had figured that Chicago would come to suit Liza just fine and that the sooner Molly got used to the distance between them, the better off she'd be.

Still, Molly had always liked her friend best in those vulnerable moments, those rare reversals. She knew this didn't make her a very nice person; she'd never say it aloud. It was just that . . . well, usually it was she who counted on Liza to hold her together. To whisper corny jokes in the dark when the slumber party included a slasher film. To force-feed her orange slices when nerves rendered her light-headed before her walk down the aisle. To brightly greet her hangover mere hours after that shouting walk home with coffee and croissants. Prepping for this dinner tonight, for what should have been a thank-you but was instead a silent apology, her shame had come to a head. And Daniel—was he *really* so oblivious, about everything? Could he honestly not tell something was off?

Maybe it wouldn't matter. Maybe tonight could salvage things between her and Liza.

Or maybe it would simply finish the job of ruining everything between them.

The doorbell sounded, and the kids took off running to answer while Molly stood rooted, rearranging the cheese once more with shaky fingers. *No turning back now.* She heard Daniel's heavy jog down the stairs, his pleasant exclamation in greeting, Liza's "Hey, little man!" hello to Grant, the slapping of high fives, and the music box notes of Nori's infectious giggle. Then, Liza again: "You said I could bring a guest. . . ."

"Absolutely. Daniel Perkins." He'd be offering his hand now, and Molly was glad of the empty room to roll her eyes into. A date, after only a couple weeks in town? Classic Liza, to set her sights on something like a hiatus and then change her mind—not that she didn't have a right to. You could do that, when you were untethered. When backing out of a bad call didn't drag someone you cared about with you.

"Max Miller."

"Max is a good friend from Chicago. He ended up being in town, so I thought I'd bring him along rather than canceling."

Molly brightened, retracting her judgment. This wasn't nonchalance from Liza—it was brilliance. Max was the sort to diffuse the tension, keep things light. Maybe they could actually have fun tonight, and she and Liza could have things out some other time. With no one listening.

"Are you and Max *best friends*?" Grant demanded. "I thought you were *Mom's* best friend."

"Well." Liza laughed uncomfortably. "I think you can have more than one."

They filed into the kitchen doorway, and Molly faltered. Though that awful morning hovered between them like fog, a part of her brain registered Liza's presence with something akin to relief: *Oh, this isn't some dreaded adversary—it's just Liza.* Molly smiled, holding out her arms to greet her guests with a proper hug.

"Good to see you, Max!" she said brightly. "And Liza, holy moly . . ." Had she really said *holy moly*? She'd had a teensy glass of wine while preparing dinner and then another when watching the clock—but usually these turns of phrase didn't surface until at least three drinks in. "I'm so glad you're okay. . . ." Liza's eyes held some unreadable challenge. Was she daring Molly to clear the air now, in front of everyone, or was she daring her *not* to? Molly looked back to Max, desperate for some sign of warmth, but his eyes were on Liza, in a *ready to defend your honor* sort of way. Maybe he wouldn't be such a great tension diffuser after all.

"Likewise," Liza said tightly, the challenge still burning behind narrowed lids.

Grant tugged at Molly's sleeve. "Do you and Aunt Liza get in trouble together?" Molly looked down at him and then back at Liza, eyebrows raised. After an awkward beat, Liza gave in to a little laugh, which Molly echoed, gratefully.

"Who, us?" Liza asked, all mock innocence.

"My teacher says she can tell who's *really* best friends by who's in trouble together."

Liza laughed again, while Molly bit back the urge to ask what exactly had prompted that observation. She hoped it didn't involve Grant, whose best friend, as far as Molly knew, was a studious Pokémon card collector named Stevie who saved him a seat on the bus every day. She should have hosted more playdates, vetted him more thoroughly. . . .

"I'm not sure I want to get into a trouble competition with your mom," Max said good-naturedly. It would have been funny under different circumstances.

"I'm not a very good listener," Nori announced, as if on cue.

Liza's eyes were back on Molly's, requesting permission to laugh. She knew enough to ask, at least. Molly smiled ruefully. "You think you have her pinned down here . . . but she bobs up right away over there somewhere!" she quipped. It was one of their favorites from her dog-eared quote book—FDR's warning that no one should dare enter an argument with Eleanor—and a handy over-the-kids'-heads stand-in for actual laughter. She turned to Nori. "That's something you're supposed to be working on, not boasting about," she told her, and with a shrug Nori was off and skidding in her socks down the hallway.

"I listen when I'm with Rosie!" she called over her shoulder. "And don't say she isn't my real best friend, Grant. She is too!"

"How can she be your best friend if she doesn't even *talk*?" Grant shot back, trailing after her.

Max turned to Daniel. "Is Rosie a dog? Because a dog is an acceptable best friend."

Molly didn't want her husband to answer, didn't want to know if his old smugness about the "troubled girl" his daughter spent time with remained. Maybe this wouldn't be so bad, feeling awkward around Liza and Max, if only she didn't feel that way around her own husband, too. "No, no, just a quiet child," she said quickly. "What can I get everyone to drink?"

By the time the natural topics for forced small talk petered out, they were seated around the table with wine and salads. As they stared into their romaine with exaggerated appreciation, it was Max who had either the courage or the audacity to pull everything into the open.

"I have to ask," he said, sounding apologetic. "I don't mean to bring up a topic you'd rather avoid, but that incident on the webcam gave Liza quite a scare. Is there any news? Who might have done that, or why?"

Daniel cleared his throat loudly from the head of the table, and Molly stole a glance at Liza, who'd never liked being spoken for, even when the speaking was a fair approximation of what she would have said herself. Molly half-expected her to put Max in his place with a sharp comment or a warning look, but she didn't. There was a solidarity between the two of them, as if they'd come into this together, with a plan, and resolved to go out the same way, and Molly wondered not for the first time if they were *really* just friends. She'd understood Liza's reservations early on, that Max hiding his own questions about his sexuality could be a sign of struggling to come to terms with it, but as time solidified the connection between the two Molly had caught herself questioning how much that even mattered. All relationships involved saying yes to one person and saying no to everyone else. What difference did it make precisely who you were directing every *no* to if you were focused on your *yes*?

"No news," Daniel answered, tacking on the kind of passive gesture that tries to say, *Guess it was just one of those crazy things.* Unlike Liza, Molly had never minded being spoken for as long as the words weren't inaccurate. In fact, she could appreciate being saved the trouble. She nodded, hoping to put forth the impression of a unified front akin to Max and Liza's. But the current that had once flown invisibly between her and Daniel had weakened until it was nothing more than a fading SOS signal. "Best guess is that it was a random burglar and Liza scared him off, thank goodness."

Molly tried to smile at her friend, who was watching her carefully. Now would be the time to show belated gratitude for Liza's all-night drive and to apologize for the way she'd treated her that morning. To blame it on shock or perhaps—though it was reaching—on the inexplicable shame that can follow such violations of personal security. But she could see in Liza's expression that it was too late for that, that there was no point in laying her sins bare in front of Daniel now, because it wouldn't make a difference anyway.

"Huh," Max replied, scrunching his face in thought. "I didn't think burglars entered the homes of people who were clearly awake. With lights on downstairs? I thought for sure it had to be someone who knew Daniel was out of town. Someone with some other purpose." He gave Molly another apologetic look. "Not that I'm trying to scare you."

She swallowed hard. "It's nothing that hasn't crossed our minds," she said, trying to keep the tremor from her voice. "But they haven't found anything to indicate that."

"How hard have they looked?" *Why was he not letting this go?*

"I'm not sure they've looked all that hard," Daniel conceded. "Given that no crime was committed, I think they have more pressing cases to investigate."

"Forcibly entering someone else's home isn't a crime?" Max scoffed.

"Well, yes, but then he walked right back out," Daniel said. "And nothing since."

Liza remained quiet. Too quiet. Molly could see how deeply her friend had *not* wanted to come, and understanding her reasons didn't make it hurt less. Molly wanted, impossibly, to go back, to behave differently that night, and the next day, to fix it all at the source. She could see that there might not be another way.

Max smiled teasingly at Daniel. "Are you sure the kinky burglar hooker you hired didn't get her dates mixed up? I *hate* it when that happens." Daniel's smile faltered, and Molly felt the blood drain from her face as he held her eyes in his. Her husband's expression took on a strange quality: not that *he* had been caught in something bad, but that *she* had.

Max burst out laughing. "The look on Molly's face!" he hooted. "It's like I finally said what she's been thinking all along!" Daniel went on looking right through her, seeing for the first time what she had really believed, at least at first, to have happened that night. That it was *her* visitor who'd timed his arrival poorly. It wasn't far from the truth, damn it, and she didn't know how in this wordless, caught-off-guard moment to pretend it was. His cheeks paled to match her own, and she wanted to lash out at Max and run from the table at the same time. "Fess up, Daniel," Max went on. "What's it you're into exactly?"

"Ha-ha," Daniel said dryly, his eyes not leaving Molly's. He didn't quite pull off the good-natured tone this time, and she answered the question in his gaze with a silent one of her own. *You're the one who invited them. Happy now?*

She turned to Max. "You're kind of right that this isn't my favorite topic," she said. "Can we talk about something else?"

"Sorry," he said. "I don't mean to make a joke of it. It's just that—I feel as if you and Liza have this in common, both having just dodged something. Her apartment burned down, for God's sake, and no one's talking about that, either."

"I don't know how much caffeine you drank on the way down here, but I'm hoping it wears off soon," Liza told him darkly, and there it was, the spark Molly had known was in there somewhere. "Ease up on everyone, will you?" Max looked so chastised that Molly felt sorry for him, though she still wasn't sure if he'd genuinely been trying to help or merely to push buttons. Maybe the solidarity between him and Liza did not, after all, extend further than a shared distaste for Molly's recent missteps.

Molly had planted the kids in front of a movie, promising they could join the adults for dessert. But here was Grant, wielding a stack of crudely safety-scissored construction paper rectangles. "I've got your tickets!" he announced. He bounded over to Liza and slid a red one next to her salad plate, which only served to highlight that her food was virtually untouched. She'd been rolling the cherry tomatoes across the bed of lettuce with her fork, but now she dutifully stabbed one and shoveled it into her mouth.

"Tickets to what?" Max asked, clearly grateful for the interruption. But Molly could barely hear him over Daniel's, "Not now, kiddo."

"To the After-Dinner Ninja Show," Grant said, handing a green one to Max importantly. "The stealth brother-sister ninja team puts on a performance the likes of which the world has never seen." A mask had been drawn in thick black marker across the length of the "ticket," the eyeholes colored in an unsettling bright red.

"Sounds impressive," Max said, but Daniel's "*After* dinner" was louder.

"That's what I said. The *After-Dinner* Ninja Show." Still smiling proudly, Grant handed Daniel an orange ticket. "Nori is the purple ninja, and I'm blue. Her favorite color *was* purple, but now she says it's pink, but I don't have a pink ninja mask, so she has to be purple anyway."

"You may *hand out the tickets* after dinner," Daniel told him sternly.

Grant presented a final pink rectangle to Molly. "I've already handed them out, Dad," he said, rolling his eyes as if Daniel were the one missing the point, and then ran from the room, calling again over his shoulder, "The likes of which the world has never seen!"

"I'd say a fire would be enough to make anyone anxious," Daniel said as if they'd never been interrupted at all.

Liza looked longingly at the doorway, clearly wishing she could follow Grant. "I'm not used to it," she said finally, the vulnerability in her tone catching Molly off guard. "Feeling so anxious, I mean. I hope it wears off soon." Molly's feelings showed on Max's face—a fallen smile, a wrinkle of concern. *I'm so glad you're okay,* Molly had greeted Liza, naïvely. Molly could see now that she'd chosen the wrong opening, that her friend was not okay. She was not herself.

"Molly's tried plenty of ways to help that sort of thing along," Daniel said. "Maybe she can recommend something."

"What does he mean?" Max asked her.

"Oh, I've had a run of bad luck, this past year or two," she said.

"Or five," Daniel said, lifting his wineglass congenially. She shot him a look.

"What?" he said. "That's how old Grant is. That's when the trouble started."

"I didn't realize you'd been keeping track so closely," she said coolly.

"It's been a lot to keep track of," he shot back.

Max was studying them both. "Are you—is he saying you're a hypochondriac, Molly?"

"Nothing like that," she said at the same time that Daniel said, "Somewhat."

"Who isn't, these days, with online symptom checkers," Liza said, and Molly heard the conflict in her words. It was force of habit for Liza to defend her, yet she was—rightly—unsure if Molly deserved defending just now. Molly offered a grateful smile that she hoped conveyed that she understood the sacrifice.

"Unfortunately, most of what I've worried was wrong with me was confirmed to be wrong with me," she told Max. True, she'd once convinced herself she was going blind in one eye because she'd noticed it was slow to adjust to the dark. And she'd had a suspicious mole or two—fine, three—removed only to find out they were nothing. But it was like that saying: Just because you're paranoid doesn't mean they're not out to get you. The dermatologist agreed that the coloring of those marks was questionable—well, all but one of them. And the optometrist had actually been impressed that she'd noticed the lag in her night vision, though it wasn't cause for concern. The other symptoms were more undeniable—in-your-face pain that no one other than the most reluctant patient would ignore. Daniel had seen them, too.

Hadn't he?

"What sorts of things?" Max asked, showing far too much interest.

"That's where Daniel's right that it's too much to keep track of," she replied.

"But anxiety? That's how we got started on this."

"I do *not* need treatment for anxiety," Liza cut in. "I hardly think being freaked out by a fatal fire counts, in the medical sense." She sounded too defensive, and Molly had the thought again: *She's not okay.* This made it seem suddenly crucial, somehow, that they reconcile. Liza needed her. No matter that this dinner was one disaster after the next.

"What was that meditation?" Daniel pressed. "The thing you said you thought could actually help with the worry, if not the pain?" She blinked at him, surprised that he'd not only heard her thoughts on the matter but retained them.

"Transcendental Meditation," she said. "It's not *for* anxiety, exactly, but it can help with it."

"Why did you stop, anyway? I thought you liked it." He sounded almost suspiciously curious, and Molly bristled. Of the many remedies she'd told him about over the years, trying to ignore his bored expression, he'd picked a fine one to recall. *Because I couldn't afford the session fees anymore. Because even if I could, I was afraid of who I might run into. Because I made a mistake, costing me the one treatment I hadn't tapped out yet—not to mention every other type of meditation practiced at the center—and I'm still paying for it. But like you say, I'm sure they were all a bunch of quacks anyway.*

"What *is* it?" Max asked, and she was glad of a question she could actually answer.

"They describe it with this analogy: All the thoughts that flow through your head on any given day—your to-do list and the notifications on your phone and everything else—they're like waves on the surface of the ocean, right? Always rolling, and it can be pretty impossible to stop them, though some kinds of meditation try to. The Transcendental method teaches you to simply sink below them to where it's quiet, to take a little break instead of getting tossed around on the surface." She turned to Liza. "Some people swear by it. It's hot among celebrities, actually."

"Huh," Max said. "I guess anything is worth a try."

"Molly believes *everything* is worth a try." Daniel twitched, as if remembering that he'd decided to be nicer about this stuff, but quickly recovered. "You two could go together." He seemed to think this was such a brilliant idea that Molly half-expected him to slap himself on the back, as if he'd made up for his misstep and then some.

"Oh, no," Molly and Liza said at the same time.

"You don't have to do that," Liza said, while Molly was blurting out, "It's better that you go alone."

"It's not like it's any trouble," Daniel said. "Molly can't get enough of that kind of stuff."

"Yes, I can," Molly said, narrowing her eyes. "I have had enough, actually." She turned to Liza. "But that doesn't mean you shouldn't try it. It does help some people."

"Step right up, ladies and gentlemans. To the most amazing ninja show in the *world*!" Grant was gliding back in through the kitchen, clad head to toe in black, and Molly caught Liza's flinch. It was too close of a trigger to what Liza had seen, what Molly had been trying not to imagine: the taller masked man who'd stood right there not three weeks ago, just long enough to ruin everything.

"*After dinner,*" Molly and Daniel chimed in unison.

"Aren't you done?" Grant said, pointing at their plates, which by now were mostly clear.

Nori poked her head around the doorway, her hazel eyes smiling out at them from a slot cut in a purple hood. "It's purple, but pretend it's pink, okay?" she hissed.

"Those were just salads," Molly told Grant. "We haven't even started the main course."

"Auntie Liza, what color do I look like?" Nori prompted, undeterred, in a stage whisper.

"Pink?" Liza guessed.

"That's right!" Nori said, forgetting the whisper entirely. "Pink ninja hi-ya!"

Molly pointed a stern finger in the direction of the living room, and Grant grabbed Nori by the arm and dragged her out of the frame.

"It's really okay," Liza said. "They're cute."

"Who was it that told you not to go to a dinner party where children would be present?" Max teased Liza. "You've been throwing that quote around for years."

Liza hid a smile. "That was Molly."

Max laughed as if it were the best thing he'd heard all night, while Daniel looked predictably baffled.

"I stand by that advice," Molly said. "Speaking of the main course, I'd better get it before we're full-out attacked. Be forewarned that Grant just got a whole kit of foam throwing stars."

"He won't be back until dessert," Daniel said with far too much confidence, and Molly was satisfied that even Liza and Max were looking at him as if he was an amateur.

"I'll help," Liza said, springing to her feet.

Molly looked, inexplicably, at Daniel, as if he might take Liza's place or at least come along so they wouldn't be alone. But Max was on about the Cubs, and no way would Liza stick around for that.

Molly headed for the oven with Liza on her heels and sneaked a glance into the living room, hoping the kids might come at them with another round of karate kicks or an impromptu song, a litany of questions, anything—but for once they were sitting obediently, albeit too close to the TV, cross-legged on the floor, engrossed in the animation.

Liza came up close behind her. Too close. "I have *no* idea why I'm playing along with this, not arguing in front of Daniel," she hissed into Molly's ear, lifting whatever sheer curtain of normalcy had remained between them.

As usual, Liza had called her out on exactly the right thing. Molly could hardly justify why *she* was doing it, either.

21

"SINCE WHEN DO YOU KEEP SECRETS FROM DANIEL ANYWAY?" LIZA PERsisted. She didn't know what she'd expected tonight—certainly her expectations hadn't been high—but this energy between Molly and Daniel felt precariously vicious. Her own plus one wasn't exactly playing nice, but this was something else.

Molly didn't answer, and Liza stepped back, shaking her head in disgust. "I can't believe you're still going around quoting Eleanor Roosevelt," she said, hitting where she knew it would hurt, in hopes that Molly might show herself at last. "Quite the feminist life you've made for yourself here. I really admire how forthcoming you've become about absolutely nothing."

"I was quoting *Franklin,*" she shot back, in lieu of a real defense. She opened her mouth to speak again, but in place of words a pool of tears filled her eyes, about to spill over.

There. It was just a glimpse, but all the same, at last: There she was.

"Molly. What's going on? What aren't you telling me?"

"I'm in trouble," she said quietly, pulling on a pair of oven mitts with a matter-of-fact precision that matched little else about her. She sounded exhausted. Broken.

"What kind of trouble?"

"Among other things, I need—well, money."

"For what?"

"It's a long story culminating in a ridiculous amount of debt."

Just like that, the glimpse disappeared. And in its place materialized the kind of fast-mounting rage Liza wasn't in the habit of holding in. She took a deep breath. "It's been a while since the season finale, so I'll give you a recap. Where we left off, I was living paycheck-to-paycheck in an overpriced town I could barely afford. Now I need to replace everything I owned, and I have to *prove* to my insurance company that I owned it all in the first place, and I'm living in my brother's guest room. And you're asking to *borrow money*?"

"No," Molly said calmly, as if Liza were one of the children, getting worked up for no reason. She retrieved the dish from the oven, and Liza entertained a brief fantasy of upending the whole thing down the front of her friend's pastel cashmere sweater—not to burn her, not to ruin the outfit, just to finally do something she couldn't ignore. "I'm not asking. I'm just answering your question. That's what's going on. And I know it's wrong to keep it from Daniel, but I also know he'd never trust me again if he knew." Setting the dish on the stovetop, she pulled at the edge of the foil and steam billowed out, traveling in a fog across the glass microwave suspended over the cooktop.

"So the guy in the mask was here to collect or something?" Liza couldn't keep the alarm from her voice, though she sounded hysterical by comparison.

Molly sighed. "I don't think so? I honestly don't know."

Liza glanced over her shoulder toward the dining room, where a friendly argument over batting order was heating up. "Are you and Daniel having problems? Besides money, I mean?"

Molly slid a serving spoon between rolls of manicotti and stood watching the sauce bubble up around it. "It's like you and me," she said finally. "We've grown apart over the years, and I hate that. Can we find our way back to the way things were? I'd like to think so, but who knows."

Liza swallowed hard. She decided to ignore the *like you and me* part—if Molly was looking for a denial, she wasn't going to get it—and confront the energy that was so off-balance in this house she couldn't wait to get out of. "You and Daniel have grown apart?"

That tearful, exhausted look was back. "That's the wrong analogy. It's not a distance, like you and I have. And with you and me, some of that wasn't even our fault, right? Though we could have done better." Liza bristled at the *we,* though she knew she wasn't free of culpability. It was just that she hadn't slammed a door in Molly's face recently. "This thing between me and Daniel, it's a wall. And we built it. At the end of the day, the question is the same, though. If we decide we want to knock it down, can we? Can we climb over? Or were we both so stubborn about piling on the bricks that we made it too strong for our own good?"

"Are we going to talk in metaphors or real terms? What did you do?"

"I might have laid the final brick. Or two. I don't know if he'll forgive me."

Liza was growing impatient. "What did you *do*? Does *this* relate to the intruder?"

"I don't know," she said again.

Liza shook her head, confused. "How can you not know?"

Molly whipped toward her. "What are you even doing here?" she hissed. "If you're so furious with me, why come?"

"Max made me."

"Why does Max care?"

She squared her shoulders. She might not have had her usual solid footing lately when it came to standing her ground, but for Max she could rally. "I think he'd like some answers about why you treated me like a door-to-door salesman when I came to check on you. As would I."

"He's only met me a few times, Liza. I think he's the last person I owe answers to."

"He would have met you once more if you'd let me in that morning." They were glaring at each other now, their faces inches apart. They should separate if they didn't want someone to notice. But they just stood there, chests heaving with angry breaths.

"What do you mean? He was with you?"

"He was in the car."

"What the hell did he come with you for?"

Was she *annoyed*? That did it. "He didn't want me driving through the no-man's-land of Indiana at all hours by myself. And he didn't know what I'd find when I got here. I was worried you'd been taken hostage or—I didn't know what!" The words came out in a rush—everything she'd been wanting to say, everything she'd been thinking. "It made no sense that you wouldn't call me back that night, after the police were gone. And it made no sense that you turned me away when I got here, like I was nothing. Like I was ridiculous for caring about you. Like I was ridiculous for being the best friend you've ever had. I don't know *what* the hell is going on here, but you are *seriously* messed up if you think I'm gonna just forget it."

She could see the wave of humiliation rolling over Molly. And she did not, as she had at the table, allow herself to feel sorry for her. In fact, she hoped Molly *was* imagining it all, just as it had happened: Max watching from the curb, in disbelief. The two of them talking about her, the whole drive back to Chicago. Five, six hours of pure speculation, lurid gossip. And now, in a new light, the two of them here, Max making what appeared to be uncomfortably on-point jokes. Though the heat of the pasta was thick in the air around them, Molly shivered, and Liza felt satisfied that her friend had accurately pictured it all. And now that Molly had seen it, Liza wanted her to explain it.

"So, what?" Liza pressed. "You wanted me gone because you knew who the masked guy was, and you didn't want Daniel to know, and you thought you could handle it? Kinky rendezvous, debt collector, all of the above?"

Molly's eyes darted around the kitchen, anywhere but Liza's face. "It's not like I'm the only one who isn't myself right now, okay? What's going on with you and Max anyway? I thought you were just friends. I thought you were on some big-deal dating hiatus."

She had never said it was a *big deal.* In fact, it had come too easily to be big. Before she met Henry, that is. "We *are* just friends."

"Friends don't drive twelve hours round-trip on a weeknight just to keep somebody company."

Liza bristled. "That's exactly what they do. And if you can't see why, then it's becoming clear he's the only real one I have."

Why was Molly doing this, lashing out when she was so clearly in the wrong? She was losing her, really losing her. Their friendship had been slowly evaporating over the years, but now it was as if someone had knocked over a water glass. Even if you tried to right it a split second later, it was already too late. Most of the fluid was gone, spreading itself so thin it was miraculous to think that the glass had ever contained it all.

"Please," Molly said, pleading. "Can we just call a truce?"

It took so much audacity Liza had to replay the words to be sure she'd heard them correctly. "Why would I want to do that?"

"To avoid one of those horrible 'friend breakups' we promised ourselves we'd never have?" It was a lame attempt at an inside joke, and it fell short by a mile. They'd read an article on the subject, in college, passing the issue of *Cosmopolitan* and a lit cigarette back and forth until they were both light-headed and teary eyed. They'd vowed that such a thing would never happen to them, proclaimed the featured women fools for letting such stupid things tear them apart. More often than not, the culprit was a man. Sometimes it was something that should have been happy, like the specifics of wedding plans, or a new baby—often offset by some badly timed rotten luck on the other side. A cheating fiancé. An infertility struggle. One woman, though, had been inconsolable that her so-called best friend had somehow jumped the line on the waiting list with an in-demand hairdresser. Of all things! "They were never really friends in the first place," Liza had said back then, rolling her eyes.

She'd been so secure in the fact that she and Molly were true blue.

"This is hardly at the hairdresser level," Liza said now. "And like you said, it's been happening for a while. This is just—the last brick, I guess. Maybe you're wrong that it isn't a wall."

Molly closed her eyes, and Liza wondered if she was thinking of that stupid mantra of hers. *Easy. Easy.* Liza had never once liked it when someone had told her to *take it easy,* much less had any inclination to lecture herself. She'd always thought it sad Molly hadn't latched on to kinder self-talk.

"Look," Molly huffed. "I'll go with you to the damn meditation class."

Liza blinked. "Who said I wanted to go? Daniel is full of bad ideas lately." *As evidenced by this dinner.*

"It's potentially life-changing stuff, Liza. With the worry cycles you've always dealt with at night, and now this? I'm sure it hasn't been easy, putting your life back together."

Nothing about her life was *back together.* The fact that Molly didn't know this made her grudge dig in its heels. "You told Daniel you'd had enough of it."

"Well, I might have misled him."

"What else is new?"

"Look, let me do this one thing for you, okay? I'm sorry about the way I acted. I know it's too little too late, but it didn't have anything to do with you. It's hard to convince you of that without telling you things I can't say right now, but please, don't give up on me. Please."

It was obvious—to everyone but Daniel anyway—that whatever the meditation sessions were or weren't capable of, Molly really didn't want to go back. Which meant she must be willing to do anything she could think of to smooth this over.

But Liza was not.

"No," she said. "I can't do this. Any of it."

"Liza—"

"Let's just get through dinner, okay? Here's some of that unsolicited advice you're so fond of giving: Consider yourself lucky I'm not making a scene in front of your family. And don't you dare ask me for anything else."

—

Max surveyed the contents of Luke and Steph's fridge. "Cheap wine or expensive beer?" he asked. They hadn't said much on the drive home—there had been a window, as soon as they were buckled in and on their way, to immediately launch into what they'd just endured, and when neither of them opened it they plunged instead into a contemplative silence. Coming in through the back door, they'd found the house quiet, the dim light over the sink left on for them, and Liza slid into a seat at the table in the dark.

Watching Max consider the options in the glow of the refrigerator, she finally felt free—and not just of the awkwardness over dinner. Not since Liza had arrived had Luke and Steph's kitchen felt like the refuge it suddenly seemed. Finally, for this moment, she didn't feel like a charity case or a third wheel, though it wasn't anything they'd said or done that had made her feel that way. It was simply true: She was both, especially as the date neared for Steph's corrective procedure, which was scheduled for Tuesday morning. Liza would have taken Max to the pub around the corner if she hadn't been sure Steph and Luke would already be in bed, though it wasn't late. A part of them still believed that if Steph did everything she could to model a healthy pregnancy, eating fresh organic produce and getting plenty of rest and taking brisk walks to get her blood pumping *just* enough—then she would have one. A part of Liza believed it, too, even though she'd seen for herself the gravity of the Perinatal Center. Even though Steph had lashed out at her yesterday when she'd mentioned Henry.

"Must be nice for your biggest concerns to revolve around a second date," she'd snapped.

Liza had been knocked off-balance by the blow—it was Steph, after all, who'd encouraged her to pursue him in the first place, who'd bounded down the stairs the morning after their date at the winery last weekend to find out how it went. But as the days crawled by, Steph's nerves had visibly frayed. And she looked so instantly horrified at her own words that Liza couldn't muster anything but sympathy.

Besides, maybe Liza *had* mentioned him more than was tolerable lately. This kind of giddiness over a man was unfamiliar, and she wasn't sure what to do with it, even as she had a general sense that *this* had been what everyone else was fussing about all along. Not love, of course, not this soon, but the *possibility* of something that might lead to it. He'd kissed her good night, long and slow, and now . . . Well, her heart jumped at every ping of her phone—which often was in fact a text from him. Her head turned toward every plane rolling by the Sky Galley window. He'd managed to join her for lunch twice this week—though she took her break uncommonly late, after they'd recovered from the rush—and hadn't hidden his disappointment that she was unable to set another date for this weekend. She'd taken a small, *hard to get* satisfaction in saying no, even as she'd wished she could say yes.

Still, the idea that he was her *biggest* concern was a gross mischaracterization. Just this afternoon, Max had run late without calling from the road and Liza had been beside herself, sure he'd been in a brutal crash like the one she'd passed on her own last drive from Chicago. By the time he'd arrived, she'd broken out in actual hives beneath her shirt.

Not that she'd shown them to anyone. That would be . . . embarrassing.

Max turned toward her, holding a bottom-shelf pinot grigio in one hand and a locally brewed IPA in the other. It really was a toss-up, as she and Max were of like minds on this, as many other matters: Good wine wasn't always superior enough to warrant the upcharge—her night out with Henry a wonderful exception, not that she'd paid—but good beer definitely was.

"Well, I've had my fill of cheap *talk,*" she began.

"Beer it is." He popped the tops onto the counter with an efficient *hiss clink, hiss clink*, and took the seat across from her.

"Cheers." They tapped the bottles together and each took a long swig, the way you do when you've really earned that first sip working in the yard all day or moving into a new apartment. Or, evidently, enduring a painful dinner party.

"You were kind of an asshole back there," she said. "I'm not saying it wasn't called for. Only a little surprising."

He flashed a sorry-not-sorry smile and took another drink. "I was," he agreed. "I don't know what came over me. As soon as we got there, my head just went back to that morning—to the way you looked the whole drive back to Chicago. Like she'd physically punched you in the gut." He set the bottle on the table. "I know you going tonight was my idea, but once we got there, I felt like she was getting off too easy. And like it was my fault, for talking you into going."

"So you just came right out the gate with the burglar hooker jokes, huh?"

He made an exaggerated cringe face, and she laughed. People really didn't give enough credence to how friendship could be as nuanced as romance, as complicated as family. She could be kind of annoyed with him and a twisted sort of grateful at the same time, just as she could be *done* with Molly and yet still feel sorry for her somehow.

"Whatever is going on in that house, it's not good," she conceded. "I got this feeling that we should back away slowly. Almost like she was *right* to turn me away that morning, crazy as that sounds." She shrugged. "But, you know, sweeping in and stirring things up like we were on some reality TV show was also a viable option."

"Sorry," he said, focusing intently on the label of his beer. "It wasn't my place."

"Well, I appreciate your loyalty. And I guess a part of me is glad you made me go. A very deranged part." He laughed, and the air between them was cleared. She wished it were always so easy. How nice that with Max it sort of always was.

"So are we back to worrying about Molly now? Did she win you over with that *hostess with the mostess* routine?"

A cackle burst out of Liza, louder than she'd intended, and she clasped a hand over her mouth, not wanting to wake anyone. When they'd left, Molly had been holding a flailing Nori, who'd been yelling something about sleeping on the floor as if it were a great luxury she was being forbidden, while Daniel fended off a shower of ninja stars behind her in the doorway.

"I wish you were moving here with me," she blurted out. She hadn't known she was going to say it, and she ducked her head sheepishly. "It would just make everything . . . better."

"What if I did?" It might have been a throwaway statement, one said after too much dinner wine, or it might have been an act of kindness, to make her feel less embarrassed about having said it at all.

Or it might have been a daydream, finally mustering the confidence to voice itself.

"What do I have going on back in Chicago that's so great?" he went on. "Maybe you had the right idea, getting a fresh start."

She laughed again, and she meant it as good-natured, going along with a joke, but it came out as awkward, unnatural. "If you *did* want a fresh start," she said, "you could probably come up with better than Cincinnati."

"I used to think about moving to San Francisco," he said, surprising her. So there was a side of him he'd kept to himself after all. A side that happened to have its wanderlust set on the country's most gay-friendly town. She instantly chided herself for the assumption. She'd long ago come to terms with the fact that Max still didn't seem to know what he wanted, and that it was none of her business when or how or if he figured it out. Plus, didn't his employer have an office there? It was possible she'd had one drink too many at dinner herself. Maybe this beer wasn't the greatest idea. She pushed the bottle away. "San Francisco doesn't have you, though," he added.

"Cincinnati does have that going for it," she agreed. "But. Friends don't follow friends several states away."

"True," he said. "Friends don't."

The words felt heavier than they should have, and the air around them took on the weight, as if this could be a moment of significance. It was too close to what Molly had said not long before: *Friends don't drive twelve hours round-trip on a weeknight just to keep somebody company.* Liza's counterargument hadn't been untrue, but Molly's observation wasn't invalid, either. And here she and Max were again: in a moment when the meaning of *friend* was questioned or—more dauntingly—when the label as it pertained to them was up for discussion.

Liza felt it, felt the mass of it pulling down on her arms, pressing on the top of her head, squeezing her lungs, and she held her breath, hoping with everything she had that it would pass and then they'd be in a different moment, a moment in which they'd be talking about something else and nothing would have changed. A moment that would spare them from forever looking back at this one and remembering the question that turned the invisible molecules around them into something with substance.

For all the ways she'd always be attracted to him, no physical pull was left between them. Not anymore.

At least she didn't think so.

"So. Are we going to talk about it?" he asked gently, and she froze.

"Talk about what?" *Don't ruin it, Max, please.*

"The pile of fire ladders in the guest room."

She burst out laughing. "I'm trying to figure out how to dispense them to Luke and Steph without them thinking I'm a head case."

"*Are* you a head case?"

"No. I'm just—I'm following some advice, actually."

"From Fireman Sam?"

She hesitated. Not mentioning Henry up until this point had been a conscious decision—one she told herself had *nothing* to do with a fear that Max would rather keep her to himself. It just seemed insensitive, when Max was still getting used to the idea of her moving away, to rub in anything unexpectedly good about the new start.

Just as seeing Max be anything but happy for her *about* Henry would dull the shine of the one novelty she was allowing herself.

"Not quite," she said. "But someone who seemed like he knew something about risk assessment. He thought they might make me feel better. And honestly? They kind of do."

Max's expression turned serious. "I walked by your old address the other day. There's a memorial now. Flowers, teddy bears, sheet music—I guess to honor those musicians, you know? It was the first time I let myself *really* think about what could've happened if you'd been in there. . . ." She shook her head and he allowed the sentence to fade out. For him it might have been the first time, but for her it was stuck on repeat, and she'd been trying desperately to shut it off. He looked as if he wanted to say more, maybe even to pull her into his arms, but he didn't. "I think you should do whatever makes you feel okay, is all I'm saying," he said finally. "Don't worry about what anyone else thinks."

She'd always told herself that she'd *never* cared what anyone else thought of her—an extension of her whole no-strings-attached persona—but it wasn't true. Otherwise she'd have thrown in the towel and returned to Cincinnati long ago. Early on, when she'd been in Chicago for only a few weeks, she'd been so homesick she came back on one of her days off without telling anyone. She'd worn a baseball cap and dark sunglasses, a poor proxy of a celebrity who didn't want to be recognized, and sat on the wall at Eden Park overlooking the muddy river far below. She'd purposely chosen a neighborhood she no longer had friends in—but what would anyone have said if they saw her? *Back so soon?* And why did that seem such a slight? She'd told herself sticking things out in Chicago was the independent thing to do, but the minute it stopped being what she wanted was the minute it stopped being an independent choice. And the idea that these new insecurities filling her days had been there all along was the most unsettling, the most difficult to face.

"I don't feel like myself," she admitted. "I kind of miss her."

He sat up straighter. "Yourself is right here," he promised her. "I was missing her, too, back home, and now I'm not, so she must be." Tears pricked her eyes, and before she could hide them he reached across the table and tapped his finger on the top of her hand. "Cut her some slack," he said. "She's dealing with a lot right now. And she might have gotten some bad advice, about subjecting herself to Molly's bullshit. My bad."

Oh, Max. It would have been better for him, too, if she'd been brave enough to back away months or even years ago, rather than clinging to him even as she told herself that she was not. She met his eye. "No, you were right. I have so much dread hanging over me right now, it's better that we got that much over with. And—even though I can't see a way past things with her right now, I don't know . . . Maybe she and I are the same amount of messed up."

His hand covered hers solemnly. "Don't ever say that again," he said, his eyes wide with alarm, and she began to giggle, the laugh escaping her in a flood that swept him up, too, until they were both wiping away tears with the backs of their hands, gasping for air.

"What would I do without you?" she asked, rubbing at her cheeks. She'd been smiling so big they hurt, and she realized how out of practice they must be.

"We're never going to find out," he said, with so much conviction she could almost feel the tiny crack appear in her heart. She already knew how easy it would be, with the miles between them, to grow apart.

22

MOLLY LOVED IT HERE AT KRIPPENDORF LODGE WHEN NO ONE ELSE WAS around, when the only sound was the trickle of water in the fountain—no children tossing coins in today—and the wind whipping the leaves overhead into a frenzy. A hike seemed risky on a day like this, when branches could easily dislodge and fall, but she'd felt a longing to be out here someway, and so here she was, stretched on the steps at the end of the wraparound porch, gazing into the forest.

The trees, she'd learned just hours ago, were communicating. Right now. Always. This morning's naturalist program discussed the phenomenon, and she'd come here in the manner of a gumshoe who has to see something for herself once a crucial piece of new information has been revealed.

She didn't usually hear the programs—only snippets of fascinated chatter afterward, when attendees wandered over for coffee or a souvenir—but today she'd been in her boss's office, waiting for him to brief her on the aviary that would be setting up an exhibit in front of the nature shop. His box of a room was around the corner from the auditorium, and when he was delayed by a complaint at the membership desk she overheard most of the presentation through the open door. By the time he finally materialized, it took restraint not to shush him. What she'd really wanted was to slip into a vacant seat in the back row and return only after all her questions had been answered.

Because she did have questions, all of a sudden. Lots of them. Things she should have asked before. Things she hadn't allowed herself to consider until the possibilities had been pointed out to her.

The forest led a secret life as a network—everything interconnected in ways so complex no one fully understood them. No tree in a well-populated habitat stood alone. What appeared to be independent organisms stretching into the sky were in actuality part of an intensely interdependent system not just of communication but also of life itself. Underground, through the roots, through the soil that nourished and held them all fast, they were all in this together. Talking, sharing. They even helped one another when they were sick.

People would say the word with a snarl, like it was a bad thing, pathetic: *codependent.* It conjured sitcom-esque clichés of a woman without a mind of her own, a man without a spine. *Interdependence* sounded nicer, *was* nicer. Ecologists had found, to their amazement, that it was the buzzing, thriving, flowing network beneath the surface that made all its parts resilient.

In all the hours Molly had spent wandering the forest, she'd never known this. And yet now that she did, she couldn't help but wonder if she'd intuited its power, longed to be pulled into its network so she'd no longer have to stand and fight alone.

Certainly she'd wished people worked that way. She'd longed to belong among the other moms, the ones who could get through a stroller-fit class without tears of frustration, who could speak fondly of their husbands without feeling like frauds, who concerned themselves too much with their children and not at all with themselves. Even her counterparts at therapeutic yoga classes seemed to be on this other plane she couldn't reach, where they were fully immersed in something that for her was a hesitant test run.

If she were a tree, she'd be one that had never rooted well on its own. That had first leaned toward the sunshine surrounding Liza and then grown into the comfortable, soft shade of Daniel's until, somehow, she'd found herself outside the network, and those poorly planted roots had weakened and begun to rot. The ecologist said that many individual problems could be traced to a breakdown in "cooperative two-way communication." She couldn't stop thinking about it: how effort from one side would never be enough. It took two fully invested, engaged individuals to sustain a bond.

Everything is connected, the naturalist assured them, *even if it doesn't look like it.*

She'd never proven this to be true in the time she'd spent pining for things that never took hold of her. But it hadn't occurred to her, until now, to look for connections she *didn't* want.

She thought of the way Daniel had come back from Chicago, his easy shade turned darker and colder, and how she'd convinced herself she didn't want to know why.

She thought of watching him through the window, after she'd spotted Toby walking by, panning the street like a bull looking for a waving red flag to charge.

And she thought of the intruder. After discarding her initial theory as to his identity—once she'd decided Rick must be telling the truth—she'd considered few others. The hope that it had been random. The nagging worry that the man with the walking stick had been speaking figuratively with his *perhaps you didn't get the message?* comment.

But now things were coming to a head. Her request to work extra shifts went nowhere. Evidently, there was no shortage of part-timers looking to boost their paychecks; she could get in line, but it was long. In the meantime, she'd made a measly couple hundred dollars reselling the herbal supplements she'd given up on. There *were* people in her predicament desperate enough to trust a stranger on the internet to send them an open bottle of pills—to gamble that the contents matched the label—and she knew where to find them: under-the-radar message boards, far from the better-policed marketplaces. Undiscerning customers, however, demanded a can't-pass-it-up price; she took a steep loss and no satisfaction in making this week's payment. The next one would be due so very soon.

If only there were some way to unload her unused prescriptions. But the last thing she needed was to get involved with anyone else unscrupulous.

For people who were so eager for her to pay up, these lenders were not easy to reach. Calls went through an answering service where messages were returned from "unknown" numbers. Her requests to be put through to a supervisor were dismissed as "not possible." When she inquired about renegotiating the terms of her loan, the "customer service" rep actually laughed.

She grew more uneasy, less certain the attorney's warning had been overblown. Putting her savings at risk was one thing, but this was something else. She was haunted by the unaddressed matter of collateral—half-expecting to wake up one day to a boot on her car or a stranger on her lawn. Breaking down and telling Daniel was looking more and more like the inevitable next step.

But what if the lenders *were* harmless? She had made her latest payment, after all. She'd bought time, if nothing else. What if there was another viable theory as to the intruder's identity—one she had overlooked?

Before she sacrificed everything to pay off her debts, she had to be sure she wasn't addressing the wrong source of her biggest fear. That it wasn't connected to a different part of the forest, underground, where no one could see.

Where no one would think to look.

What would she do if Daniel saw her here? Or if he caught wind of it from someone who recognized her from the annual holiday party she always seemed to be, to her chagrin, feeling well enough to attend? The chart in the lobby indicated that Human Resources was on the first floor, so at least she wouldn't have to risk the close quarters of the elevator. She'd hope for the best with no real way to plan for the worst. What else was new.

The receptionist had stepped away, and the phone on her desk was ringing. Molly strode past it with what she hoped looked like confidence and started reading placards outside office doors. It didn't take long to find Toby's—he was supposed to be accessible, after all. His door was open, and inside he was smiling so intently at his computer screen that whatever was on it couldn't possibly pertain to work. She knocked on the doorway and watched as he took a second to place her.

"Mrs. Perkins?"

She nodded. "Molly."

"Molly. Daniel's office is up on Four. Would you like me to have someone escort you?"

"I'm here to see you, actually. I—" She took a deep breath. Was she really doing this? "I have some questions about our medical benefits. About the family plan."

"Oh, well. It's, uh—" His eyes flitted past her to the deserted hallway, then back. "It's unorthodox for us to work with spouses, but I'm sure we can answer your questions. Why don't you write them down for Daniel, and if he can't find the answers in the materials we've distributed, I'd be happy to meet with him."

She crossed to one of his guest chairs and slid in, clutching her purse in her lap. "You know those privacy policies they make you sign at the doctor now? Giving permission for who can access your health information?" He nodded. Though she spoke quietly, he had the look of someone who was being embarrassed in public by a tantrum-prone child or a day-drunk companion. "Well, I'm hoping there's an equivalent where Human Resources is concerned. I realize I'm not an employee, but I am covered by your plan, and I'd rather not relay these particular questions to my husband, as they allude to medical information I'd rather he not know. Do you have a similar policy that requires you to keep this conversation private?"

"Uh . . ." His eyes were on the empty hallway again, where the ringing phone persisted from the lobby. "Well, I suppose just because it's unorthodox doesn't mean it isn't possible. Let me see if someone is available—" He made a move to stand, but she shook her head, quickly.

"I'd really rather talk with you. I have to tell you I've called the provider a few times already and I've had my fill of people telling me they have to check with their supervisor and call me back. You *are* the supervisor, correct?"

He sighed and glanced at the clock mounted on his wall. "I have fifteen minutes until my next meeting."

"Great." She stood to shut his door, then seated herself again.

"First, the Health Savings Account. Are we able to use those funds to cover alternative medicine treatments?" She already knew, through painstaking hours spent poring over the paperwork year after year, exactly what was and wasn't covered as it pertained to her treatment preferences. But she made him go through it all, line by line, no by no, just for the satisfaction of making him realize how short their offerings fell, how their *resources* weren't so great after all—though she suspected he already knew that. By the time they were finished, he looked exasperated, as he should have.

But she thought his exasperation misplaced. It had come together for her, under the trees: The brokers Toby had been courting when Daniel was coming home complaining about his spending. The change in her husband after his trip to Chicago: jumpy, antsy, and speaking no name but Toby's. Daniel's instant stiffening at her mention of the man walking by their home. She might feel as if her spouse barely knew her anymore, but she still knew him. She was going to gamble that she'd drawn the right conclusion. Now or never.

"And the Bank of Toby fund you've added to the 401(k) plans. I'm assuming you'll start exempting Daniel from those withdrawals? If you haven't already, of course." Toby's face froze as if, maybe, if he didn't acknowledge that she'd spoken she might vanish from his office, all of this a bad dream.

She was simultaneously relieved and horrified. She had guessed correctly.

"I beg your pardon?"

"You should beg everyone's pardon. Doubt you'll get it, though."

His eyes narrowed, and she could imagine his crooked mind racing ahead, plotting his next move.

"Coming into your husband's employer and throwing meritless accusations around is pretty off-the-handle stuff, Mrs. Perkins," he said, their first-name basis behind them. "This meeting is over, and if we both agree there won't be another, you'll be getting off easy."

"*I'll* be getting off?" She dared to laugh. "I've done nothing wrong. But I'm here so you know that I'm well aware you have. And I can't think of an impetus for me to keep that information to myself."

"Can't you?" he said coldly. "I strongly suggest you speak with your husband before you make any snap decisions to that end. Your *culpable* husband."

She tried to hold steady. She'd come here hoping to flip the switch on Toby—but what if Daniel had already compromised himself somehow, beyond his complacent-as-always guilt-by-inaction? It wasn't possible—was it? Daniel had flaws, but he wasn't a crook. The fact that he was *bothered* by Toby was the reason she'd known to come here at all.

"Is there proof of that?"

Now it was his turn to laugh. "You mean aside from his sign-off on *all* the company's finances?"

She shrugged. "You seem sure I care if my husband goes down with the ship. I just gave you a pretty decent idea of what my life is like—of everything that's wrong with me, of everything my husband would prefer to stay out of, everything I don't want him to know, to touch, even to have an opinion on. Does that sound like a happy marriage to you?"

He leaned back in his chair. "I can't make out why you're here. Did he put you up to this?"

"My husband doesn't put me up to things," she snapped. "That would imply he thinks I'm capable of handling them."

"If he could see you now." Sarcasm dripped from Toby's voice.

"Let's just say whatever you're lording over Daniel isn't going to work on me. And I work for one of the city's most beloved nonprofits, with top donors from all over the business community. Make no mistake that you won't go quietly. You won't work in this town again."

She could see in his eyes that he wanted to test her, but something seemed to be holding him back. Perhaps he really did have something on Daniel, a card up his sleeve he was debating whether to play. She didn't like the idea of it, not at all. But she had to keep up this front.

"What *would* work on you?" he asked finally.

She hesitated. She hadn't realized this would be so tempting: The shiny-red-apple prospect of arranging for her debts to be paid, right now. Of making another *big* problem go away. Skim the skimmer, blackmail the blackmailer, come down to the opponent's level.

But no. She was better than that, even at her worst. She'd already fallen so much further than she wanted to face. And she was here to reduce the risk to her family, not increase it.

She leaned forward. "If you've made any kind of bad judgment call that has extended your ill-conceived threats from Daniel to the rest of my family? Or if you've so much as *thought* of doing so—sending a friend to do your grunt work, or stirring up that nosy sister of yours? You'd better never do it again. If you *ever* show up at my house, speak to my children, speak *about* me or my children to anyone, I will ruin you. Whatever game you're playing, you play it here, in this building. Anything to do with our family is out of bounds. Including Daniel's 401(k)." She wasn't just saying so on principle. They needed every cent.

"You've got the wrong guy, Mrs. Perkins," he said evenly. "I think I know what you're referring to, in terms of your after-hours visitors, and I can assure you, I've done no such thing."

She had an unsettling feeling that he was telling the truth—he seemed almost *entertained* by the suggestion. She couldn't trust it, though. He was someone who'd stood up in front of the whole company, looked them in the eye, and siphoned away their money. "And you never will again," she said, her voice as strong as she could muster.

His hands, she noticed, were shaking, almost imperceptibly—but at what part of her affront she couldn't tell. *Damn it. She couldn't tell.* She'd hoped coming here would let her discern whether he'd been behind the mask, metaphorically or literally. But it had only affirmed that he was an asshole. Which everyone already knew.

"It's too bad we've had to cut back our budget for social functions this year," he said dryly. "I do always look forward to seeing the spouses at the holiday party."

She got to her feet. If he'd been the intruder or had anything to do with it, perhaps this visit would deter him from anything further. Otherwise, this had done nothing but call more attention to Daniel's place on Toby's watch list. Which might even make things worse.

The reprieve she'd been hoping for slipped away. She would leave here still afraid. Still in debt, still in pain, still dreading a race with a finish line that seemed out of reach, still walled off from two of the people she cared about most.

Still not knowing what to do next.

"I know how closely you watch every cent," she said pointedly, and had the satisfaction of seeing something of her own fear mirrored in Toby's expression before she made for the door.

23

HOSPITALITY MANAGEMENT HAD ITS PERKS, BUT A FORGIVING SCHEDULE wasn't among them—least of all when you were the newest hire. Liza had spent consecutive Thanksgivings catering to families who considered it a luxury to forgo home cooking. She'd worked the Fourth of July every one of her Chicago summers, never once seeing the fireworks light up the lake. She'd volunteered to run Valentine's dinners and dances, grateful for the excuse to keep busy; she'd bartered for Christmas and New Year's off; she'd reluctantly handed over coveted concert tickets on nights when she was called in to choreograph damage control. She accepted this as part of the life she'd chosen and rarely complained—though enduring the disappointment of her parents, significant others, and friends meant that she never missed an occasion without, at minimum, a twinge of guilt. Sometimes it actually made her *glad* of having so few attachments, and at that, she could appreciate her career even for its flaws.

But when she looked over the week's schedule on Monday and saw that she was the only one available to open the restaurant Tuesday morning, she minded. Luke and Steph would be headed to the hospital, to resolve the incarcerated uterus—Liza would never get used to *thinking* those awkward words, much less saying them—one way or the other. And she'd be able to offer them nothing but a good-bye and good luck.

After Max had returned to Chicago, the drawn-out stillness of anticipation filled the house. They all moved quietly among each other, knowing these could be the last days with the baby, and while Liza knew this potential loss would never mean to her what it meant to Steph and Luke, she shared in their fear—while doing her best to behave as if she did not. She continued to do Steph's "hope yoga" alongside her, and after dark downed without argument the stiff drinks her brother poured them both, so he wouldn't have to steel his nerves alone.

Liza planned to stay out of their way tonight, to let them have the final hours to themselves. But come tomorrow's procedure, she'd hoped to be on call, on hand to celebrate or mourn, whatever the day would bring. She sat in the tiny back office off the Sky Galley kitchen, paging through the planner, looking to switch shifts, but could see no one available. A reluctant yet strong dread began to fill her, and she tried to put the emotion in check, to give it a swift kick. It wasn't as if Luke and Steph *asked* her to be there, after all. It wasn't as if they wouldn't understand . . .

And that's when she realized the dread was not coming from the schedule.

It was coming from the smoke.

She smelled it nightly—the fatal scent of her worst dreams, accompanied by the terrible sound of crackling destruction. Sometimes she imagined screams. A baby crying. Distant sirens that would arrive too late. She'd wake and repeat over and over to herself that it wasn't real, yet still she could smell it, hear it, even taste it.

Just like now. Only she was wide awake.

Shouting came from the kitchen, where the cooks had been prepping for lunch service, and a second after she registered the ashy air as *real* she could see it, thick and billowy, filling the doorway of her windowless office, blocking the exit. The smoke detectors began to bleat.

Fear pinned Liza to her chair even as the blur of a white chef's coat ran past the doorway, then back again, carrying a shiny glint of red. She heard the fire extinguisher discharging in several bursts, followed by masculine cheering. Liza should jump to her feet, get out, go check, take charge. But she couldn't breathe.

A young line cook appeared in the doorway. "Don't worry, boss, it's out. Sorry about that. Overheated the grease, then spilled it when I tried to clamp on the lid."

The earsplitting beeping of the alarms went on. She licked her lips, squinting at him through the smoky air. She couldn't speak.

"That alarm will have notified the fire department. We're supposed to wait in the parking lot until they give the all clear."

Then the approaching siren was real, too—it was so like the one in her dream. The one that wouldn't get there in time. The one that might as well not come at all.

"Boss? We'd better go."

She got to her feet, numbly, and managed a nod.

Henry found her in the parking lot, standing apart from the group, as far from the massive fire engine as she could reasonably be without drawing attention. He'd been in a meeting at the opposite end of the terminal, evacuated too. He looked from her to the flashing lights and back again and wrapped a silent arm around her shoulders. *Don't you cry,* she commanded herself. *Don't you dare cry.*

—

Henry's apartment did not smell like smoke. It smelled like cinnamon and sugar.

"Cinnamon rolls?" she asked as he took her jacket.

"My weakness," he admitted. "Most days breakfast is the only meal I cook at home, and there's this great recipe I can't resist—so my kitchen kind of permanently smells like them."

"Yum." When she'd brushed off his concerned suggestion that she beg off work for the day—though she'd already known she would tremble through the entirety of her shift—he'd invited her over for dinner instead. "Helluva start to the week," he'd said, not commenting further on her pallid state. "Give me a chance to help turn it around." Before she could wonder if she should say no until she'd pulled herself together more tightly, she heard herself say yes.

His one-bedroom in a high-rise on the edge of downtown was compact but clean. Almost *too* clean—but the signs of life she did see passed inspection. A bookcase so crammed full of thrillers and biographies, no amount of tidying would declutter it. A worn gray throw she could imagine a grandmother or an aunt laboring over, crochet hook in hand. A wine fridge that was, as revealed through the glass door, filled with an assortment of microbrew bottles. At that, she pointed and smiled. "So the date to the winery was just for show, huh?"

"Not at all. That was for fun—a wine adventure!" She laughed. "But on a normal day, the wine I drink hardly needs its own fridge. My parents gifted me this, so I figured it would be of better use perfectly chilling my expensive beer."

She cocked her head at him. "Those are my exact spending proportions for adult beverages."

"Then next time I'll take you to Taft's Ale House. It's gorgeous." He opened the little glass door. "What's your fancy? I have an early release of a summer lager. . . ."

"Sold." She crossed the room to examine a series of vintage aerial photos framed on the wall. They were all islands: some sandy, surrounded by turquoise waters, others lush and mountainous, and a few encrusted with snow.

"Even paradise can look lonely from the sky, can't it?" he said, coming to stand next to her. "Reminds me not to wish myself away too much." He held out a pilsner glass, and she took a sip.

"Perfectly chilled," she said.

"Right? Okay, so this isn't a line, but you have to follow me into the bedroom."

She laughed. "How is that not a line?"

"It's the best place to check out the view. No funny business, I promise." Never mind that she was already fantasizing, in spite of herself, about sticking around long enough to try the cinnamon rolls. She followed him in and stopped short. His view was panoramic, from the football-shaped stadium across the bridges to the levee. It did not make Cincinnati look like a backup plan, and this only endeared him to her more.

"It's a very Chicago apartment by Cincinnati standards," she said approvingly.

"You didn't like Chicago," he pointed out.

"I liked the view."

"Well, so do I." But he wasn't looking out the window. His eyes were on her.

—

Liza did not stay the night, but she did stay long enough that Luke and Steph were asleep when she got home. Come morning, she followed them as far as the front porch, where she waved, trying not to look like she was sending them off to some make-or-break fate, though they all knew that's exactly what she was doing. Their hugs were quick and tight; they promised to call.

Work, at least, was better. Nothing remained of yesterday's smoke, and she was relieved to find she could start her shift with a steady hand—printing half sheets of the lunch specials, taking inventory behind the bar, brewing coffee and tea for the busser stations because the opener had called in sick. She distracted herself with flashes of Henry last night—how he'd somehow known to both keep a distance and stay close, down to holding her hand as he'd walked her to her car. Still, her stomach churned with a different worry, and she broke her own staff rule and kept her phone on hand, though she wasn't supposed to hear anything until closer to lunch.

At 9:30, though, it rang, Steph's name flashing on the screen. Liza was in the office retrieving register drawers from the safe, and lunged to answer.

"I'm not having it done." Steph was talking so fast Liza could hardly process the words. "It worked! The yoga actually, finally *worked*! Talk about sliding in under the buzzer!"

"You fixed it on your own?" She pulled a clenched fist toward her and squeezed her eyes shut—*yessssss!*—and when she opened them, the head cook was in the doorway, eyebrows raised. He was a hulking, ponytailed kitchen lifer named Keith who, when she'd asked how long he'd worked there, had responded by counting managers, not years. Thank God he hadn't witnessed her incompetence during the grease fire. *Good news,* she mouthed, pointing at the phone, grinning as if he'd been stopping in to check on her all along.

"I did! Or the baby did. Either way, my uterus is *free*!"

Liza did a little dance, and the cook's mouth twitched in something between a smile and a smirk before he disappeared from view. Let him think her ridiculous. Something she really cared about had gone the *right* way, when it so easily could have gone the other. Sliding back into the groove of not censoring herself was an indescribable comfort.

"We have to celebrate tonight," Liza gushed. "Whatever you want!"

"Luke and I are headed to Original Pancake House now," Steph bubbled. "I'm going to order one of everything. I really might." Liza laughed. "But tonight, you and I: sister celebration."

The word seized her. *Sister.* Molly had used it for her in affection; Luke had mainly said it in jest; she couldn't remember the last time she'd heard it. "Thank you," Steph whispered. "For everything. You've been great."

"I don't know about that," Liza said. "But I've been meaning to say the same to you. I chose such a bad time to show up at your door—"

"How many times do I have to tell you I'm *glad* you're here?" Steph interrupted. "But I'll be gladder if you come home with really good chocolate. Champagne being off-limits and all." No one had ever sounded so thrilled to be forbidden alcohol.

"Done," Liza said. It was nice to be needed. Maybe *that* was what she'd been missing these past few years. She'd been so accustomed to the way Molly relied on her, before she'd left. Maybe she hadn't found her friend's tagalong ways as cloying as she'd let herself believe.

"What's the good news?" Keith asked. He was back in the doorway. "Did you get a better job offer after all?"

She laughed. "My brother is going to be a dad," she said.

And she was going to be a damn good aunt.

—

For the chocolate, Liza stopped at the Kenwood Graeter's, not just because it was decadent, though it was, but also because it was conveniently located near a big-box baby store. Steph wouldn't be the only one getting presents today. Liza had thought through the rest of her shift about the way she'd blurted Steph's news to Keith as if she'd just heard it for the first time. All of them—their parents and friends included—had spoken of the pregnancy as a *maybe* ever since the complication had arisen, avoiding mention of the end result. She'd gone along with it to protect Steph as much as to guard against her own disappointment, but now she felt ashamed and wanted to make it up to her future niece or nephew.

Liza hadn't set foot in the store in years, but it was just as she remembered: fluorescently lit, primary colored, and plastic, with the overall feel of a sales circular that used too many exclamation points. She sidestepped the seasonal toy sale—inflatable floats and sand buckets already—and followed the signs past a dizzying array of formula and diapers to the *real* baby gear. The good stuff.

Outfits were a no go, without knowing the gender, and stuffed animals seemed generic. She wanted something useful but also meaningful. Her first insurance check had arrived, and she had money to spend—but the more extravagant necessities, the car seats and strollers and swings, seemed like things Steph and Luke would want to choose themselves. The arrays of features were dizzying; pros and cons would need to be weighed, preferences specified. And of course Luke and Steph hadn't registered yet; no one had made noises about a shower for a baby no one dared talk about.

Finally, at the end of one of the aisles, she saw it. A tall display topped by a flowery sign that said simply: "Peace of Mind." These were baby monitors, high-end ones: with video features, remote monitoring through smartphone apps, and two-way voice. She reached for one with a glittery twilit sky on the package and turned it over. This model tracked more than just sound. Breathing, movement: a safeguard against SIDS. *So you can rest easy while your baby does,* the box promised. It was perfect. As one of the most expensive options, it was one they might not buy for themselves. What better than some extra "peace of mind" to celebrate the weeks of worrying Steph now could put behind her?

Liza smiled the whole way home, the box gift bagged beside her next to the ribbon-tied chocolate-covered pretzels and buttery buckeyes. Henry was right—it did help, in a weird way, to prepare for the worst. Like how she always tried to have an umbrella along, because that way, it wouldn't rain—sudden downpours preferred catching her unawares. She'd gotten up the nerve to give the fire ladders to Luke, and he'd simply sized her up for a moment before admitting they were probably something every house should have. No big deal; nothing to read into.

She burst through the front door clumsily, her rustling bags and jingling keys disturbing the peace as she maneuvered inside. She'd expected—well, noise. Music. Laughing. Everything that had been missing as they'd tiptoed around the complication. But though the lights were on, the house was quiet and looked just as it had when she'd left that morning. Steph's yoga mat was still unrolled in front of the couch in tribute to the awkward poses she would no longer have to assume.

Liza found Luke upstairs, sitting on her bed in the guest room, looking sadder than she'd expected. When she stepped into the doorway, he looked up and pressed a finger to his lips. "She's taking a nap," he said, his voice low. "I think it's the first good sleep she's had in weeks."

Liza nodded and shut the door behind her. "What are you doing in here?" she asked. "Have I violated house rules?"

When they were growing up, their father had proclaimed things "house rules" willy-nilly, too often for anyone to keep track of them, and usually only after they'd been broken. If Luke came home from one of Dad's favorite restaurants without offering to bring takeout, he'd tsk, "Come on, kid. House rules," and then help himself to Luke's Styrofoamed leftovers. If Liza bought a Madonna concert on pay-per-view without asking, he'd say, "Damn it, Liza. House rules!" and then hover around, mimicking the backup dancers until she wasn't sure which of them looked sillier.

Luke, too, would be a *great* father: funny, good-natured, and just this side of embarrassing in public. She realized she wasn't the only one who hadn't been herself these past weeks. Luke had traded his irreverent side for a more guarded one. It'd be nice to have him back.

"Oh, my." He laughed. "How did I almost forget about house rules?"

"You've had a few other things on your mind." She plopped onto the bed across from him, dropping the bags to the floor, and gave him a smile. "I'm so relieved, I can't even imagine how you must feel." They hadn't had much time just the two of them since she'd arrived, and the familiarity of Luke without the still newness of Steph was nice. She breathed it in.

He nodded. "I walked down to Pipkin's Market to grab some

flowers for Steph and got some for you, too." He gestured at the vase of pink tulips on the nightstand and tapped his index finger on the miniature notepad she'd left sitting on the edge. "I wasn't snooping," he continued. "Just putting them here. But I couldn't help but see . . ."

He took the pad into his hands and raised an eyebrow. How careless of her to leave it out.

"'Deer struck on overpass fell on car passing below,'" he read. "'Fall on basement stairs with laundry basket. Baby pool after a rainstorm.'" His eyes returned to hers. "What are you listing, exactly?"

She looked down at her hands, self-conscious. He wouldn't like this. But she could think of no explanation but the truth. She cleared her throat. "I keep checking the Chicago news sites for some update on the fire—the cause, the litigation, whatever. But there's never any news." She shrugged. "This stuff jumps out at me instead."

"These are ways actual people have actually died?" She nodded. "Jesus, Liza."

"Yeah, well. Turns out he doesn't always take the wheel."

He blinked at her. "You know fear is a defensive response, right? You're going to render it useless if you make yourself afraid of *everything.*"

"Who said I was afraid?"

"You're keeping a list of odd, random ways to die."

If he turned the page, he'd find the scribbled backstory she'd imagined for the woman who'd fallen—how it had been years since she'd gone through a day without doing some household chore that had gone unnoticed by everyone else, and how they sure as hell were going to notice now. She hoped suddenly and intensely that he wouldn't. Best to keep him talking.

"I keep lists for lots of things," she said. "Groceries. Errands. Reasons I should move out at the soonest opportunity." The teasing came out of habit, but the instant she said it she knew she wasn't ready to go. Three weeks had passed, though, almost a month—they'd be within their rights to ask her to move on.

"I have that list, too," he said dryly. "We should compare notes. Wonder if you thought of any I missed."

"Doubt it."

He shook his head, turning serious again. "The fire ladders were one thing, but this . . . are you okay, Sis?" The verbal sparring was more familiar for both of them than the heart-to-heart, and hers sank, knowing he wouldn't attempt this lightly.

"Of course I'm okay."

"Are you, though? It's understandable if you're not. But we can't help if you don't open up. A lot has happened in a short time."

She hadn't really hidden the way she was feeling, had she? Maybe a little, but mostly they'd just been preoccupied with other things. More important things.

"You've even—maybe—lost your best friend," he continued. "My personal thoughts on Molly notwithstanding, I know this isn't how you ever imagined coming back."

She averted her eyes. She was touched, in a way, that he'd ask. But that didn't mean she wanted to talk about it. "Look," she said. "Today I'm just happy for you guys. Can't we just enjoy it for a minute?" He looked uncertain, and she mustered her best encouraging smile. "Come on. I even have presents. For Steph *and* baby." She reached down for the bags and flopped them onto the bed between them.

"Aww, you didn't have to do that." He returned the smile. Success. "Can I peek?"

"Peek away."

Rustling the tissue paper in the gift bag, he took out the monitor's box and held it in both hands, his head bowed over the package, reading the features.

For an uncomfortably long time.

She cleared her throat. "I know you'll want to pick things yourselves, but this is top-of-the-line. Every feature you could possibly want."

When he looked up at her, his eyes did not hold gratitude. Instead, they reflected something between sadness and suspicion, and her breath caught. What had she done wrong?

"You celebrated the end of us monitoring a complication by giving us a way to monitor for more complications?" The words sounded strained, pulled taut across astonishment and anger and disgust, and she drew back, caught off guard.

"Everyone has a baby monitor, Luke. I just got the best one—"

"This monitors *vital signs,* Liza. It's for parents who are freaked out about SIDS. Regular monitors just let you know if the baby is awake. They don't check for you that your kid is still *alive.*" He was looking at her as if she'd lost her mind. "You literally just asked if we could just be happy for a day—this is your way of being happy for a day? Jumping straight to the next thing we should worry about?"

"No!" *Was* that what she was doing? If she'd thought of it in those terms even for a fleeting instant, she'd have chosen something else. "You're blowing this out of proportion. It's not about worrying; it's about peace of mind. That's even what the store display was called."

Luke shook his head and held the box in front of her face, tapping angrily on its logo. "The second you see this, you feel like you're supposed to be worried your baby will die." He dropped it back into the bag. "We just got done with that. I appreciate the gesture, but please. Take it back."

"Luke—"

"Liza, we've honestly liked having you here. But if you're really keeping a list of reasons you shouldn't stay, put this at the top. Whatever paranoid tendencies you're fighting in the wake of this fire, do not force them onto my expectant wife. Do not force them onto me." He tossed her notepad back onto the nightstand, where it jostled the tulips in their vase. "Nobody wants to think about this stuff. And neither should you."

"It's like bringing an umbrella . . . ," she said weakly. But she could see there was no point in finishing the thought.

"I don't think safeguarding against premature death is like expecting rain," he said. "Seriously, Liza. Maybe you should talk to somebody. A professional. I'm not good at this."

She shook her head. "Not my thing."

"It doesn't have to be a traditional counselor. Even some kind of—I don't know, meditation or something. Something to calm your brain down."

She hesitated, reeling from how poorly she'd misjudged the gift, the situation, her brother's whole point of view. She still wasn't sure Luke wasn't overreacting, but even so, she felt awful—because when it came to being a houseguest, egregious offenses were in the eye of the beholder, and she owed the beholder a lot. It didn't matter at this moment which one of them was right. It mattered that Luke was upset with her and she desperately didn't want him to be. "Molly did offer to take me to a class . . . ," she began, against her better judgment.

He looked surprised. "So you've made up? You and Max said that dinner was a disaster."

"It was. And no, we didn't make up. But Daniel latched on to this idea of her taking me to this thing."

"Was he wanting you to go along to help Molly, or Molly to help you?" Liza thought back to the common denominator between that conversation and this one. *Damn it.* When she didn't answer, Luke nodded. "Maybe you could do it for me. I need to feel like you're doing something. Besides buying fire ladders."

She bristled, suddenly furious not with Luke, but with Henry. Damn his theories, his misguided attempts to put training for the air into practice on the ground. Maybe when it came to what was and was not a good idea, she couldn't trust herself just now. It was disconcerting to have something that had seemed so right turn out to be absolutely wrong, yet again. She was starting to think she could put her whole friendship with Molly in that column, let alone her time in Chicago, her efforts since returning home . . .

She grabbed the baby's gift bag and jammed it underneath the bed, where Steph wouldn't see. At least she had the chocolate to show for herself. She might not be operating independently very well, but hey, she could follow instructions.

"I'll call Molly," she said.

Only a fool would have believed she was looking forward to it, but Luke did her the courtesy of pretending.

24

HE'D HAD A FEW DAYS TO STOP REELING, BUT DANIEL WAS STILL PRO-cessing what this could mean.

He knew now for certain why Molly hadn't told him about the intruder. Why she'd shut the door in Liza's face the next morning, running away with her feet firmly in place. And why—for some reason, this poked under his skin most of all—Rick had given him the damn book, ostensibly to help him help Molly.

He'd seen all of it and more on Molly's face when Max made that crass joke at dinner. No, no one had been caught off guard by a sex-on-call delivery boy. But a lover? She'd flinched as if a searchlight had landed on her, and Daniel had thought, *No, certainly not,* but, *Then again, that explains everything,* followed by, *But who?* The only logical answer he could think of was at the other end of the footpath leading out of their backyard and through the woods to someone else's.

Had the affair been under way or just getting started? Either way, the outcome was the same: Molly spinning into a frenzy of trying to cover up something that had no cover. Rick backpedaling—had he and Molly cooled things off for now or for good?—and trying to make nice with Daniel out of, what, proximity?

Looking back, maybe Daniel *had* suspected, even before the

incident. He'd just resisted acknowledging his mistrust, his fears—even as they turned up the volume on his wake-up call, even as they egged him on into his subsequent about-face. He couldn't very well confront the fact that Molly may have strayed without owning up to the circumstances that may have led her to. And he hadn't wanted to do that; he'd only wanted to find a reset button for them both.

He hadn't wised up yet, back then, to what a bad idea it was to kick things into gear with a shortsighted plan and hope they'd turn his way from there.

But he was wiser now.

Daniel had risked so much for Molly. His conscience—or was it just selfish paranoia?—had turned on him at the office. When Jules snagged him the best donut before the vultures descended on the box, or proudly showed him her daughter's senior pictures, he'd think of how much she'd detest him if she knew. He was supposed to be on her side—one of the few, the proud, the good guys, not the butt of the jokes they liked to make about everyone else.

He'd have gone back on his arrangement with Toby, come what may, were he not certain the man would make good on his threat to take a wrecking ball to Daniel's marriage. He reassured himself again and again that no one else in the company was in a position to spot the things he'd spotted—that was part of the problem, after all—but it did little to lessen the pressure. For all he'd endured to be for *nothing* was simply not acceptable. Not anymore.

Whether that dark night had been the false start of Rick and Molly's affair or some later stage of it seemed almost a technicality. The feelings existed. They had to, because unlike Daniel, his wife couldn't separate the emotional and physical aspects of a bond. The downward slope of his marriage had shown him that, if nothing else. It followed, then, that while Daniel was one of those people who could buy into the claim, hypothetically of course, that a tryst meant nothing, Molly was not.

He'd thought he was past feeling this desperate. He'd thought he was coming out on the other side.

But there was still time. She wasn't gone yet—if she were, she'd have reacted to all of this differently. *You caught us. I was trying to work up how to tell you. I'm sorry.*

He was at a dead end anyway. He'd called the number on the statement he'd found, navigated the automated system with Molly's Social Security number and zip code, and found out she'd paid it in full—but somehow the zero balance didn't set his mind at ease. He'd tried and failed to access her separate accounts, to guess at her passwords and log-ins; he'd combed their joint assets for signs of odd payments, undisclosed debts. He couldn't help but question *how* she'd managed such a big sum, all at once. He'd be a fool not to wonder if there were others like it.

Still. Maybe she'd just been bad about keeping up with the month-to-month. If she'd paid, however she'd done it, things couldn't be that bad, financially speaking.

Could they?

In for a penny, in for a pound was one of Molly's classic drunkisms. He'd laughed as she'd slurred it cheerfully at the late-night burrito counter with her upsized order, on the eggnog-filled Christmas Eve she overstuffed his stocking until it ripped and fell, even on the full-moon night they decided to conceive a sibling for Grant.

So it was for Daniel now. In for a pound, or more—whatever it took to tip the scales back in his favor.

He had not come this far only to lose her.

25

MOLLY STOOD IN FRONT OF THE BODY-LENGTH MIRROR MOUNTED ON HER closet door and bent her legs, pulsing a few times before straightening up. The copper sleeves she'd ordered felt uncomfortably tight, but the fit *looked* right. They didn't roll down when she moved, and the flesh of her quadriceps wasn't billowing around the top. Was this how they were supposed to feel? And could she really run in these things, if she could run at all? The copper zigzags shone across the black fabric, catching the glow of the Himalayan salt lamps she'd installed on their bedside tables some months prior. She'd forgotten by now precisely what the illuminated crystals were supposed to do—something about ridding the air of negative ions, allowing for more cleansing sleep—but she still liked the way they gave the bedroom a sort of spa quality, in appearance if nothing else. Daniel had never expressed an opinion on them one way or another, aside from a flat-falling wisecrack about kryptonite the day they arrived. She should have tried to have a better sense of humor about it, maybe. Probably.

"Mom!" Grant burst through the door without knocking—a habit she was going to curb one of these days—and stopped short. "Hey, *cool.* LeBron James wears those! Are they for the race?"

She nodded, taking a more critical look at her otherwise standard athletic wear. Did the knee sleeves make her look like a parody—a suburban mother who fancied herself in the NBA? Maybe she should wear long pants to cover them, even if race day proved as hot as the extended forecast guessed it would be.

"Can I have some?" Matching Grant could be cute. If only these hadn't cost a bundle—she'd gone for quality so as not to risk that the copper wasn't legitimate. Even in spending dollars she didn't have, why throw good money after bad?

"I don't think they sell them for kids. But anyway, these are supposed to support Mommy's bad knees. Your knees are fine." She bent her legs again, frowning. Maybe she'd try the sleeves on a hike first—she'd be meeting Rick and Rosie again after work tomorrow, and this time they'd have company. Molly hadn't expected Liza to change her mind about the meditation class, but she'd called yesterday, and Molly was so relieved to realize she might have another shot at her friend's forgiveness that she blurted out the first, fastest alternative she could think of. Liza had sounded uncharacteristically hesitant, even needy, but Rick had made up for her lack of enthusiasm, as having a new face join their brave talking was Rosie's prescribed next step. Molly hoped she wouldn't regret melding worlds this way, but it was better than melding *herself* back into a place she didn't want to go. And maybe seeing Rosie's struggle with things the rest of them took for granted *would* help Liza get some perspective. It was worth a try.

Daniel appeared in the open doorway behind Grant and surveyed her. This was how it always went—she'd sneak away for a five-minute shower or to try something on, and next thing she knew, she had an audience.

"Auditioning for the Lakers?" he said brightly, and Grant beamed up at him. "That's what I said, Dad! Doesn't Mom look cool?"

"Totally cool." Molly smiled weakly. How many years before Grant couldn't think of a single "cool" thing about her? She'd seen the eye rolls at the bus stop when the older kids' parents appeared even at their most helpful, brandishing a forgotten lunch or library book. She dribbled an imaginary basketball and passed it to Grant, who mimed the catch and a jump shot.

"Three-pointer!" he yelled, and Molly joined in his victory dance, ignoring the twinge in her lower back.

"Speaking of, there's a basketball game going in the cul-de-sac. Ryan's older brother said he'd keep an eye on you if you want to go out."

"Ooh, yeah! Can I?"

Molly started to shake her head, but Daniel nodded. "We'll call you when it's time for dinner."

Grant pounded down the stairs, and Daniel's smile fell. "Are you really going to run this thing?" he asked. "I'm not sure copper sleeves are going to cut it, Mols."

Of course he wouldn't believe support would help. In *any* of its forms. "I told him I would," she said simply.

"Most people don't run even a short race without training at least a little bit. I'm not trying to sound cruel, but when's the last time you ran anywhere?"

"That's the point, I guess," she said. Her hands had found their way onto her hips. "I'm tired of disappointing him. I'll just have to rally." He opened his mouth to speak again, and she held up a hand. "Let's not, okay? Your budget meetings—you can't get out of them, can you?"

Daniel genuinely looked sorry. "The start of the fiscal isn't flexible, unfortunately. And neither is the exec board."

"Right. So. You can't do it. He really, really wants someone to do it. Ergo, I will do it. Let me worry about how." She hiked a leg onto the bed and peeled off the sleeve. The release of the suction felt strange. Maybe it had been doing something useful after all. "Also, since when are we okay with sixth-graders being responsible for our kid playing in the street? I should get down there."

"He'll be fine," Daniel said. He cleared his throat. "There's something I want to talk to you about."

Her heart dropped. Here it came. She'd practically held her breath for the whole rest of the day following her visit to Toby, but Daniel had shown no signs that he'd heard anything about it—not then or the next day, either. But she couldn't remember the last time any variation of *we need to talk* had led to something good. "I was going to start dinner . . . ," she began, but he was shaking his head. Adamant.

"There's never a good time, is there? Once the kids are asleep, either one of us is, too, or we're both distracted with other things. I set Nori up with a movie—she's sucked in." He looked too proud of himself for this to be entirely bad. With a quick nod, Molly sank onto the bench at the foot of their bed and busied herself with yanking off the second sleeve.

"I have a surprise for you," he said. "Something I want for us to do together, I mean." He perched on the opposite end of the bench and dropped a brochure onto the varnished wood between them. On the cover was the name of a wellness center she'd never heard of, set against the backdrop of, she was pretty sure from the shape and the tint, the Blue Ridge Mountains.

"What's this?"

He took a deep breath and let it out in a gust. "After I put my foot in my mouth suggesting you take Liza to one of those meditation classes, I got to thinking. About how that was the one thing *I* haven't offered to do, the whole time you've been going through all this." He didn't qualify what his interpretation of "all this" was, but that was probably for the best. "I've never offered to go with you." She tried to brush past the way he said *the one thing* as if he'd exhausted all other outlets. Instead, she pictured skeptical Daniel, peering over her shoulder—over all the shoulders—from the corners of acupuncture rooms and yoga studios and healing massage parlors. She could picture her favorite therapeutic yoga instructor, whose very presence brought the word *zen* to mind, shaking her head, pointing a finger at the door.

"I appreciate the thought," she said. And in some off-center way, she did. "But it's okay. That's not something I've been secretly longing for. If I had been, I would have asked." Of course she wouldn't have asked. But the first part was true.

"This is different from anything you've done," he said. "It's a healing retreat, a weekend away. And it's not just about physical treatments, though they have those. It's about having time to get lost in the mountains, to unplug for a while. They have spiritual guides, to help you—*center,* I think they call it. And they also have these people—not therapists, exactly, but coaches, sort of. You can tell them about everything that's happened, and everything you've tried, and get their feedback. What do you think?"

She opened the brochure and let her eyes touch the photographs inside, one by one. Rocky creeks and fire circles and morning tai chi and intimate conversations in valley-view tearooms. What she thought was that this must be enormously expensive and that she wished he had offered it two years ago, or even one—back when she'd looked with longing at such offerings, unable to fathom how she could manage to get away, let alone justify her desire to. What she thought was that financially speaking she could not let herself consider this possibility, even if she wanted to. What she thought was that she couldn't resist digging just a little bit more.

"This is something you'd actually want to do?" she asked. She laid the brochure back in the space between them and met his eyes. "I don't think it does anyone any good to go to these things and then act like they're bunk."

"I'd want to do it if you wanted to do it," he said, and she could see that he meant it. Or at least he thought he did. "I'd be willing to try. And if you're worried about me judging the retreat, judging you, don't. I know I've been guilty of it before, but you have my word that I'd look for the good in it. That I'd try to learn something."

She squinted at him. "This is where the wife character says, 'Who are you and what have you done with my husband?'"

"I know. I'm sorry."

They fell into silence, both of them staring at the brochure. The hope on his face was almost too much to bear. She'd cycled through her whole supply, and it was tempting to dip into his, to hold herself over until she could replenish her reserves. If only it were that simple.

"Do you know," she said, "what they would tell me if I went? Those coaches, those guides?"

"No," he said, "but I'd be interested to find out. Only if you wanted to share those parts with me, of course."

"I can share it with you now. They'd tell me I've been doing it wrong."

"Doing what wrong?"

"All of it."

He searched the air for a response. "I guess they'd teach you how to do it right, then."

"I'm not talking about techniques. I'm talking about my whole approach. These treatments, they're supposed to become a part of your lifestyle. Every practitioner warns you that you need to implement them consistently before you'll see benefits. But do I listen? No. I flit from one to the next in something like a panic, worried that what I'm trying isn't working fast enough, convincing myself that it won't fix me, that it's the wrong solution, setting my sights too soon on the next thing that will. Everything I've tried that hasn't worked? It isn't that this stuff doesn't work. It works for plenty of people. It's that I've been doing it wrong."

He blinked at her. "Why?" he asked finally.

"I don't know," she said. "I know I'm going about it wrong, yet I can't seem to stop."

"Well, this could be the perfect chance to start fresh."

He sounded so sure, and it was so ironic, coming from him, and she was filled with a rush of the rage she'd been holding back. "You know what?" she said, her spine stiffening, her stomach roiling. "I *do* know why I've been doing it wrong. It started with you. You'd ask how it was going after two classes and I'd tell the truth and it'd be written all over your face, what a waste of time this was, what a waste of money.

You were impatient with it, and that made me impatient with it. I had to find something that would prove to you, and to myself, that I could do it. What I should have done was just stop. I was too vulnerable to be put in a place to have to defend something that I had no idea would be effective. But I didn't stop. Instead, I just stopped telling you about it. I just stopped telling the truth. But I could hear your voice anyway."

The muscles at the corners of his mouth twitched. "I've been making a real effort, since the night we had that scare. . . ." His voice was so level it seemed designed to make her sound irrational by comparison. "But you keep bringing up everything I did wrong before. Doesn't it count that I'm trying to do better now?"

"We can't just go on as if the past few years never happened!" she exploded. "A part of me wants to, but we can't! You *eroded the empathy from our marriage.*" He drew back, wounded, but she didn't feel sorry for saying it. In some ways it was the truest confession she could make, regardless of everything she still had yet to tell.

These past years, he had looked at her and seen a woman in pain. A woman who couldn't get by without certain kinds of help on certain kinds of days. A drain on their family's energy, a drag on their productivity, a leap that fell short, over and over. And she *had* been those things. She'd seen them, too, hated them, too. But it wasn't *all* she'd seen. She still knew who else she was. She was a mother who loved her children with an intensity that kept her alive. She was a warm smile at the visitor center. She was a woman who liked to walk alone in the woods, who was grateful for the hidden beauty she found there, who was proud that no hindrance had kept her from seeing it. She was a helper, a listener, to others in her therapeutic classes, to middle-of-the-night regulars on message boards, to the widower who lived behind them.

She was a whole person. She was not *only* a sufferer. But even now, when he was priding himself on looking at the pain in a more understanding way, he wasn't seeing the rest. He seemed to believe she had been *replaced* by all the negatives rather than complicated by them.

"You eroded the empathy," she repeated, lowering her volume to match his. "And no spiritual retreat in the mountains is going to put it back."

"That's not fair." He geared up, giving in to the fight. "If you're telling me you stopped telling the truth, then *you* eroded the *trust.*"

"Did I?" Evidently, she'd been braced for this challenge. For once, she knew what to say. "How can you trust somebody with your emotions, with anything, when they don't *feel* for you? What is a marriage even supposed to be, if not *feeling* for somebody?"

He jumped to his feet. "If you felt like I was 'eroding' something essential, why not say something? Even at my soulless office, you don't get fired out of the blue. They tell you when you aren't meeting expectations. They give you a chance to improve."

"It's telling, that you'd compare our marriage to a job."

"Stop twisting everything. All I'm saying is to give us a chance now. On this retreat."

She shook her head, incredulous. It was one thing for him to feel sincere about going with good intentions, but the reality of being there together would be a test of their combined lack of patience and faith. In spite of everything—even if they could afford to go, which they definitely couldn't—she didn't want to so obviously fail. Because *then* what would they do?

"Look," he continued. He had that desperate glaze he'd had the day he'd brought her flowers, the day she'd started to believe maybe they could fix this. Had she stopped believing again? "You don't have to forgive me to go. Maybe it's good, to have this out in the open instead of tiptoeing around it. They can teach us to fight better, or . . . whatever they do at these places."

There it was. The slightest hint of the verbal eye roll she'd known had to be coming. Her fury grabbed it by the tail and swung. "So you think the way to bring our marriage back together is for you to do something on my behalf that we both know will make you miserable? Dragging people along to things they aren't into isn't my idea of a good time."

"Since when is compromise bad for a relationship?"

"Compromise is agreeing on something that would make us both halfway happy. Your idea is that first I make you miserable doing something you don't want to do and then, what, now you have the Make Molly Miserable card to play whenever you want?"

He closed his eyes and sighed. Loudly. "Fine. This retreat is now officially the thing that will make me happy. Be miserable about it if you want to. I'll play my card now."

"I don't get *why.*" Molly's frustration thickened her voice into a gurgle of hostility.

"Because I already paid for it, okay? You've been chasing this shit for years; I honestly didn't think you were going to pick now of all times to decide you're doing it wrong. What is it you're really done with, Molly? The treatments, or me?"

The wall between them was not as sturdy as she'd imagined it to be. Because now it swayed as if caught in a sudden storm, hovered off-balance for a terrible moment, and crushed Molly beneath its weight. Until she couldn't move. Until she couldn't breathe.

26

A SQUARE WHITE BOX TIED WITH A THICK RED RIBBON SAT AT THE FOOT OF the Sky Galley door when Liza arrived to open the restaurant Thursday morning. She shifted her traveler cup of coffee, her dripping-wet umbrella, and the staff key ring to lift the thin, glossy cardboard between her fingertips and saw her name on the tag—no message, no signature. But the doughy smell of cinnamon reached her even before she untied the bow, and she knew who it was from.

The perfectly well-meaning man she'd been avoiding since leaving his house late Monday. Or, more specifically, since Luke had rebuked her equally well-meaning gift on Tuesday. Henry had texted her later that night, before bed, asking how things had gone with Steph, and when she sent the shortest possible response—*Everything A-OK!*—the excitement and relief he shot back made her heart twinge. He'd had no stake in the game other than knowing she did. He'd cared enough to follow up. And he'd checked in several times since, initiating conversations that were easy enough to shut down with a non-conversational response.

He'd also been out of town for the past couple days, which had given her time to think. About how maybe she was putting too much stock into not just Henry's theories, but Henry himself. Maybe, with no home address, zero furniture, a meager wardrobe, and a climbing anxiety level, she wasn't in a position to be putting stock into anything right now. Maybe, given how emotionally attached she was feeling, against both odds and reason, in under a month, she should get out now—simply take the safer route, in a time when danger suddenly seemed to be everywhere.

Inside her office, she lifted the lid to find a still-warm, generously iced cinnamon roll. It seemed disingenuous to accept the gift when her feelings on its sender had grown murky, but then again, no point letting it go to waste. The first bite was soft and not too sweet, even as she tried not to picture Henry rising from bed to make them, donning his uniform, taking the time to package the pastry, thinking of her.

A text chimed into her phone, and she knew without looking that it was from Max. He had an uncanny knack for following Henry's gestures with his own, a fact that had to be purely accidental—least of all because she hadn't alerted him to Henry's existence—but that she couldn't help but think might mean something. She'd been happy enough on her dating hiatus partly because Max was in many ways enough for her. Maybe that wasn't healthy, but then again, who was qualified to assess that? She knew of women who'd lived their entire adult lives in loves based solely in friendship, a different kind of commitment, and as they aged those couples could seem so affectionate, so fortunate to have found each other—even operating under a certain understanding of what would or would not be happening in the bedroom. Maybe it was silly not to pursue that kind of happiness if you could see it within reach. Maybe the more foolish thing was to drag yourself out on other limbs that, for all you knew, could bend and break under your weight.

She'd felt the creaking already, under her brother's scrutiny. And if all it had taken was a few pointed questions, maybe she should recognize the signs that the branch wouldn't hold her—at least not now, when she was carrying so much else on her shoulders. Maybe she should just slowly back off.

Taking another guilty bite of the roll, she lit the screen of her phone, expecting some sort of morning wisecrack to cheer her, but saw that she'd been wrong. It *wasn't* from Max. The little airplane icon she'd assigned to Henry glowed next to the message.

Pretty good, right?

She couldn't argue with that. *You shouldn't have,* she sent back, meaning it, even as she uncoiled the outer layer and folded it onto her tongue.

Laughter came from the doorway, and she jumped. Henry was leaning on the frame, his pilot's cap tipped down so his grin shone brighter than his eyes. She'd left the door unlocked for the chef and prep crew, but they weren't due in for half an hour.

She swallowed the bite too soon and tried to cough into her fist without sputtering as she got to her feet. "I thought you'd be in the air by now?"

"Rain delay. Seemed like a good excuse to see what you're up to this weekend."

If only he hadn't caught her so clearly enjoying the breakfast. She didn't return his smile. "Trying to figure out how to make my brother less pissed at me, maybe. Or apartment hunting? They kind of go hand in hand."

"Why is he pissed at you?"

"Let's just say he didn't find *pre-mortem thinking* to be the best motivation for a baby gift."

Henry's eyebrows shot up. "What was the gift?"

She sighed. "A top-of-the-line baby monitor. But it had SIDS detection features that he thought were a little *over*-the-top."

He shrugged. "Sounds like a pretty generous gift to me. And not a cheap one, either."

"Of course it sounds okay to *you*. You're the one who gave me the advice."

She expected him to step back, but instead he approached the desk, concern softening his features. "I don't remember you asking me what you should buy your brother and his wife. In fact, I haven't heard much from you this week. I thought we had a nice time Monday. . . ."

"You know what I mean. Maybe pilot's training *doesn't* translate to life."

"You can't be blaming me because your brother is mad at you?"

Her eyes dropped to the cinnamon roll, which seemed to have deflated. Sometimes that happened. You took a bite, it seemed good at first, but then the appeal just kind of leaked out. It didn't have to be anyone's fault. She knew it was hers as much as his.

"I'm not blaming anyone," she said, though her tone did sound sort of accidentally angry. "I just think—I'm not really in a good place right now. So the place that I'm in, I should probably just occupy it by myself for a while. Until I figure out how to get to a better one."

He let silence fill the room for what seemed an eternity before he spoke. "I'm always in transit," he said finally. "It's not often I meet someone who so instantly makes me want to stay where I am. So it must not be *that* bad of a place. Not when all I can think about is being there."

She knew what he meant—getting him off her mind had been surprisingly difficult from the start, so much so that she *might* have subconsciously, foolishly taken this job because of him—and yet she didn't want to. Why couldn't he just get mad right back, like everybody else? Why did he have to be so—well, so *Henry*?

"Please just give me a little space," she said, her voice barely audible even to her own ears.

"Liza—"

"I have to get to work. The kitchen staff will be here soon. I haven't done a single useful thing since I got here."

The last sentence landed with a thud as she turned to open the safe. As if it had been some great inconvenience to pause her morning to accept a gift, to thank the person who gave it to her, to chat with him just long enough to send things between them south. Her bad mood had much more to do with Luke and even Molly than with him, and she regretted her tone immediately.

But when she turned back, he was gone.

—

Liza shifted her weight from one foot to the next at the base of the dock, wondering how long this was going to take. And also, what she was really doing here, on the side of a lake, waiting for a silent little girl to speak. Molly had briefed her on Rosie's situation and on how she and Nori had been helping, but none of it quite explained why she'd brought Liza here rather than to a free introductory meditation class.

"Nothing after the intro presentation is cheap," Molly had warned. "I'm not saying it isn't worth it, but in your situation, with so many other expenses coming? Just come along to this first. Something about it restores my faith in—in faith, I guess. It'll lend perspective, at the very least."

But Liza didn't lack perspective; her new eyes-wide-open view of the world seemed to be the very source of the problem. And Molly hadn't told her enough, clearly, about Rick. Now that Liza was here, at the edge of this odd dock that forked in three directions, she especially didn't want to be. Sharing space with Molly and Rick made her feel as if she was intruding on a private moment. Even though they'd invited her. Even though the children were here, huddled obediently in the center of the dock, contemplating their options with the seriousness of adults.

"Boat ride," Molly said for the third time, pointing to the first end of the dock, where a rowboat was tied. "Feed the turtles," she said again, pointing to the food pellets piled on the middle prong. "Explorer packs." On the third arm of the dock were backpacks filled with binoculars, magnifying glasses, bug jars, the works. "Which will be our adventure today?"

Rosie did not look at Liza, but the child was obviously hyperaware of her presence even as she watched a pair of mallard ducks swim by.

When she still didn't answer, Molly's face broke into a reassuring smile. "Take your time, sweetheart. We'll wait until you decide." She perched nonchalantly on the edge of a nearby bench, and Rick settled in the middle, gesturing for Liza to join them. She tried not to look sullen as she landed as far from him as the seat would allow and crossed her ankles beneath her. On the dock in front of them, Nori whispered something into Rosie's ear and the two of them sank to the wooden planks, cross-legged. None of them seemed to be in a hurry to proceed.

"I was so sorry to hear about what brought you back to town," Rick said quietly. "Do they know what caused the fire yet?"

Liza shook her head. "Did you say you were a contractor?"

"I did." Not her favorite profession at the moment. She straightened her spine.

"Well, there were initial reports that this contractor was negligent."

He cringed. "So Molly said. There were fatalities, right?" She looked down at her lap, and he sighed. "In an old building like that . . . I hope it was just a freak accident."

Liza didn't raise her eyes. "Is it weird that I almost don't hope that? I almost want someone to be held responsible. I don't like the idea of life or death being a dumb-luck thing."

"Even if someone was at fault, it'd still be dumb luck for everyone else," he said.

"I guess that's true." She shuddered again. "I can't stop thinking about it. Not the fire, exactly, but the odds of it happening the way it did." As usual, she'd said too much. She braced herself for him to ask what she meant. As far as she knew, Molly hadn't put the timing together with Liza's fated through-the-night drive, which was fine by her. She didn't want to give her the satisfaction of being *glad* about the silver lining.

On the other side of Rick, Molly had inched closer, ostensibly to lean across him to hear Liza. But Molly's eyes were on the girls, watching to see what they'd do when they thought no one was paying attention, and the small space between her and Rick seemed intimate in a way that made Liza uneasy.

"I remember when we brought Rosie home from the hospital," Rick was telling her. "It was snowing, and there was this orderly on the night shift who took a liking to us in the maternity ward. We were there a few days longer than normal—we didn't know about the cancer yet, but we did know something wasn't right—and she'd been sneaking me meals even though I wasn't a patient. The last night, when she knew we were about to be discharged into the storm, she gave us a string of beads. Said they'd been hanging from her rearview mirror during *two* collisions that should have been fatal. Said they would keep us safe, bring us luck."

The story was oddly moving. Maybe Rick had that sense of intimacy with everyone he met, not just Molly. Maybe something about him made people want to get close, want to help.

Maybe.

"Did you feel like they worked?" she asked.

He gave her a guilty half smile. "We never hung them," he admitted. "She was in more than one near-fatal car crash with those things. She believed they were good luck because she survived, but what if they were *bad* luck because she had the crashes in the first place? That's the thing about luck. It's flimsy."

At the other end of the bench, Molly had turned her intent gaze on Rick. "Do you ever think maybe you should have hung them?" she asked. Her voice held curiosity without judgment. A pitch-perfect strumming of that hard-to-reach chord had always been one of Molly's best qualities.

"All the time," Rick said.

Liza was the first to notice Rosie approaching them. She wasn't finding the girl particularly inspiring thus far, but she did relate—uncomfortably strongly—to her reluctance to make a choice. The girl shot her a nervous glance, then ran and buried her head in her dad's lap.

"Nori wants to do the turtles," came the tiny, muffled voice.

Molly had described this moment as one that was nearly impossible *not* to cheer for, but Liza was too distracted by the way Molly was nudging Rick, by the way he extended the fondness in his eyes from his daughter straight over to Molly in such an unguarded way that he must not even realize he was doing it. Molly didn't seem to know he was doing it, either. She was biting back her own smile, lowering her head to Rosie's.

"It's not Nori's turn to pick," Molly said gently. "What do *you* want to do?"

The girl turned her face just out of his pant leg to meet Molly's eye, then nodded once. "Turtles," she whispered.

"I love how you told us that. Turtles it is!" Molly got to her feet and led Rosie by the hand out to the dock, turning to flash Liza and Rick a thumbs-up.

"It probably doesn't seem like a big deal," Rick said, not looking at her. "But she hasn't talked in front of a stranger since—well, maybe ever. Thanks for coming."

This exercise was clearly everything to him—it wasn't an act, or an excuse to get close to Molly, or a front for something else between them. Liza could see all of that had happened by accident. It was understandable, she had to admit, how he would have fallen for her friend along the way. She saw, too, that he knew the depths he'd stepped into, but that this revelation was relatively new. His gaze at Molly was weighed down with wistfulness but also a sort of shock, a justified alarm. Regret, too.

Molly's, meanwhile, held a willful denial. Maybe even negligence for the effect this could have on him even as she leaned into it, a crutch to prop up the less happy moments in her own life, something to get her by until she sorted things out on her own.

"You're welcome," Liza told Rick. For a moment, she felt nothing but sorry for him.

27

"EVER NOTICE HOW YOUR BODY CAN ONLY FOCUS ON ONE PAIN AT A TIME?" Molly knew she was rambling but couldn't stop. Now that Rick had taken the girls and left the two women to follow the trail around the lake, Liza seemed unnaturally tight lipped, as if withholding some sort of judgment. And so it fell to Molly to withhold Liza.

"Whatever hurts worst at the moment kind of fills up your brain," she went on. "You trip over something hard, and right away your foot hurts where you hit it. Then a few minutes later, once that subsides, you realize you've twisted your ankle pretty good, too. And once you've iced that, you're walking up the stairs and notice your knee is also popping. They're not happening one after the other, but you experience them that way, like your body thinks it would be too much for you otherwise." She risked a sidelong glance at her friend as they made their way across a wooden footbridge. Liza was peering over the rail at the muddy rut left by heavy rains.

"Never really thought about it," Liza said.

"I envy you. But actually, I think it's been kind of like that with what you've had going on. You know, maybe in Chicago . . ." Liza obviously hadn't been moved by Rosie's efforts earlier. Molly had to make *something* about this outing resonate, lest the conversation turn back to the meditation center. Or, worse, lest Liza beg off and never call her again. "Sometimes you'd feel homesick for Cincinnati. And then, other times you'd be down on dating, or your boss taking you for granted. One small pain at a time when really they were all at once. And even though some of those resolved when you came back, a whole new set has been thrown at you. It'll take a while to cycle through, have a look at everything you're dealing with."

"Gee," Liza said flatly. "How comforting."

"I never said it was comforting," Molly replied, frowning. "But a near-death experience can be pretty profound."

Liza sighed. "Let's not pretend I've been impacted in any *meaningful* way. I haven't changed careers to become an ER nurse. I'm not volunteering my time to help put fire and flood victims in new homes. If I am enlightened, it hasn't made me noble. It's only made me neurotic."

"You're not starring in a movie about rising from the ashes, Liza. You're just living your life. Sometimes that's the most noble thing a person can do, especially on her own terms. Nobody's looking for more from you. No one's expecting a hero or a miracle. We just want for you to be okay."

"And what's your movie about?"

"What?"

"The one *you* are starring in. What's it about?"

Molly brushed her hair back from her face, uneasy. "I guess I'm still figuring that out."

"Let me help. You thought it was *Rick* in the mask that night, didn't you? Max was on the right track with his kinky-affair jokes, only it wasn't Daniel. It was *you.*"

Molly stopped walking. She shook her head.

"Come on, Mols. That explains a lot. Not everything, but a lot."

Liza's eyes bored into hers, and she saw there was no point in denying it. Had there ever been? Molly never had the upper hand—not with Daniel, Liza, or anyone else she could think of. "But it wasn't Rick," she said, giving in. "He says it wasn't him, and I believe him."

Liza didn't react, only tilted her head. "Are you having an affair?"

Tears sprung to Molly's eyes. The way Liza was looking at her . . . "No. I might have come close, and I'm not proud of it. But we're only friends."

"You might want to tell Rick that," she shot back. "He's the one who's going to get hurt here. Don't you think the guy has been through enough?"

Over Liza's shoulder, a smear of color caught Molly's eye: a chalked design on an ancient tree trunk as wide as her arm span. It might have passed for the doodle of a free spirit, perhaps a tribal-looking sun, but Molly would know that spiral anywhere.

She knew its deceptive comfort from the contract she'd signed bearing its name. And she knew its desperation, from every mounting bill she had yet to pay. Its outer rim of arrows mocked her, relentlessly, a ring of fire disguised as an emergency exit.

She pushed past Liza, trancelike, to the tree, and touched the chalk with a tentative finger. The bright blue came off easily on her fingertip; it had to be fresh, as it had rained all morning, and it wouldn't last long, as the forecast held more. Someone had intended for her to see it *now*.

"Molly? Are we not *finally* having a real conversation?" She whirled not toward Liza, but away, panning beneath the canopy of the trees, searching for the mark's maker. But everything these people did seemed so carefully untraceable—leaving Molly to question whether she had really experienced it at all, until another sign appeared. Or until, as now at last, she had a witness.

Not unlike her pain itself.

She turned in a slow circle, and another blur of color caught her eye. More chalk, at the bend ahead; bright yellow this time. She began to move toward it, picking up speed as her panic grew.

"What are you *doing*?" Liza called.

She didn't answer. The symbol was repeated here, this time with two words under it: *Try harder.*

She pushed ahead, catching sight of another, leaving Liza behind. They'd chosen only the trunks that were too big to miss, too centered in any walker's line of vision to overlook. This one was an electric orange and said simply: *Find a way.*

At that, she had to laugh. They were supposed to *be* the way. *Your Way Back* Financial. Clearly the *YWBF* stood for something else. You're Way Beyond Fucked.

Or maybe: You Will Be Found.

Someone was coming, up ahead, straight toward her—but it was only a pair of spry-looking elderly bird watchers. One saw her looking at the mark and smiled. "They're all around," she said. "Some new age hiking group or something?"

"I'm all for motivation, but it's a little heavy on the tough love for my taste," her companion said, chuckling. Molly tried to smile, but she felt dizzy, outside of herself. She stood aside to let them pass, and by the time they did, Liza had caught up and was turning her by the shoulder.

"Molly!" The impatience drained from her expression at the sight of Molly's tears, just spilling over. "What is it? You're freaking me out."

She took a shaky breath, lifting her eyes to the branches above, away from the symbols, the spinning trees, the muddy ground. "I'm in way over my head," she managed. It came out as a whimper.

"With Rick?"

"No. I mean, maybe. But—" The tears kept coming. She was so tired. Tired of being afraid, of everything. Tired of deceiving herself into thinking everything would somehow be fine. Tired of feeling alone.

"The money problems you mentioned?" Liza supplied.

She nodded, swallowing hard. "It isn't ordinary debt. I accepted help from . . . some *alternative* methods. They've been here today." She pointed at the chalk. "And they've been here before."

Liza's eyes widened. "And at your house? That night?"

The sobs were coming harder now. They'd been pent up too long.

She could barely get the words out. "I really didn't think so. I didn't want to believe . . . I still don't know for sure."

Liza looked skeptical. "What kind of alternative methods? Have you been gambling?"

"Nothing like that. I thought it was this small loan company for people with medical expenses like mine. But it was a scam." She gestured at the trunk in front of them. "This is their logo. These messages are for me. Though for all I know they have other clients here, too."

"They're *threatening* you? You need to call the police."

She shook her head quickly, sniffing hard. She had to pull herself together, or Liza would take control. She didn't want to relinquish what few decisions she had left. She searched her jacket pockets for an old tissue, a napkin, anything, but came up empty. "I don't know that they are. No overt threats about my safety, anything like that. They just want their money. Which, in fairness, I do owe. I signed a contract."

Liza looked from one chalked symbol to the next, then back at Molly. "I don't know, Mols. This seems crazy creepy to me."

Well, she was right about that. And in the one place Molly had always felt unafraid. She officially had no safe harbor left. Not Daniel, not Rick and Rosie, not these woods, not even Liza. She could tell from the look on her friend's face that this predicament wasn't tugging at her sympathetic heartstrings. If anything, it would make her glad she already had a grudge of an excuse to maintain a safe perimeter. And who could blame her?

Still. Holding back had gotten Molly nowhere. Nowhere but here.

"I don't know if these people were behind the intruder, but I am more and more convinced it wasn't random," she ventured. "There are too many other options."

Liza threw up her hands. "More than this one?"

She nodded. "There's something underhanded going on at Daniel's work, too. I think he found out, and—I don't know." If only her visit to Toby had yielded any peace of mind at all. She'd only felt more on edge ever since. Unsure what to believe.

Liza pulled a face. "Well, I highly doubt they hired a thug. It's the nontoxic furnishings business, for crying out loud."

"But it could have been this guy he's caught on to. I actually saw him in our neighborhood, and . . ." She stopped short. She sounded crazy. "All I know is someone was either trying to scare Daniel or trying to scare me. Either way, it worked." She gestured toward the trees. "I know I have to make this right, but I've been caught up like an idiot in damage control. I'm so embarrassed. And I'm terrified they'll be back. Whoever *they* are."

"*Nonthreatening* lenders don't follow people into the woods and chalk messages on trees," Liza persisted. "Where did you find these people?" She fished a pocket-sized pack of tissues out of her jacket and handed it over. Molly took one gratefully and pressed it to her face.

"They found me. Outside the meditation center. That's why I didn't want to take you. They *lurk* there, looking for easy prey. I don't know what they'll do if they see me. And I don't want them to see you, either, because—"

Terror gripped her, abrupt and hard. "Liza. Oh my God, your apartment fire. You don't think he somehow knew who you were and came after you, too? Because you saw him on the webcam?" She lifted a shaky hand to her mouth, feeling the blood drain from her face. She really might faint. "Oh, God . . ."

"No! Molly, no. It's not possible." Liza had her by the shoulders again. "The fire was the same night. Do you hear me?"

Confusion clouded Molly's watery view. "The same night?"

She nodded. "While I was driving to check on you. Unless he time traveled somehow to Chicago, you can rule that one out."

Molly pulled away. "There *is* a flight that gets you to Chicago in an hour, though! Daniel took it for work—he *said* it was like time travel. Those were his exact words." She stepped back, fully engrossed in the horror. "Oh my God. *Toby* has taken that flight. . . . That might mean—"

Liza held up a hand. "Molly, I don't know who Toby is, but that Chicago shuttle doesn't fly late at night."

"How do you know?"

"I work at Lunken, remember?"

"You might not know all the schedules."

"Mols, I'm dating that shuttle's pilot. Or I was."

Dating a pilot? Since when? Molly knew next to nothing about Liza's life since her return, and all because Molly was too much of a coward to explain herself. She'd never been so ashamed, about so many things.

"Hey," Liza said more gently. "You're really scared, aren't you? What does Daniel think?"

Molly pulled another tissue from the pack. "Just what he told you at dinner. That you saved us from an entirely random intruder. No reason for future concern."

"He's your *husband*. What happened between you two that you can't talk to him about something like *this*?"

"He will never forgive me this," Molly said.

"You don't know that. And I'm not seeing other options here. You can't go on this way."

She shook her head, knowing Liza was right but unable to imagine any outcome that was better. She'd be less afraid, maybe, but more alone than ever. "I told you, there's a wall."

"Well, the Molly I know can't be stopped by a little wall."

She laughed weakly. Guilt *had* been chipping away at her fortress ever since she'd declined Daniel's overture of the retreat, but she had so many things to feel guilty about, it was getting hard to separate one from the next.

"Can *you* forgive me?" she asked. It was one of many things she'd have been better off asking sooner. Much sooner. "I know I don't deserve it. I never should have treated you the way I did. It wasn't about you, and it wasn't fair to you. I just—panicked."

Liza looked away. She didn't have to say that she wasn't sure she could, that she wasn't sure she wanted to. She was never one to mask her feelings, and Molly could read them as if they were her own.

In fact, they *had* been her own—toward Daniel. But never toward Liza.

"I'm trying to figure out how to sell this to Luke," Liza said finally. A conspicuous non-answer. And perhaps an apt subject change. Luke had never liked Molly—had always seen her for what she was. A pathetic excuse for a friend. "I promised him I'd go to that meditation class with you. Which is obviously not happening. But it was either that or see a therapist. And I'm not sure this Rosie thing counts as therapeutic. No offense."

A therapist? Luke wasn't a touchy-feely sort. He must be convinced that Liza needed help. Significantly. So much of their limited time together, since Liza's return, had been focused on wading through Molly's debris field. No wonder her friend was reluctant to bury bygones. Molly was lucky Liza was standing here at all, bothering to change the subject, putting off hurting her feelings. She cleared the lump from her throat, trying to keep her voice neutral. "Well, if you want to find the least-offensive-to-you self-help option available, I'm your girl. Ask me anything—I've tried it all."

"You know, maybe that's the problem. Maybe it's like . . . well, I have this new beef with news headlines. I've been rewriting them—just for myself. Trying to make them more honest."

"How do you mean?"

"To be less about what happened, and more about who it happened to—and why, I guess. Ever since the fire . . . it bothers me that we get the facts, but not the humanity behind them."

Hmmm. This might explain Luke's concern. But Molly wasn't in a position to judge.

"Maybe it's the same with the self-help stuff. It's spelled out for you, and it might seem cut-and-dry, but that stuff works differently for everyone. And if you take it all as gospel, maybe you're sending yourself the message that if you've read all the relevant books and articles and you're still unwell, it's *your* fault."

"It *is* my fault."

Liza shook her head. "Maybe this debt is your fault, maybe this line you're teetering on with Rick is your fault, but your pain isn't your fault. And how your husband has reacted? I don't doubt he's given you a few hard shoves toward Rick, or toward the next fix, or whatever. I'm not saying you don't bear any responsibility, but you can't blame yourself for everything."

If only. "You've *never* liked self-help. You once told me it felt 'oppressive.'"

"Well, you haven't proven me wrong."

Maybe Molly *was* putting too much emphasis on the *self* part. She could only have gotten in this deep without someone else to snap her out of it. She managed a smile.

"If I have to lay off the self-analysis, then so do you."

"Mine's different."

"Is it? I've become an expert at *not* thinking through consequences—self-delusion all the way. But you've convinced yourself every decision you make is life-or-death. No wonder you're feeling so anxious."

A beat of something like understanding passed between them. "One pain at a time," Liza said softly. "Like you said. You deal with one at a time, but you deal. Okay? And I will, too."

Hearing Liza say the words made it seem doable, possible, if only Liza would still be there, by her side.

But she still hadn't answered that part. And Molly knew better than to ask again.

28

ONE DAY TO GO UNTIL THE BIG-DEAL MEETING WITH THE BIG-HEADED SUITS, and Daniel's budget presentation had never been so . . . creative.

Damn it. On top of everything, now he was borrowing Toby's word.

The math was all there, and everyone knew numbers didn't lie. It reflected twelve solid fiscal months of widespread profits dwarfing spotty losses and forecasted an even better year ahead: streamlined expenses without a reduction in staff, and acquisition-driven growth that had remarkably little blowback on existing resources. A whole desktop folder full of meticulously zipped-up spreadsheets, and there was no reason to be nervous about a thing in any of them. He'd never seen the company in such a safe, healthy place—an anomaly in today's corporate climate, an executive board's dream. If they were to request a change, it should be to add a little something extra for his troubles. That's how good it looked. That's how lucky the employees were.

The creativity, of course, was in what it did *not* reflect. The transgressions in HR were buried—down to the travel expenses that had first drawn Daniel's attention. The omissions were too small to be line items unless someone requested a closer look, which wouldn't happen, as they were for things that weren't supposed to have transpired. And the fact that employee deductions didn't add up as they should? The bogus fees that made the provider a bad deal all the way around? Well, that information didn't get reviewed at this level. That's how unlucky the employees were.

Still, he needed this day, all eight, nine, or ten hours of it, and the rest of the office knew not to disturb him, the star of tomorrow's show. Ostensibly he was looking it all over once more. In actuality he was sitting with what he was about to do. It wasn't his first point of no return in recent memory, and the others hadn't gone particularly well. He needed this to be different.

The call buzzed through on his desk line, and as soon as he picked it up Daniel knew this could not be good news: Liza, of all people, calling him at work, of all places.

Was this a bad time? she wanted to know. It was a horrible time, but he wasn't about to put her off without finding out what she had to say. And he could always count on Liza to get right to the point. Which she did.

"I'm worried about Molly."

He'd once had a boss who'd respond *Welcome to my world!* when anyone dared voice a complaint—in blatant negligence of the reality that his "world" was largely daisies and rainbows, thanks to his long-suffering support staff. Daniel had come to loathe the phrase, and yet it was what leaped to his mind now: *Welcome to my world.* He resisted the urge to say it aloud.

Molly's rejection of his retreat idea had felt like a final attempt failed, in part because, while the invitation hadn't been insincere—far from it—it had also been a test. He'd been hoping she'd turn to him with the status of her pain, tallying its figurative *and* literal costs. But not only had Molly *not* come clean, she'd turned somewhere far darker. It threw him, the way she dismissed the idea, along with all her other attempts, with a simple *I've been doing it wrong,* as if it were out of her hands, no longer a problem worth fixing. An alarming category she seemed on the verge of lumping their marriage into while she was at it.

And her accusations—they hurt, in part because she was right. Not about every single thing she said, but about too much of it. He hadn't brought up the retreat since. In spite of the fact that the thing was prepaid, he had no idea if they were going.

"I don't understand why she's not telling you this herself," Liza went on, "and I don't like betraying a confidence. But Daniel, she's *scared.* She thinks that intruder was someone who's out to get her. She's terrified they'll be back."

Well now, hang on a second. He'd been bracing himself to hear that Molly wasn't herself anymore, that she seemed weary, exhausted, defeated. But terrified?

"You're sure? I didn't even think this was still on her mind. You heard her at dinner. A random thing. Bullet dodged."

"She doesn't really believe that," Liza said. "Do you?"

This was uncomfortably direct. "Well, I don't have any other theories," he said, trying to sound unbothered, if perplexed. So Molly didn't believe the intruder was Rick after all. Or, more likely, she didn't believe it *anymore*—Rick had convinced her otherwise. Either way, she was still hanging out with the guy. Nori had mentioned Rosie just yesterday.

"That makes one of you," Liza said. "You're not involved in anything that might have put you both at risk? At work, maybe?" There wasn't real conviction behind the question, but still it put him on edge. It implied Molly had alluded to the possibility.

"Of course not," he said, even as his palms grew clammy at the thought of who else Molly might have mentioned it to. "That's ridiculous."

"Well, Molly doesn't think so. She's freaked out," Liza said. "And that freaks *me* out. You can't let on that I called you about this, but you need to find a way to bring it up with her."

"I—"

"If there's any truth at all to what she's afraid of, she shouldn't be facing it alone. But I don't know how to help. I think you're the only one who can do that."

He was nodding, slowly, into the empty room, an action no more futile than anything else he'd done in recent memory. This week marked a month since the incident, a month of failing to correct their course. His nudges, his overtures, his tiptoed dances around things no one wanted to say—all of it had amounted to nothing.

"Thanks for the call," he said, all business. It was an unnatural tact to take with someone who had once climbed through their apartment window without so much as a knock every weekend morning. But so much had changed. "I'll look into it."

Left to the silence of his office, he stared unseeing at his computer screen and categorized the cause and effect in the Molly spreadsheet of his mind.

Rick might not be the only thing Daniel had missed. Something else might have spooked her. Toby? In spite of the unsettling but explained-away sighting on their street, Daniel couldn't work out a reason his adversary would breach their deal and approach Molly. Toby was getting what he wanted, after all.

Daniel, however, was not.

It was time to do what he should have done in the first place. In more ways than one.

29

THE CONGESTION AT THE STARTING LINE—PEOPLE SECURING THEIR NUMbers with pins, double-knotting their shoes, stretching their hamstrings, high-fiving their partners—was almost enough to mask Molly's mounting panic.

Almost.

Why had she thought she could do this?

Long before any real kind of pain ever gripped her, she'd dreaded the timed mile runs in phys ed. She was an active enough student, with ballet and biking, to think of herself as healthy, even fit, but running seemed to require a set of skills her body was programmed to reject. Her breath would too quickly become shallow. Her sides would clench into stitches, bending her at odd angles. Her shins would splint no matter how diligently she walked on her heels before or after. She'd manage to finish, but inevitably among the stragglers, and never without collapsing like a gasping fish on the other side of the stopwatch.

She'd been so much younger then. And that had only been one mile. People talked about 5Ks as if they were short jaunts, so she'd been more shocked than she should've been to look up the distance conversion and find she'd agreed to run 3.1 miles. Three times as far as those miserable gym classes back when she'd been *at least* three times more in shape.

Grant was punching the air next to her Rocky Balboa style, jumping on his tiptoes like a slingshot ready to release. School had let out a half hour ago, and the midafternoon heat was intensified here on the blacktop of the bus lot. He was wearing a kindergarten class T-shirt the PTO peddled for monthly "spirit days," color blocked in the school's signature orange. To match she'd worn the only orange shirt in her closet, a Bengals tee Daniel had gifted her one Christmas in spite of her disdain for the NFL. If gifts could talk, most of the ones she'd received from her husband would have purred *If you can't beat 'em, join 'em.* Daniel hated that expression—he had a tendency to be personally affronted by idioms, especially at work—so why he'd foist the intent behind it upon her was a mystery best left unexplored.

Grant beamed at her. "Okay, Mom, so the plan is for *me* to match *your* pace," he said importantly. He'd been spouting recommendations from his after-school club for days. *There will be water stations and we shouldn't skip them, even if we don't feel thirsty. We should not wear new shoes in case they give us blisters. Even though it's a race, we shouldn't worry about winning, only about finishing.* The last part was no comfort. Winning was obviously out of the question, but she'd started to worry Grant didn't see it that way. "Our time doesn't get recorded until our slowest runner crosses the line." This, too, she'd heard no fewer than a dozen times, and every time, her heart sank lower. If she didn't finish, Grant wouldn't get credit. And though he'd first received her offer to run the race with an appropriate amount of skepticism, somewhere along the line he'd convinced himself that she could do it. While her own doubts had grown, his had been absorbed by youthful enthusiasm. If she disappointed him, what would that do to his ability to keep faith in any unlikely thing?

What would it do to his faith in her?

"Got it," she said, bending again to touch her toes. Shades of orange swirled around her, and she felt suddenly light-headed. Her airway was dry, but there was no water station here and wouldn't be for the first mile. This was a terrible mistake. She straightened and searched the spectators for Rick, who was holding Rosie in one arm and Nori in the other. The girls pointed and waved, but Rick's expression mirrored her own. He hadn't tried to talk her out of this, but nor did he share Grant's belief that she'd wished her way into a vastly improved human vessel overnight.

She had to find a way out, a way that would save face for her and Grant both. Something that had nothing to do with being weak, that might occur through no fault of her own. She scanned the sidelines for options and saw nothing more promising than a golf cart manned by volunteers. If she were to maneuver in front of it, then stumble . . .

No. This was ridiculous. She had only two options: go through with it, somehow, or tell Grant now that she couldn't. Yet true to form, it seemed she could do neither of those things. She could only stand rooted, about to humiliate herself and her son in front of his entire school. The heat filled her lungs and threatened to explode. She wondered what hyperventilation felt like, even as she told herself to stay calm, that panic would only beget panic, just as doubt would only beget doubt, and pain would only beget pain.

Easy. She hated this damn mantra. She needed a new one, but it was all she had. *Easy.* A hand clapped her on the back, and she turned.

The stranger who'd confronted her in the nature center parking lot was dressed exactly as he had been that day—as if this time it was more important to be sure she recognized him than it was to blend with his surroundings. He tipped his Panama hat and flashed an icy smile, his fingers curling around his binoculars as he leaned closer. The panic that had already begun to grip her squeezed harder.

"You know what they say about how you can run but not hide," he chided, giving her a wink. "It's wonderful to see you healed enough to attempt the running part. But the latter half would be unwise to try."

Grant was dancing around again, oblivious, so close to this horrible man—too close. Molly wanted to wrap her son in the protection of her arms and fight her way through the waiting racers, to get away, but what if there was still some chance the man didn't know which child was hers? She didn't dare point Grant out with so much as a glance, just in case. She was unable to move anyway, frozen in her terror.

One pain at a time, she and Liza had decided. Molly's calendar mandated that the race be the one she dealt with first. But what if she'd already dragged her feet too long?

"Final warning to pay up," the man said, his voice an eerily pleasant singsong.

"What if I can't?" Her words were a low rasp. She should have asked the first time he'd appeared. But the vagueness of his warning had, somehow, allowed her to slip back into her denial, uncomfortable though it was.

"Well, we don't bust up knees." He gestured toward her copper sleeve–wrapped legs, and chuckled. "Though maybe you're wishing I would." He took a step closer, his voice lower still. "We're more about taking *temporary* custody of something of value. A vehicle, perhaps—though we'd need more than one in your case. Of course, sometimes it's the things that have *no* monetary value that are the greatest motivators."

There was a flurry of motion at her side, and she looked down with horror to see Grant looking up at her expectantly. Before she could sweep him out of view, the man dropped a firm palm onto the top of his head and left it there. "Good luck with your race today, son," he said warmly.

"Thanks!" Grant replied.

The last of Molly's denial disintegrated, too late.

"Good luck to you, too," he told Molly, winking again. "I expect we'll be hearing from you soon. Say, within the week?" Just like that, he turned and began weaving his way through the crowd. She watched the top of his hat bob until she couldn't see it anymore. She risked a glance over at Rick, but his attention was on the girls. Somehow, no one had seen.

She might still be safe. They *all* might be safe. For now.

But only for now.

Grant had thought nothing of the encounter, was giggling with a friend who'd called his name. She looked down at her body, becoming aware of the adrenaline coursing through her veins, the primal fight-or-flight curling itself into every muscle. And her next thought, bizarrely, was not that she no longer had a choice but to come clean to Daniel, to pay her debts by *any* means necessary, to stand guard in the meantime. None of that was going away—*final warning, custody, motivators*—but it could wait for her at the finish line.

Because what she *actually* thought next was that maybe she could run this thing after all. Maybe, the sheer fear could fuel her.

Either that, or it would lay her flat right here.

"Looking good, you two!"

The voice came from behind, familiar and strong, and she turned to see Daniel, clad in a matching Bengals T-shirt, black shorts, and even, to her surprise, copper knee sleeves. Pinned to his chest was a white square with the number 176 on it. Identical to hers and Grant's.

"Dad!" Grant cried. "What are you doing here?"

When Daniel grinned this broadly, he and Grant looked an awful lot alike. The shock of it reminded her how seldom Daniel smiled anymore with such abandon. "Turns out my budget meeting wasn't unskippable after all."

Grant let out a whoop and hopped over to a set of twins from his class, who were bookending their hulk of a father. "My dad is here, too!" Grant boasted. "My dad is here, too!"

"It wasn't?" Molly asked, still whirling in adrenaline, but not so fast as to mask her incredulity. "Really?"

"No, it totally was," Daniel admitted, his smile unwavering. "But all of a sudden it seemed like this was, too. So I made a choice."

He stepped closer to Molly and leaned into her ear. She skimmed the crowd over his shoulder once more, but there was no sign of the hat. Daniel had come at the perfect time—not too soon and not too late.

She breathed him in, steadying herself. *Not too late.*

"Listen," he said. "I'm not trying to step on your toes. I just didn't want you to feel alone. I know how much you don't want to disappoint Grant." She nodded, still looking out at the crowd. *It's okay. He's really gone.* She took another deep breath, another. "We can do this one of three ways," Daniel murmured, inching closer still. "I got someone on the phone earlier, explained we might have a health issue. They said they'll call us finished, for Grant's sake, if only two of us cross." She pulled back to look at him, surprised. "They just want to encourage the kids to do good for charity," he said. "It's not *American Ninja Warrior.*" She managed a laugh, and he splayed a reassuring hand across the small of her back. "So, option one, the two of you can run it, as planned, and I'll follow on the sidelines as an alternate, just in case you reach a point where you can't go on. Option two, all three of us run and if you decide to drop back or stop at some point, no worries. Option three, we plan it right now as a relay; Grant never knows anything more than the fact that we decided to take turns. Not because of you, but because of me. Because I joined the team at the last minute."

Tears filled her eyes as she nodded, her heart still pounding. "You knew. That I wouldn't be able to do it," she whispered.

"That's *not* why I'm here." He looked at her seriously. "I *know* you can do pretty much anything you want to do. But I also know that everything you've been dealing with is real. It's not necessarily something you can push through just because you want to. If you could, you would have by now. I'm sorry for acting like you just needed to suck it up. You *have* been. I want to help, whether that means taking your place or running at your side."

The tears spilled over, and she began, bizarrely, to laugh. She clutched at his elbows and touched her forehead to his as relief of all kinds washed over her.

He wiped at her cheeks with his thumbs and kissed her lightly on the mouth. "Which do you prefer?" he asked.

"I still want to try," she said. He peered at her as if searching for some sign that she was referring to something bigger than the race. She felt lighter just knowing he was there, even as the weight of her encounter and its implications hung over her.

Tomorrow. She'd confront that tomorrow, and not a day beyond.

But this, this one day, would *not* become about her or her mistakes or even, if she by some miracle managed to pull this off, her triumph. It would be about Grant. It would be about her family becoming a team again, even if for the last time.

"Notice you not trying wasn't one of the three options," Daniel pointed out, smiling. "Do you want me at your side, or do you want me to wait you out?"

Their eyes locked, and she knew—this *was* bigger than the race. After this, she'd have to tell him everything. She might lose him again, might lose it all. But in this moment . . .

"At my side," she said.

He slid his steady hand into hers, and she was finally ready.

30

LIZA WAS ENCASED IN LUKE AND STEPH'S GUEST ROOM, WHERE SHE'D spent the better part of the last week hiding from her hosts, pleading one excuse or another—a headache, a long day, a can't-put-it-down book. In truth she'd spent as much time staring aimlessly out the window as she had resisting the urge to analyze grim headlines—on that topic, at least, she was fairly certain Luke had been correct—and she lunged for the phone when it rang, grateful for company.

"Got a second?" Max asked.

"I have a lot of them," she replied. She was itching to tell him about the bizarre outing with Molly and her neighbor, the mysterious chalk trail, the call she'd placed to Daniel—though the guilt of that one was still nagging at her, in spite of her certainty that she'd done the right thing. Stronger was the worry that Molly's fears were founded, but Liza reasoned that she'd done all she could. Daniel would get involved, make things okay. Whatever happened from here was between Molly and Daniel. Liza had spent too much time in the middle as it was. "What's new?"

"Well, I think you might have inspired me."

She laughed. "Are you sure? I can't even inspire myself."

"Stop that," he said, and he wasn't returning her laugh. He was *scolding* her. Her smile faded. "You've been so down on yourself since the fire. Or since our disastrous drive-athon. I understand why, but it isn't you."

This was why she and Max had gotten on so well from the start. If one of them had something to say, they came out with it. She could hardly fault him for it now, when she was the one who'd lost that spark. "I'm sorry," she said automatically.

"See? Now you're apologizing. Why don't you tell me to—I don't know, *stop fucking judging you*?"

She squared her shoulders. "Stop *fucking judging me,* Max."

"Doesn't that feel better?"

She turned her eyes to the ceiling and shook her head, the corners of her mouth twitching. "Don't tell me how to feel."

"*There* you are." He laughed. "Anyway. Listen." He let out a deep breath—a *whew, here goes nothing*—and a hand's length of tension spread itself across the back of her neck. "I haven't been able to stop thinking about our talk when I was visiting. About your move. And me." She closed her eyes. She'd thought of it plenty, too, though she'd been trying to forget—the unpursued questions, the sudden precariousness of their status. *Friends don't follow friends.*

"Okay," she said slowly, bracing herself. It had been a good call not to tell him about Henry. If he was about to make her turn him down, he wouldn't confuse why. Not that Henry was a factor anymore. She'd seen to that, though she halfway wished she hadn't.

More than halfway, if she was honest. She missed him.

"I'm thinking about doing it," he announced. "Moving to San Francisco."

She blinked, reorienting herself in the conversation. "You're *what*?"

"Here's the thing: I shouldn't be this bereft here with you gone. It makes me realize how little else is tying me to Chicago. In fact, the biggest disadvantage I can think of to California is being a plane ride away from you instead of a drive away. And I can afford a ticket every few months."

"Wow. And your job—"

"They're willing to transfer me. It's a call away from being arranged."

"That's so . . . easy. They must love you as much as I do."

Why had she chosen the very words she'd been afraid that *he* was going to say? What Freudian bullshit was this? As soon as they were out, she was back in the kitchen on that night after Molly's dinner, holding her breath.

He cleared his throat. The pause that followed went on for a few seconds too long. "That call I mentioned? Standing between me and the move? This is it." The room tilted as she absorbed the words, bracing for their impact. He took an audible breath. "Can you give me any reason at all not to go?"

She closed her eyes, expecting the tilt to grow steeper, dizzying, but instead, when she opened them, she found the room had righted itself.

She could have given him a reason. But it wouldn't have been the right one.

"I can't," she said softly. She owed him more than that, though. "Did you—did you really want me to?"

"I'm not sure," he said, and he didn't seem upset. "I guess I just wanted to know. And now I do." He laughed, sounding almost proud of himself. Happy. Resolute. A relief filled her chest as the invisible hand on her neck loosened its grip.

"If my nickname is going to stay Cincinnati, do I get to call you Frisco?"

"I heard that term actually annoys the Friscans."

"Frisco it is." It was an odd combination, this relief and the sudden lump in her throat. "Seriously, Max? Good for you."

"Thanks, 'Nati. I'm not leaving without a good-bye party. In a month, right before I go. Say you'll come? Bring whoever and stay here if you want—just fair warning that most of my furniture will be on a truck. But hey, an empty living room will make for an epic dance party."

He'd drive that truck all the way across the country, set up a whole new life—one she'd hardly be part of. She knew how this would go, how it would escalate the trajectory she'd denied having set in motion by coming here. How they would slowly grow apart in spite of their best efforts, how one day their daily lives would be unfamiliar to each other in a way that would fill her heart with longing.

Molly, all over again.

Yet she'd still hold out hope that maybe things would be different somehow. Because that was what friends did. Significant others, sometimes, too. And if she and Max *ever* had a chance to find themselves back in the same city and to reclaim what they'd had? How sad and petty it would be for either of them to pass that up, no matter the reason.

"Wouldn't miss it," she said.

After they'd hung up, Liza's stomach rumbled, reminding her of the worst thing about hiding here: It was too far from the kitchen. To hell with it. She headed down in search of a snack.

Steph was at the table, eating chocolate peanut butter ice cream straight from the carton, and she brightened when Liza came in. "I'm just an ordinary pregnant cliché now," she said. "Isn't it great?"

Liza laughed. "Pretty great," she agreed.

Her sister-in-law raised a mischievous eyebrow. "Want to just grab a spoon? Luke's playing basketball at the rec center—he'll never know."

"Sold." Liza took one from the silverware drawer, joined Steph at the table, and helped herself to a big bite. "Mmm," she said, grabbing a napkin to wipe her chin. "And now I'm just an ordinary freeloader cliché."

"Nah," Steph said good-naturedly. She hesitated. "Though I *have* been wanting to get you alone." Liza peered into the carton and stabbed her spoon into the center of the thickest peanut butter ripple. She scooped it into her mouth before she could say anything stupid.

"I was vacuuming and I knocked over the bag under your bed. I hadn't seen it there, and when I hit it, the gift fell out. Luke told me why you hadn't given it to me."

"I'm sorry," Liza said, setting her spoon on the table with a metallic clink. "I guess I'm not very good at imagining what you might . . . I mean, I didn't think about—"

"Oh, please." Steph waved the words away with her spoon. "Luke told me because I was so geeked out, I went running into the bedroom to show him. He tried to break it to me that we weren't getting the present after all."

Liza squinted at her. "You mean, you like it?"

Steph's head bobbed enthusiastically. "It was the model my coworkers pitched in to buy my boss when she was pregnant. That thing is *deluxe*! And more money than you should have spent."

"I was just so happy for you guys and wanted to help celebrate. I never meant it the way Luke took it."

Steph sighed. "I set him straight. The thing is, all of this is new to your brother. He's been worried about me, and he's been worried about you, too, and, you know . . ." She grappled for the right words. "He doesn't know what he doesn't know, really," she said finally.

Liza shrugged, even as she bit back a laugh. "To be fair, he might have been right about me. Dealing with things wrong, I mean."

"Deal with things however you want to," Steph said, surprisingly firm. "Luke is always trying to tell me the right and wrong ways to cope. Like there's an appropriate amount of worry or sadness to allot to something. He means well, but he also needs to understand he doesn't get to decide that for anyone else. We respect his opinion, but we don't need his stamp of approval."

Liza gave Steph's forearm a grateful squeeze and picked up her spoon again. Steph had said *we* as if they were unquestionably in this together.

"I know I'm supposed to be leaning on my husband during this time, but I really like having a girlfriend here right now," Steph said. "I understand if you're ready to get your own place, but I hope you won't let any weirdness from Luke pressure you to."

Liza smiled. They'd put up with her for a month, in spite of everything. Where would she be without them? "I'm so grateful for both of you. And you don't have to apologize for my brother. The flip side is that he's kind of awesome, for worrying the way he does."

"So sweet and yet so clueless," Steph sighed.

Liza laughed, then winced. "It *might* run in the family. I think I was a little harsh on someone who meant well, too."

"Not the dashing pilot?"

"I'm afraid so."

"Thank goodness for second chances," Steph said, getting to her feet. She grabbed a bag of pretzels from the bread box, opened it noisily, and popped one in her mouth.

"What makes you so sure I'll get one?"

Steph plopped back into her chair with a grin. "Because he's a regular," she said simply. "And because, more often than we realize, people do."

—

It had been the kind of day Liza wanted to tell someone about before drifting off to tomorrow. She passed over her options—Max, Luke, Steph, Henry, all of whom knew some of what had happened but none of whom knew it all—and the urge to rehash the in-between started to subside. She thought again of Max moving so far away, and about second chances and how sure Steph seemed that they weren't as rare as people thought.

And then, she picked up the phone and called Molly. Not for any reason, really. Just to hear an old, familiar voice.

31

MOLLY WAS ON THE PHONE WITH LIZA, IN THE MIDST OF A REMARKABLY animated conversation for someone who was propped on the couch by virtue of a pyramid of pillows and ice packs. She was gushing, if Daniel was not mistaken, about him, though she should've been singing her own praises instead. The genuine smile she flashed as he entered the living room filled him with a reciprocal gush, that light-headed happiness far more common in early-stage romance than in slog-status marriages.

In other words, he'd finally gotten something right. But then again, so had she.

She'd finished the race as if carried by sheer will. In stride, the three of them had run the first three kilometers, walked the fourth, and resumed their jog for the final stretch. Daniel was just as proud of Grant as he was of Molly. When she could no longer run, the boy did *not* repeat his earlier admonition that races were not for walking but instead piped up with an "I was getting tired anyway, Mom!" and though it may have been true—his legs were so little to run so far, and he could see that plenty others were walking by then, too—Daniel and Molly had exchanged a wordless look at his grace. They had made this little person, and though neither of them had been at their best since he'd come along, they had made him kind. *That* was why his earlier words about his mother's lack of strength had cut them both so deep: because he hadn't meant anything malicious by them. He'd only believed them. And now he didn't.

Molly was paying for it now, though. The swelling in her knees was pronounced—hues of purple that reflected Daniel's shame at having ever, at any point, doubted her claims of discomfort—but she'd all but laughed it off, saying it was worth it. She still seemed delicate, beneath the laugh, but there was a resolve to her now. He supposed that for someone who'd been suffering largely in solitude, the support alone was an analgesic, and he finally understood how different things might have been all along, if only he'd listened.

If it was up to him, and he hoped it was, he'd be doing more of that from now on.

She hadn't asked again about how he'd gotten out of the presentation, which was just as well, and as he crossed to the closet for his coat he bargained that she wouldn't ask where he was going now, either. They often took turns running simple errands after the kids were asleep—getting gas, a prescription, a few groceries—extolling the benefits of not dealing with the whining of kids in tow, or with crowds, while keeping mum on the added bonus of avoiding alone time with each other. He hoped they wouldn't be needing that avoidance strategy again, at least not on a regular basis. This particular errand would help see to that. He gave her a nonchalant wave, and though she looked about to call him back, she instead raised a silent hand in return, giving in to a laugh at something Liza said, and he slipped out, one step closer to home free.

Rick answered the door looking impressively more haggard than he had on the sidelines that afternoon—unshaven, with the button-up job on his lumberjack flannel misaligned so that one side hung lower than the other. He looked surprised to see Daniel, guardedly so, until Daniel offered back his book and saw a disproportionate relief wash across his face.

"Oh, you didn't have to go out of your way to return that." Rick took it into his hands with an odd reluctance. "But thanks. Was it helpful at all?"

Daniel nodded. "Very. Got a minute?"

Rick gestured for him to enter. The living room was a mess, the cushions pulled off the couches and piled in the center of the floor beneath a mound of blankets. Stuffed animals and doll clothes were strung through the room, and an empty rocks glass was sweating onto a cocktail napkin atop the piano. "I'd offer you a seat, but Rosie was really into fort building today," he said, perching on the edge of the piano bench. "I'm under strict instructions not to take it down." A gold metallic light illuminated the sheet music open on the tray, and his eyes shone glassy in the adjacent shadows. Daniel wondered how many drinks he'd had and whether they might work in his own favor or against it.

"I'll stand," he said.

"Some race, huh? You're probably beat." Daniel nodded. His leg muscles were taking on that jelly quality, reminding him that he'd been right about training, at least—it wasn't overrated. "Molly did great," Rick added. "Nori was cheering her head off."

Daniel nodded. "Molly's tougher than she thinks." He slid his hands into his pockets and leveled his eyes with his neighbor's. "That night the intruder entered our house, I know she thought it was you."

The shadows across Rick's face deepened. "It's not what you think. It was such a stupid thing. . . ."

"You're right about that."

"Just let me—" He sighed, then started again. "That afternoon, the girls were playing on the deck. We came in to get them a snack and I turned on the TV, just for background noise. We weren't even really watching, but it was some low-budget movie, and there was this over-the-top scene where the love interest posed as a burglar. The main character was into it." Daniel tried to keep his breath even as he pictured his wife watching any sex scene—even a campy one—with another man. With *this* man. "We were laughing at how masochistic it was, and Molly made this joke in defense of the movie, about how she could see the appeal."

Daniel's mouth dropped open, but Rick rushed ahead. "She was joking! But the break-in happened *that* night, so that's what she thought of, and—she assumed I hadn't taken it as a joke. She assumed I had taken it as an invitation." Rick averted his eyes, and Daniel considered him for a long moment.

"Was it an invitation?" he asked quietly.

"I swear to you, I have never laid a hand on your wife." He was telling the truth. Daniel could tell by how *proud* he seemed. As if this were a great achievement: mind over matter.

"But you're in love with my wife," Daniel said. It wasn't a question, and Rick didn't answer. He merely stared down at the piano keys as if they might play themselves.

"Here's the thing," Daniel said. "Molly has convinced herself that this intruder was not random. She's genuinely afraid someone is out to get her. And it's your fault. Because if she hadn't had *reason* to think it was you, she would have urged the police to pursue it. She would have come to me, right away. But instead, she ran scared, thinking she was going to get caught on the verge of an affair."

"She wasn't on the verge of anything," Rick insisted. "She knows it wasn't me."

"She knows that *now.* Point is, she missed her chance to see it through *then,* and couldn't explain her way into bringing it back up. So now she's miserable, terrified. She thinks they're going to come back. She's gone paranoid, and she doesn't even know that I know any of this."

Rick did meet his eyes then. "Well, now that you do, you can bring it back up, let her off the hook. The police can look into it again—"

"Absolutely not. It's old news by now; I think they're satisfied that they've looked into it plenty. They were here, weren't they?"

"Yes, but—"

"Look, I'm not worried. If someone was out to target us, they would've been back by now. And people don't come much more innocuous than Molly. But you know as well as I do how relentless she is with this stuff. How unhealthy it can be for her, once she gets something into her head, some unsolvable problem to solve. We're finally working through a lot of things, and I'll level with you: This is the last big hurdle. This, and you. Two birds, one stone."

Rick looked longingly at his empty glass. "What do you mean? What's the stone?"

"Convince her it was you. Let her let go of her fear, close this chapter, and move on. Her first guess was right, end of story. And you and I never had this talk. I know nothing."

"I would never—"

"It's like the saying," Daniel interrupted. "'If you love something, set it free.'" His words were icicles: pointed, cold. "It *was* never yours to begin with."

Rick shook his head. "I'm not sure you understand what you're asking. You wouldn't believe how far my daughter has come with Molly and Nori's help."

"Exactly," Daniel said. "She's going to be fine. I heard she even talked in front of Liza." Rick looked so bereft he *almost* pitied the guy. "Look, you did me a solid lending me that book, and now I'm doing you one. You can't find a partner when you're hung up on someone else's."

Rick was quiet for a long moment. "She'd never forgive me," he said finally.

Daniel raised an eyebrow, holding his eyes until Rick looked away.

"You might have the wrong idea about me, but make no mistake, I love my wife. I would never give her up without a fight, and I've sat by and let this continue long enough. It's over, one way or another. As far as I can tell, you're getting off easy. I've heard of jealous husbands doing far worse."

The man was deflating before his eyes, until he was flat enough to see through. Barely an obstacle at all.

Daniel forced a smile. "All settled, then. Proceed at your earliest convenience. As long as it's first thing tomorrow."

32

GRANT ALWAYS WAVED AT MOLLY FOR AS LONG AS HE COULD SEE HER WHEN the school bus pulled away, and this morning was the same, only different. It was better, because there was a new affirmation between them, in his bright eyes, in his wide smile—that she had not, would not, let him down. And it was worse, too, because she couldn't claim the same where Daniel was concerned—and by the end of the day, her husband would know that she had failed, would fail, them both.

She hated the thought of endangering this new softening between her and Daniel. She hated it so much that she'd let herself be *glad* he stepped out last night while she was on the phone with Liza. She'd never meant to tie herself up with a call, but then there her friend was, on the line, and Molly's heart had been filled with the kind of gratitude that only came with redemption. How could she put Liza off, when they'd finally reached this point of repair?

The conversation with Daniel couldn't wait any longer, though. The hat man had given her a week, but pulling her rescue hatch would take only moments. As of yesterday, telling Daniel about the still-to-be-tabulated cost of the secrets she'd kept had officially become less scary than continuing to keep them. And as of yesterday, she'd glimpsed *some* reason, however small, to hope that maybe, just maybe, this did not have to be their breaking point after all.

That he would forgive her had seemed such a far-fetched possibility. But then again, his coming around to *some* understanding of her pain, his admission that he could have done more, his willingness to put her first even when the heat was on at work—those had seemed long shots, too, yet they'd materialized.

As had Liza's phone call. It seemed like a sign—to never assume someone was lost for good.

She was amazed she'd slept at all last night, but the race had leveled her, and she'd drifted off still waiting for Daniel to come home. She'd barely come to when he left for the office this morning, early to compensate for yesterday, but he'd already called once—just as they were filing out to the bus stop—simply to say he loved her. If only she'd been able to hear it without the deafening roar of trepidation crashing down around her—at *all* she'd put in danger, at his blissful lack of awareness that they were in so deep. Tonight, she would sit him down and tell him everything. Unburdening herself would be no small relief, come what may.

"Mommy, can I have another waffle?" Nori tugged at her pant leg as the bus disappeared from view, and Molly tried not to grimace as she shifted her weight. She was all soreness from the hips down and pining for an anti-inflammatory her stomach couldn't handle.

"Well, you can't have any more syrup," Molly said, summoning a mischievous smile. "I saw you licking it from your plate."

"But I'm still hungry. And waffles are yucky without syrup."

"Remember that next time you're slurping up a syrup puddle."

Nori laughed and skipped up the walk ahead of her. "Slurping syrup slurping syrup slurping syrup . . . Mommy, can you say that five times fast?"

Molly was laughing her way through an exaggeratedly botched attempt when she caught sight of Rosie's tricycle turning out of Rick's long driveway. Nori's eyes lit up. "Ooh, can I ride my bike, too, until school? Please? Please?" They'd done this a few times in the fall, but the mornings had been too chilly since. Funny how Molly hadn't even stopped earlier to appreciate the novelty of no longer needing a coat, to drink it in and be grateful. Some warmings were so slow you didn't notice them until you found yourself sweating. It was too easy to skip right over the midpoint when, if you'd stop to think about it, you'd realize you were quite comfortable. Rick appeared behind Rosie and guided her onto the street, headed this way.

"Sure," Molly said. "Let me just run in and grab some coffee."

Moments later, she and Rick were sipping from steaming mugs in companionable silence on the front stoop, watching the girls trace figure eights with their wheels on the flat end of the driveway. Toby's obnoxious sister with the equally obnoxious dog power walked past, calling out a greeting even as she eyed them with outward suspicion. Molly registered her own uneasiness that until this very moment a stranger might have been right to wonder about her and Rick's closeness. But the current between them was noticeably absent today—finally, she supposed, one or both of them had succeeded in switching it off. Just as well.

"There's something I have to tell you," Rick said. She glanced at him to find his eyes fixed on his mug, his knuckles white around the handle.

And then, he rewired that current. For a few horrible moments, while he talked into his coffee and she listened, speechless, the live wire flailed between them, shooting off sparks of revelation that reached her beyond the buzz, above the noise. "It was me" and "stupid idea" and "I panicked" and "I was wrong" and "didn't want to lose you" and, finally, obviously, "I know this changes everything." Her mind spun in protest, flashing confused images of the man in the Panama hat disappearing into the crowd, and of Toby smirking behind the desk, *but what about* and *is this true* and *could it be* losing their power before she could voice them. By the time he was finished speaking, the wire was grounded and the space between them, once electric with forbidden possibility but also compassion and friendship and gratitude and respect and affection, was nothing more than just that: space. Deeply singed space.

"Why are you telling me this now?" she whispered. They were so exposed here, everything about it wrong, from the sunshine down to the girls' giggles. Rosie had pulled up alongside Nori, and they were trying to synchronize their pedaling. They would, too. They'd always been in sync, and she couldn't even claim they'd been fueled by any energy generated by Molly and Rick. The girls' bond had come first, right on the other side of this yard, before their parents had spoken more than a couple of harried sentences over the din of the tree cutters another lifetime ago. But now their bond would come last. Thanks to those same selfish parents, it would have to be broken. And as much as Molly wanted to lay the blame on Rick, scream at him, even flail her fists at him, they both knew she was at fault, too.

"All I can say is . . . how embarrassed I was. And how furious with myself. Not only had I misread the situation, but—if I'd ever have imagined the possibility of someone else seeing me, I'd never have taken that risk. Not for you, having to deal with the fallout, and not for Rosie and me, losing you and Nori both. I guess I thought if I denied it, everything could go back to normal." Rick's eyes were pleading, as if there might still be some way back, though they both knew there was not. "You assured me you thought it was random, so I figured the anxiety I'd caused would fade when nothing else happened. I didn't realize, though . . . Daniel mentioned how terrified you've been, that you *haven't* been convinced you weren't targeted, and I felt awful. If I'd known, I'd have come clean earlier."

She scooted over on the stoop, putting more distance between them before turning to him with narrowed eyes. "*Daniel* mentioned it?" She tried to recall Daniel ever speaking to Rick for longer than thirty seconds. But that aside, how had her relatively imperceptive husband perceived her fear, even a hint of it? Up until yesterday anyway, she'd been so careful to brush this off as nothing. Had that bastard Toby said something to him after all?

Rick's jaw muscles twitched, his eyes shifting away, then down. "Just in passing. I don't think he suspected me or anything, don't worry." The last syllables warbled, and she realized she'd never had occasion to witness what a horrible liar he was. Rick had always been honest with her.

Until now.

She peered at him in confusion. Why this of all things to be untruthful about? And again, why *now*? Had Liza been right that Molly was guilty of stringing him along, and he'd gotten tired of it? Or, worse to contemplate somehow, could Rick have been the one with *her* on the hook? And now that Rosie was improved, he was reaching for a way to release her, just like that?

The migraine saw its opening; the aura slipped inside. She needed Rick to leave before it took hold of her, so she could take a pill and think this through. If this was what he wanted, for whatever reason—if he was sacrificing himself for the good of them both—maybe it was better not to stop him, screaming instincts be damned.

"Nori and I are going to miss Rosie," she said quietly.

He held her gaze for a long minute before giving a somber nod. "And Rosie and I are going to miss Nori," he said. His voice broke in place of the name he did not say—her own—and something in Molly did, too. Would they have been better off without each other all along?

She got to her feet, every aching muscle crying in protest, and called to her daughter.

In spite of everything, she didn't like to think so.

In spite of everything, she wouldn't.

33

A PAIR OF COFFEE MUGS SAT FORGOTTEN ON THE EDGE OF MOLLY'S FRONT stoop, the shallow dredges inside beginning to curdle in the glaring sun, and Liza gathered them up as she made her way to the front door and knocked curtly, three times. She dismissed the fleeting memory of the last time she'd stood here in the morning light, of the vague sense of dread that still accompanied any hint of that day. This time was different.

This time, Molly had *asked* her to come. In fact, her request had seemed almost ordinary, as if they'd never stopped consulting each other over every crisis du jour.

And this time, Molly looked relieved to see her, opening the door with a genuine, grateful smile, even though she'd sounded numbly distressed on the phone, saying only that some "interesting developments" had occurred and she was wondering if Liza might be up for putting their heads together after Nori's preschool drop. Liza assumed it was about Daniel—Molly had told her last night about her steeled resolve to come clean about the debt, and it must not have gone well. Liza was glad she'd scheduled herself for the closing shift today and her morning happened to be free. She'd stopped at Servatii's bakery on the way, planning to grab some of Molly's favorite cheese Danishes, but the smell of sugar and dough filled her with such regret over how she'd treated Henry that she turned right around and left empty handed.

"Come in, come in!" Molly caught sight of the mugs and her smile wavered, then recovered as she rushed to take them from her. "So glad you could come. I was just thinking I should've asked you to bring some cheese Danishes. I'm kind of in the mood to eat my worries."

Whoops. Well, what Molly didn't know wouldn't hurt her.

"You've earned the calories after yesterday," Liza said, following her to the kitchen. Molly moved with visible effort, as if tethered to the ground with resistance bands, but she voiced no complaint. The kitchen was a mess, the fixings for what Liza guessed to be Grant's packed lunch and Nori's breakfast still spread on the counters, but Molly seemed not to notice.

"Coffee? I could reheat you some."

"Sure." Liza crossed behind her and began putting things back together. The lid on the peanut butter. The twist tie on the bread. The cap on the syrup. "So tell me about these developments," she said. "Is it Daniel? Did you tell him?"

Molly shook her head. The microwave beeped, and she extracted a steaming mug and brought it to the table with a carton of half-and-half. She slid into a chair and gestured for Liza to leave the mess and join her. "Allegedly the mystery is solved. About who you saw on camera that night."

"What?" This was the last thing she'd expected. She thunked into the opposite chair. "How? Who?"

"I remember hearing this detective say on TV that his first, most obvious theory is often the correct one. . . ."

"Rick?"

Molly nodded, and Liza tried to ground her thoughts, landing somewhere between skepticism and disappointment. "But I thought he *insisted* it wasn't him?"

"Right up until this morning, when he came over and confessed. Out of nowhere, like it was suddenly urgent to fill me in. He said he misread my signals, then got embarrassed and tried to cover it up."

Liza blinked at her. "So that's it? The whole thing thanks to a non-starter affair?"

"I don't know."

She'd said *allegedly,* Liza realized. "Do you not believe him?"

Molly massaged her temples, whether from a stress headache or out of habit Liza couldn't tell. "I don't know," she said again. "I think back to confronting Rick about this, straight off—and him confronting me, too. He tracked me down to have it out, and kind of put me in my place. Plus, he seemed just as freaked as I was—I mean, beyond back-pedaling. Why would he have done any of that if it was him, and if he truly wanted to brush it under the rug?"

Liza poured some cream into her coffee and gave the cup a swirl. She hadn't been around for any of that and had only just met Rick. She felt ill equipped to offer advice.

"But then I think," Molly went on, "that he was also asking a lot of questions that day. About the police, whether they had a record of the video, whether I'd mentioned to anyone in public that Daniel was going to be out of town. So maybe it was a front for him to fish around and make sure he *could* just deny it. And to try to get me thinking of other theories."

"Sounds like," Liza said, taking a sip.

"Plus, Rick and I used to talk about everything. And he never asked me about it again. I took it as him not wanting to dredge it up because I'd accused him. *Awkward.* But maybe it was because once he'd talked me out of suspecting him, he didn't want to press his luck."

"He didn't ask me about it, either," Liza agreed. "Even though he knew I was the one on the webcam, right?"

"Right. It's just that . . ." Molly squinted at her. "You know when a kid is lying to you and you can just tell? They're not very good at it. That's how it felt."

Liza shook her head. "Why the hell would anyone falsely confess to something so twisted?"

Molly shrugged. "I'm not saying he did. I just don't get it." She sighed. "If he really did this, it's not like I wasn't on to him. It would've been so much easier for him to just fess up and ask forgiveness straight off, to save both of us all this grief. Then again, given the mess I'm in with Daniel, who am I to talk?"

Liza rolled it over in her mind. "It's easier for me to understand why he *wouldn't* have admitted it before than it is for me to conjure a reason for him to own up to something he didn't do," Liza said carefully. "Especially this far after the fact."

"That's just it. I asked him, *Why now?*"

"And?"

"He said Daniel mentioned I was afraid. Said he'd never meant to traumatize me that way. The weird thing is, for starters, I didn't realize Daniel was aware of how I'd been feeling."

Liza felt the guilty rush of color to her cheeks. "Maybe he's more perceptive than you think," she offered quickly. "He did come to the race."

"That's true. Maybe. But also, Daniel and Rick don't usually talk. I tried to ask him how it came up, but he was vague." Her eyes squeezed shut. "I don't like the idea of the two of them talking about me. Especially since it turns out Rick and I . . ."

She let the sentence trail off, and a crawling sensation pricked at the back of Liza's neck. What if she *could* conjure a reason for Rick to have suddenly spilled his *alleged* guts? One that began with her own well-intended phone call to Daniel?

"Forget trying to think of a reason," she said slowly. "You really got the sense that Rick was lying today? For sure?"

"I did. Takes one to know one, maybe." Tears came into Molly's eyes. "I guess I should just let it go. You said yourself Rick and I should cool it, and I know you were right. But our friendship meant a lot to me, and for it to end like *this* . . ." She took a shaky breath and looked away.

The contrast from their jubilant conversation last night was heartbreaking, confusion and hurt eclipsing the rare relief Molly had exuded just hours before, and Liza wanted to find the man responsible and grind his face in it. Her anger only intensified the prickling, which was working its way up her hairline, clawing at her to pay attention.

"Anyway." Molly straightened her shoulders, though her jaw was still trembling. "I should focus on my own, very true, confession that I have to make to Daniel tonight."

"You chickened out last night?" Liza asked gently.

"I didn't get the chance to chicken out. Daniel went out, when you and I were on the phone. Wasn't home until late."

On a weeknight? After their big reconnection at the race? "Where'd he go?" Liza asked, trying to keep her voice even.

"No idea. An errand, probably. We've gotten out of the habit of keeping track of each other." The prickling sensation had climbed up to Liza's scalp now, and her whole head was tingling with dread. She was afraid she knew exactly where he'd gone. And she could think of only one reason why.

"But there's no way around telling him tonight," Molly went on, seemingly talking to herself as much as to Liza. "Even if these awful lenders weren't behind the intruder, who knows what they'll do next. I can't brush them off anymore. I need help. Plus, if Daniel and I are going to rebuild, he needs to know everything." She swiped at her wet eyes, sniffing hard. "It was so bittersweet yesterday, him showing up that way, knowing that once he knows the whole truth, he might never look at me like that again."

To know everything. The whole truth. Molly deserved that, too.

Liza stood. "Listen, Mol, I have to run. Are you going to be here? I could maybe come by again before work. I hate to think of you stewing alone."

Molly nodded and stood to clench her in a tight hug.

She let Liza show herself out. After all, it's not like she was company.

She was practically family.

34

DANIEL'S COLLECTED FACADE HAD FINALLY FAILED HIM, BUT HE SUPPOSED it didn't really matter. No one would dare disturb him behind his closed office door just now; they were merely *imagining* the way his heart was racing as he bided his time until ten o'clock, when he was to report to the CEO's office, presumably to be terminated. The admin who'd sent the meeting request had the biggest mouth in the place, though in this case the rumor mill would have gotten on fine without her. Bowing out of the budget meetings the way he had—leaving a table full of board members and investors sipping lukewarm coffees and glancing impatiently at the clock, until Jules ventured in to make his apologies—hadn't left much room for guessing at possible outcomes.

But he also knew something no one else did: that while the stunt he'd pulled would have a casualty, it wouldn't be him.

They had the racing-heart part right, though. His cold hands had trembled as he'd placed the call to Molly using the recording app that would tap her smartphone's microphone—a connection that, once covertly made, only he could disconnect. He'd timed the call *just so* and kept her on the line long enough to be sure she carried the phone with her to the bus stop. He'd known that once it was in her pocket, it would likely stay there long enough to suit his purposes, as long as Rick didn't get cold feet. And good ole Rick did prove reliable. Daniel had the whole, heartfelt confession on tape, down to the *if I'd known, I'd have come clean earlier.* A nice touch.

Toby had nothing on him now. Granted, Daniel didn't know exactly how Toby had retroactively booked him that alibi hotel room for the night the intruder broke in—he'd merely left a printed confirmation in Daniel's in-box to show that he was holding up his end of the bargain—but even if he'd had help, Daniel was betting no one in the travel-booking arm would admit to assisting with a fraudulent reservation. Toby could *try* to cry to Molly or even to the police that Daniel had not in fact left town that night, but after today it would just sound like sour grapes. The ultimate safeguard was that now, even if they did look into it, no one would suspect Daniel of anything Rick had already fessed up to—and should Rick try to retract his admission, Daniel had it right here in the audio file he was at this moment backing up to his storage cloud, his heart still racing, but with purpose, racing *toward* something, not away. Toby, meanwhile, was about to have plenty to be sour about. And his purpose thwarted.

Once you took the court of public opinion into consideration, an all-employee email seemed the best way to blow the whistle. It put Daniel in control of who knew what when. And when everyone knew who had come to their rescue, none of them would stand for the hero being fired. Especially as it related to his reasons for skipping out yesterday. If anyone found out about the 5K, he'd simply say he'd joined his family on a whim.

The adrenaline pressed the keyboard keys for him.

It has come to my attention that our individual 401(k) deposits are, paycheck by paycheck, a fraction of a percentage less than they should be—an amount that may sound small until you look at the totals over time. . . .

He swallowed the irony of making such a big deal out of honesty in accounting when his own wife had yet to come clean about the depths of her debt at home.

A corrupt deal cut in Human Resources in exchange for going with this particular provider, after no small amount of wining and dining of our esteemed HR head himself, whose pockets are being lined by skimming our savings, while the provider piles on nonsense fees, which no doubt he gets a cut of, too . . .

It wasn't the same thing, though. When it came to love, money was secondary. When it came to business, money was the only damn reason any of them were here.

I sat with this discovery, worrying I could be held responsible for not catching it sooner. Worrying about my job, my family . . . I wanted to be absolutely sure, so I gathered all the evidence I could, all the while hoping I would prove my suspicions wrong, find some other explanation. . . . I didn't want to believe anyone would stoop so low. . . .

A file of the aforementioned evidence would be emailed to the board simultaneously.

It came down to the wire, but when the moment arrived just as my fears were confirmed, I could not in good conscience face the board. . . .

Daniel had let Toby too deep inside his head. Plenty of people were overextended in their jobs. Daniel might have had a hand in making his own shoes too big to fill, but in some ways it *had* been an honest mistake. He certainly hadn't thought real harm would come of it. He would help make the necessary adjustments to their oversight systems so this sort of thing wouldn't happen again; he would use what he'd learned about their blind spots to illuminate them. Every day in corporate America, people embezzled and defrauded and lied, while exponentially more people looked the other way. After more than a month of rolling in all that mud, it felt good to get clean.

Molly would be proud of him for it. It was what she'd been pulling for from the start, even without knowing the extent of the corruption. Molly 2.0 was a good person. She had more in common with Molly 1.0 than he'd realized.

It had been such dumb luck, the way he'd first met Molly, when her being in the wrong place at the wrong time equated to his own stars aligning in a way that couldn't have been more right. She'd been stranded outside her running car in that dark parking lot, waiting for Roadside Assistance to come pop open the locked door, and he'd been pumping gas when he'd seen the man encroach. The stranger was drunk, he was tall and broad enough to easily overpower Molly, and he was not taking no for an answer. So adamant was he on getting that *yes* that he seemed to have forgotten he was in a public space. A dark corner, sure, but not a private one.

Daniel acted before he could think it through, and it was doubly lucky that the man had been too drunk to *really* fight, that he'd been unarmed, and that Roadside Assistance pulled up just in time to help restrain the asshole as he got to his feet from Daniel's falsely confident first blows.

Molly had looked at him like he was her knight in shining armor—*her* person, her backup, her heart—for a long time after that. Not for moments or hours or weeks. For *years.*

And then, she'd stopped looking at him with any kind of light in her eyes at all. Darkness moved in, and he grew afraid. It seemed so impenetrable. Now he knew that wasn't true. He'd finally acknowledged the reasons the lights had gone out, at least some of them, and in doing so had seen at last how to turn them back on, one by one.

It would take some time, but he could do it.

He read over every letter of the email, nipping and tucking until he was satisfied it took precisely the right shape. He concluded with an apology for good measure, though his coworkers would be thanking him by the time this was over. His superiors would have no choice but to show their appreciation, too. He made sure the attachments in the separate message they'd receive were in perfect order. As was the budget presentation he'd be hand-delivering in lieu of getting fired.

With a deep breath, he hit Send, and waited for the racing of his heart to begin to slow.

The door to his office flung open, and he startled in his chair—surely no one read that fast? But the ball of anger coming at him through the doorway wasn't Toby, or Jules, or anyone from the board.

The door swung shut heavily behind her, and he winced, already on his feet, crossing the room to open it again.

"Liza, this is *really* not a good time. The worst possible time, actually."

She laughed. "I'm *always* showing up at the worst possible times, aren't I?"

"I don't—"

"It was you, wasn't it? In the mask that night?"

He froze. "*Excuse* me?"

"Answer the question."

Jesus. "Okay. No. That's absurd."

"If you really don't have time to talk now, you'd better skip over the part where you insult my intelligence. Cut to the part where you explain. Because I'm not leaving until you do."

They squared off, both of them breathing hard, for a terrible moment. He'd been so close to extracting himself from this mistake. He didn't want to let it go, the improbable hope that he still could.

"Whatever you think, you're wrong," he said. But he could hear the panic in his voice. And so could she. She appraised him through her fury, as if he were a cataclysmic problem she'd only just become aware of, and it was the next worst thing to Molly herself looking at him this way. He'd always liked Liza, genuinely. Only once before had he ever minded having her in the picture—and even that he'd tried to repent for, to extend an olive branch where Molly would not. And this was where it had gotten him.

"No one other than Molly was supposed to see me," he said finally, his eyes not leaving hers, his voice barely above a whisper. It had been a stupid plan, relying too heavily on desperate emotion and not enough on rational thought. Molly was only meant to catch a glimpse of him that night, at which point he'd blunder his little invasion enough to let her save herself, call the cops, watch him scurry off into the woods before they arrived. In that moment, she'd prove to herself what she could no longer see: That she was still that woman from the gas station parking lot, perfectly capable of fixing things under the hood. But also that he was still that man from the parking lot—that when things got ugly, she didn't have to be alone in the dark. She could still run back to his arms—which would feel warm and safe again.

"What on earth were you trying to *do*? What were you after?"

His eyes flitted to the door. How long did he have before the full whistle blow had been heard loud and clear? Surely not more than a couple minutes, tops. He had to talk fast.

"Nothing! I don't know. I know it sounds crazy to say that faking that business trip and putting on that mask made sense at the time, but all I knew was that I had to do *something* to jolt us both out of this place we were in. It was—too drastic, I know. That was immediately clear." He'd had the decency to be ashamed from the start. But shame never got anyone anywhere good. He'd only been digging further into his hole, trying to find a way out the other side.

"Don't tell me this has to do with your hero complex."

"You know I'd never hurt her."

"Terrifying her doesn't count as hurting her? Do you know what you've put her through? How *could* you?"

The worst part was that she wasn't wrong. "I didn't think it through."

"I know you're big on 'grand gestures' as shortcuts, but this—"

He shook his head. "You weren't there. You don't know!"

"What do you mean? I saw the whole thing!"

"Before, I mean! We were *losing her,* Liza. People talk about waking up one day and realizing what they've let go, and that's exactly what happened. It's like I was sleepwalking through my life, and one day there was this moment—a little moment that turns big, you know? Grant, our sweet, sensitive kid, said this un-sweet, insensitive thing, and it *killed* her to hear it. And it was because he *sounded like me.* I wanted to reach her, to make it all up to her, and I couldn't even get her to *look* at me. Not that day, or the next . . . She wouldn't let me reach her anymore. She'd already *been* dying, little by little, this person who mattered most to me in the world, and I had *let* that happen. I had *helped* it happen. And I wanted to fix it, but I could see it might be too late. My replacement was already on deck."

Liza was still glaring at him. He was failing at this. At conveying what it was like to watch a panorama of your most precious memories fade before your eyes. The refracted sunlight in Molly's hair each sleepy-perfect morning of their honeymoon. The giddy triumph in first turning the key in the door of their very own house. The shared wonder at meeting their newborn children, each tiny being miraculously just as much him as her.

He'd done it as a last attempt to hang on, to hold tight. The ball had been in his hand, the count full, and he'd panicked and thrown a wild pitch.

But no one had seen. Or at least no one had known what they saw. He'd rationalized that good intentions could compensate for bad judgment, even as he'd promised himself that no one would *ever* know.

He'd been wrong. But today, in the moments before Liza stormed in, it hadn't felt wrong. It had felt *worth it.* A twisted, backward way back to Molly, back to the man he had meant to be, out of this awful arrangement with Toby and on his way to a fresh start all the way around. It had almost worked, which was the craziest thing of all. And that had made it hard to be sorry.

It was easier now.

"What did you say to that poor man last night to make him come over and confess this morning? *That* might be the most messed-up thing. His hands are heartbreakingly full without your bullshit."

"That was—a means to an end. I didn't like doing it. Even if he was after my wife. But it solved some very complicated problems for me. One of which has nothing to do with Molly and is the reason you really shouldn't be here right now."

"You know, it's not like you've never shown your manipulative side before, but I always liked you anyway," she said, exaggerating her tone as if to marvel at her own naïveté.

"For what it's worth," he said, "Rick agreed it was for the best. He wouldn't have done it otherwise."

"Now you're trying it on *me,*" she said, eyes wide with incredulity. "Let's set Rick aside and back up. Do you know what you put *me* through? I still don't follow what you would have done if I didn't see you. What would have happened if—"

She stopped short, and he watched the realization dawn across her face. He'd thought of it a lot, himself, ever since the day he'd run into her at Lunken, looked up reports of the fire upon landing in Chicago, and put the dates together. "My harebrained scheme saved your life," he said for her. "That, I don't regret."

She stood, motionless, her eyes clouded over. "Look," he told her. "You know deep down I'm right that we were losing her. I did the stupid thing, you saw me, and then what did Molly do? Nothing! Are you aware she didn't even *tell me* about the intruder at all?" Liza stared through him. "I came home and heard it from the cop parked outside, and then she acted like he wasn't even out there, like nothing even happened. If I didn't confront her later that day, I probably *still* wouldn't have heard any of this from her. Meanwhile, you show up to check on her and she slams the door in your face." Surprise flickered in Liza's eyes. She was listening. He kept going. "Does that sound like someone who was in a place to talk things through, work things out? If you hadn't moved back, where do you think you two would be now?"

Liza stepped back. She wouldn't want anything to do with this line of reasoning, but she couldn't deny it, either. "If there'd been *any* doubt we were two seconds away from losing her, the morning after erased it. What I did was messed up, but how she reacted was, too. Who doesn't tell her own husband about an intruder? Who doesn't welcome her worried best friend inside when she's been driving all night? Don't tell me nothing drastic was necessary. I'm not saying what I did was right, but I also know that's not true."

There was a commotion, outside his office. The email had landed. People were talking. They'd be coming here soon, the ones at the top, to hear it straight from him all over again. Liza turned toward the closed door, her head cocked, attuned to the energy shift.

"You're going to have to go," Daniel said, his urgency rising. Now or never. "I'm begging you, Liza, please don't tell Molly. There's no reason for her to know. What does it change? And she's doing better now. *We're* doing better now. And you two are, too. What's done is done."

"Oh no. You're not pulling me into this."

"You're already in it. Please at least think about it. What's to be gained from telling her?"

She shook her head, incredulous. A knock sounded on the door.

"Please," he said again.

The door opened and Liza walked out before he could say another word. All he could do was watch her go as the line of waiting suits filed inside.

35

IN THE CONTEMPLATIVE VACUUM OF SILENCE LEFT BY LIZA'S DEPARTURE, Molly had turned to another strong woman for company.

In all her years of paging through the Eleanor Roosevelt quote book—the one that had inspired the name of her daughter, the one that had followed her from bedroom to dorm room to apartment to house—she'd managed to skip over the First Lady's "Ten Rules for Success in Marriage," reprinted from a 1931 edition of *Pictorial Review.* Not *all* advice was evergreen, after all. Even the feminist icon had listed housekeeping among a wife's three fundamental roles and asserted that having children was not a choice but a duty in matrimony.

Molly read them now, however, with an initial skepticism that grew into the kind of intense discomfort you want to wriggle swiftly out of, leaving your skin behind if that's what it takes to be free.

The rules, for the most part, were still relevant, smart. Yet *both* she and Daniel had broken every one. *Apportion your time and energy. . . . Expect to disagree. Be honest. Talk things over. Keep alive the spirit of courtship, that thoughtfulness which existed before marriage.*

Also, this prescient understatement: *Remember that sooner or later money is apt to be a cause of friction.*

Right.

It was as if they, but most literally she, had had the answers all along, yet blatantly disregarded them. What audacity, for either her or Daniel to have expected a better outcome.

This was doing nothing to help her mind-set for their sit-down tonight. It only made her feel less worthy of forgiveness, her sense of hope waning as her dismay at their mistakes grew wider and deeper. Their breaking points were not, as she'd told herself, the product of a few escalated bad decisions, but the result of systematic failures in their fundamental core.

But Molly was meant to be psyching herself up, not tearing herself down—and thank God for Liza, yet again. Here her friend was back, calling out a greeting in lieu of a knock, brandishing a white paper bag darkened with splotches of pastry grease. One look at her face, though, and Molly sensed she was about to lose her appetite.

"This goes against the grain for delivering bad news, but I don't think you should get this sitting down," Liza said. "Let's walk."

So they did, like they used to—down the manicured sidewalks, where everything seemed maddeningly ordinary. The pungent, woody smell of freshly spread mulch and the drone of a lawn mower and the tiny lawn signs the schools were fond of doling out: "Home of an All-Star Reader" and "Congrats to Our Graduate" and "Team Spirit: We Bleed Orange!" The people in these houses had followed Eleanor's rules, certainly. At least *some* of them.

"Something you said earlier tipped me off," Liza began. "But I had to be sure. Too many false accusations have been flung already."

She pieced it all together for Molly as they walked—what Daniel had put her through, and sustained somehow, and his backward rationale, and whatever the hell he must have said to Rick last night, no doubt proving to the guy that he was better off without the mayhem that came with Molly. Their pace slowed as Liza picked up steam, gesturing in front of them wildly, a hand talker in times of stress, tearing truth through the air. Back on the couch or at the kitchen table, Molly might have absorbed the shock like a blow, but Liza had been right to keep her moving this way. The forward momentum carried Molly into the thick and through, and the soreness of yesterday and the reckonings of this morning fell away until she was left with only this. The words. The walk. The reality.

Liza stole a quick glance at her. "Are you okay? This is a lot."

Molly concentrated on the rhythm of their sneakers on the pavement. *One, two. One, two.* She realized she hadn't thought of her mantra once today—not even while Rick was unloading his false confession, and most telling of all not now—and was glad to be rid of it. Even counting to two was more soothing than constantly reminding herself nothing was easy. And it was comforting to have Liza in stride beside her. *Step, step.* Had a part of Molly suspected Daniel? Had a part of her known? She didn't think so. If she had, maybe the rage that was heating to a rolling boil now would be tempered by some unsurprised emotion—the satisfaction of a hunch panning out, even in a heartbreaking way.

"I don't know what to be angriest about," Molly said, her voice slippery, barely under her control. "It's taken years to hear him own up to having done *anything* to contribute to the state we're in. Now I'm supposed to believe he was so aware of it, so desperate about it, he did *this*?"

Liza shrugged. "I caught him off guard, but he was *ardent* at explaining himself. Something's going down at his office today, too. Seemed serious. Maybe to do with that scandal you mentioned?"

It was. He'd texted with the bombshell: Toby caught in an illegal scheme, and Daniel helping do the catching. Said he needed to make some statements, on the record. He'd be home late. Possibly very late.

Said she'd inspired him yesterday, at the finish line, to be the sort of person others could put their faith in, even when it was hard to come through. Said he loved her, so much.

Had he typed those words before or after Liza's visit?

"Does he honestly think there's a chance in hell you didn't come straight here and tell me everything?"

Liza shrugged. "He *begged* me not to."

"Well," Molly said dryly. "Thank you for not succumbing to his charms." She meant it as a joke, but Liza didn't laugh. A woman with a jogging stroller raised a hand in greeting as she passed, and they waited until she was behind them before speaking again.

"I'm on your side," Liza said. "In case that isn't obvious."

"It is. I'm sorry." Molly hugged herself, though the air was sticky. Her arms seemed to need some purpose, and swinging them felt bizarrely cheerful. "What do I *do* with this?"

"Molly, he—maybe you've already thought of it." She cleared her throat. "He saved me from that fire. *Saved my life.*"

She'd *not* thought of it. *My God.* She turned her attention to Liza, trying to discern if this exacerbated the way Liza had been feeling since her near miss, or if it helped somehow. Her sudden gratitude at her friend's very presence overwhelmed her, and she reached out and gave Liza's hand a squeeze. Liza squeezed back.

"So you can't be mad at him, is what you're saying."

"Oh no," Liza said. "I'm mad. And I'm—I'm more sad, if I'm honest. For both of you. Last night, the way you were talking about him had me thinking that turnarounds were possible, under any circumstances. But now . . ." She shook her head. "I can't cast a vote, is all. However you handle this has to be your call."

Under any circumstances. She'd almost dared to think so, too, and she wanted to scream at having it ripped from her grasp. "This is insane," she said. "I swear I used to be a normal person. With room to talk."

"Maybe," Liza said. She never did mince words. "But even if? You both did something desperate to try to save something you loved. You both got in over your heads. You'd both change it if you could."

It was a charitable perspective, begging to be challenged. But Liza had already done so much. Molly wouldn't press her, though she wanted to: *Tell me again why you believe the best about him—or even about me. Tell me why I should. Tell me if any of that is enough.*

Tell me how to forget I know this.

"Say he could forgive you everything. Could you forgive him? What do you *want*?"

"I don't know." What *did* she want? She was furious. Heartbroken. And . . . was she *relieved*? She'd been about to take her place in the hot seat, but now Daniel would be joining her there. Was it wrong to feel less alone?

Still, she couldn't visualize the next steps. She let out something between a moan and a growl. "What I want is to skip ahead," she said. "To where we have no *real* worries, not in our finances, not in our marriage. Where Daniel is like he was at the starting line yesterday: in it all the way. Where I'm like I was then, too: capable of things I thought I couldn't do."

"So you don't want to skip to the part where you're divorced and over it," Liza pointed out.

Molly pursed her lips. "But maybe that's the shock talking. It's not that simple. How could I trust him again? And even if I could, what does that say about me? That I'm a doormat?"

"Doormats don't open and shut doors," Liza said firmly. "And *you* are the one here with your hand on the knob."

Was she? With Daniel on the other side, wanting in?

The person who wants less from the relationship holds the power.

"Besides," Liza went on. "Maybe simplicity is overrated. Or maybe things can be as simple as we want them to be."

Number one on Eleanor Roosevelt's list of marriage rules was to have a plan. A clear objective for the future.

For that, Molly had two choices. And one, she could suddenly see, had a big advantage over the other.

36

MORE THAN ANY OTHER PLACE SHE'D WORKED, LIZA LIKED CLOSING UP THE Sky Galley. Mornings here were de rigueur as anywhere—the preparation, the inevitability of some ingredient or service revealing itself to be in short supply—but after dark, after the last patrons had departed and her staff had cashed out and rolled the next day's silverware, the space took on an air of novelty. With the background din silenced every footfall echoed under the old ceilings, and the picture windows framed a panorama of lights blinking and blurring down the runways.

They closed fairly early—weeknights at nine—and Liza liked to linger after everyone else had gone, as she did tonight. She straightened the line of high-backed barstools running the length of the galley that gave the restaurant its name, pausing to watch a plane take off and finding, at last, that she had more curiosity about where it was headed than worry about whether it would get there.

Seeing Steph so unburdened had restored for Liza *some* of her faith that things were more likely to go right than wrong. And Daniel—*oh, Daniel*—had proven that even a terrible mistake could result in some improbable thing to be grateful for. If not for that, she wouldn't be here.

She'd had to relearn that letting go didn't necessarily make you naïve, only hopeful.

She didn't know what might happen between Molly and Daniel tonight, but she was happy to be free of the questions that had tormented her since she'd been their witness. Free of a lot of things. Lighter.

After another almost summer day, the dinner crowd had arrived in a good mood. Liza was growing to like them—the loyal regulars, the hungry trail runners, the unhurried travelers, who didn't forget to appreciate Lunken for what it was, a last-man-standing symbol of a less complicated time. She'd worried, signing on, that this job might not feel like enough, but for now it was exactly enough—nothing less and nothing more.

If only she could break her habit of watching the door, foolish though it was to hope Henry would reappear. She owed him an apology at the very least, and had gotten as far as scrolling to his name on her phone, but that was where she clammed up. She'd been in such disarray since they'd met, she couldn't even think of a convincing argument to coax him back.

Satisfied the restaurant was ready for another day, she headed to where she'd stashed her purse beneath the bar and retrieved the rental application a prospective landlord had faxed over. She had appointments to see two of his properties in Mount Lookout tomorrow. Nothing good stayed on the rental market there for long, though she wasn't otherwise in a hurry to move. Since her talk with Steph, Luke had warmed again, and Liza worried less about wearing out her welcome and more about making the most of this time they had together.

She grabbed a pen from the hostess station and crossed to a table by the window, but before she could pull out a chair something caught her attention beyond the patio.

Or, rather, someone.

Henry lifted one hand in a sheepish wave, indicating with the other, through elaborate finger walking, that she should come out and join him. He wasn't exactly smiling, but then again, he was here, and anticipation surged through her at the sight of him. She held up a finger and rushed to gather her things, turning out the lights and locking the door behind her.

Her breath caught as she headed down the walk toward the dark airfield. Waiting at the open gate, Henry was out of uniform but still somehow looked the part with his light zip jacket hanging open over his T-shirt in the warm night air.

"I didn't want you to think I was a creeper, waiting out here for you," he said, preempting her while she was still a few strides away. "But there's something I want to show you."

"I don't think you're a creeper," she said, grinning. "Yet. Guess it depends on what this something is."

"Fair enough." She followed him through the opening and toward the first hangar. Lights dangled high overhead into the cavernous, shadowy space, revealing an assortment of small planes in various colors and body styles. They passed one that might have belonged to Snoopy's Red Baron, then two more modern silver models, and stopped next to a white and blue two-seater with disproportionately long wings. Just looking at them conjured an image of the plane gliding aloft, tilting back and forth in constant search of center, and so Liza focused her gaze on the cockpit, where Henry stood next to the open door.

"On loan from a friend," he said. "A beauty, isn't she?"

Liza nodded. She'd never thought of a plane as beautiful, but this one looked as if someone had showered it with love. There wasn't so much as a scuff on the paint, and polished leather beckoned from the seats.

"I was hoping you might reconsider," he said, gesturing inside, and her eyes widened. He held up a hand. "Don't answer yet. I've brought provisions. In the event of the most common mishaps, you'll be prepared." He turned and reached into the space behind the passenger seat, procured a large cardboard box, and set it at his feet.

She gaped at him. "Um. Is the plane not equipped with those things in the first place?"

He cleared his throat. "Well, yes and no. I didn't say anything about a flight, did I?" He grinned and added, "Yet."

Before she could respond, he bent to rummage through the box and came up holding a slender hand-painted vase. He held it out to her, and she took it gingerly into her hands, examining the fine brushstrokes that swirled the surface.

"When we have our first argument, probably something small and silly, I'm going to bring you a single flower. Just one, nothing showy. I'm guessing you haven't replaced your housewares yet, so this will give you something to put it in."

She wrapped her fingers around its thin neck, feeling the cool ceramic against her skin. "That's sweet," she said. "But I think we just had our first argument. Though you're right that it was small and silly." She hesitated. "*I* was small and silly," she said more quietly.

"No, you weren't. But I figured you might say this one counted." He bent over again, removed a hydrangea blossom from the box, and presented it to her with a flourish. "For you."

She laughed in weak protest. "But this one was my fault!"

"I don't know about that," he said, and his voice was kind—kinder than she deserved. "Pre-mortem thinking is not for everyone, and I kind of already knew that. In fact, I'm taking a chance here. But go with it, okay?"

"I'm with it," she assured him.

"Good. So, I hate to bring this up now that we're back on track, but one day, I'm really going to piss you off." He tapped his finger on an envelope and handed it over. "Open this then."

She peeked at the back, but it was sealed. "May I ask what's inside?"

"A list of everything I like about you so far. Maybe it'll remind you of something you like about me, even if I'm being stupid. Failing that, there's also a movie gift card. Treat a friend to a girls' night instead of sitting home with no date."

She shook her head. "Henry, you didn't have to—"

"Moving on to a better problem: A day I'm doing everything right but have to leave for my overnight flight schedule. A day you're sad to see me go." He reached back into the box and presented her with a glossy trifold bearing the air shuttle's logo. "You can use this voucher to come along. No need to ask. Surprise me sometime."

Liza opened it to look inside, almost not believing this was real, and when she looked up he was holding a pink toothbrush. "I debated this one," he said. "Don't want to seem presumptuous. But we're adults, right? So, should you ever want to stay over, unplanned, I'll keep this at my place. Just in case."

She rolled her eyes, laughing, and he dropped it back into the box. When he straightened, he was holding the gaudiest reindeer sweater she'd ever seen. He pressed Rudolph's nose, and the wreath framing the animal lit up red.

"What on earth . . ."

"Further ahead of myself, but if all goes well, you'll need this for *any* get-together my family throws at Christmastime. I apologize in advance."

She shook her head, though she wasn't succeeding in masking her grin. "I think I'm starting to realize how Luke felt when I gave him that monitor."

"Too much?" His eyes twinkled, but his face was serious as he stepped closer. "I figured I might only get one shot to prove my point, which is this: I know this hasn't been an easy time for you, and maybe on paper it *isn't* good timing to meet someone. But we did meet. And if you want to lend your heart on the safest possible terms—"

One step forward was all it took to bury her head in his chest. He wrapped his arms around her and she tipped her face up to his. When they finally pulled back, the least of her worries was whether this decision was right, or safe. She had already made it regardless.

"One more thing," he said, reaching into his pocket. He opened his hand, and in his palm was one of those little gold pins presented to children on airplanes. Stripes and wings. She let him pin it to her collar.

"This could come loose and stab me," she said, stifling a smile. "It has just this one fastener. Not two. Definitely not seven."

He shrugged. "I've never seen it happen, in all my years of flying."

"So we *are* going up?" She eyed the precarious aircraft behind him and thought about what it would be like to buckle in right now, to perch in the balance between those teetering wings and look down on the blanket of lights that just moments before had been outside the restaurant window. Frightening. But exhilarating.

"Only if you want to."

She kissed him again, feeling his lips smile beneath hers, and she could see it, then, how his "preparation" for the bad had really been a preview of the good that was *always* possible on the flip side. She already knew what she'd use her flight voucher for: to take him along to Max's good-bye party. And maybe they wouldn't date long enough for her to ever venture out in that hideous holiday sweater—but then again, maybe they would.

He touched his forehead to hers, and she looked him in the eye and nodded.

"I'll take my chances."

37

MOLLY HAD BEEN THINKING A LOT ABOUT THE NIGHT IN QUESTION. HOW she'd gone into it wondering if it was ever possible for two people who'd grown apart to reverse course. Not with the relationships you were content to outgrow, but with the ones you couldn't even think of relegating to memory without a lump catching in your throat.

She'd been so reluctant that night to face Liza, even through the filter of the webcam, and she'd viewed Daniel's business trip as a reprieve from the strain of their marriage. In hindsight, the Molly of that night had all but made up her mind that it *wasn't* possible. That these small efforts to reconnect only prolonged the inevitable.

The man in the mask changed all that.

Not right then, of course. But the fallout from his brief appearance stirred stagnant things into motion. Things that had *needed* to move.

She knew now that there *were* ways back, though they may not be pretty, with no precedent to follow. As with any chemistry, a catalyst was required, the right conditions. The chain reaction, once begun, could still fizzle, but not if you reassessed the components, fueled the fire with stubbornness, sheer will, even force of habit—anything you had on hand.

Liza would remain back in her life. And Daniel—well, he wanted to. A turnaround as miraculous as any other.

What if you found out it all had been a reckless experiment, but you couldn't deny the end result was an improvement? Aside from, that is, the mess you'd made in your own lab, the one you still needed your partner to help you clean up?

You could reject the whole thing, on principle.

Or you could dig out your Bunsen burner, strap on your safety goggles, and see what happened next.

She let the kids prolong bedtime. She was in no hurry to sit alone with her apprehension, awaiting Daniel's return, and the children had taken on that fairy-dusted quality they had in moments that already felt like memories. Grant was still riding the high of the race, carefully hanging his "Finished!" ribbon on his nightstand knob before joining her and Nori on his bed for extra stories, extra snuggles, extra songs. Molly built Nori's little nest on her doorway floor without being asked, only to have Nori leap over the pile and bounce into her bed. She admired this kid's own-mindedness. Molly's job was not to tame it, but to nurture it. To protect what was strong in her daughter in a world that *would* try to wear it away.

Daniel texted that he was headed home. Fair warning. She polished off the last cheese Danish for fuel. Thought of opening a bottle of wine, decided against it. Settled on the couch with the TV off, the lights on. Heard the automatic garage door go up, then down. The slug of the car door. The shuffle of loafers on concrete. A pause and some tinkering. A sudden need, perhaps, to declutter the tool bench. Stalling.

She smiled into the empty room, eerily calm. Even at this moment she'd long been dreading, she could take solace in the small miracle that he was dreading it more.

Here he was. A bit unnerved by her smile. A hesitant grin in return, his eyes investigating the room. Looking for signs of Liza, perhaps. Molly would not be the one to break the silence. What happened next would be up to him, just not the way he thought.

"Boy," he said. A voice strained through wire mesh. "What a day."

She gestured to the cushions next to her. "Tell me everything." His eyes shifted again, trying to discern her meaning, fearing the worst—that this was his one chance to fess up before she flew off the couch, clawing at him, *How could you?* "Start from the beginning," she prodded. "Does this go back to those expense reports you told me about?"

She'd never seen him so relieved at the mention of Toby. He sank onto the couch a short distance away and sat stiff as a door, walking her through the excitement of the day without the slightest hint of excitement. Hard to muster emotion while so preoccupied, but he managed the details. She tsked at what Toby had been up to. Gasped at how Daniel had found out. Nodded with approval at his masterpiece email. Knitted her brow at the hours of questioning he'd endured.

She *did* know the right things to say. She'd memorized her lines.

She even smiled as he relayed how Toby had yelled, as they escorted him from the building, some unintelligible nonsense about Daniel "and his crazy wife." At this, Daniel shook his head. "I don't even think he could pick you out of a lineup, could he?" he asked.

She could end the whole charade right now. But if you thought about it, that was letting him off easy. He still didn't know where he stood, knew only that his position was one too easily transported to the other side of the door.

"You don't look happy," she observed. "I thought you'd be proud of yourself."

He cleared his throat, still eyeing her sideways. Halfway sure she must know, halfway convinced he still had time, even if only tonight.

This was the place to do it. Here, on this line.

"As long as things are getting out in the open, there's something else you should know."

She couldn't help it: She cried when she told him. Everything rushing back. The initial mounting debt, the bad call to consolidate it in the most unsavvy of ways. The desperation, the loneliness, the fear.

Also, the regret. Nothing she'd learned today had made her less sorry. She'd betrayed them both. No wrong on his part could ever make that right.

He interrupted, at salient moments. "*All* of your retirement savings?" He ran a hand through his hair. "What about the IRAs?"

"I'm sorry," she said again. The words seemed just as inadequate now as they'd sounded coming from Daniel these past few years.

"And this alternative solution you were approached with—in a parking lot—it didn't seem off? Too good to be true?" His voice was convincingly calm, but his eyes gave away his struggle to keep his disbelief in check.

"It should have," she said. "All I can say is I was blinded by panic. And pain. I did show the paperwork to a lawyer. Not promising, unfortunately."

He went pale as she neared the end. The threats she'd grown sure she wasn't reading too much into. The urgent need to pay, immediately. And the amount still due—his bereft silence confirmation that he could produce it, but scarcely a cent to spare.

The tears still falling—this would be the last of them—she lifted her head and locked her eyes on their target.

Go ahead, she dared him. *Lay into me.*

And he saw. That she knew. Or he didn't see—he'd gone paranoid. Had he actually convinced Liza to keep quiet? He couldn't take the chance. But he didn't want to confess needlessly. She saw it all: The internal boxing match, the relentless back-and-forth.

Every jab proof that in spite of all she'd done, he still had hope for them.

Which meant he still had love for her.

Suddenly Daniel was the one crying. On his knees, on the floor, at her feet. Noble-effort Daniel, whom she'd loved since the first time she saw him, until she almost stopped. Saying her name, over and over. "Forgive me," over and over. "I know you didn't get out on that ledge without my help." He peered up at her through wet eyes, pleading.

"And I know how desperate it can be, an urge to fix something broken. I know how it can drive a person to do crazy things."

The apology wasn't just for shunning her pain, for piling on its cost. It was for everything she may or may not know, might or might not discover. Anguish radiated from him as the words fell around her. And she knew he was sincere, because she always had been partial to the vulnerable sides of the people she most loved. She'd missed this one so—she'd know it anywhere. "I *love* you, Molly. I don't *care* about the money."

She still wanted to rail at him, to hell with the plan. To complete her catharsis with a string of accusations, every one of them valid and true.

But if she did, she wouldn't have this.

This tip in the balance. Slanting, at last, in her favor.

Good-bye to weak Molly. Abandoned Molly. *I'll do anything* Molly.

She would tell him that he *should* care about the money. That she certainly did. She would offer to go back to a rat race of a career, knowing he wouldn't let her. They would squeak by, start again. It would nag at him, though, what these predators had gotten away with. Her pain would ebb and flow, but they'd meet it together. They'd go on the retreat, paid for anyway, and in a moment of mountaintop solace she'd gently suggest he visit the attorney she'd consulted. See if one of those regulatory agencies couldn't use his keen financial eye. A more suitable fit than the corporate world anyone could see he loathed. Besides, he'd need to satiate his hero complex somewhere.

Better them than her.

All the while he'd wonder about the card in her pocket. If he was imagining it there. If she would ever play it. He wouldn't bring himself to ask Liza, but if he did, she'd probably just say the same thing she'd told Molly.

That the option was interesting. Full of possibilities.

There was one rule, it turned out, on Eleanor's list that Molly decided to take issue with.

Let neither husband nor wife strive to be the dominating person in the household.

After years of the pendulum pulling back one way, straining the gear, showing off its might, a swing to the other side was required to restore the equilibrium. Things would even out eventually. Just not quite yet.

Following the rest of the rules would help. And they both would, from now on. She'd see to that. *Talk things over. Keep alive the spirit . . .* Nine out of ten ain't bad.

One day, she'd come home to a whole truckload full of those same yellow tulips Daniel had brought her at the point of no return. Not cut stems, but potted plants, fresh and healthy. A real grand gesture, at last, and she'd smile. She'd been wrong to scoff that she preferred roses. She'd forgotten about the thorns. And she hadn't put enough stock in the fact that tulips were springtime pioneers, risk-takers, not afraid to go first because someone had to, doggedly reaching up through the soil even knowing nature's unpredictable April whims could bury them in snow.

Together she and Daniel would transfer them to the flower beds. She'd water them daily until she was sure they'd bloom next year, and the year after that, regardless of how harsh the winter, to remind her that things could always be restored.

And, of course, of what they stood for.

Hopeless love.

Acknowledgments

MY DEEPEST GRATITUDE TO THE FOLLOWING:

My agent, Barbara Poelle: The doer to my (over)thinker. Not a day goes by that I don't thank my lucky stars (and garters) that I have you in my corner.

My two talented editors: Holly Ingraham, whose enthusiasm for this project from the start meant everything, and April Osborn, whose insightful eye helped to transform the final draft.

The whole team at St. Martin's Press: in particular Sally Richardson, Jennifer Enderlin, Katie Bassel, Jordan Hanley, Danielle Christopher, Sarah Grill, and the dedicated group at Macmillan Audio.

Janice Bocskor at the Cincinnati Nature Center's Nature Shop, who graciously spent a morning answering my questions about her days working there (though I've taken some creative license with my rendering, of course). And the many unnamed employees and volunteers who always greeted me with a smile when I came in to observe, enjoy, and write, once even holding on to a forgotten-behind coffee mug for me until I could reclaim it.

Brad Moeller at State Farm for—quite like a good neighbor—lending insight into Liza's situation as an insured renter.

The talented and prolific writer Bob Mayer for a fascinating cocktail hour chat that veered into his "Rule of Seven," and for gifting me thereafter his books *Stuff Doesn't Just Happen 1* and *2,* which helped to inspire Henry's theory. Both are available as ebooks from Cool Gus Publishing, and offer interesting further reading for anyone intrigued by a glimpse into that way of thinking.

Kelly Fields, for her good-humored explanations of the inner workings of human resources, and Scott Strawser for his expertise, always, on the financial side. Any perceived inconsistencies or liberties taken are mine alone.

Kim Dinan, the most gracious of hostesses, whose writing retreat reinvigorated this story (and its author) at just the right time. And fellow retreat writers Cat Johnson and Meghan McNamara, whose ideas at our group brainstorm helped to give Molly and Daniel a push.

My beta readers, Lindsay Hiatt, Amy Price, and Megan Rader, for their thoughtful feedback on an earlier draft, and for cheering me on between reads.

Sharon Short and Katrina Kittle for their writerly sisterhood; the Tall Poppy Writers for welcoming me into their fold; fellow writers turned friends via 17 Scribes and WFWA; and my colleagues at *Writer's Digest,* whose continued support means more to me than I can say.

The Quotable Eleanor Roosevelt, edited by Michele Wehrwein Albion, proved a wonderful desk reference as Molly cites the occasional quote from her daughter's namesake. Published by the University Press of Florida in 2013, this book was years too late to have been the dog-eared quote book Molly so treasured, but I imagine hers to be one quite like it, and recommend the title to anyone who'd like one of their own.

My brother, Evan Yerega, has been a wonderful support over the past year in particular; I feel lucky to have, in my only sibling, such a level head and good heart. My parents, Michael and Holly, have shown us both how much strength and resilience we have in our blood, and I'm ever grateful for all they've done for me in my roughly four decades on this planet.

And, always, the three people who carry my heart with them everywhere they go: my husband, Scott, who took a big leap with me into this new career—never once flinching at the unknown—and our children, the best of us both, who bring to every day pure joy.

1. How does Liza and Molly's friendship differ from that of Liza and Max? How do these different friendships represent and reflect Liza as a person?

2. Do you think Molly and Rick's friendship would have progressed to an affair had they continued on the path they were on? Or, by your definition of infidelity, were they already having one?

3. How is Molly's worsening pain a mirror of her relationships with Liza, with Daniel? Do you believe that all of her pain was real, or to some extent did it become a self-fulfilling prophecy?

4. What does Rosie and her reluctance to speak mean to Molly? Whom do you think Molly ultimately needs more: Rick or Rosie?

5. Put yourself in Liza's shoes. Would you have driven all night to Molly's after seeing the intruder? After being turned away so dismissively, would you have given Molly a chance to redeem herself, at any point?

6. Have you ever had a near-death experience or a close call, the way Liza did? How did you react afterward—and can you relate to the way it rattled her?

7. How do you feel about Henry's theory that truly bad things are the result of a series of missteps—nothing more, nothing less? Do you find it worrisome, or reassuring? Is there a difference between luck and fate?

8. At what point would you have told Daniel about the mounting debt? In your opinion, is Molly ultimately more untrustworthy than Daniel, or did she do the best she could?

9. Molly is drawn to the nature center when she needs to feel grounded. Do you have a place like that—and do you go there often enough? Do you prefer to go alone or to share the experience?

10. What is the most complicated relationship in the novel? Molly and Liza? Molly and Daniel? Liza and Max? Molly and Rick?

ST. MARTIN'S GRIFFIN

11. Why do you think Luke never liked Molly? How much attention should we pay to what our family thinks of the relationships we choose?

12. Molly accuses Daniel of "erod[ing] the empathy" from their marriage. Can a relationship really recover from the worst kinds of betrayals—negligence, infidelity, dishonesty? What is unforgiveable in love?

13. What do you think Molly running the race means for her family and friendships in the future? For her sense of self?

14. Do you agree at all with Daniel's justification for doing what he did? Even if you don't, would you begrudgingly admit that it worked?

15. Where do you imagine the characters ten years from now? Are Molly and Daniel still married? Are Liza and Molly close? Does Liza still live in Cincinnati, or did she move on to another city?